EERIE CANAL

Abivard looked back over his shoulder again. Here came the whole army up out of the canal. There, on the far bank, the Videssians still sat on their horses, quietly, calmly, as if nothing in the least out of the ordinary had happened. No, not quite like that: a couple of them were sketching circles over the left side of their chests, the gesture they used when invoking their god.

Seeing that made Abivard's wits, stunned till then, begin to work once more. Whether well or poorly he could not guess, but thought started replacing the blank emptiness between his ears. He shouted the first word that came into his mind: "Magic!" A moment later he amplified it: "The Videssians have used magic to keep us from crossing the canal and giving them what they deserve!"

By Harry Turtledove
Published by Ballantine Books:

THE THOUSAND CITIES

Book Three of
The Time of Troubles

Harry Turtledove

A Del Rey® Book
BALLANTINE BOOKS • NEW YORK

A Del Rey® Book
Published by Ballantine Books
Copyright ©1997 by Harry Turtledove

http://www.randomhouse.com

Library of Congress Catalog Number: 96-93123

ISBN: 0-345-38049-5

Map by Christine Levis

Manufactured in the United States of America

First Edition: June 1997

10   9   8   7   6   5   4   3   2   1

THE
THOUSAND
CITIES

I

ABIVARD SON OF GODARZ STARED THROUGH SEA MIST TO THE east over the strait called the Cattle Crossing toward Videssos the city. The sun gleamed off the gilded globes the Videssians had set on spires atop the countless temples they had built to honor Phos, their false god. Abivard's left hand twisted in the gesture Makuraners used to invoke *the* God, the only one they reverenced.

"Narseh, Gimillu, the lady Shivini, Fraortish eldest of all, let that city fall into my hands," he murmured. He'd lost track of how many times he'd beseeched the Prophets Four to intercede with the God on his behalf, on behalf of Makuran, on behalf of Sharbaraz King of Kings. As yet his prayers remained unanswered.

Beside him Roshnani, his wife, said, "It seems close enough to reach out and pluck, like a ripe fig from a tree."

"Scarcely the third part of a farsang from one side of that water to the other," he agreed, setting a hand on her shoulder. "Were it land, a man could walk thrice so far in an hour's time. Were it land—"

"It is not land," Roshnani said. "No point wasting time thinking what you might do if it were."

"I know," he answered. They smiled at each other. Physically they were very different: she short, round-faced, inclined to plumpness; he lean and angular, with brooding eyes beneath bristling brows. But they shared a commonsense practicality unusual both in their own folk—for Makuraners were given to extravagant melodramatics—and in the devious, treacherous Videssians. After a decade and more of marriage no one knew Abivard's mind better than Roshnani, himself often included.

The sun beat down on his head. It was not nearly so fierce as the summer sun that blazed down on Vek Rud domain, where he'd grown to manhood. Still, he felt its heat: he'd lost the hair at the back of his crown. Godarz had boasted a full head to his dying day, but the men of his mother, Burzoe's, family, those who lived long enough, went bald. He would rather not have followed in their footsteps, but the choice did not seem to be his.

"I wonder how the domain fares these days," he murmured. Formally, he was still its *dihqan*—its overlord—but he hadn't seen it for years, not since just after Sharbaraz had overthrown Smerdis, who had stolen the throne after Sharbaraz' father, Peroz King of Kings—along with Abivard's father, Godarz, along with a great host of other nobles, very nearly along with Abivard himself—had fallen in an attack gone disastrously awry against the Khamorth nomads who roamed the Pardrayan plain north of Makuran.

His younger brother, Frada, ran Vek Rud domain these days. Sharbaraz had flung Abivard against the Empire of Videssos when the Videssians had overthrown Likinios, the Avtokrator who'd helped restore the King of Kings to his throne in Mashiz. Videssian civil strife made triumphs come easy. And so, these days, all of Videssos' westlands lay under the control of Makuran through the armies Abivard commanded. And so—

Abivard kicked angrily at the beach on which he walked. Sand spurted under the sole of his sandal. "Back in Mashiz that last third of a farsang looks easy to cross to Sharbaraz. What a tiny distance, he's written to me. May his days be long and his realm increase, but—"

"And who has done more than you to increase his realm?" Roshnani demanded, then answered her own question: "No one, of course. And so he has no cause to complain of you."

"If I do not give the King of Kings what he requires, he has cause to complain of me," Abivard answered. "His Majesty does not understand the sea." Through Makuran's long history, few men had ever had occasion to understand the sea. A handful of fishing boats sailed on the landlocked Mylasa Sea, but, before Videssos' recent collapse, the writ of the King of Kings had not run to any land that touched the broad, interconnected waters of the ocean. Sharbaraz thought of a third of a farsang and saw only a trivial obstacle. Abivard thought of this particular third of a farsang and saw—

Oars rhythmically rising and falling, a Videssian war dromon centipede-walked down the middle of the Cattle Crossing. The choppy little waves splashed from the greened bronze beak of its ram; Abivard could see the dart thrower mounted on its deck and the metal siphons that spit liquid fire half a bowshot. Videssos' banner, a gold sunburst on blue, snapped in the breeze from a flagstaff at the stern.

He did not know how many such dromons Videssos possessed. Dozens, certainly. Hundreds, probably. He did know how many he possessed. None. Without them his army could not leap over that last third of a farsang. If he tried getting a force across in the few fishing boats and merchantmen he did command—most of those had fled away from the westlands whither he could not pursue them—there would be a great burning and slaughter, and the green-blue waters of the Cattle Crossing would redden with blood for a while.

And so, as he had for almost two years, he stared longingly through sea mist over the water toward Videssos the city. He had studied the single seawall and the great double land wall not only with his eyes but also through detailed questioning of scores of Videssians. Could he but put his siege engines alongside those walls, he thought he could breach them. No foreign foe had ever sacked Videssos the city. Great would be the loot from that plundering.

"Let me but put them alongside," he muttered.

"May the God grant that you do," Roshnani said. "May she grant you the wisdom to see how it can be accomplished."

"Yes, may he," Abivard said. They both smiled. The God, being of unlimited mutability, was feminine to women and masculine to men.

But then Abivard turned his gaze back toward the capital of the Empire of Videssos. Roshnani's head swung that way, too. "I know what you're looking for," she said.

"I expected you would," Abivard answered. "Old Tanshar gave me three prophecies. The first two came true years ago, but I have yet to find a silver shield shining across a narrow sea." He laughed. "When Tanshar spoke those words, I'd never seen any sea, let alone a narrow one. But with so much that glitters in Videssos the city, I've never yet seen light sparking from a silver shield. Now I begin to wonder if the Cattle Crossing was the sea he meant."

"I can't think of any other that would be," Roshnani said, "but then, I don't know everything there is to know about seas, either. Pity we can't ask Tanshar what he meant."

"He didn't even know what he'd said in the prophetic fit, so strongly did it take him," Abivard said. "I had to tell him, once his proper, everyday senses came back." He sighed. "But even had he known, we couldn't call him back from his pyre." He kicked at the sand again, this time with a frustration different from that of a man thwarted of his prey. "I wish I could recognize the answers that spring from foretelling more readily than by spotting them as they've just passed. I shall have to speak to my present wizard about that."

"Which one?" Roshnani asked. "This new Bozorg or the Videssian mage?"

Abivard sighed again. "You have a way of finding the important questions. We've spent so long in Videssos since Likinios' fall, we've come to ape a lot of imperial ways." He chuckled. "I'm even getting a taste for mullet, and I ate no sea fish before these campaigns began."

"Nor I," Roshnani said. "But it's more than things like fish—"

As if to prove her point, Venizelos, the Videssian steward who had served them since they had drawn near the imperial capital, hurried up the beach toward them. The fussy little man had formerly administered an estate belonging to the Videssian logothete of the treasury. He'd changed masters as readily as the estate had.

If the Videssians ever reclaimed this land, Abivard had few doubts that Venizelos would as readily change back.

The steward went down on one knee in the sand. "Most eminent sir," he said in Videssian, "I beg to report the arrival of a letter addressed to you."

"I thank you," Abivard answered in Makuraner. He probably would have used Videssian himself had he and Roshnani not been talking about the Empire and its influence on their lives. He'd learned that speech in bitter exile in Serrhes, after Smerdis had driven Sharbaraz clean out of Makuran. Then he'd wondered if he'd see his homeland again or be forced to lived in Videssos forevermore.

He shook his mind off the past and followed Venizelos away from the beach, back toward the waiting dispatch rider. The suburb of Across, so called from its position relative to Videssos the city, was a sad and ragged town these days. It had gone back and forth between Makuran and Videssos several times in the past couple of years. A lot of its buildings were burned-out shells, and a lot of the ones that had escaped the fires were wrecks nonetheless.

Most of the people in the streets were Makuraner soldiers, some mounted, some afoot. They saluted Abivard with clenched fists over their hearts; many of them lowered their eyes to the ground as Roshnani walked past. That was partly politeness, partly a refusal to acknowledge her existence. By ancient custom, Makuraner noblewomen lived out their lives sequestered in the women's quarters first of their fathers' houses, then of their husbands'. Even after so many years of bending that custom to the breaking point, Roshnani still found herself an object of scandal.

The dispatch rider wore a white cotton surcoat with the red lion of Makuran embroidered on it. His whitewashed round shield also bore the red lion. Saluting Abivard, he cried, "I greet you in the name of Sharbaraz King of Kings, may his years be many and his realm increase!"

"In your person I greet his Majesty in return," Abivard answered as the horseman detached a leather message tube from his belt. The lion of Makuran was embossed there, too. "I am delighted to be granted the boon of communication from his flowing and illustrious pen."

No matter how well the Makuraner language lent itself to flowery flights of enthusiasm, Abivard would have been even more delighted had Sharbaraz let him alone and allowed him to get on with the business of consolidating his gains in the westlands of Videssos. Mashiz lay a long way away; why the King of Kings thought he could run the details of the war at such a remove was beyond Abivard.

"Why?" Roshnani had said once when he had complained about that. "Because he is King of Kings, that's why. Who in Mashiz would presume to tell the King of Kings he cannot do as he desires?"

"Denak might," Abivard had grumbled. His sister was Sharbaraz' principal wife. Without Denak, Sharbaraz would have stayed mured up forever in Nalgis Crag stronghold. He honored her still for what she had done for him, but in their years of marriage she'd borne him only daughters. That made her influence on him less than it might have been.

But Sharbaraz might well not have heeded her had she given him sons. Even in the days when he had still been fighting Smerdis the usurper, he'd relied most of all on his own judgment, which, Abivard had to admit, was often good. Now, after more than a decade on the throne, Sharbaraz did solely as his will dictated— and so, inevitably, did the rest of Makuran.

Abivard opened the message tube and drew out the rolled parchment inside. It was sealed with red wax that, like the tube and the messenger's surcoat and shield, bore the lion of Makuran. Abivard broke the seal and unrolled the parchment. His lips moved as he read: "Sharbaraz King of Kings, whom the God delights to honor, good, pacific, beneficent, to our servant Abivard who does our bidding in all things: Greetings. Know that we are imperfectly pleased with the conduct of the war you wage against Videssos. Know further that, having brought the westlands under our hand, you are remiss in not extending the war to the very heart of the Empire of Videssos, which is to say, Videssos the city. And know further that we expect a movement against the aforementioned city the instant opportunity should present itself and that such opportunity should be sought with the avidity of a lover pursuing his beloved. Last, know also that our patience in this regard, appearances to the contrary notwithstanding, can be exhausted. The crown stands in urgent need of the last jewel remaining to the downfallen Empire of Videssos. The God grant you zeal. I end."

Roshnani stood beside him, also reading. She was less proficient at the art than he was, so he held the parchment till she was through. When she was, she let out an indignant snort. Abivard's glance warned her to say nothing where the dispatch rider could hear. He was sure she wouldn't have even without that look, but some things one did without thought.

"Lord, is there a reply?" the dispatch rider asked.

"Not one that has to go back on the instant," Abivard answered. "Spend the night here. Rest yourself; rest your horse. When morning comes, I'll explain to the King of Kings how I shall obey his commands."

"Let it be as you say, lord," the dispatch rider answered submissively.

To the messenger Abivard was *lord*, and a great lord at that: brother-in-law to the King of Kings, conqueror of Videssos' westlands, less exalted by blood than the high nobles of the Seven Clans, perhaps, but more powerful and prestigious. To every man of Makuran but one he was somebody with whom to reckon. To Sharbaraz King of Kings he was a servant in exactly the same sense as a sweeper in the royal palace in Mashiz was a servant. He could do more things for Sharbaraz than a sweeper could, but that was a difference of degree, not of kind. Sometimes he took his status for granted. Sometimes, as now, it grated.

He turned to Venizelos. "See that this fellow's needs are met, then join us back at our house."

"Of course, most eminent sir," Venizelos said in Videssian before falling into the Makuraner language to address the dispatch rider. These days Abivard was so used to lisping Videssian accents that he hardly noticed them.

The house where he and Roshnani stayed stood next to the ruins of the palace of the hypasteos, the city governor. Roshnani was still spluttering furiously when she and Abivard got back to it. "What does he want you to do?" she demanded. "Arrange a great sorcery so all your men suddenly sprout wings and fly over the Cattle Crossing and down into Videssos the city?"

"I'm sure the King of Kings would be delighted if I found a wizard who could work such a spell," Abivard answered. "Now that I think on it, I'd be delighted myself. It would make my life much easier."

He was angry at Sharbaraz, too, but was determined not to show it. The King of Kings had sent him irritating messages before, then had failed to follow up on them. As long as he stayed back in Mashiz, real control of the war against Videssos remained in Abivard's hands. Abivard didn't think his sovereign would send out a new commander to replace him. Sharbaraz knew beyond question that he was loyal and reliable. Of whom else could the King of Kings say that?

Then he stopped worrying about what, if anything, Sharbaraz thought. The door—which, but for a couple of narrow, shuttered windows, was the only break in the plain, to say nothing of dingy and smoke-stained, whitewashed facade of the house—came open, and his children ran out to meet him.

Varaz was the eldest, named for Abivard's brother who had fallen on the Pardrayan steppe with Godarz, with so many others. He had ten years on him now and looked like a small, smooth-faced, unlined copy of Abivard. By chance, even his cotton caftan bore the same brown, maroon, and dark blue stripes as his father's.

"What have you brought me?" he squealed, as if Abivard had just come back from a long journey.

"The palm of my hand on your backside for being such a greedy thing?" Abivard suggested, and drew back his arm as if to carry out that suggestion.

Varaz set his own hand on the hilt of the little sword—not a toy but a boy-sized version of a man's blade—that hung from his belt. Abivard's second living son grabbed his arm to keep him from spanking Varaz. Shahin was three years younger than his brother;

between them lay another child, also a boy, who'd died of a flux before he had been weaned.

Zarmidukh grabbed Abivard's left arm in case he thought of using that one against Varaz. Unlike Shahin, who as usual was in deadly earnest, she laughed up at her father. In all her five years she'd found few things that failed to amuse her.

Not to be outdone, Gulshahr toddled over and seized Varaz' arm. He shook her off, but gently. She'd had a bad flux not long before and was still thin and pale beneath her swarthiness. When she grabbed her brother again, he shrugged and let her hold on.

"Our own little army," Abivard said fondly. Just then Livania, the Videssian housekeeper, came out to see what the children were up to. Nodding to her, Abivard added, "And the chief quartermaster."

He'd spoken in the Makuraner language. She answered in Videssian: "As far as that goes, supper is nearly ready." She hadn't understood the Makuraner tongue when Abivard's horsemen had driven the Videssians out of Across, but now she was fairly fluent.

"It's octopus stew," Varaz said. The name of the main ingredient came out in Videssian; as Makuran was a nearly landlocked country, its language had no name for many-tentacled sea creatures. All Abivard's children used Videssian as readily as their own tongue, anyhow. And why not? All of them save Varaz had been born in formerly Videssian territory, and all of them had spent far more time there than back in Makuran.

Abivard and Roshnani glanced at each other. Both of them were easily able to control their enthusiasm for octopus. As far as Abivard was concerned, the beasts had the texture of leather with very little redeeming flavor. He would have preferred mutton or goat or beef. The Videssians ate less red meat than did Makuraners at any time, though, and years of war had diminished and scattered their herds. If the choice lay between eating strange beasts that crawled in tide pools and going hungry, he was willing to be flexible.

The stew *was* tasty, full of carrots and parsnips and cabbage leaves and flavored with garlic and onions. Abivard, his family,

Livania, and Venizelos ate in the central courtyard of the house. A fountain splashed there; that struck Abivard, who had grown up in a dry country, as an extravagant luxury.

On the other hand, no bright flowers bloomed in the courtyard, as they would have in any Makuraner home this side of a hovel. Livania had started an herb garden. Most of the plants that grew in it were nondescript to the eye, but their spicy scents cut through the city and camp stinks of smoke and men and animals and garbage and ordure.

Abivard snapped his fingers. "Have to find artisans to repair that broken sewage main or the smell will get worse and the men will start coming down sick by companies. We've been lucky we haven't had anything much going through them, because we've stayed in one place a long time."

"That's true, most eminent sir," Venizelos said gravely. "If once a few men are taken ill with a disease, it can race through a host like fire."

"May it not come to pass." Abivard twisted his left hand in a sign intended to avert any evil omen.

"When do we get to fight the Videssians again, Father?" Varaz asked, once more setting hand to sword hilt.

"That's up to Maniakes Avtokrator more than it is up to me," Abivard answered. "We can't get at his soldiers right now—" *However much Sharbaraz doesn't care for the notion*, he added to himself. "—and he won't come to us. What does that leave?"

Varaz frowned, seriously considering the question. The past couple of years Abivard had taken to asking him more and more questions of that sort to get him used to thinking like an officer. Some of his answers had been very good. Once or twice Abivard thought they were probably better than the ones the officer facing the real situation had come up with.

Now Varaz said, "If we can't go over the Cattle Crossing and Maniakes won't cross over here to fight us, we have to find some other way to get at his army and beat it."

"Wishing for something you can't reach doesn't make it fall into your lap," Abivard answered, reminded that his eldest son was still a boy, after all. "There is another way for us to get to

Videssos the city, but it's not one we can take. It would mean bringing an army over the Pardrayan steppe, all the way around the Videssian sea, and then down into Videssos from the north. How would we defend ourselves from the nomads if we tried that, or keep the army supplied on the long journey it would have to take?"

"We keep our armies supplied here in Videssos," Varaz said, reluctant to abandon his notion.

"Yes, but here in Videssos they grow all sorts of things," Abivard said patiently. "This coastal lowland is as rich as the soil of the Thousand Cities between the Tutub and the Tib, I think. And they have towns here, with artisans to make every kind of thing an army needs. It's different on the steppe."

"What's it like?" Shahin asked. He knew Videssos and little else.

"It's—vast," Abivard said. "I was only out there once, on the campaign of Peroz King of Kings, the one that failed. Nothing but farsang after farsang of rolling grassland, none of it very rich but so much of it that the nomads can pasture great flocks out there. But it has no cropland, no towns, no artisans except for the few among the Khamorth—and all they know is connected to the herds one way or another."

"If the country is that bad, why did Peroz King of Kings want it?" Varaz asked.

"Why?" Across a decade and more remembered anger smoldered in Abivard's voice. "I'll tell you why, Son. Because the Videssians spread gold among the Khamorth clans, bribing them to cross the Degird River into Makuran. You can never be too sure about Videssians."

"Well! I like that," Livania said indignantly.

Abivard smiled at her. "I didn't mean people like you and Venizelos. I meant the people in the palaces." He waved east, toward the imperial residence in Videssos the city. "They are devious, they are underhanded, they will cheat you three different ways in a minute's time if they see the chance—and they commonly do see it."

"But didn't Maniakes Avtokrator help put Sharbaraz King of

Kings, may his years be many and his realm increase, back on the throne?" Varaz persisted.

"Yes, he did," Abivard said. "But that was your mother's idea."

Varaz had heard the story before. He looked proud, not astonished. Abivard thought Shahin had heard it, too, but he must not have understood what it meant, for, with his smaller sisters, he stared at Roshnani with enormous eyes. "*Your* idea, mother?"

"Smerdis' men had beaten us," she said. "They'd driven us away from Mashiz and across the Thousand Cities to the edge of the badlands that run between them and the border of the Videssian westlands. We were doomed if we stayed where we were, so I thought we couldn't do worse and might do better if we took refuge with the Videssians."

"And look what's become of that," Abivard added, driving the lesson home. "A lot of people—men mostly, but a surprising lot of women, too—think women are foolish just because they're women. They're wrong, all of them. If Sharbaraz hadn't taken your mother's advice, he probably wouldn't be King of Kings today."

Varaz pondered that with the same careful attention he'd given Abivard's question on strategy. Shahin just nodded and accepted it; he was still at the age when his parents' words had the authority of the Prophets Four. Maybe, if he heard such things often enough when he was small, he would pay more heed to his principal wife once he grew to be a man.

With luck, he would have a principal wife worth heeding. Abivard glanced fondly over at Roshnani.

Twilight deepened to darkness. Servants lit torches. They drew moths to join the clouds of mosquitoes that buzzed in the courtyard. Because the coastal lowlands were so warm and damp, the droning pests flourished there in swarms unknown back at Vek Rud domain. Every so often a nightjar or a bat would dive out of the night, seize a bug, and vanish again. There were more bugs, though, than creatures to devour them.

Livania put Zarmidukh and Gulshahr to bed, then came back for Shahin, who made his usual protests over going to sleep but finally gave in. Varaz, grave in the responsibility of approaching adulthood, went off without a fuss when his own turn came half an hour or so later. Roshnani chuckled under her breath. Abivard understood why: in another couple of weeks—or couple of days, for that matter—Varaz was liable to forget his dignity and go back to squawking.

"Will there be anything more, most eminent sir?" Venizelos asked.

"Go to bed," Abivard told him. "Roshnani and I won't be up much longer ourselves." Roshnani nodded agreement to that. As the two of them got up and headed for their bedchamber, the torches that had been lighted were doused. The stink of hot tallow filled the courtyard. The servants left a torch burning near the entrance to the house. Abivard paused there to light a clay lamp filled with olive oil.

Roshnani said, "I'd sooner burn that stuff than cook with it or sop bread in it the way the Videssians do."

"I'm not fond of it, either," Abivard answered. "But you'll notice all the children love it." He rolled his eyes. "They should, seeing how Livania stuffs it into them every chance she gets. I think she's trying to turn them into Videssians from the stomach out."

"I wonder if that's a kind of magic our wizards don't know." Roshnani laughed, but the fingers of her left hand twisted in the sign to turn aside the evil idea.

She and Abivard walked down the hall to their bedchamber. He set the lamp on a little table by his side of the bed. The bed had a tall frame enclosed by gauzy netting. There were usually fewer mosquitoes inside the netting than outside. Abivard supposed that was worthwhile. He pulled off his caftan and lay down on the bed. Sweet-smelling straw rustled beneath him; the leather straps supporting the mattress creaked a little.

After Roshnani lay down beside him, he blew out the lamp through the netting. The room plunged into darkness. He set a hand on her hip. She turned toward him. Had she turned away or lay still, he would have rolled over and gone to sleep without worrying about it. As it was, they made love—companionably, almost lazily—and then, separating to keep from sticking to each other once they were through, fell asleep together.

The Videssian in the blue robe with the cloth-of-gold circle on the left breast went down on one knee before Abivard. "By the lord with the great and good mind, most eminent sir, I beg you to reconsider this harsh and inhuman edict," he said. The early-morning sun gleamed off his shaved pate as if it were a gilded dome topping one of false Phos' temples.

"Rise, holy sir," Abivard answered in Videssian, and the hierarch of Across, a plump, middle-aged cleric named Artanas, grunted and got to his feet. Abivard fixed him with what he hoped was a baleful stare. "Now, see here, holy sir. You should be glad you are allowed to practice your religion in any way at all and not come whining to me about it. You will obey the decree of Sharbaraz King of Kings, may his days be long and his realm increase, or you will not be allowed to worship and you will be subject to the penalties the decree ordains." He set a hand on the hilt of his sword to make sure Artanas got the idea.

"But, most eminent sir," Artanas wailed, "forcing us to observe heretical rituals surely condemns us to Phos' eternal ice. And the usages of the Vaspurakaner heretics are particularly repellent to us."

Abivard shrugged. "If you disobey, you and all who worship with you will suffer." In the abstract, Sharbaraz had been clever to force the Videssian temples in the westlands to conform to Vaspu-rakaner usages if they wanted to stay open: it had split them away from the Empire of Videssos' central ecclesiastical authority. As for the Vaspurakaners themselves— "As I say, holy sir, count yourself lucky. In the land of Vaspurakan we require the worship of the God, not your false spirits of good and evil."

"That serves the Vaspurakaners right for their longtime treach-ery against the true faith," said Artanas, who did not object when the Makuraners interfered with someone else's belief, only when they meddled with his own.

For his part, Abivard was not sure the King of Kings was acting rightly in imposing the cult of the God in Vaspurakan. He did not doubt for a moment that faith in the God was the only guarantor of a happy afterlife, but he also had no reason to doubt the fanaticism of the Vaspurakaners for their own faith: all the followers of Phos struck him as being passionately wedded to their own version of error, whatever it happened to be. If one pushed them too far, they were liable to snap.

That same thought also applied to Artanas, though Abivard didn't care to admit as much to himself. Sharbaraz might have done better not to meddle in any matters of religion till after the war against Videssos had been won. But if Abivard did not carry out the policies the King of Kings had set forth, word of his failure would soon head for Mashiz—after which, most likely, he would, too, in disgrace.

He said, "We shall attend closely to what you preach, holy sir. I am not schooled in your false beliefs, but we have men who are. No matter what you say or where you say it, some of them will hear you. If you do not preach the doctrine you are ordered to preach, you will suffer the consequences. Perhaps I shall send to Mashiz for a special persuader."

Artanas' skin, already a couple of shades paler than Abivard's, went almost fish-belly white. Sweat gleamed on his shaved skull. Makuraner torturers and their skill in torment were legendary in Videssos. Abivard found that amusing, for Videssian torturers enjoyed a similar reputation in Makuran. He did not tell that to the Videssian hierarch.

"You ask me to preach what I know to be untrue," Artanas said. "How in good conscience can I do that?"

"Your conscience is not my concern," Abivard answered. "Your actions are. If you do not preach of Vaspur the Firstborn and the place of the Vaspurakaners as his chiefest descendants, you shall answer to me."

Artanas tried another tack: "The people here, knowing the Vaspurakaners' claims to be ignorant, empty, ignoble, and impious, will not heed this preaching and may rise up not only against me but also against you."

"That is my affair, not yours," Abivard said. "Where the armies of Videssos have not been able to stand against the brave warriors of Makuran for lo these many years, why should we fear a rabble of peasants and artisans?"

The local prelate glared at him, then said, "Videssian arms won a great victory against the barbarians of Kubrat earlier this year, or so I have heard."

Abivard had heard that, too, and didn't care for it. He knew more than he'd ever wanted to learn about nomad horsemen pouring down out of the north. After the Khamorth had destroyed the flower of Peroz King of Kings' army out on the steppe, they'd raided over the Degird and into Makuran. The flocks and fields of his own domain had come under attack. Since Videssian meddling out on the steppe had set the clans in motion, he was anything but sorry to see the Empire having nomad troubles of its own and anything but glad to see those troubles overcome.

Making his voice hard, he said, "We are stronger than the barbarians, just as we are stronger than you Videssians. Heed what I say, holy sir, in your services and sermons, or you will learn at first hand how strong we are. Do you understand me?" When Artanas did not say no, Abivard made an abrupt gesture of dismissal. "Get you gone."

Artanas left. Abivard knew that the hierarch remained rebellious. That edict of Sharbaraz' imposing Vaspurakaner usages on the Videssian westlands had already sparked riots in a couple of towns. Abivard's men had put them down, true, but he wished they hadn't had the need.

Since Sharbaraz was King of Kings, the God was supposed to have blessed him with preternatural wisdom and foresight. If the God had done that, the results were moderately hard to notice. And here the sun was, not a third of the way up the sky from rising, and Abivard already felt like having a mug of wine or maybe two.

Hoping to escape any more importunate Videssians, he went out to the encampment of his own troops, not far from the field fortifications Maniakes had run up in a vain effort to hold the armored horsemen away from Across. The Videssian works were not so strong as they might have been; Maniakes, realizing they were too little, too late, had neither completed them nor defended what his engineers had built. Abivard was grateful for the wasted effort.

Back among the Makuraners, Abivard came as close to feeling at home as he could within sight of Videssos the city. The lean, swarthy men in caftans who groomed horses or sat playing dice in what shade they could find were of his kind. His own language filled his ears. Many of the warriors of the army he and Sharbaraz had so painstakingly rebuilt spoke with a northwestern accent like his own. When Sharbaraz had been a rebel, the Northwest had rallied to him first.

But even in the camp not all was as it would have been near Vek Rud domain or near Mashiz or between the Tib and the Tutub. A lot of the servants and most of the camp women were Videssians who had been scooped up as his army had traveled back and forth through the westlands. Some of those women had children seven and eight and nine years old. The children used a weird jargon of their own, with mostly Videssian words but a grammar closer to that of the Makuraner tongue. Only they could understand most of it.

And here came the man Abivard perhaps least wanted to see when he was fed up with things Videssian. He couldn't even show it, as he could with Artanas. "I greet you, eminent Tzikas," he said, and presented his cheek for the Videssian officer to kiss, a token that he reckoned Tzikas' rank but little lower than his own.

"I greet you, Abivard son of Godarz, brother-in-law to Sharbaraz King of Kings, may his years be many and his realm increase," Tzikas answered in Makuraner that was fluent and only slightly lisping. He kissed Abivard's' cheek just as a minor noble from Mashiz might have, though that was not a practice the Videssians followed among themselves.

"Have you learned anything new and interesting from the other side, eminent sir?" Abivard asked, pointing with his chin east over the Cattle Crossing toward Videssos the city.

Tzikas shook his head. He was a solidly made middle-aged man with a thick head of graying hair and a neatly trimmed gray beard. He seemed quite ordinary till one looked at his eyes. When one did, one discovered they had already looked through one, weighed one's soul, measured it, and assigned one to one's proper pigeonhole in the document file of his mind. The turncoat Videssian was, Abivard had reluctantly been forced to conclude, nearly as clever as he thought he was—no mean assessment.

"Too bad," Abivard said. "Anything I can find out about what Maniakes is planning for this summer will help. I've seen him in action. If he has steady troops behind him, he'll be difficult."

"That pup?" Tzikas made a dismissive gesture that irritated Abivard, who was not far from Maniakes' age. "He has a habit of striking too soon and of thinking he's stronger than he really is." His face clouded. "It cost us dear in the Arandos valley not long after he took the crown."

Abivard nodded, though Tzikas was rewriting things in his memory. For years the garrison Tzikas commanded at Amorion, at the west end of the valley, had held off Abivard's force: Abivard had developed a healthy respect for the Videssian general's skill. But at last Amorion had fallen—before Maniakes' army, pushing west up the line of the Arandos, could reinforce it. Abivard's men had beaten Maniakes after that, but it had not been the Avtokrator's fault that Amorion had at last been taken.

What Abivard said was, "If he's as hasty and headstrong as you say, eminent sir, how did he smash the Kubratoi as he did?"

"Easy enough to win a fine name for yourself fighting savages," Tzikas answered. "What you get from it, though, won't help you much when you come up against soldiers with discipline and generals who can see farther than the ends of their noses."

Abivard took his own nose between thumb and forefinger for a moment. It was of generous size, though in no way outlandish for a man of Makuran. He hoped he could see past the end of it. "You do have a point," he admitted. "Fighting the Khamorth is nothing like coming up against you Videssians, I must say. But I worry about Maniakes. He made fewer mistakes against me last year than he had before—and tried to accomplish less, which is almost another way of saying the same thing, considering how unsteady his soldiers were. I fear he may be turning into a good commander."

Tzikas' lip curled. "Him? Not likely."

The first question that came to Abivard's mind was, *No? Then why did you fail when you tried overthrowing him this past winter?* He didn't ask it; on the orders of his sovereign, he was treating Tzikas with every courtesy in the hope that Tzikas would prove a useful tool against Maniakes. Had many Videssian garrisons in the westlands been left, Tzikas might have persuaded their commanders to go over to Makuran, as he had. But the only Videssian troops here these days were raiding bands largely immune to the renegade general's blandishments.

A traitor Tzikas might be; a fool he was not. He seemed to have a gift for plucking thoughts from the heads of those with whom he conversed. As if to answer the question Abivard had not asked, he said, "I would have toppled the pervert from the throne had his protective amulet not warded him just long enough to reach his wizard and gain a counterspell against my mage's cantrip."

"Aye, so you've said," Abivard replied. To his way of thinking, an effective conspirator would have known about that amulet and found some way to circumvent it. Saying that to Tzikas, though, would surely have offended him. If only Tzikas took similar care when speaking to Abivard.

Again the Videssian replied to what Abivard had not said: "I know you Makuraners think nothing of first cousins marrying, or uncles and nieces, or even brothers and sisters among the Seven Clans." He pulled a face. "Those usages are not ours, and no one will convince me they are not perverse. When Maniakes bedded his uncle's daughter, that was incest, plain as day."

"So you've said," Abivard repeated. "More than once, in fact. Has not your Mobedhan Mobedh, or whatever you call your chief priest, given leave for that marriage?"

"Our patriarch," Tzikas answered, reminding him of the Videssian word. "Yes, he has." Tzikas' lip curled again, more this time. "And no doubt he gained a fitting reward for the dispensation." Abivard picked up the meaning of that Videssian term from the context. Tzikas went on: "I stand with true righteousness no matter what the patriarch might say."

He looked very righteous himself. He was never less believable than when he donned that mantle of smug virtue, for it did not fit him well. He'd made his play, it hadn't worked, and now he seemed to want a special commendation for pure and noble motives. As far as Abivard was concerned, if one tried killing a man by magic, one's motives were unlikely to be pure or noble—odds were, one just wanted what he had.

Tzikas said, "How I admire Sharbaraz King of Kings, may his days be long and his realm increase, for maintaining the imperial dignity of the true heir to the throne of Videssos, Hosios the son of Likinios Avtokrator."

"How generous of you to recognize Hosios' claim," Abivard answered tonelessly. If he had to listen to much more of Tzikas' fulsome good cheer, he'd need a steaming down at the closest bathhouse. The real Hosios was long years dead, executed with his father when Genesios had butchered his way to the Videssian throne. As far as Abivard knew, three different Videssians had played Hosios at Sharbaraz' bidding. There might have been more. If one started to think one really was an Avtokrator rather than a puppet—

"I would recognize any claim in preference to that of Maniakes," Tzikas said seriously. But that was too much of a courtier's claim even for him to stomach. Shaking his head, he corrected himself: "No, were I to choose between Maniakes and Genesios, I would choose Maniakes."

Abivard knew that he ought to despise Genesios, too. The man had, after all, murdered not only Likinios, the benefactor of Makuran, but also all his family. But had it not been for Genesios, he would not be able to look over the Cattle Crossing and see Videssos the city. Under what passed for the murderer's reign, Videssos had dissolved in multicornered civil war, and more than one town in the westlands had welcomed the Makuraners in the hope that they would bring peace and order to replace the bloody chaos engulfing the Empire.

When Tzikas saw that Abivard was not going to respond to his preferences for the Videssian throne, he changed the subject, at least to some degree: "Brother-in-law to the King of Kings, when may I begin constituting my promised regiment of horsemen in the service of Hosios Avtokrator?"

"Soon," Abivard answered, as he had the last time Tzikas

had asked that question, and the time before that, and the time before *that*.

"I have heard there is no objection in Mashiz to the regiment," Tzikas said delicately.

"Soon, eminent sir, soon," Abivard repeated. Tzikas was right; Sharbaraz King of Kings was happy to see a body of Videssian troops help give the current Hosios' claim to the throne legitimacy. The hesitation lay on Abivard's part. Tzikas was already a traitor once; what was to keep him from becoming a traitor twice?

Roshnani had used a homelier analogy: "A man who cheats *with* a woman and then marries her will cheat *on* her afterward—not always, maybe, but most of the time."

"I trust I shall not have to appeal directly to Sharbaraz King of Kings, may his years be many and his realm increase," Tzikas said exactly as a Makuraner noble might have—the Videssians knew how to squeeze, too.

"Soon I said, and soon I meant," Abivard replied, wishing that some hideous disease—another bout of treason, perhaps—would get Tzikas out of his hair. For the Videssian renegade to use the word *trust* when he was so manifestly unworthy of it grated. What grated even more was that Tzikas, who was so perceptive elsewhere, seemed blind to Abivard's reasons for disliking him.

"I shall take you at your word," Tzikas said, "for I know the nobles of Makuran are raised to ride, to fight, and to tell the truth."

That was what the Videssians said of Makuraners. The men of Makuran, for their part, were told that Videssians sucked in mendacity with their mothers' milk. Having dealt with men from both sides of the border, Abivard had come to the reluctant conclusion that those of either nation would lie when they thought that was to their benefit or sometimes merely for the sport of it, those who worshiped the God about as readily as those who followed Phos.

"Everything I can do, I will," Abivard said. *Eventually,* he added to himself. He did not enjoy being imperfectly honest with Tzikas, but he did not relish the prospect of the Videssian's commanding troops, either. To take the moral advantage away from Tzikas, he went on: "Have you had any luck in finding ship's carpenters, or whatever the proper name for them is? If we are going to beat Maniakes, to beat Videssos once and for all, we'll have to get our men over the Cattle Crossing and assault Videssos the city. Without ships—"

Tzikas sighed. "I am making every effort, brother-in-law to the King of Kings, but my difficulties in this regard, unlike yours concerning horsemen, are easy to describe." Abivard raised an eyebrow at that jab. Unperturbed, Tzikas went on, "Videssos separates land and sea commands. Had a drungarios fallen into your clutches, he could have done better by you, for such matters fall within his area of responsibility. As a simple soldier, though, I fear I am ignorant of the art of shipbuilding."

"Eminent sir, I certainly did not expect you to do the carpentry on your own," Abivard answered, working hard to keep his face straight. Tzikas' describing himself as a simple anything would have drawn a laugh from any Makuraner—and probably from most of the Videssians—who had ever had to deal with him. "Learning where to gather the men with the requisite trades is something else again."

"So it is, in the most literal sense of the word," Tzikas said. "Most of the men who practice these trades have left the westlands in the face of your victorious advance, whether by their own will or at the urging of their city governors or provincial chiefs."

Such urging, Abivard knew, had probably been at a sword's point. "The Videssians dug a hole and pulled it in after themselves," he said angrily. "I can see them over there in Videssos the city, but I can't touch them no matter what I try. But they can still touch me—some of their seaborne raids have hurt."

"They have a capacity you lack," Tzikas agreed. "I would help you remedy that lack were it in my power, but unfortunately it is not. You, on the other hand, have the ability to allow me to recruit a suitable number of horsemen who—" Without apparent effort, he turned the tables on Abivard.

By the time Abivard managed to break away, he'd decided he would gladly let Tzikas recruit his long-desired cavalry regiment provided that the Videssian swore a frightful oath to take that regiment far, far away and never come nagging any man of Makuran again.

* * *

Abivard missed Tanshar. He'd always gotten along well with the fortune-teller and wizard who'd lived for so long in the village below Vek Rud stronghold. But Tanshar now was five years dead. Abivard had been searching ever since for a mage who could give him results that matched Tanshar's and not make him feel like an idiot for asking an occasional question.

Whether the wizards who traveled with the army suited him or not, it had a fair contingent. Battle magic rarely did an army any good. For one thing, the opposition's sorcerers were likely to block the efforts of one's own mages. For another, no magic was very effective in the heat of battle. When a man's passions were roused to fever pitch as he fought for his life, he scarcely sensed spells that might have laid him low had they taken him at his ease.

The wizards, then, did more in the way of finding lost rings—and occasionally lost toddlers—for the camp women than they did in hurling sorcerous fireballs at Maniakes' men. They foretold whether pregnant women would bear boys or girls—not with perfect accuracy but better than they could have done by random guessing. They helped heal sick men and sick horses and with luck helped keep camp diseases from turning into epidemics. And, being men, they boasted about all the other things they might do if only they got the chance.

Every so often Abivard summoned one of them to see if he could make good on his boasts. One hot, sticky high-summer day he had called to his residence the mage named Bozorg, a young, eager fellow who had not accompanied the army in all its campaigns in the Videssian westlands but was newly arrived from Mashiz.

Bozorg bowed very low before Abivard, showing he recognized that his own rank was low compared with that of the general. Venizelos fetched in wine made tangy with the juice of oranges and lemons, a specialty of the coastal lowlands. Over the past couple of years Abivard had grown fond of it. Bozorg's lips puckered in an expression redolent of distaste.

"Too sour for me," he said, and then went on, "unlike my gracious and generous host, whose kindness is a sun by day and a full moon by night, illuminating by its brilliance all it touches. I am honored beyond my poor and humble worth by his invitation and shall serve him with all my heart, all my soul, and all my might, be my abilities ever so weak and feeble."

Abivard coughed. They didn't lay compliments on with a trowel in the frontier domain where he'd grown up. The Videssians weren't in the habit of quite such cloying fulsomeness, either; their praise tended to have a sardonic edge to it. But at the court of Mashiz flattery knew no bounds.

Bozorg must have expected him to take it for granted, too, for he continued. "How may I serve the valiant and noble lord whose puissance causes Videssos to tremble, whose onset is like that of the lion, who strikes with the swiftness of the goshawk, at whose approach the pale easterners who know not the God slink away like jackals, who overthrows city walls like an earthquake in human form, who—"

Abivard's patience ran thin. "If you'll give me a chance to get a word in edgewise, I'll tell you what I have in mind." He was glad Roshnani wasn't listening to Bozorg; he would have been a long time living down *earthquake in human form*.

"Your manner is harsh and abrupt," Bozorg said sulkily. Abivard glared at him. He'd sent looks less hostile toward the Videssian generals whose armies he'd overthrown. Bozorg wilted. Shifting from foot to foot, he admitted, "I am of course here to serve you, lord."

"That's a relief," Abivard said. "I thought you'd come to stop up my ears with treacle." Bozorg assumed a deeply wounded expression. He hadn't practiced it enough; it looked plastered on rather than genuine. Abivard did him a favor: he ignored it. After pausing to marshal his thoughts, he went on, "What I need from you, if you can give it to me, is some sort of picture of what Maniakes has in mind to do to us this year or next year or whenever he decides he's strong enough to face us in open battle."

Now Bozorg really did look worried. "Lord, this is no easy task you set me. The Avtokrator of the Videssians will surely have his plans hedged around with the finest sorcery he can obtain from those small fragments of the Empire still under his control."

"If what I wanted were simple, I could give silver arkets or Videssian goldpieces to any local hedge wizard," Abivard said, looking down his long nose at the mage from Mashiz. "You, sirrah, come recommended for both talent and skill. If I send you back to the capital because you have not the spirit to essay what I ask of you, you shall get no more such recommendations in the future."

"You misunderstand me, lord," Bozorg said quickly. "It is not to be doubted I shall attempt this task. I did but warn you that the God does not guarantee success, not against the wizards Maniakes Avtokrator has under his command."

"Once we're born, the only thing the God *guarantees* is that we'll die and be judged on how we have lived our lives," Abivard answered. "Between those two moments of birth and death we strive to be good and true and righteous. Of course we can't succeed all the time; only the Prophets Four came close, and so the God revealed himself to them. But we must strive."

Bozorg bowed. "My lord is a Mobedhan Mobedh of piety," he said. Then he gulped; had he laid his flattery on with a trowel again? Abivard contented himself with folding his arms across his chest and letting out an impatient sigh. Hastily the wizard said, "If my lord will excuse me for but a moment, I shall fetch in the magical materials I shall require in the conjuration."

He hurried out of Abivard's residence, returning a moment later with two dust-covered leather saddlebags. He set them down on a low table in front of Abivard, undid the rawhide laces that secured them, and took out a low, broad bowl with a glistening white glaze, several stoppered jars, and a squat jug of wine.

After staring at the jug, he shook his head. "No," he said. "That is wine of Makuran. If we are to learn what the Avtokrator of the Videssians has in his mind, Videssian wine is a better choice."

"I can see that," Abivard said with a judicious nod. He raised his voice: "Venizelos!" When the steward came into the chamber, he told him, "Fetch me a jar of Videssian wine from the cellar." Venizelos bowed and left, returning shortly with an earthenware jar taller and slimmer than the one Bozorg had brought from

Mashiz. He set it on the table in front of the wizard, then disappeared as if made to vanish by one of Bozorg's cantrips.

Abivard wondered if a Videssian mage might not serve better than a Makuraner one, too. He shook his head. He couldn't trust Panteles, not for this.

Bozorg used a knife to cut through the pitch sealing the stopper in place. When the stopper was freed, he yanked it out and poured the white bowl nearly full of wine as red as blood. He also poured a small libation onto the floor for each of the Prophets Four.

He opened one of the jars—there was no pitch on its stopper—and spilled out a glittering powder from it into the palm of his hand. "Finely ground silver," he explained, "perhaps a quarter of an arket's worth. When polished, silver makes the finest mirrors: Unlike bronze or even gold, it adds no color of its own to the images it reflects. Thus, it also offers the best hope of an accurate and successful sorcerous view of what lies ahead."

So saying, he sprinkled the silver over the wine, chanting as he did so. It was not the ritual Tanshar had used in his scrying but seemed a shoot from a different branch of the same tree.

The powdered silver did not sink but stayed on the surface of the wine; Abivard got the idea that the incantation Bozorg had made had something to do with that. The mage said, "Now we wait for everything to become perfectly still." Abivard nodded; that, too, was akin to what the wizard from the village under Vek Rud stronghold had done.

"Will you tell me what you see?" he asked. "When the bowl is ready, I mean."

Bozorg shook his head. "No. This is a different conjuration. You will look into the bowl yourself and see—whatever is there to be seen. I may see something in the depths of the wine, too, but it will not be what you see."

"Very well," Abivard said. Waiting came with dealing with wizards. Bozorg studied the surface of the wine with a hunting hawk's intensity. At last, with a sudden sharp gesture, he beckoned Abivard forward.

Holding his breath so he wouldn't spoil the reflective surface, Abivard peered down into the bowl. Though his eyes told him the floating specks of silver were not moving, he somehow sensed them spinning, spiraling faster and faster till they seemed to cover the wine with a mirror that gave back first his face and the beams of the ceiling and then—

He saw fighting in mountain country, two armies of armored horsemen smashing against each other. One of the forces flew the red-lion banner of Makuran. Try as he would, he could not make out the standards under which the other side fought. He wondered if this was a glimpse of the future or of the past: he'd sent his mobile force into the southeastern hill country of the Videssian westlands, trying to quell raiders. His success had been less complete than he'd hoped.

Without warning, the scene shifted. Again he saw mountains. These, at a guess, were in hotter, drier country than those of the previous vision: the hooves of the horses strung out in the line of march kicked up sand at every step. The soldiers atop those horses were unmistakably Videssians. Off in the distance—to the south?—the sun sparkled off a blue, blue sea filled with ships.

There was another shift of scene. He saw more fighting, this time between Makuraners and Videssians. In the middle distance a town with a mud-brick wall stood on a hill that rose abruptly from flat farmland. *That's somewhere in the land of the Thousand Cities,* Abivard thought. The settlements there were so ancient that these days they sat atop mounts built up of centuries' worth of accumulated rubble. Again, he might have been seeing the future or the past. Videssians under Maniakes had fought Smerdis' Makuraners between the Tutub and the Tib to help return Sharbaraz to the throne.

The scene shifted once more. Now he had come full circle, for he found his point of vision back at Across, staring over the Cattle Crossing toward Videssos the city. He could see none of the dromons that had held his army away from the imperial capital. Suddenly, something flashed silver across the water. He knew that signal: the signal to attack. He would—

The wine in the bowl bubbled and roiled as if coming to a boil. Whatever it had been about to show Abivard vanished then; it was once more merely wine. Bozorg smacked his right fist into his left palm in frustration. "My scrying was detected," he said, angry at himself or at the Videssian mage who had thwarted him or maybe both at once. "The God grant you saw enough to suit you, lord."

"Almost," Abivard said. "Aye, almost. You confirmed for me that the 'narrow sea' of a prophecy I had years ago is indeed the Cattle Crossing, but whether the prophecy proves to be for good or ill I still do not know."

"I would hesitate before I sought to learn that, lord," Bozorg said. "The Videssian mages will now be alerted to my presence and watchful lest I try to sneak another scrying spell past them. For now, letting them ease back into sloth is the wiser course."

"Let it be as you say," Abivard answered. "I've gone without knowing the answer to that riddle for a long time now. A little longer won't matter—if in fact I can learn it before the event itself. Sometimes foreseeing is best viewed from behind, if you take my meaning."

Before, Bozorg had shown him flattery. Now the wizard bowed with what seemed genuine respect. "Lord, if you know so much, the God has granted you wisdom beyond that of most men. Knowing the future is different from being able to change it or even to recognize it until it is upon you."

Abivard laughed at himself. "If I were as wise as all that, I wouldn't have asked for the glimpses you just showed me. And if you were as wise as all that, you wouldn't have spent time and effort learning how to show me those glimpses." He laughed again. "And if the Videssians were as wise as all that, they wouldn't have tried to keep me from seeing those glimpses, either. After all, what can I do about them if the future is already set?"

"Only what you have seen—whatever that may be—is certain, lord," Bozorg warned. "What happened before, what may come after—those are hidden and so remain mutable."

"Ah. I understand," Abivard replied. "So if I saw, say, a huge

Videssian army marching on me, I would still have the choice of either setting an ambush against it or fleeing to save my skin."

"Exactly so." Bozorg's head bobbed up and down in approval. "Neither of those is preordained from what you saw by the scrying: they depend on the strength of your own spirit."

"Even if I do set the ambush, though, I also have no guarantee ahead of time that it will succeed," Abivard said.

Bozorg nodded again. "Not unless you saw yourself succeeding."

Abivard plucked at his beard. "Could a man who was, say, both rich and fearful have a scryer show him great chunks of his life to come so he would know what dangers to avoid?"

"Rich, fearful, foolish men have indeed tried this many times over the years," Bozorg said with a scornful curl of his lip worthy of Tzikas. "What good does it do them? Any danger they do so see is one they cannot avoid, by the very nature of things."

"If I saw myself making what had to be a dreadful error," Abivard said after more thought, "when the time came, I would struggle against that course with all my might."

"No doubt you would struggle," Bozorg agreed, "and no doubt you would also fail. Your later self, having knowledge that the you who watched the scryer lacked, would assuredly find some reason for doing that which was earlier reckoned a disaster in the making—or might simply forget the scrying till, too late, he realized that the foretold event had come to pass."

Abivard chewed on that for a while, then gave it up with a shake of his head. "Too complex for my poor, dull wits. We might as well be a couple of Videssian priests arguing about which of the countless ways to worship their Phos is the single right and proper one. By the God, good Bozorg, I swear that one flyspeck on a theological manuscript of theirs can spawn three new heresies."

"They know not the truth and so are doomed to quarrel endlessly over how the false is false," Bozorg said with a distinct sniff, "and to drop into the Void once their foolish lives have passed."

Abivard was tempted to lock Bozorg and Artanas the hierarch in a room together to see which—if either—came out sane.

Sometimes, though, one had to sacrifice personal pleasure for the good of the cause.

Bozorg bowed. "Will there be anything more, lord?"

"No, you may go," Abivard answered. "Thank you for your service to me."

"It is my pleasure, my privilege, my honor to serve a commander of such great accomplishment, one who excites the admiration of all who know of him," Bozorg said. "Truly you are the great wild boar of Makuran, trampling down and tearing all her foes." With a final bow the wizard reassembled his sorcerous paraphernalia, loaded it back into the saddlebags in which it had traveled from Mashiz, and took his leave.

As soon as his footsteps faded down the hall, Abivard let out a long sigh. This sorcerer wasn't a Tanshar in the making, either, being both oily as what the Videssians squeezed from olives and argumentative to boot. Abivard shrugged. If Bozorg proved competent, he'd overlook a great deal.

Abivard's marshals sprang to their feet to greet him. He went down their ranks accepting kisses on the cheek. A couple of his subordinates were men of the Seven Clans; under most circumstances he would have kissed them on the cheek, not the other way around. They might even have given him trouble about that had he been placed in command of them—were his sister not Sharbaraz' principal wife. As brother-in-law to the King of Kings, he unquestionably outranked them. They might resent that, but they could not deny it.

Romezan was a scion of the Seven Clans, but he had never given Abivard an instant's trouble over rank. Thick-shouldered rather than lean like most Makuraners, he was a bull of a man, the tips of whose waxed mustaches swept out like a bull's horns. All he wanted was more of Videssos than Makuran had yet taken. As he did at every officers' gathering, he said, "How can we get across that miserable little stretch of water, lord?"

"I could piss across it, I think, if I stood on the seashore there," another general said. Kardarigan was no high noble; like Abivard, he was a *dihqan* from the Northwest, one of so many young men forced into positions of importance when their fathers and brothers had died on the Pardrayan steppe.

Romezan leered at him. "You're not hung so well as that." Laughter rose from the Makuraner commanders.

"How do you know?" Kardarigan retorted, and the laughter got louder. The generals had reason to make free with their merriment. Up to the Cattle Crossing they'd swept all before them. Sharbaraz might be unhappy because they'd not done more, but they knew how much they had done.

"We must have marble in our heads instead of brains," Abivard said, "not being able to figure out how to beat the Videssians, even if only for a little while, and get our men and engines across to the eastern shore. Can we but set our engines against the walls of Videssos the city, we will take it." How many times had he said that?

"If that accursed Videssian traitor had built us a navy instead of stringing us along with promises, we might have been able to do it by now," Romezan said.

That accursed Videssian traitor. Abivard wondered what Tzikas would have done had he heard the judgment against him. Whatever he thought, he wouldn't have shown it on the outside. It would have to hurt, though. The Makuraners might use him, but he would never win their trust or respect.

A messenger, his face filthy with road dust, came hurrying up to Abivard. Bowing low, he said, "Your pardon, lord, but I bear an urgent dispatch from the *marzban* of Vaspurakan."

"What does Vshnasp want with me?" Abivard asked. Up till then Sharbaraz' governor of Vaspurakan had done his best to pretend that Abivard did not exist.

He accepted the oiled-leather message tube, opened it, and broke the wax seal on the letter inside with a thumbnail. As he read the sheet of parchment he'd unrolled, his eyebrows climbed toward his hairline. When he was through, he raised his head and spoke to his expectantly waiting officers: "Mikhran *marzban* requests—begs—our aid. Vshnasp *marzban* is dead. The Vaspurakaners have risen against him and against the worship of the God. If we don't come to his rescue at once, Mikhran says, the whole province will be lost."

II

ABIVARD STORMED THROUGH THE CORRIDORS OF HIS RESIDENCE. Venizelos started to say something to him but got a good look at his face and flattened himself against the wall to let his master pass.

Roshnani was embroidering fancy flowers on a caftan of winter-weight wool. She glanced up when Abivard came into the chamber where she was working, then bent her head to the embroidery once more.

"I told anyone who would listen that we should have left the Vaspurakaners to their own misguided cult," he ground out. "But no! We have to ram the God down their throats, too! And now look what it's gotten us."

"Yes, you told anyone who would listen," Roshnani said. "No one back in Mashiz listened. Are you surprised? Is this the first time such a thing has happened? Of course it's not. Besides, with Vshnasp over them, it's no wonder the Vaspurakaner princes decided to revolt."

"All the Vaspurakaners style themselves princes—the God alone knows why," Abivard said, a little less furious than he had been a moment before. He looked thoughtfully at his wife—his principal wife, he supposed he should have thought, but he'd been away from the others so long that he'd almost forgotten them. "Do you mean the Vaspurakaners would have rebelled even if we hadn't tried to impose the God on them?"

Roshnani nodded. "Aye, though maybe not so soon. Vshnasp had a reputation in Mashiz as a seducer. I don't suppose he would have stopped that just because he was sent to Vaspurakan."

"Mm, likely not," Abivard agreed. "Things were better with the old ways firmly in place, don't you think?"

"Better for men, certainly," Roshnani said, unusual sharpness in her voice. "If you ask the wives who spent their lives locked away in the women's quarters of strongholds and saw no more of the world than what the view out their windows happened to give, you might find them singing a different tune." She gave him a sidelong smile—she had never been one to stay in a bad humor. "Besides, husband of mine, are you not pleased to be on the cutting edge of fashion?"

"Now that you mention it, no," Abivard answered. Roshnani made a face at him. Like it or not, though, he and Sharbaraz *were* on the cutting edge of fashion. Giving their principal wives leave to emerge on occasion from the women's quarters had set long-frozen Makuraner usage on its ear. At first, ten years ago now, men had called noblewomen who appeared in public harlots merely for letting themselves be seen. But when the King of Kings and his most successful general set a trend, others would and did follow it.

"Besides," Roshnani said, "even under the old way, a man determined enough might find out how to sneak into the women's quarters for a little while, or a woman to sneak out of them."

"Never mind that," Abivard said. "Vshnasp won't sneak in now, nor women out to him. If such sneakings were what touched off the Vaspurakaner revolt, I wish some of the princes had caught him inside and made him into a eunuch so he would stay there without endangering anyone's chastity, including his own."

"You *are* angry at him," Roshnani observed. "A man says he wants to see another man made a eunuch only when his rage is full and deep."

"You're right, but that doesn't matter, either," Abivard answered. "Vshnasp is in the God's hands now, not mine, and if the God should drop his miserable soul into the Void . . ." He shook his head. Vshnasp *didn't* matter. He had to remember that. The hideous mess the late *marzban* of Vaspurakan had left behind was something else again.

As she often did, his wife thought along with him. "How much of our force here in the westlands will you have to take to Vaspurakan to bring the princes back under the rule of the King of Kings?" she asked.

"Too much," he said, "but I have no choice. We ought to hold the Videssian westlands, but we must hold Vaspurakan. We draw iron and silver and lead from the mines there and also a little gold. When times are friendlier than this, we draw horsemen, too. And if we don't control the east-west valleys, Videssos will. Whoever does control them has in his hands the best invasion routes to the other fellow's country."

"Maniakes has Vaspurakaner blood, not so?" Roshnani said.

Abivard nodded. "He does, and I wouldn't be the least surprised to find the Empire behind this uprising, either."

"Neither would I," Roshnani said. "It's what I'd do in his sandals. He doesn't dare come fight us face to face, so he stirs up trouble behind our backs." She thought for a moment. "How large a garrison do you purpose leaving behind here in Across?" Her voice was curiously expressionless.

"I've been chewing on that," Abivard answered. The face he made said that he didn't like what he'd been chewing. "I don't think I'm going to leave anyone. We'll need a good part of the field force to put down the princes, and on the far side of the Cattle Crossing the Videssians have soldiers to spare to gobble up any small garrison I leave here. Especially after they beat the Kubratoi earlier this summer, I don't want to hand them a cheap victory that would make them feel they can meet us and win. It's almost sorcery: if they feel that, it's halfway to being true."

He waited for Roshnani to explode like a covered pot left too long in the fire. She surprised him by nodding. "Good," she said. "I was going to suggest that, but I was afraid you'd be angry at me. I think you're right—you'd be throwing away any men you leave here."

"I think I'll name you my second in command," Abivard said, and that got him a smile. He gave it back, then quickly sobered.

"After we leave, though, the Videssians will come back anyhow. One of my officers is bound to write to Sharbaraz about that, and Sharbaraz is bound to write to me." He rolled his eyes. "One more thing to look forward to."

A wagon rolled up in front of the residence that had belonged to the Videssian logothete of the treasury. Abivard's children swarmed aboard it with cries of delight. "A house that moves!" Shahin exclaimed. None of them remembered what living in such a cramped space for weeks at a time was like. They'd find out. Roshnani did remember all too well. She climbed into the wagon with much less enthusiasm than her offspring showed.

Venizelos, Livania, and the rest of the Videssian servants stood in front of the house. The steward went to one knee in front of Abivard. "The lord with the great and good mind grant you health and safety, most eminent sir," the steward said.

"I thank you," Abivard answered, though he noted that Venizelos had not prayed that Phos grant him success. "Perhaps one day we'll see each other—I expect so, at any rate."

"Perhaps," was all Venizelos said. He did not want to think about the Makuraners' return to Across.

Abivard handed him a small heavy leather sack, gave Livania another, and went down the line of servants with more. Their thanks were loud and effusive. He could have forced them to go along with him. For that matter, he could have had them killed for the sport of it. The coins inside the sack were silver arkets of Makuran, not Videssian goldpieces. The servants would probably grumble about that once he was out of earshot. Again, though, he could have done far worse.

He swung up onto his horse, a stalwart bay gelding. With knees and reins, he urged the animal into a walk. The wagon driver, a skinny fellow named Pashang, flicked the reins of the two-horse team. Clattering, its ungreased axles squealing, the wagon rattled after Abivard.

Abivard's soldiers had broken camp many times. They were used to it. The loose women they'd picked up and the Videssian servants they'd swept up were another matter altogether. The army was late setting out. Abivard willingly forgave that on the first day. Afterward, he'd start jettisoning stragglers. He also suspected that the racket his force made could be heard in Videssos the city on the far side of the Cattle Crossing.

That didn't much worry him. If Maniakes couldn't hear the Makuraner army departing, he'd be able to see it. If he didn't watch personally, the captains of those accursed dromons would notice that the camp at the edge of Across had been abandoned.

Abivard had thought about leaving men behind to light fires and simulate one more night's occupancy. What point was there to it, though? Already, very likely, men were slipping into little rowboats they'd hidden from the Makuraners and hurrying across the strait to tell the Avtokrator everything they knew. He wouldn't have been a bit surprised to learn that Venizelos was one of those men.

At last, far more slowly than he'd hoped, his force shook itself out into something that approximated its future line of march. Light cavalry, archers riding unarmored horses and wearing no more protection than helms and leather jerkins themselves, formed the vanguard, the rear guard, and scouting parties to either flank.

Within that screen of light cavalry rode the heavy horsemen who made the red lion of Makuran so feared. Neither riders nor horses were armored now, for Abivard did not expect battle any time soon. The weight of iron warriors and beasts carried into battle was plenty to exhaust the horses if they tried bearing it day in, day out. The riders still bore their long lances in the sockets on the right side of their saddles, though, even if their armor was wrapped and stored in the supply wagons.

Those, along with the wagons carrying noncombatants, made up the core of the army in motion. If Abivard suddenly had to fight, he would maneuver to put his force between the baggage train and the foe, regardless of the direction from which the foe came.

He ordered the army southwest on the first day's march, away from the coast. He did not want Maniakes' dromons watching every move he made and reporting back to the Avtokrator. He assumed that Maniakes already knew he was heading off to avenge Vshnasp. How fast was he going, and by what route? That was his business, not Maniakes'.

Peasants who had been busy in the fields took one look at the outriders to Abivard's army and did their best to make themselves invisible. Any who lived near high ground fled there. Those who didn't either hid in their houses or ran off with their wives and families and beasts of burden and whatever they could carry on their backs or those of their oxen and donkeys and horses.

"Take what you need from those who have run away," Abivard told his men, "but don't go setting fires for the sport of it." Some of the warriors grumbled; incendiarism was one of the sports that made war entertaining.

All was quiet the first night on the march and the second. On the third night someone—a couple of someones—sneaked past the sentries and lobbed arrows into the Makuraner camp. The archers wounded two men and escaped under cover of darkness.

"They will not play the game that way," Abivard declared when the unwelcome news reached him. "Tomorrow we burn everything along the line of march."

"Well done, lord," Romezan boomed. "We should have been doing that all along. If the Videssians fear us, they'll leave us alone."

"But if they hate us, they'll keep on hitting back at us no matter what we do," Kardarigan said. "It's a fine line we walk between being frightful and being despised."

"I was willing to treat them mildly," Abivard answered, "but if they shoot at us from ambush out of the night, I won't waste much sympathy on them, either. Actions have consequences."

Smoke from a great burning rose the next day. Abivard supposed that sailors on Videssian dromons, looking in from the waters of the Videssian Sea, could use that smoke to figure out where his army was. That made him regret having given the order, but only a little: Maniakes would have learned his whereabouts soon enough, anyhow.

When darkness fell, several more men shot at the encamped Makuraners. This time Abivard's troops were alert and ready. They swarmed out into the night after the bowmen and caught three of them. The Videssians were a long time dying. Most of the soldiers slept soundly through their shrieks.

Abivard ordered another day of burning when morning came. Kardarigan said, "If we trade frightfulness for frightfulness, where will this end?"

"We can hurt the Videssian in the westlands worse than they can hurt us," Abivard told him. "The sooner they get that idea, the sooner we can stop giving them lessons."

"Videssians are supposed to be a clever folk—you'd certainly think so from hearing them talk about themselves," Romezan added. "If they're too stupid to see that raids against the armies of the King of Kings are more trouble than they're worth, whose hard luck is it? Not ours, by the God. Drop me into the Void if I can work up much sympathy for 'em."

For the next couple of days the local Videssians left the Makuraner army alone as it passed through their land. Abivard didn't know what happened after that; maybe his men outrode the news of what they did to the countryside when someone harassed them. Whatever the reason, the Videssians again took to shooting at the army by night.

The next day the Makuraners sent pillars of smoke billowing up to the sky. The day after that the Videssians caught two men from the vanguard away from the rest, cut their throats, and left them where the rest of the Makuraners would find them. That afternoon a medium-size Videssian village abruptly ceased to be.

"Lovely sort of fighting," Kardarigan remarked as Abivard's army made camp for the night. "I wish Maniakes would come forth and meet us. Fighting a real battle against real soldiers would be a relief."

"Wait till we get to Vaspurakan," Abivard told him. "The princes will be happy enough to oblige you."

Dispatches from Mikhran reached Abivard every day. The *marzban* kept urging him not to delay, to rush, to storm, to come to his rescue. All that proved to Abivard was that Mikhran hadn't yet received his first letter promising aid. He began to wonder if his courier had gotten through. If the Videssians harassed his army, what did they do to lone dispatch riders? On the other hand, if they habitually ambushed couriers, how did the ones Mikhran sent keep reaching him?

The army forded the Eriza River not far south of its headwaters. The Eriza would grow to become a stream of considerable importance, joining the Arandos to become the largest river system in the Videssian westlands. A bridge spanned the river a couple of farsangs south of the ford, or, rather, a bridge had spanned it. Abivard remembered watching it go up in flames as the Videssians had tried to halt his army's advance in one of the early campaigns in the westlands. It had yet to be repaired.

Tzikas remembered the bridge burning, too; he'd ordered it set afire. "You didn't know about the ford then, brother-in-law to the King of Kings," he said, still proud of his stratagem.

"That's so, eminent sir," Abivard agreed. "But if I'd pressed on instead of swinging south, I would have found out about it. The local peasants would have given it away, if for no other reason than to keep us from eating them out of house and home."

"Peasants." Tzikas let out a scornful snort amazingly like the one his horse would have produced. "That's hardly a fit way to run a war."

"I thought you Videssians were the ones who seized whatever worked and we Makuraners were more concerned with honor," Abivard said.

"Give me horsemen, brother-in-law to the King of Kings," Tzikas answered. "I will show you where honor lies and how to pursue it. How can you deny me now, when we shall no longer be facing Videssians but heretical big-nosed men of Vaspurakan? Let me serve the King of Kings, may his years be long and his realm increase, and let me serve the cause of Hosios Avtokrator."

Whatever the topic of conversation, Tzikas was adept at turning it toward his own desires. "Let us draw closer to Vaspurakan," Abivard said. The Videssian turncoat scowled at him, but what could he do? He lived on sufferance; Abivard was under no obligation to give him anything at all, let alone his heart's desire.

And while Tzikas scornfully dismissed the Vaspurakaners as heretics now, might he not suddenly develop or discover the view that they were in fact his coreligionists? Down under the skin, weren't Phos worshipers Phos worshipers come what may? If he did something of that sort, he would surely do it at the worst possible moment, too.

"You do not trust me," Tzikas said mournfully. "Since the days of Likinios Avtokrator, may Phos' light shine upon him, no one has trusted me."

There were good and cogent reasons for that, too, Abivard thought. He'd met Likinios. The Videssian Emperor had been devious enough for any four other people he'd ever known. If anyone could have been confident of outmaneuvering Tzikas at need, he was the man. After fighting against Tzikas, after accepting him as a fugitive upon his failure to assassinate Maniakes, Abivard thought himself justified in exercising caution where the Videssian was concerned.

Seeing that he would get no immediate satisfaction, Tzikas gave Abivard a curt nod and rode off. His stiff back said louder than words how indignant he was at having his probity questioned constantly.

Romezan watched him depart, then came up to Abivard and asked, "Who stuck the red-hot poker up his arse?"

"I did, I'm afraid," Abivard answered. "I just don't want to give him the regiment he keeps begging of me."

"Good," Romezan said. "The God keep him from being at my back the day I need help. He'd stand there smiling, hiding a knife in the sleeve of his robe. No thank you."

"Sooner or later he *will* write to Sharbaraz," Abivard said gloomily. "Odds are, too, that his request will get me ordered to give him everything his cold little heart desires."

"The God prevent!" Romezan's fingers twisted in an apotropaic sign. "If that does happen, he could always have an accident."

"Like the one Maniakes almost had, you mean?" Abivard asked. Romezan nodded. Abivard sighed. "That could happen, I suppose, though the idea doesn't much appeal to me. I keep hoping he'll want to be useful in some kind of way where I won't have to watch my back every minute to make sure he's not sliding that knife you were talking about between my ribs."

"The only use he's been so far is to embarrass Maniakes,"

Romezan said. "He doesn't even do that well anymore; the more the Videssians hear about how we came to acquire him, the more they think we're welcome to him."

"The King of Kings puts great stock in Videssian traitors," Abivard said. "Having had his throne usurped by treachery, he knows what damage it can do to a ruler."

"If the King of Kings is so fond of Videssian traitors, why don't we ship Tzikas off to Mashiz?" Romezan grumbled. But that was no answer, and he and Abivard both knew it. If Sharbaraz King of Kings expected them to encourage and abet Videssian traitors, they had to do it no matter how much Tzikas raised their hackles.

The road swung up from the coastal lowlands onto the central plateau. Resaina lay near the northern edge of the plateau, about a third of the way from the crossing of the Eriza to Vaspurakan. Like most good-sized Videssian towns, it had a Makuraner garrison quartered within its walls.

A plump, graying fellow named Gorgin commanded the garrison. "I've heard somewhat of the Vaspurakaners' outrages, lord," he said. "By the God, it does my heart good to see you ready to chastise them with all the force at your command."

Abivard sliced a bite of meat from the leg of mutton Gorgin had served him—cooked with garlic in the Videssian fashion instead of Makuraner style with mint. He stabbed the chunk and brought it to his mouth with the dagger. While chewing, he remarked, "I notice you do not volunteer the men of your command to join in this chastisement."

"I have not enough men here to hold down the city and the countryside against a real revolt," Gorgin answered. "If you take some of my soldiers from me, how shall I be able to defend Resaina against any sort of trouble whatever? These mad easterners riot at the drop of a skullcap. If someone who fancies himself a theologian rises among 'em, I won't be able to put 'em down."

"Are you enforcing the edict ordering their holy men to preach the Vaspurakaner rite?" Abivard asked.

"Aye, I have been," Gorgin told him. "That's one of the reasons

I feared riots. Then, a few weeks ago, the Videssians, may they fall into the Void, stopped complaining about the rite."

"That's good news," Abivard said.

"I *thought* so," Gorgin replied gloomily. "But now my spies report the reason why they accept the Vaspurakaners' rituals: it's because the men from the mountains have revolted against us. The Videssians admire them for doing it because they'd like to get free of our yoke, too."

"You're right," Abivard said. "I don't fancy that, not even a little bit. What are we supposed to do about it, though? If we order them to go back to their old rituals, we not only disobey Sharbaraz King of Kings, may his days be long and his realm increase, we also make ourselves look ridiculous to the Videssians."

"We don't want that, let me tell you," Gorgin said. "They're hard enough to govern even when they know they have good reason to fear us. When they're laughing at us behind our backs, they're impossible. They'll do any harebrained thing to stir up trouble, but half the time their schemes end up not being harebrained at all. They find more ways to drive me crazy than I'd ever imagined." He shook his head with the bewildered air of a man who knew he was in too deep.

"After we beat the Vaspurakaners, the Videssians will see that the revolt didn't amount to anything," Abivard answered. "As soon as they realize that, the princes will look like heretics again, not heroes."

"The God grant it be so," Gorgin said.

A moment later Abivard discovered that not all Videssians willingly accepted the Vaspurakaner liturgy. "Torture! Heresy! Mayhem!" a man shrieked as he ran into Gorgin's residence.

The garrison commander jerked as if stuck by a pin, then exchanged a glance full of apprehension with Abivard. Both men got to their feet. "What have they gone and done now?" Gorgin asked, plainly meaning, *What new disaster has fallen on my head?*

But the disaster had fallen on the head of a Videssian priest, not that of Gorgin. The fellow sat in an antechamber, his shaved scalp and part of his forehead puffy and splashed here and there with dried blood. "You see?" cried the Videssian who had brought him in. "Do you see? They captured him, kidnapped him, however you like, and then they—" He pointed.

Abivard did see. The swelling and the blood came from the words that had been tattooed into the priest's head. Abivard read Videssian only haltingly. After some study, he gathered that the words came from a theological text attacking the Vaspurakaners and their beliefs. The priest would wear those passages for the rest of his life.

"Do you see?" Gorgin exclaimed, as the local had before him. "Every time you think you have their measure, the Videssians do something like this. Or something not like this but just as hideous, just as unimaginable, in a different way."

"We may even be able to make this outrage work to our advantage," Abivard said. "Take this fellow out and show him off after he heals. We can make him out to be a martyr to his version—our version—of the Videssians' false faith. When you take the heads of the men who did this, people will say they had it coming."

"Mm, yes, that's not bad," Gorgin said after a moment's thought. He looked at the priest who had just become, however unwillingly, a walking religious tract. "If he'd let his hair grow out, after a while you'd only be able to see a little of that."

He and Abivard had both been using their own language, assuming that the Videssian priest did not speak it. He proved them wrong, saying in fair Makuraner, "A bare scalp is the mark of the good god's servant. I shall wear these lying texts with pride, as a badge of holiness."

"On your head be it," Abivard said. The priest merely nodded. Gorgin stared at him as if he'd said something horrid. After a moment he realized he had.

The Videssian central plateau put Abivard in mind of the country not far from Vek Rud domain. It was a little better watered and a little more broken up by hills and valleys than the territory in which he'd grown up, but it was mostly herding country, not farmland, and so had a familiar feel to it.

He didn't think much of the herds of cattle and flocks of sheep moving slowly over the grasslands. Any *dihqan* back in Makuran would have been ashamed to admit he owned such a handful of ragged, scraggly beasts. Of course, the flocks and herds of Makuran hadn't been devastated by years of civil war and invasion.

The Videssians certainly thought like their Makuraner counterparts. As soon as they got wind of the approach of Abivard's army, they tried to get their animals as far out of the way as they could. Foraging parties had to scatter widely to bring in the beasts that helped keep the army fed.

"That's the way," Romezan said when the soldiers led in a good many sheep one afternoon when the highlands of Makuran were beginning to push their way up over the western horizon. "If they won't give us what we need, we'll bloody well take it—and we'll take so much, we'll make the Videssians, crazed as they are with their false Phos, take starvation for a virtue because they'll see so much of it."

"These lands are subject to the rule of Sharbaraz King of Kings and so may not be wantonly oppressed," Abivard reminded him. But then he softened that by adding, "If the choice lies between our doing without and theirs, we ought not to be the ones going hungry."

From the west Mikhran *marzban* still bombarded him with letters urging haste. From the east he heard nothing. He wondered if Maniakes had retaken Across and whether Venizelos had resumed his post as steward to the logothete of the treasury.

Farrokh-Zad, one of Kardarigan's lieutenants, said, "Let your spirits not be cast down, lord, for surely this fool of a Maniakes, seeing us departed, will overreach himself as has been his habit of old. After vanquishing the vile Vaspurakaners, with their noses like sickles and their beards like thickets of wire, we shall return and take from the Videssian whatever paltry parts of the westlands he may steal from us. For are we not the men of Makuran, the mighty men whom the God delights to honor?"

He puffed out his chest, twirled the waxed tip of his mustache, and struck a fierce pose, dark eyes glittering. He was younger than Abivard and far more arrogant: Abivard had been on the point of laughing at his magniloquent bombast when he realized that Farrokh-Zad was in earnest.

"May Fraortish eldest of all ask the God to grant your prayers," Abivard said, and let it go at that. Farrokh-Zad nodded and rode off, a procession of one. Abivard stared after him. Farrokh-Zad probably hadn't set foot in Makuran since his beard had come in fully, but being away hadn't seemed to change his attitudes in the slightest. Those had probably set as hard as cast bronze before he had gotten big enough to defy his mother.

About half the officers in the army were like that; Romezan was a leader among them. They clung to the usages they'd always known even when those usages fit like a boy's caftan on a grown man. Abivard snorted. He was in the other faction, the ones who had taken on so many foreign ways that they hardly seemed like Makuraners anymore. If they ever did go home to stay, they were liable to be white crows in a black flock. But then, Abivard thought, he'd been getting around Makuraner traditions since the day he had decided to let Roshnani come along when he and Sharbaraz had launched their civil war against Smerdis the usurper.

Such concerns vanished a little later, for an armored rider approached the Makuraner army from the west, carrying a white-painted shield of truce. He was not a Videssian, although the army was still on what had been Videssian soil, but a warrior of Vaspurakan—a noble, by his horse and his gear.

Abivard had the fellow brought before him. He studied the Vaspurakaner with interest: he was not a tall man but thick-shouldered, with a barrel chest and strong arms. Abivard would not have cared to wrestle with him; he made even the bulky Romezan svelte by comparison. His features were strong and heavy, with bushy eyebrows that came together above a nose of truly majestic proportions. His thick beard, black lightly frosted with gray, spilled down over the front of his scale mail shirt and grew up to within a finger's breadth of his eyes. He looked brooding and powerful.

When he spoke, Abivard expected a bass rumble like falling rocks. Instead, his voice was a pleasant, melodious baritone: "I greet you, Abivard son of Godarz, brother-in-law to Sharbaraz King of Kings, may his years be many and his realm increase," he said in Makuraner fluent enough but flavored by a throaty accent quite different from the Videssian lisp to which Abivard had grown used. "I am Gazrik son of Bardzrabol, and I have authority to speak for the princes of Vaspurakan."

"I greet you, Gazrik son of Bardzrabol," Abivard said, doing his best to imitate the way the Vaspurakaner pronounced his name and that of his father. "Speak, then. Enlarge yourself; say what is in your mind. My ears and my heart are open to you."

"You are as gracious as men say, lord, than which what compliment could be higher?" Gazrik replied. He and Abivard exchanged another round of compliments, and another. Abivard offered wine; Gazrik accepted. He took from a saddlebag a round pastry made with chopped dates and sprinkled over with powdered sugar; Abivard pronounced it delicious, and did not tell him the Videssians called such Vaspurakaner confections "princes' balls." At last, the courtesies completed, Gazrik began to come to the point. "Know, lord, that the cause of peace would be better served if you turned this host of yours aside from Vaspurakan, the princes' land, the heroes' land."

"Know, Gazrik son of Bardzrabol, the cause of peace would be better served if you left off your rebellion against Mikhran *marzban* and handed over to him the vile and vicious wretches responsible for the assassination of his predecessor, Vshnasp *marzban*."

Gazrik shook his head; Abivard was reminded of a black bear up in the Dilbat Mountains in back of Mashiz unexpectedly coming upon a man. The Vaspurakaner said, "Lord, we do not repent that Vshnasp *marzban* is dead. He was an evil man, and his rule over us was full of evils."

"Sharbaraz King of Kings set him over you. You were in law bound to obey him," Abivard answered.

"Had he stayed in law, obey him we would have," Gazrik said. "But you, lord, if a man took women all unwilling from your women's quarters for his own pleasure, what would you do?'"

"I do not know that Vshnasp did any such thing," Abivard said, deliberately not thinking of some of the reports he'd heard. "A man's enemies will lie to make him seem worse than he is."

Gazrik snorted, not a horselike sound but almost the abrupt, coughing roar of a lion. Abivard had rarely heard such scorn. "Have that however you will, lord," the Vaspurakaner said. "But I tell you this also: any man who seeks to lead the princes away from Phos who first made Vaspur, that man shall die and spend eternity in Skotos' ice. If you help those who would force this on us, we shall fight you, too."

Uneasily, Abivard answered, "Sharbaraz King of Kings has ordained this course. So he has ordered; so shall it be."

"No," Gazrik said—just the one word, impossible to contradict. He went on in an earnest voice: "We were loyal subjects to the King of Kings. We paid him tribute in iron and silver and gold; our soldiers fought in his wars. We would do this again, did he not interfere in our faith."

Abivard hoped his frown concealed what he was thinking, for he agreed with Gazrik and had tried to persuade Sharbaraz to follow the course the Vaspurakaner had suggested. But the King of Kings had not agreed, which meant Abivard had to conform to the policy Sharbaraz had set regardless of what he thought of it. Abivard said, "The Videssians make all their subjects worship in the same way: as they have one empire, so they also have one religion. Sharbaraz King of Kings has decreed this a good arrangement for Makuran as well. Let all worship the God; let all acknowledge the power of the King of Kings."

Gazrik stared down his nose at him—and a fine nose for staring down it was, too. With magnificent contempt the Vaspurakaner said, "And if the Avtokrator of the Videssians chose to leap off a cliff, would Sharbaraz King of Kings likewise cast himself down from a promontory?" By his tone, he hoped it would be so.

Several of the Makuraner generals behind Abivard growled angrily. "Hold your tongue, you insolent dog!" Romezan said.

"Some day we may meet without shield of truce, noble from the Seven Clans," Gazrik answered. "Then we shall see which of us teaches the other manners." He turned back to Abivard. "Brother-in-law to the King of Kings, Mikhran *marzban* holds only the valley containing the fortress of Poskh, and not all of that. If he will withdraw and leave us in peace, we will give him leave to go. This will let you turn back to the east and go on with your war against Videssos. But if he would stay and you would go on, we shall have war between us."

The trouble was that Abivard saw the course Gazrik proposed as most expedient for Makuran. He exhaled slowly and angrily. He could either obey Sharbaraz in spite of thinking him mistaken or rebel against the King of Kings. He'd seen enough of rebellion both in Makuran and in a Videssos too ravaged by uprising after uprising to oppose the forces of the King of Kings.

And so, wishing he could do otherwise, he said, "Gazrik son of Bardzrabol, if you are wise, you will disband your armies, have your men go home to the valleys where they were born, and beg Sharbaraz King of Kings to show you mercy on the grounds that you rebelled against his appointed *marzban* only because of the outrages he committed against your women. Then perhaps you will have peace. If you continue in arms against Sharbaraz King of Kings, know that we his soldiers shall grind you as the millstones grind wheat into flour, and the wind will blow you away like chaff."

"We have war now," Gazrik said. "We shall have more. You will pay in blood for every foot you advance into the princes' land." He bowed in the saddle to Romezan. "When the time comes, we shall see who speaks of insolence and of dogs. Skotos hollows a place in the eternal ice for you even now."

"May the Void swallow you—and so it shall," Romezan shouted back. Gazrik wheeled his horse and rode away without another word.

Soli, on the eastern bank of the Rhamnos River, was the last town in Videssian territory through which Abivard's army passed before formally entering Vaspurakan. The stone bridge over the river had been destroyed in one of the campaigns in the war between Makuran and Videssos, or perhaps in a round of Videssian civil war. But the Makuraner garrison commander, an energetic officer named Hushang, had spanned the ruined arch with timbers. Horses snorted nervously as their hooves drummed on the planks, but they and the heavily laden supply wagons crossed without difficulty.

Abivard did not feel he was entering a new world when he reached the west bank of the Rhamnos. The mountains grew a little higher and the sides of the valleys seemed a little steeper than they had on the Videssian side of the river, but the difference as yet was small. As for the people, folk of Vaspurakaner blood were far from rare east of the Rhamnos. The marketplace at Soli had been full of dark, stocky men, many of them in the three-peaked cap with multicolored streamers that was the national headdress of Vaspurakan.

"That's an ugly hat, isn't it, Father?" Varaz said one evening as a Vaspurakaner rode away after selling some sheep to the Makuraner army. "If you're not going to wear a helmet, you should wear a pilos the way we do." His hand went to the felt cap shaped like a truncated cone that sat on his own head.

"Well, I don't much fancy the caps the Vaspurakaners wear, I admit," Abivard told him, "but it's the same as it is with horses and women: not everybody thinks the same ones are beautiful. The other day I found out what the Vaspurakaners call the pilos." Varaz waited expectantly. Abivard told him: "A chamber pot that goes on the head."

He'd expected his son to be disgusted. Instead Varaz giggled. For boys of a certain age the line between disgusting and hilarious was a fine one. "Do they really call it that, Father?" Varaz demanded. Regretting he'd mentioned it, Abivard nodded. Varaz giggled even louder. "Wait till I tell Shahin."

Abivard decided not to put on a pilos for the next several weeks without upending it first.

He and the army pressed on toward the valley of Poskh. At first, in spite of what Gazrik had threatened, no one opposed them. The Vaspurakaner *nakharars*—nobles whose status was much like that of the *dihqans* of Makuran—stayed shut up in their gray stone fortresses and watched the Makuraners pass. To show them that he rewarded restraint with restraint, he kept the plundering by his men to a minimum.

That wasn't easy; the valleys of Vaspurakan were full of groves with apricots and plums and peaches just coming to juicy ripeness, full of sleek cattle and strong if not particularly handsome horses, full of all sorts of growing things.

Most of the valleys ran from east to west. Abivard chuckled as he passed from one into the next. A great many Makuraner armies had gone into battle heading east, roaring through Vaspurakan into the Videssian westlands. But never before in all the days of the world had the minstrels had the chance to sing of a Makuraner army moving into battle from the east: out of Videssos and into Vaspurakan.

His riders were entering the valley that held the town and fortress of Khliat when the princes first struck at them. It was not an attack of horsemen against horsemen; that his force would have faced gladly. But the Vaspurakaners were less eager to face them. And so, instead of couching lances and charging home on those unlovely horses of theirs, they pushed rocks down the mountainside, touching off an avalanche they hoped would bury their foes without their having to face them hand to hand.

But they were a bit too eager and began shoving the boulders too soon. The rumble and crash of stone striking stone drew the Makuraners' eyes to the slopes above them. They reined in frantically, except for some in the van who galloped forward, hoping to outrun the falling rocks.

Not all escaped. Men shouted and wailed in agony as they were struck; horses with broken legs screamed. But the army, as an army, was not badly harmed.

Abivard stared grimly ahead toward the walls of Khliat as his men labored to clear boulders from the track so that the supply wagons could go forward. The sun sparkled off the weapons and armor of the warriors on those walls.

He turned to Kardarigan. "Take your soldiers and burn the fields and orchards here. If the Vaspurakaners will not face us in battle like men, let them learn the cost of cowardice as we taught it to the Videssians."

"Aye, lord," the great captain said dutifully, if without great enthusiasm. Before long flames were licking through the branches of the fruit trees. Great black clouds of smoke rose into the blue dome of the sky. Horses rode through wheatfields, trampling down the growing grain. Then the fields were fired, too. Come winter, Khliat would be a hungry place.

The Vaspurakaners shut up in the fortress shouted curses at Abivard's men, some in the Makuraner tongue, some in Videssian, but most in their own language. Abivard understood hardly a word of that, but it sounded fierce. If the sound had anything to do with the strength of the curse, Vaspurakaner was a fine language in which to wish harm on one's foes.

"The gloves have come off," Romezan said. "From now on we fight hard for everything we get." He sounded delighted at the prospect.

He also proved as good a prophet as any since the Four. Khliat was not well placed to keep invaders from moving west; that showed that it had been built in fear of Makuran rather than Videssos. Abivard and his army were able to skirt it, brush aside the screen of Vaspurakaner horsemen trying to block the pass ahead, and force their way into the valley of Hanzith.

As soon as he saw the shape of the mountains along the jagged boundary between earth and sky, Abivard was certain he'd been this way before. And yet he was just as certain that he'd never passed through this part of Vaspurakan before in all his life. It was puzzling.

No—it would have been puzzling had he had more than a couple of heartbeats to worry about it. No cavalry screen lay athwart the valley here; the Vaspurakaners had assembled an army of their own to block his progress toward the valley and fortress of Poskh. The riders were too many to be contained in the pair of fortresses controlling the valley of Hanzith. Their tents sprawled across what had been cropland, a few bright silk, more dun-colored canvas hard to tell at a distance from dirt.

When the Makuraners forced their way into the valley, horns cried the alarm up and down its length. The Vaspurakaners rushed to ready themselves for battle. Abivard ordered his own lightly armed horsemen ahead to buy time for himself and the rest of his heavy horse to do likewise.

If you rode everywhere in iron covering you from head to toe, if you draped your horse in what amounted to a blanket and headpiece covered with iron scales, and if you then tried to travel, you accomplished but one thing: You exhausted the animals. You saved that gear till you really needed it. This was one of those times.

Supply wagons rattled forward. Warriors crowded around them. Drivers and servants passed their armor out to them. They helped one another fasten the lashings and catches of their suits: chain mail sleeves and gloves, finger-sized iron splints covering the torso, a mail skirt, and iron rings on the legs, all bound to leather.

Abivard set his helmet back on his head after attaching to it a mail aventail to protect the back of his neck and a mail veil to ward his face below the eyes. Sweat streamed from every pore. He understood how a chicken felt when it sweltered in a stew pot. Not for nothing did the Videssians call Makuraner heavy cavalry "the boiler boys."

He felt as if he were carrying Varaz on his shoulders when he walked back to his horse and grunted with the effort of climbing into the saddle. "You know," he said cheerfully as he mounted, "I've heard of men who've had their hearts give out trying this."

"Go ahead, lord," someone said close by. With metal veils hiding features and blurring voices, it was hard to tell who. "Make me feel old."

"I'm not the one doing that," Abivard answered. "It's the armor."

He surveyed the Vaspurakaners mustering against him. They did not have his numbers, but most of them and their horses wore armor like that of his heavy horsemen and their mounts. Iron was plentiful and cheap in Vaspurakan; every village had a smith or two, and every fortress had several of them, mostly busy making armor. Merchants sold Vaspurakaner cuirasses in Mashiz, and he'd seen them in the marketplaces of Amorion, Across, and other Videssian towns.

"Come on!" he shouted to his men. "Fast as you can." Who deployed first and by how much would say a lot about how and where the battle was fought.

Vaspurakaner horsemen began trotting toward his screening force of light cavalry before he had more than half his force of heavy horse ready for action. The Makuraners whooped and made mock charges and shot arrows at the oncoming princes. One or two Vaspurakaner horses screamed; one or two riders slid from their saddles. Most kept right on coming, almost as if the foes before them weren't there. Their advance had a daunting inevitability to it, as if the Makuraners were trying to hold back the sea.

Lances in the first ranks of the Vaspurakaner force swung from vertical down to horizontal. The princes booted their horses up from a slow trot to a quick one. Up ahead steel flashed from drawn swords as the Makuraner light cavalry readied itself to receive the charge.

It broke. Abivard had known it would break. Some of the Makuraners were speared out of their saddles, and some were ridden down by men and horses too heavily armed and armored to withstand. Most of his light horse simply scattered to either flank. The men were brave, but asking them to stop such opponents for long was simply expecting too much.

They had already done as much as he'd wanted them to do, though: they'd bought time. Enough of his own heavy horsemen had armed themselves to stand up against the Vaspurakaners. He waved the riders ahead, trotting at their fore. If they could hold the princes in place for a while, he'd soon have enough men to do a proper job of crushing them.

Next to him a proud young man carried the red-lion banner of Makuran. The Vaspurakaners fought under a motley variety of standards, presumably those of the *nakharars* who headed their contingents. Abivard saw a wolf, a bear, a crescent moon . . . He looked farther down their battle line. No, he couldn't make out what was on those banners.

He stared at them nonetheless. Those indecipherable standards set against these particular notched mountains—this was the first of the scenes Bogorz had shown him. The wizard had lifted the veil into the future, but so what? Abivard had no idea whether he was destined to win or lose this battle and hadn't realized he was in the midst of what he had foreseen till it was too late to do anything about it.

"Get moving!" he called to his men. The momentum that came from horse, rider, and weight of armor was what gave his lancers their punch. The last thing he wanted was to be stalled in place and let the Vaspurakaners thunder down on him. To meet them on even terms he had to have as much power in his charge as they did.

The collision sounded like a thousand smiths dumping their work on a stone floor all at the same time and then screaming about what they'd done. The fight, as it developed, was altogether devoid of subtlety: two large bands of men hammering away at each other to see which would break first.

Abivard speared a Vaspurakaner out of the saddle. His lance shattered against a second man's shield. He yanked out his long, straight sword and lay about him. The Videssians, whose archers and javelin men were between his heavy and light forces in armor and other gear, had delighted in feints and stratagems. He'd smashed through them all. Now the Vaspurakaners were trying to smash him.

One of the princes swung at him with the ruined stump of a lance much like the one he'd thrown away. He took the blow in the side. *"Aii!"* he said. The finger-sized iron splints of his armor and the leather and padding beneath them kept him from having broken bones –at least, no fractured ribs stabbed at him like knives when he breathed—but he knew he'd have a great dark bruise when he took off his corselet after the fight was done.

He slashed at the Vaspurakaner backhanded. The fellow was wearing a chain mail veil like his own. That meant Abivard's sword didn't carve a slab off his face, but the blow surely broke his nose and probably his teeth, too. The Vaspurakaner screamed, clutched at his hurt, and reeled away before Abivard could finish him.

Locked in a hate-filled embrace, the two armies writhed together, neither able to force the other back or break through. Now the lightly-armed Makuraners whom the men of Vaspurakan had so abruptly shoved aside came into their own. From either wing those of them who had not fled plied the Vaspurakaners with arrows and rushed stragglers four and five against one. The princes had no similar troops to drive them back.

A shout of "Hosios Avtokrator!" rose from the Makuraner left. That had to be Tzikas; none of the Makuraners cared a candied fig about Sharbaraz' puppet. But Tzikas, even without the prestige of Makuraner rank or clan, was able to lead by courage and force of personality. He slew a Vaspurakaner horseman, then swarmed in among the princes. Makuraners followed, wedging the breach in the line open wider. The men of Vaspurakan began falling back, which encouraged the Makuraners to press ahead even harder than they had before.

In the space of what seemed only a few heartbeats, the fight went from battle to rout. Instead of pressing forward as doughtily as their opponents, the Vaspurakaners broke off and tried to flee. As often happens, that might have cost them more casualties than it saved. Abivard hacked down a couple of men from behind; how could you resist with your foes' back to you?

Some of the Vaspurakaners made for the castles in the valleys, which kept their gates open wide till the Makuraners got too close for comfort. Other princes rode up into the foothills that led to the ranges separating one valley from another. Some made stands up there, while others simply tried to hide from the victorious Makuraners.

Abivard was not interested in besieging the Vaspurakaner castles. He was not even interested in scouring the valley of Hanzith clean of foes. For years, for centuries, Vaspurakan had been full of men with no great love for Makuran. The King of Kings had derived great profit from it even so. Sharbaraz could derive great profit again—once his *marzban* was freed to control the countryside. Getting Mikhran out of the castle of Poskh came first.

The valley of Poskh ran southwest from Hanzith. Abivard pushed his way through the pass a little before sunset. He saw the fortress, gray and massive in the distance, with the Vaspurakaners' lines around it. They hadn't sealed it off tightly from the outside world, but supply wagons would have had a rugged time getting into the place.

"Tomorrow we attack," Romezan said, sharpening the point of

his lance on a whetstone. "The God grant I meet that churlish Vaspurakaner envoy. I shall have somewhat to say to him of manners."

"I'm just glad we hurt the Vaspurakaners worse than they hurt us," Abivard said. "It could have gone the other way about as easily—and even if we free Mikhran, will that do all we want?"

"How not?" Romezan said. "We'll get him out of the fortress, join forces with his men, thump the Vaspurakaners a few times, and remind them they'd better fear the God." He slammed his thick chest with one fist; the sound was almost like stone on wood.

"They may fear the God, but are they going to worship him?" Abivard asked. "We ruled them for a long time without demanding that. Now that we have demanded it, can we make them obey?"

"Either they obey or they go into the Void, which would prove to 'em the truth of our religion if only they could come back whence none returneth." Romezan was a typical man of the Seven Clans: he took his boyhood learning and beliefs as a given and expected everyone also to take them the same way. Within his limits he was solid.

"We should be trying to keep the princes quiet so we can fight Videssos, not antagonizing them, too," Abivard said. "We should—" He shook his head. "What's the use? We have our orders, so we follow them." He wasn't so different from Romezan, after all.

If Gazrik was in the fight the next day, Abivard didn't know it. With his force attacking the Vaspurakaners who besieged the fortress of Poskh, with Mikhran and his fellow Makuraners sallying from the fortress to grind the princes between two stones, the battle was easier than the previous fighting had been. Had he commanded the Vaspurakaners, he would have withdrawn in the night rather than accept combat on such terms. Sometimes headlong courage was its own punishment.

By noon his soldiers were gathering in the mounts of unhorsed Vaspurakaners and plundering bodies of weapons and armor, rings and bracelets, and whatever else a man might think of some value. One soldier carefully removed the red-dyed plumes from a prince's helm and replaced the crest of his own headgear with them.

Abivard had seen and heard and smelled the aftermath of battle too often for it to astonish or horrify him. It was what happened. He rode over the field till he found Mikhran *marzban*. He did not know the new Makuraner governor of Vaspurakan by sight, but like him, Mikhran had a standard-bearer nearby displaying the banner of their country.

"Well met, lord," Mikhran said, realizing who he must be. The *marzban* was a few years younger than he, with a long, thin face made to hold worried wrinkles. That face had already acquired a good many and probably would gain more as the years went by. "Thank you for your aid; without it, I should have come to know the inside of that castle a great deal better than I wanted."

"Happy to have helped," Abivard answered. "I might have been doing other things with my force, I admit, but this was one that needed doing."

Mikhran nodded vigorously. "Aye, lord, it was. And now that you have freed me from Poskh valley and Poskh fortress, our chances of regaining rule over all of Vaspurakan are—" Abivard waited for him to say something like *assured* or *very good indeed*. Instead, he went on, "—not much different from what they were while I was holed up in there."

Abivard looked at him with sudden liking. "You are an honest man."

"No more than I have to be," the *marzban* answered with a wintry smile. "But whatever else I may be, I am not a blind man, and only a blind man could fail to see how the princes hate us for making them worship the God."

"That is the stated will of Sharbaraz King of Kings, may his years be many and his realm increase," Abivard said. "The King of Kings feels that as he is the sole ruler of Makuran and as this land has come under Makuraner sway, it should be brought into religious conformity with the rest of the realm: one realm, one faith, one loyalty." He looked around at the scattered bodies and the spilled blood now turning black. "That one loyalty seems, um, a trifle hard to discover at the moment."

Mikhran's mournful features, which had corrugated even further as Abivard set forth the reasoning of the King of Kings, eased a bit when he admitted that the reasoning might not be perfect. "The one loyalty the princes have is to their own version of Phos' faith. It got them to murder Vshnasp *marzban* for trying to change it." He paused meditatively. "I don't think, though, that was what made them cut off his privates and stuff them into his mouth before they flung his body out into the gutter."

"They did that?" Abivard said. When Mikhran nodded, his gorge tried to rise. None of the *marzban*'s dispatches had gone into detail about how Vshnasp had met his untimely demise. Picking his words with care, Abivard observed, "I've heard Vshnasp *marzban* was of . . . somewhat lustful temperament."

"He'd swive anything that moved," Mikhran said, "and if it didn't move, he'd shake it. Our nobles would have served him the same way had he outraged their womenfolk as he did those of the *nakharars* here."

"No doubt you're right, Gazrik said as much," Abivard answered, thinking what he'd do if anyone tried outraging Roshnani. Of course, anyone who tried outraging Roshnani might end up dead at her hands; she was nobody to take lightly nor one who shrank from danger.

"I warned him." Mikhran's words tolled like a sad bell. "He told me to go suck lemons; he'd go get something else sucked himself." He started to say something more, then visibly held his tongue. *He got that, all right, and just as he deserved,* was what ran through Abivard's mind. No, Mikhran *marzban* couldn't say that no matter how loudly he thought it.

Abivard sighed. "You proved yourself wiser than the man who was your master. So what do we do now? Must I spend the rest of this year going from valley to valley and thrashing the princes? I will if I must, I suppose, but it will lead to untold mischief in the Videssian westlands. I wish I knew what Maniakes was doing even now."

"Part of the problem solved itself when Vshnasp's genitals ceased to trouble the wives and daughters of the Vaspurakaner nobles," Mikhran said. "The *nakharars* would willingly return to obedience, save that . . . "

Save that we have to obey Sharbaraz King of Kings. Again Abivard supplied a sentence Mikhran *marzban* didn't care to speak aloud. Disobeying the King of Kings was not something to be contemplated casually by any of his servants. In spite of the God's conveyance of preternatural wisdom to the King of Kings, Sharbaraz wasn't always right. But he always thought he was.

Mikhran opened a saddlebag, reached in, and pulled out a skin of wine. He undid the strip of rawhide holding it closed, then poured a tiny libation for each of the Prophets Four down onto the ground that had already drunk so much blood. After that he took a long swig for himself and passed the skin to Abivard.

The wine went down Abivard's throat smooth as silk, sweet as one of Roshnani's kisses. He sighed with pleasure. "They know their grapes here, no doubt about that," he said. On the hillsides in the distance were vineyards, the dark green of the grapevines' leaves unmistakable.

"That they do." Mikhran hesitated. Abivard gave him back the wineskin. He swigged again, but that wasn't what he'd wanted. He asked, "What will the King of Kings expect from us now?"

"He will expect us to restore Vaspurakan to obedience, nothing less," Abivard answered. The golden wine mounted swiftly to his head, not least because he was so worn from the morning's fighting. He went on. "He will also expect us to have it done by yesterday, or perhaps the day before."

Mikhran *marzban*'s slightly pop-eyed expression said he hadn't just stepped over an invisible line, he'd leapt far beyond it. He wished he'd held his tongue, a useless wish if ever there was one. But perhaps his frankness or foolishness or whatever one wanted to call it had finally won the *marzban*'s trust. Mikhran said, "Lord, while we are putting down this rebellion in Vaspurakan, what will the Videssians be doing?"

"I was wondering the same thing myself. Their worst, unless

I'm badly mistaken," Abivard said. He listened to himself in astonishment, as if he were someone else. If his tongue and wits were running a race, his tongue had taken a good-sized lead.

But Mikhran *marzban* nodded. "Which would Sharbaraz King of Kings, may his days be long and his realm increase, sooner have: war here and Videssos forgotten or peace here and Videssos conquered?"

"Both," Abivard replied without hesitation. But in spite of his tongue's running free as an unbroken colt, he knew what Mikhran was driving at. The *marzban* didn't want to be the one to have to say it, for which Abivard could hardly blame him: Mikhran was not Sharbaraz' brother-in-law and enjoyed no familial immunity to the displeasure of the King of Kings. How much did Abivard enjoy? He suspected he'd find out. "If we give up trying to compel the princes to follow the God, they'll be mild enough to let me get back to fighting the Videssians."

When Mikhran had said the same thing earlier, he had spoken of it as an obvious impossibility. Abivard's tone was altogether different. Now Mikhran said, "Lord, do you think we can do such a thing and keep our heads on our shoulders once the King of Kings learns of it?"

"That's a good question," Abivard observed. "That's a very good question." It was *the* question, and both men knew it. Since Abivard didn't know what the answer was, he went on: "The other question, the one that goes with it, is, *What is the cost of not doing it?* You summed that up well, I think: we will have warfare here, and we will lose the gains we made in Videssos."

"You are right, lord; I'm certain of it," Mikhran said, adding, "You will have to draft with great care the letter wherein you inform the King of Kings of the course you have chosen." After a moment, lest that seem too craven, he added, "Of course I shall also append my signature and seal to the document once you have prepared it."

"I was certain you would," Abivard lied. And yet it made sense that he should be the one to write to Sharbaraz. For better or worse—for better *and* worse—he was brother-in-law to the King of Kings; his sister Denak would help ease any outburst of wrath from Sharbaraz when he learned that for once not all his wishes would be gratified. But surely Sharbaraz would see that the change of course would only do Makuran good.

Surely he would see that. Abivard thought of the latest letter he'd gotten from the King of Kings, back in Across. Sharbaraz had not seen wisdom then. But the red-lion banner had never before flown above Across. Makuran had struggled for centuries to dominate Vaspurakan. Persecutions of the locals had always failed. Surely Sharbaraz would remember that. Wouldn't he?

Mikhran said, "If the God be kind, we will be so well advanced on our new course, and will have gained such benefits from it by the time Sharbaraz King of Kings, may his years be many and his realm increase, receives your missive that he will be delighted to accept what we have done."

"If the God be kind." Abivard's left hand twisted in the gesture that invoked the Prophets Four. "But your point is well taken. Let us talk with their chief priests here; let us see what sort of arrangements we can work out to put the uprising behind us. Then, when we have at least the beginnings of good news to report, will be time enough to write."

"If we have even the beginnings of good news to report," Mikhran said, suddenly gloomy. "If not, we only bring more trouble down on our heads."

At first Abivard had a hard time imagining more trouble than Vaspurakan aflame with revolt and the Videssian westlands unguarded by his mobile force because of that revolt. But then he realized that those were troubles pertaining to Makuran as a whole. If Sharbaraz grew angry at how affairs in Vaspurakan were being handled contrary to his will, he would be angry not at Makuran in general but at Abivard in particular.

Nevertheless— "Are we agreed on our course?" he asked.

Mikhran *marzban* looked around the battlefield before answering. Most of the Makuraner dead had been taken away, but some still sprawled in death alongside the Vaspurakaners whose defeat they would not celebrate. He asked a question in his turn: "Can we afford more of this?"

"We cannot," Abivard answered, his purpose firming. "We'll

treat with the princes, then, and see what comes of that." He sighed. "And then we'll tell Sharbaraz King of Kings of what we've done and see what comes of *that*."

III

THE FORTIFIED TOWN OF SHAHAPIVAN LAY IN A VALLEY SOUTH of Poskh. Abivard approached it by himself, holding before him a white-painted shield of truce. "What do you want, herald?" a Vaspurakaner called from the walls. "Why should we talk to any Makuraner after what you have done to our people and to our worship of the lord with the great and good mind who made us before all other men?"

"I am not a herald. I am Abivard son of Godarz, brother-in-law to Sharbaraz King of Kings, may his days be long and his realm increase. Is that reason enough to talk with me?"

He had the satisfaction of watching the jaw of the fellow who'd spoken to him drop. All the princes close enough to hear stared down at him. They argued in their own language. He'd learned a few Vaspurakaner curses but nothing more. Even if he did not speak the tongue, though, he easily figured out what was going on: some of the warriors believed him, while others thought he was a liar who deserved to have his presumption punished.

Presently a man with a gilded helmet and a great mane of a beard spilling down over his chest leaned out and said in fluent Makuraner, "I am Tatul, *nakharar* of Shahapivan valley. If you truly care to do the land of the princes a service, man of Makuran, take up your soldiers and go home with them."

"I do not wish to speak with you, Tatul *nakharar*," Abivard answered. Several of the Vaspurakaners up on the wall growled like wolves at that. The growls spread as they translated for their comrades who knew only their own tongue. Abivard went on, "Is not the chief priest of Shahapivan also chief priest of all those who worship Phos by your rite?"

"It is so." Pride rang in Tatul's voice. "So you would have speech with the marvelously holy Hmayeak, would you?"

"I would," Abivard answered. "Let him come to my camp, where I will treat him with every honor and try to compose the differences between us."

"No," the *nakharar* said flatly. "This past spring Vshnasp, who has now gone to the eternal ice, sought to foully murder the marvelously holy Hmayeak, upon whom Phos' light shines with great strength. If you would be illuminated by the good god's light reflected from his shining soul, enter into Shahapivan alone and entirely by yourself. Give yourself over into our hands and perhaps we shall find you worth hearing."

Tatul's smile was broad and unpleasant. Some of the Vaspurakaners on the wall laughed. "I am not Vshnasp," Abivard said. "I agree."

"You—agree?" Tatul said as if he'd forgotten what the Makuraner word meant. The princes on the wall of Shahapivan gaped. After a moment Tatul added, "Just like that?"

"I'm sorry," Abivard said politely. "Must I fill out a form?" When she found out he was going into Shahapivan alone, Roshnani would roast him over a slow fire. She, however, was back at the baggage train, while he was up here in front of the city gate. He dug the knife in a little deeper. "Or are you afraid I'll take Shahapivan all by myself?"

Tatul disappeared from the wall. Abivard wondered whether that meant the *nakharar* was coming down to admit him or had decided he was witstruck and so not worth the boon of a Vaspurakaner noble's conversation. He had almost decided it was the latter when, with a metallic rasp of seldom used hinges, a postern gate close by the main gate of Shahapivan swung open. There stood Tatul. He beckoned Abivard forward.

The gate was just tall and wide enough to let a single rider through at a time. When Abivard looked up as he passed through the gateway, he saw a couple of Vaspurakaners peering down at him through the iron grid that screened the murder hole. He heard a fire crackling up there. He wondered what the princes kept in the cauldron above it, what they would pour down through the grid onto anyone who broke down the gate. Boiling water? Boiling oil? Red-hot sand? He hoped he wouldn't find out.

"You have spirit, man of Makuran," Tatul said as Abivard emerged inside Shahapivan. Abivard was wondering what kind of idiot he'd been to come here. Hundreds of hostile Vaspurakaners stared at him, their dark, deep-set eyes seeming to burn like fire. They were quiet, quieter than a like number of Makuraners, far quieter than a like number of Videssians. That did not mean they would not use the weapons they carried or wore on their belts.

A bold front seemed Abivard's only choice. "I am here as I said I would be. Take me now to Hmayeak, your priest."

"Yes, go to him," Tatul said. "Here, by yourself, you shall not be able to serve him as Vshnasp served so many of our priests: you shall not cut out his tongue to keep him from speaking the truth of the good god, you shall not break his fingers to keep him from writing that truth, you shall not gouge out his eyes to keep him from reading Phos' holy scriptures, you shall not soak his beard with oil and set it alight, saying it gives forth Phos' holy light. None of these things shall you do, general of Makuran."

"Vshnasp did them?" Abivard asked. He did not doubt Tatul; the *nakharar*'s list of outrages sounded too specific for invention.

"All—and more," Tatul answered. A servitor brought him a horse. He swung up into the saddle. "Come now with me."

Abivard rode with him, looking around curiously as Tatul led him through the narrow, winding streets of Shahapivan. Mashiz, the capital of Makuran, was also a city sprung from the mountains, but it was very different from the Vaspurakaner town. Though of the mountains, Mashiz looked east to the Thousand Cities on the floodplain of the Tutub and the Tib. Its builders worked in timber and in baked and unbaked brick as well as in stone.

Shahapivan, by contrast, might have sprung directly from the gray mountains of Vaspurakan. All the buildings were of stone: soft limestone, easily worked, took the place of mud brick and cheap timber, while marble and granite were for larger, more impressive structures.

The princes had not done much to enliven their town with plaster or paint, either. Even coats of whitewash were rare. The locals seemed content to live in the midst of gray.

They were not gray themselves. Men swaggered in caftans of fuller cut than Makuraners usually wore and dyed in stripes and dots and swirling patterns of bright colors. Their three-pointed tasseled hats looked silly to Abivard, but they made the most of them, shaking and tossing their heads as they talked so that the tassels, like their darting hands, helped punctuate what they said.

Peasant women and merchants' wives crowded the marketplaces, dickering and gossiping. The sun sparkled from their jewelry: polished copper bracelets and gaudy glass beads on those who were not so wealthy, massy silver necklaces or chains strung with Videssian goldpieces on those who were. Their clothes were even more brilliant than those of their menfolk. Instead of the funny-looking hats the men preferred, they wore cloths of linen or cotton or shimmering silk on their heads. They pointed at Abivard and let loose with loud opinions he could not understand but did not think complimentary.

Amid all those fiery reds, sun-bright yellows, vibrant greens, and blues of sky and water, the Vaspurakaner priests stood out by contrast. Unlike Videssian blue-robes, they wore somber black. They did not shave their heads, either, but gathered their hair, whether black or gray or white, into neat buns at the napes of their necks. Some of their beards, like Tatul's, reached all the way down to their waists.

The temples where they served Phos were like those of their Videssian counterparts in that they were topped with gilded globes. Otherwise, though, those temples were very much of a piece with the rest of the buildings of Shahapivan: square, solid structures with only upright rectangular slits for windows, having the look of being made much more for strength and endurance than for beauty and comfort. Abivard noted how many temples there were in this medium-size city. No one could say the Vaspurakaners did not take their misguided faith seriously.

They were in general a sober folk, given to minding their own business. Swarms of Videssians would have followed Tatul and Abivard through the streets. The same might have been true of Makuraners. It was not true here. The Vaspurakaners let their *nakharar* deal with Abivard.

He had expected Tatul to lead him to the finest temple in Shahapivan. When the *nakharar* reined in, though, he did so in front of a building that had seen not just better days but better centuries. Only the gilding on its globe seemed to have been replaced at any time within living memory.

Tatul glanced over to Abivard. "This is the temple dedicated to the memory of the holy Kajaj. He was martyred by you Makuraners—chained to a spit and roasted over coals like a boar—for refusing to abjure the holy faith of Phos and Vaspur the Firstborn. We reverence his memory to this day."

"I did not kill this priest," Abivard answered. "If you blame me for that or even if you blame me for what Vshnasp did, you are making a mistake. Would I have come here if I did not want to compose the differences between you princes and Sharbaraz King of Kings?"

"You are a brave man," Tatul said. "Whether you are a good man, I do not yet know enough to judge. For evil men can be brave. I have seen this. Have you not also?"

"Few men are evil in their own eyes," Abivard said.

"There you touch another truth," Tatul said, "but not one I can discuss with you now. Wait here. I shall go within and bring out to you the marvelously holy Hmayeak."

"I had thought to go with you," Abivard said.

"With the blood of Vaspurakaner martyrs staining your hands?" Tatul's eyebrows leapt up toward the rim of his helmet. "You would render the temple ritually unclean. We sometimes sacrifice a sheep to the good god: its flesh, burned in fire, gives Phos' holy light. But for that, though, blood and death pollute our shrines."

"However you would have it." When Abivard shrugged, his corselet made small rattling and clinking sounds. "I await him here, then."

Tatul strode into the temple. When he returned shortly afterward, the black-robed priest he brought with him was a surprise. Abivard had looked for a doddering, white-bearded elder. But the marvelously holy Hmayeak was in his vigorous middle years, his thick black beard only lightly threaded with gray. His shoulders would have done a smith credit.

He spoke to Tatul in the throaty Vaspurakaner language. The *nakharar* translated for Abivard: "The holy priest says to tell you he does not speak your tongue. He asks if you would rather I interpret or if you prefer to use Videssian, which he does know."

"We can speak Videssian if you like," Abivard said directly to Hmayeak. He suspected that the priest was trying to annoy him by denying knowledge of the Makuraner tongue and declined to give him satisfaction by showing irk.

"Yes, very well. Let us do that." Hmayeak spoke slowly and deliberately, maybe to help Abivard understand him, maybe because he was none too fluent in Videssian himself. "Phos has taken for his own the holy martyrs you men of Makuran have created." He sketched the sun-circle that was his sign of piety for the good god, going in the opposite direction from the one a Videssian would have used. "How now will you make amends for your viciousness, your savagery, your brutality?"

"They were not mine. They were not those of Mikhran *marzban*. They were those of Vshnasp *marzban*, who is dead." Abivard was conscious of how much he wasn't saying. The policy of which Hmayeak complained had been Vshnasp's, true, but it also had been—and still was—Sharbaraz'. And Vshnasp was not merely dead but slain by the Vaspurakaners. For Abivard to overlook that was as much as to admit that the *marzban* had had it coming.

"How will you make amends?" Hmayeak repeated. He sounded cautious; he might not have expected Abivard to yield so much so soon. To him Vaspurakan was not just the center of the universe but the whole universe.

To Abivard it was but one section of a larger mosaic. He answered, "Marvelously holy sir, I cannot bring the dead back to life, neither your people who died for your faith nor Vshnasp *marzban." If you push me too hard, you'll make me remember how Vshnasp died.* Could Hmayeak read between the lines?

"Phos has the power to raise the dead," Hmayeak said in his deliberate Videssian, "but he chooses not to use it, so that we do not come to expect it of him. If Phos does not use this power, how can I expect a mere man to do so?"

"What do you expect of me?" Abivard asked.

Hmayeak looked at him from under thick, bushy bristling brows. His gaze was very keen yet almost childlike in its straightforward simplicity. Maybe he deserved to be called *marvelously holy*; he did not seem half priest, half politician, as so many Videssian prelates did.

"You have come to me," he replied. "This is brave, true, but it also shows you know your people have done wrong. It is for you to tell me what you will do, for me to say what is enough."

Almost, Abivard warned him aloud against pushing too hard. But Hmayeak sounded not like a man who was pushing but like one stating what he saw as a truth. Abivard decided to accept that and see what sprang from it. "Here is what I will do," he said. "I will let you worship in your own way so long as you pledge to remain loyal to Sharbaraz King of Kings, may his days be long and his realm increase. If you for your priesthood make this pledge and if the *nakharars* and warriors of Vaspurakan abide by it, the rebellion here shall be as if it had never been."

"You will seek no reprisals against the leaders of the revolt?" That was not Hmayeak speaking, but Tatul.

"I will not," Abivard said. "Mikhran *marzban* will not. But all must go back to being as it was before the revolt. Where you have driven Makuraner garrisons from towns and fortresses, you must let them return."

"You ask us to put on once more the chains of slavery we have broken," Tatul protested.

"If it comes to war between Vaspurakan and Makuran, you will lose," Abivard said bluntly. "You lived contentedly under the arrangement you had before, so why not go back to it?"

"Who will win in a war among Vaspurakan and Makuran—and Videssos?" Tatul shot back. "Maniakes, I hear, is not Genesios—

he is not altogether hopeless at war. And Videssos follows Phos, as we do. The Empire might be glad to aid us against your false faith."

Abivard scowled for a moment before replying. Tatul, unlike Hmayeak, could see beyond the borders of his mountainous native land. If the past offered any standard for judgment, he was liable to be right, too—if Videssos had the strength to act as he hoped. "Before you dream such dreams, Tatul," Abivard said slowly, "remember how far from Vaspurakan any Videssian soldiers are."

"Videssos may be far." Tatul pointed toward the northeast. "The Videssian Sea is close."

That made Abivard scowl again. The Videssian Sea, like all the seas bordering the Empire, had only Videssian ships upon it. If Maniakes wanted badly enough to send an army to Vaspurakan, he could do so without fighting his way across the Makuraner-held westlands.

Hmayeak held up his right hand. The middle finger was stained with ink. The priest said, "Let us have peace. If we are allowed to worship as we please, it is enough. Videssos as our master would try to force what it calls orthodoxy upon us, just as the Makuraners try to make us follow the God and the Prophets Four. You know this, Tatul; it has happened before."

Grudgingly, the *nakharar* nodded. But then he said, "It might not happen this time. Maniakes is of the princes' blood, after all."

"He is not of our creed," Hmayeak said. "The Videssians could never stomach an Avtokrator who acknowledged Vaspur the Firstborn. If he comes to drive away the men of Makuran, be sure he will be doing it for himself and for Videssos, not for us. Let us have peace."

Tatul muttered under his breath. Then he rounded on Abivard again. "Will the King of Kings agree to the arrangement you propose?"

If he has a drop of sense in his head or concealed anywhere else about his person. But Abivard could not say that. "If I make the arrangement, he will agree to it," he said, and hoped he was not lying.

"Let it be as he says," Hmayeak told Tatul. "Vshnasp excepted, the Makuraners seldom lie, and he has made a good name for himself in the wars against Videssos. I do not think he is deceiving us." He spoke in Videssian so that Abivard could understand.

"I shall do as I say," Abivard declared. "May the Prophets Four turn their backs on me and may the God drop me into the Void if I lie."

"I believe you will do as you say," Tatul answered. "I do not need the marvelously holy Hmayeak to tell me you are honorable; by your words today you have convinced me. Would Vshnasp have trusted himself among us? It is to laugh. No, you have honor, brother-in-law to the King of Kings. But has Sharbaraz honor?"

"He is the King of Kings," Abivard declared. "He is the font of honor."

"Phos grant it be so," Tatul said, and sketched his god's sun-sign above his heart.

Roshnani stood, hands on hips, outside the wagon in which she had traveled so many farsangs through the Videssian westlands and Vaspurakan. Facing her might have been harder than entering Shahapivan. "Husband of mine," she said sweetly, "you are a fool."

"Suppose I say something like *No doubt you're right, but I got away with it*?" Abivard answered. "If I do that, can we take the argument as already over? If I tell you I won't take such chances again—"

"You'll be lying," Roshnani interrupted. "You've come back, so we can argue. That takes a lot of cattle away from the stampede, if you know what I mean. But if you hadn't come back, we would have had a furious fight, let me tell you that."

"If I hadn't come back—" Abivard was tired. He got a quarter of the way through that before realizing it made no logical sense.

"Never mind," Roshnani said. "I gather the Vaspurakaners agreed. If they hadn't, they would have started sending you out in chunks." When Abivard didn't deny it, his principal wife asked the same question the *nakharar* Tatul had: "Will Sharbaraz King of Kings agree?"

Abivard could be more direct with her than he had been with

the Vaspurakaner. "Drop me into the Void if I know," he said. "If the God is kind, he'll be so happy to hear we've brought the Vaspurakaner revolt under control without getting tied down in endless fighting here that he won't care how we did it. If the God isn't kind—" He shrugged.

"May she be so," Roshnani said. "I shall pray to the lady Shivini to intercede with her and ensure that she will grant your request."

"It will be as it is, and when we find out how that is, we shall deal with it as best we can," Abivard said, a sentence dismissing all fortune-telling if ever there was one. "Right now I wouldn't mind dealing with a cup of wine."

Roshnani played along with the joke. "I predict onc lies in your future."

Sure enough, the wine appeared, and the world looked better for it. Roast mutton with parsnips and leeks improved Abivard's attitude, too. Then Varaz asked, "What would you have done if they'd tried to keep you in Shahapivan, Father?"

"What would I have done?" Abivard echoed. "I would have fought, I think. I wouldn't have wanted them to throw me into some cell in the citadel and do what they wanted with me for as long as they wanted. But after that your mother would have been even more upset with me than she really was."

Varaz thought that through and then nodded without saying anything more; he understood what his father meant. But Gulshahr, who was too young to follow conversations as closely as Varaz could, said, "Why would Mama have been upset, Papa?"

Abivard wanted to speak no words of evil omen, so he answered, "Because I would have done something foolish—like this." He tickled her ribs till she squealed and kicked her feet and forgot about the question she'd asked.

He drank more wine. One by one the children got sleepy and went off to their cramped little compartments in the wagon. Abivard got sleepy, too. Yawning, he walked with neck bent—to keep from bumping the roof—down to the little curtain-screened chamber he shared with Roshnani. Several carpets and sheepskins on the floor made sleeping soft; when winter came, he and Roshnani would sleep under several of them rather than on top.

There was no need now. Vaspurakan did not get summer heat to match that of Vek Rud domain, where Abivard had grown to manhood. When you stepped out into the sunshine on a hot day there, within moments you felt your eyeballs start to dry out. It was warm here in the valley of Shahapivan, but not so warm as to make you wonder if you had walked into a bake oven by mistake.

Abivard would have rolled over and gone to sleep—or even gone to sleep without rolling over first—but Roshnani all but molested him after she pulled the entry curtain shut behind her. Afterward he peered through the darkness at her and said, "Not that I'm complaining, mind you, but what was that in aid of?"

Like his, her voice was a thread of whisper: "Sometimes you can be very stupid. Do you know that I spent this whole day wondering whether I would ever see you again? *That* is what that was in aid of."

"Oh." After a moment Abivard said, "You're giving me the wrong idea, you know. Now, whenever I see a hostile city, I'll have an overpowering urge to go into it and talk things over with whoever is in command."

She poked him in the ribs. "Don't be more absurd than you can help," she said, her voice sharper than it usually got.

"I obey you as I would obey Sharbaraz King of Kings, may his years be many and his realm increase," Abivard said with an extravagant gesture that was wasted in the darkness. He paused again, then added, "As a matter of fact, I'd sooner obey you. You have better sense."

"I should hope so," Roshnani said.

Panteles went to one knee before Abivard, one step short of the full prostration the Videssian wizard would have granted to Maniakes. "How may I serve you, most eminent sir?" he asked, his dark eyes eager and curious.

"I have a question I'd like answered by magical means," Abivard said.

Panteles coughed and brought a hand up to cover his mouth. Like his face, his hands were thin and fine-boned: quick hands, clever hands. "What a surprise!" he exclaimed now. "And here I'd thought you'd summoned me to cook you up a stew of lentils and river fish."

"One of the reasons I don't summon you more often is that viper you keep in your mouth and call a tongue," Abivard said. Far from abashing Panteles, that made him preen like a peacock. Abivard sighed. Videssians were sometimes sadly deficient in notions of servility and subordination. "I presume you can answer such a question."

"Oh, I can assuredly answer it, most eminent sir," Panteles replied. He didn't lack confidence: Abivard sometimes thought that if Videssians were half as smart as they thought they were, they would rule the whole world, not just the Empire. "Whether knowing the answer will do you any good is another question altogether."

"Yes, I've started to see that prophecy is about as much trouble as it's worth," Abivard said. "I'm not asking for divination, only for a clue. Will Sharbaraz King of Kings approve of the arrangement I've made here in Vaspurakan?"

"I can tell you this," Panteles said. By the way he flicked an imaginary speck of lint from the sleeve of his robe, he'd expected something more difficult and complicated. But then he leaned forward like a hunting dog taking a scent. "Why do you not ask your own mages for this service, rather than me?"

"Because news that I've put the question is less likely to get from you to Sharbaraz than it would be from a Makuraner wizard," Abivard answered.

"Ah." Panteles nodded. "Like the Avtokrator, the King of Kings is sensitive when magic is aimed his way, is he? I can understand that."

"Aye." Abivard stopped there. He thought of Tzikas, who had tried to slay Maniakes by sorcery and had been lucky enough to escape after his attempt had failed. Sovereigns had good and cogent reasons for wanting magicians to leave them alone.

"A simple yes or no will suffice?" Panteles asked. Without

waiting for an answer, he got out his paraphernalia and set to work. Among the magical materials was a pair of the round Vaspurakaner pastries covered with powdered sugar.

Pointing to them, Abivard said, "You need princes' balls to work your spell?"

"They are a symbol of Vaspurakan, are they not?" Panteles said. Then he let out a distinctly unsorcerous snort. He cut one of the pastries in half, setting each piece in a separate bowl. Then he poured pale Vaspurakaner wine over the two halves.

That done, he cut the other pastry in half. Those halves he set on the table, close by the two bowls. He tapped the rim of one bowl and said, "You will see a reaction here, most eminent sir, if the King of Kings is likely to favor the arrangement you have made."

"And I'll see one in the other bowl if he opposes?" Abivard asked. Panteles nodded. Abivard found another question: "What sort of reaction?"

"Without actually employing the cantrip, most eminent sir, I cannot say, for that will vary depending on a number of factors: the strength of the subject's feelings, the precise nature of the question, and so on."

"That makes sense, I suppose," Abivard said. "Let's see what happens."

With another nod Panteles began to chant in a language that after a moment Abivard recognized as Videssian, but of so archaic a mode that he could understand no more than every other word. The wizard made swift passes with his right hand, first over the bowl where Sharbaraz' approval would be indicated. Nothing happened there. Abivard sighed. He hadn't really expected the King of Kings to be happy about his plan. But how unhappy would Sharbaraz be?

Panteles shifted his attention to the princes' ball soaking in the other bowl. Almost at once the white wine turned the color of blood. The wizard's eyebrows—so carefully arched, Abivard wondered if he plucked them—flew upward, but he continued his incantation. The suddenly red wine began to bubble and steam. Smoke started rising from the Vaspurakaner pastry in the bowl with it.

And then, for good measure, the other half of that princes' ball, the one not soaked in wine, burst into flame there on the table. With a startled oath Panteles snatched up the jar of Vaspurakaner wine and poured what was left in it over the pastry. For a moment Abivard wondered if the princes' ball would keep burning anyhow, as the fire some Videssian dromons threw would continue to burn even when floating on the sea. To his relief, the flaming confection suffered itself to be extinguished.

"I believe," Panteles said with the ostentatious calm that masks a spirit shaken to the core, "I believe, as I say, Sharbaraz has heard ideas he's liked better."

"Really?" Abivard deliberately made his eyes go big and round. "I never would have guessed."

The messenger shook his head. "No, lord," he repeated. "So far as I know, the Videssians have not gone over the strait to Across."

Abivard kicked at the dirt in front of his wagon. He wanted Maniakes to do nice, simple, obvious things. If the Avtokrator of the Videssians had moved to reoccupy the suburb just on the far side of the Cattle Crossing, Abivard would have had no trouble figuring out what he was up to or why. As things were— "Well, what *have* the Videssians done?"

"Next to nothing, lord," the messenger answered. "I have seen as much—or, rather, as little—with my own eyes. Their warships remain ever on patrol. We have had reports they are fighting the barbarians to the north again, but we do not know that for a fact. They seem to be gathering ships at the capital, but it's getting late in the year for them to set out on a full-scale campaign."

"That's so," Abivard agreed. Before too long, storms would make the seas deadly dangerous and the fall rains would turn the roads into muck through which one couldn't move swiftly and sometimes couldn't move at all. Nobody in his right mind, or even out of it, wanted to get stuck in that kind of mess. And after the fall rains came snow and then another round of rain . . . He thought for a while. "Do you suppose Maniakes aims to wait till the rains start and then take back Across, knowing we'll have trouble moving against him?"

"Begging your pardon, lord, but I couldn't even begin to guess," the messenger said.

"You're right, of course," Abivard said. The messenger was a young man who knew what his commander had told him and what he'd seen with his own eyes. Expecting him to have any great insights into upcoming Videssian strategy was asking too much.

More dust flew up as Abivard kicked again. If he pulled out of Vaspurakan now, the settlement he'd almost cobbled together here would fall apart. It was liable to fall apart anyhow; the Vaspurakaners, while convinced of his good faith, still didn't trust Mikhran, who had served under the hated Vshnasp and who formally remained their governor. Abivard could make them believe he'd go against Sharbaraz' will; Mikhran couldn't.

"Is there anything else, lord?" the messenger asked.

"No, not unless you—" Abivard stopped. "I take that back. How was your journey across the westlands? Did you have any trouble with Videssians trying to make sure you never got here?"

"No, lord, nothing of the sort," the messenger answered. "I had a harder time prying remounts out of some of our stables than I did with any of the Videssians. In fact, there was this one girl—" He hesitated. "But you don't want to hear about that."

"Oh, I might, over a mug of wine in a tavern," Abivard said. "This isn't the time or the place for such stories, though; you're right about that. Speaking of wine, have yourself a mug or two, then go tell the cook to feed you till you can't eat any more."

He stared thoughtfully at the messenger's back as the youngster headed off to refresh himself. If the Videssians weren't doing more to harass lone Makuraners traveling through their territory, they didn't think Maniakes had any plans for this year. Maybe that was a good sign.

Rain pattered down on the cloth roof of the wagon. Abivard reminded himself to tell his children not to poke a forefinger up there against the fabric so that water would go through and run down it. He reminded them of that at the start of every rainy season and generally had to punctuate the reminders with swats on the backside till they got the message.

The rain wasn't hard yet, as it would be soon. So far it was just laying the dust, not turning everything into a quagmire. Probably it would ease up by noon, and they might have a couple of days of sun afterward, perhaps even a couple of days of summerlike heat.

From outside the wagon, Pashang the driver called out to Abivard: "Lord, here comes a Vaspurakaner; looks like he's looking for you." After a moment he added, "I wouldn't want him looking for me."

No one had ever accused Pashang of being a hero. All the same, Abivard belted on his sword before peering out. As raindrops splashed his face, he wished the pilos he was wearing had a brim.

He quickly discovered that donning the sword had been a useless gesture. The Vaspurakaner was mounted on an armored horse and wore full armor. He'd greased it with tallow; water beaded on his helmet and corselet but did not reach the iron.

"I greet you, Gazrik son of Bardzrabol," Abivard said mildly. "Do you come in search of me armed head to foot?"

"Not in search of you, brother-in-law to the King of Kings." Gazrik shook his head. Water sprayed out of his beard. "You treated me with honor, there when I bade you turn aside from Vaspurakan. You did not heed me, but you did not scorn me, either. One of your marshals, though, called me dog. I hoped to find him on the field when our force fought yours, but Phos did not grant me that favor. And so I have come now to seek him out."

"We were enemies then," Abivard reminded him. "Now there is truce between Makuran and Vaspurakan. I want that truce to grow stronger and deeper, not to see it broken."

Gazrik raised a thick, bushy eyebrow. "You misunderstand me, Abivard son of Godarz. This is not a matter of Vaspurakan and Makuran; this is a matter of man and man. Did a *nakharar* show me like insult, I would seek him out as well. Is it not the same among you? Or does a noble of Makuran suffer his neighbor to make his name into a thing of reproach?"

Abivard sighed. Gazrik was making matters as difficult as he could, no doubt on purpose. The Vaspurakaner knew whereof he spoke, too. Makuraner nobles were a proud and touchy lot, and the men of one domain often fought those of the next on account of some slight, real or imagined.

"Give me the name of the lout who styled me insolent dog," Gazrik said.

"Romezan son of Bizhan is a noble of the Seven Clans of Makuran," Abivard answered, as if to a backward child. By blood, Romezan was more noble than Abivard, who was but of the *dihqan* class, the minor nobility ... but who was Sharbaraz' brother-in-law and marshal.

In any case, the distinction was lost on Gazrik, who judged by different standards. "No man not a prince of Vaspurakan can truly be reckoned of noble blood," he declared; like Abivard, he was explaining something so obvious to him, it hardly needed explanation. He went on, "Regardless, I care nothing for what blood he bears, for I purpose spilling it. Where in this camp of yours can I find him?"

"You are alone here," Abivard reminded him.

Gazrik's eyebrows twitched again. "And so? Would you keep a hound from the track? Would you keep a bear from the honey tree? Would you keep an insulted man from vengeance? Vshnasp excepted, you Makuraners are reputed to have honor; you yourself have shown as much. Would you throw that good name away?"

What Abivard would have done was throw Gazrik out of the encampment. That, though, looked likely to cause more problems than it solved. "You will not attack Romezan without warning?"

"*I* am a man of honor, brother-in-law to the King of Kings," Gazrik said with considerable dignity. "I wish to arrange a time and place where the two of us can meet to compose our differences."

By composing their differences, he meant that one of them would start decomposing. Makuraner nobles were known to settle disputes in that fashion, although a mere *dihqan* would rarely presume to challenge a man of the Seven Clans. By Gazrik's bearing, though, he reckoned all non-Vaspurakaners beneath him and was honoring Romezan by condescending to notice himself insulted.

Abivard pointed to a sprawling silk pavilion a couple of furlongs away. Peroz King of Kings might have taken a fancier one into the field when he went over the Degird on his ill-fated expedition against the Khamorth, but not by much—and Romezan, however high his blood, was not King of Kings. "He dwells there."

Gazrik's head turned toward the pavilion. "It is very fine," he said. "I have no doubt some other man of your army will draw enjoyment from it once Romezan needs it no more."

He bowed in the saddle to Abivard, then rode off toward Romezan's tent. Abivard waited uneasily for shouts and screams to break out, as might have happened had Gazrik lied about going simply to deliver a challenge. But evidently Gazrik had spoken the truth. And if Romezan acknowledged him as noble enough to fight, the man of the Seven Clans would grant his foe every courtesy—until the appointed hour came, at which point he would do his considerable best to kill him.

Abivard wished kingdoms and empires could settle their affairs so economically.

It was a patch of dirt a furlong in length and a few yards wide: an utterly ordinary patch of ground, one occasionally walked across by a Vaspurakaner or even a Makuraner but not one to have had itself recorded in the memories of men, not till today.

From now on, though, minstrels would sing of this rather muddy patch of ground. Whether the minstrels who composed the boldest, most spirited songs would wear pilos or three-crowned caps would be determined today.

Warriors from Makuran and Vaspurakan crowded around the long, narrow strip of ground, jostling one another and glaring suspiciously when they heard men close by speaking the wrong language, whichever that happened to be. Sometimes the glares and growls persisted; sometimes they dissolved in the excitement of laying bets.

Abivard stood in the middle of the agreed-upon dueling ground. When he motioned Romezan and Gazrik toward him from the opposite ends of the field, the throng of spectators fell into expectant silence. The noble of the Seven Clans and the Vaspurakaner *nakharar* slowly approached, each on his armored steed. Both men were armored, too. In their head-to-toe suits of mail and lamellar armor, they were distinguishable from each other only by their surcoats and by the red lion painted on Romezan's small, round shield. The Makuraner's chain mail veil hid the waxed spikes of his mustache, while Gazrik's veil came down over his formidable beard.

"You are both agreed combat is the only way you can resolve the differences between you?" Abivard asked. With faint raspings of metal, two heads bobbed up and down. Abivard persisted: "Will you not be satisfied with first blood here today?"

Now, with more rasping noises, both heads moved from side to side. "A fight has no meaning, be it not to the death," Romezan declared.

"In this, if in no other opinion, I agree with my opponent," Gazrik said.

Abivard sighed. Both men were too stubborn for their own good. Each saw it in the other, not in himself. Loudly, Abivard proclaimed, "This is a fight between two men, each angry at the other, not between Makuran and Vaspurakan. Whatever happens here shall have no effect on the truce now continuing between the two lands. Is it agreed?"

He pitched that question not to Romezan and Gazrik but to the crowd of spectators, a crowd that could become a brawl at any minute. The warriors nodded in solemn agreement. How well they would keep the agreement when one of their champions lay dead remained to be seen.

"May the God grant victory to the right," Abivard said.

"No, Phos and Vaspur the Firstborn, who watches over his children, the princes of Vaspurakan," Gazrik said, sketching his deity's sun-circle above his left breast with a gauntleted hand. Many of the Vaspurakaners among the spectators imitated his gesture. Many of the Makuraners responded with a gesture of their own to turn aside any malefic influence.

"Ride back to your own ends of the field here," Abivard said, full of misgivings but unable to stop a fight both participants wanted so much. "When I signal, have at each other. I tell you this: in spite of what you have said, you may give over at any time, with no loss of honor involved." Romezan and Gazrik nodded. The nods did not say, *We understand and agree.* They said, *Shut up, get out of the way, and let us fight.*

Romezan, Abivard judged, had a better horse than did Gazrik, who was mounted on a sturdy but otherwise unimpressive gelding of Vaspurakaner stock. Other than that, he couldn't find a copper's worth of difference between the two men. He knew how good a warrior Romezan was; he did not know Gazrik, but the Vaspurakaner gave every impression of being able to handle himself.

Abivard raised his hand. Both men leaned forward in the saddle, couching their lances. He let his hand fall. Because their horses wore ironmongery like their own, neither Romezan nor Gazrik wore spurs. They used reins, voice, their knees, and an occasional boot in the ribs to get their beasts to do as they required. The horses were well trained. They thundered toward each other, dirt fountaining up under their hooves.

Each rider brought up his shield to protect his left breast and most of his face. *Crash!* Both lances struck home. Romezan and Gazrik flew over their horses' tails as the crowd shouted at the clever blows. The horses galloped down to the far ends of the field. Each man's retainers caught the other's beast.

Gazrik and Romezan got slowly to their feet. They moved hesitantly, as if half-drunk; the falls they'd taken had left them stunned. In the shock of collision Gazrik's lance had shivered. He threw aside the stub and drew his long, straight sword. Romezan's lance was still intact. He thrust at Gazrik: he had a great advantage in reach now.

Clang! Gazrik chopped at the shaft of the lance below the head, hoping to cut off that head as if it belonged to a convicted robber. But the lance had a strip of iron bolted to the wood to thwart any such blow.

Poke, poke. Like a cat toying with a mouse, Romezan forced Gazrik down the cleared strip where they fought, not giving him the chance to strike a telling blow of his own—until, with a loud cry, the Vaspurakaner used his shield to beat aside the questing lance head and rushed at his foe.

Romezan could not backpedal as fast as Gazrik bore down on him. He whacked Gazrik in the ribs with the shaft of the lance, trying to knock his foe off balance. That was a mistake. Gazrik chopped at the shaft again and this time hit it below the protective strip of iron. The shaft splintered. Cursing, Romezan threw it down and yanked out his sword.

All at once both men seemed tentative. They were used to fighting with swords from horseback, not afoot like a couple of infantrymen. Instead of going at each other full force, they would trade strokes, each draw back a step as if to gauge the other's strength and speed, and then approach for another short clash.

"Fight!" somebody yelled from the crowd, and in an instant a hundred throats were baying the word.

Romezan was the one who pressed the attack. Gazrik seemed content to defend himself and wait for a mistake. Abivard thought Romezan fought the same way he led his men: straight ahead, more than bravely enough, and with utter disregard for anything but what lay before him. Tzikas had used flank attacks to maul his troopers a couple of times.

Facing only one enemy, Romezan did not need to worry about an attack from the side. Iron belled on iron as he hacked away at Gazrik. Sparks flew as they did when a smith sharpened a sword on a grinding wheel. And then, with a sharp snap, Gazrik's blade broke in two.

Romezan brought up his own sword for the killing stroke. Gazrik, who had self-possession to spare, threw the stub and hilt of his ruined weapon at the Makuraner's head. Then he sprang at Romezan, both hands grabbing for his right wrist.

Romezan tried to kick his feet out from under him and did, but Gazrik dragged him down, too. They fell together, and their armor clattered about them. Gazrik pulled out a dagger and stabbed at Romezan, trying to slip the point between the lamellae of his corselet. Abivard thought he'd succeeded, but Romezan did not cry out and kept fighting.

Gazrik had let go of Romezan's sword arm to free his own knife. Romezan had no room to swing the sword or cut with it. He used it instead as a knuckle-duster, smashing Gazrik in the face with the jeweled and weighted pommel. The Vaspurakaner groaned, and so did his countrymen.

Romezan hit him again. Now Gazrik wailed. Romezan managed to reverse the blade and thrust it home point first, just above the chain mail veiling that warded most but not all of Gazrik's face. Gazrik's body convulsed, and his feet drummed against the dirt. Then he lay still.

Very slowly, into vast silence, Romezan struggled to his feet. He took off his helmet. His face was bloody. He bowed to Gazrik's corpse, then to the grim-featured Vaspurakaners in the crowd. "That was a brave man," he said, first in his own language, then in theirs.

Abivard hoped that would keep the Vaspurakaners in the crowd calm. No swords came out, but a man said, "If you call him brave now, why did you name him a dog before?"

Before Romezan answered, he shed his gauntlets. He wiped his forehead with the back of his hand, mixing sweat and grime and blood but not doing much more. At last he said, "For the same reason any man insults his foe during war. What have you princes called us? But when the war was over, I was willing to let it rest. Gazrik came seeking me; I did not go looking for him."

Though you certainly did on the battlefield, and though you were glad to fight him when he came to you, Abivard thought. But Romezan had given as good an answer as he could. Abivard said, "The general of Makuran is right. The war is over. Let us remember that, and let this be the last blood shed between us."

Along with his countrymen, he waited to see if that would be reply enough or if the Vaspurakaners, in spite of his words and Romezan's, would make blood pay for blood. He kept his own hand away from the hilt of his sword but was ready to snatch it out in an instant.

For a few heartbeats the issue hung in the balance. Then, from the back of the crowd, a few Vaspurakaners turned and trudged back toward the frowning gray walls of Shahapivan, their heads down, their shoulders bent, the very picture of dejection. Had Abivard had any idea who they were, he would have paid them a handsome sum of silver arkets or even of Videssian goldpieces. Their peaceful, disappointed withdrawal gave their countrymen both the excuse and the impetus to leave the site of the duel without trying to amend the result.

Abivard permitted himself the luxury of a long sigh of relief. Things could hardly have gone better: Not only had Romezan beaten his challenger, he'd managed to do it in a way that didn't reignite the princes' rebellion.

He walked up to his general. "Well, my great boar of Makuran, we got by with it."

"Aye, so we did," Romezan answered, "and I stretched the dog dead in the dirt, as he deserved." He laughed at Abivard's flabbergasted expression. "Oh, I spoke him fair for his own folks, lord. I'm no fool: I know what needed doing. But a dog he was, and a dead dog he is, and I enjoyed every moment of killing him." Just for a moment his facade of bravado cracked, for he added, "Except for a couple of spots where I thought he was going to kill me."

"How did you live, there when he was stabbing at you through your suit?" Abivard asked. "I thought he pierced it a couple of times, but you kept on."

Romezan laughed. "Aye, I did, and do you know why? Under it I wore an iron heart guard, the kind foot soldiers put on when they can't afford any other armor. You never know, thought I, when such will come in handy, and by the God I was right. So he didn't kill me, and I did kill him, and that's all that matters."

"Spoken like a warrior," Abivard said. Romezan, as best he could tell, had no great quantity of wit, but sometimes, as now, the willingness to take extra pains and a large helping of straightforward courage sufficed.

Fall drew on. Abivard thought hard about moving back into the Videssian westlands before the rains finished turning the roads to mud but in the end decided to hold his mobile force in Vaspurakan. If the princes broke their fragile accord with Makuran, he didn't want to give them the winter in which to consolidate themselves.

Also weighting his judgment was how quiet Maniakes had been. Instead of plunging ahead regardless of whether he had the strength to plunge, as he had before, the Videssian Avtokrator was playing a cautious game. In a way that worried Abivard, for he wasn't sure what Maniakes was up to. In another way, though, it relieved him: even if he kept the mobile force here in Vaspurakan, he could be fairly sure the Avtokrator would not leap upon the westlands.

Keeping the mobile force in Vaspurakan also let him present to Sharbaraz the settlement he'd made with the princes as a reconquest and occupation of their land. He made full use of that aspect of the situation when at last he wrote a letter explaining to the King of Kings all he'd done. If one didn't read that letter with the greatest of care, one would never notice that the Vaspurakaners still worshiped at their old temples to Phos and that Abivard had agreed not to try to keep them from doing so.

"The King of Kings, may his days be long and his realm increase, is a very busy man," he said when he gave the carefully crafted letter to Mikhran *marzban* for his signature. "With any luck at all, he'll skim through this without even noticing the fine points of the arrangement." He hoped that was true, considering what Panteles had told him about how Sharbaraz was likely to react if he did notice. He didn't mention that to the *marzban*.

"It would be fine, wouldn't it?" Mikhran said, scrawling his name below Abivard's. "It would be very fine indeed, and I think you have a chance of pulling it off."

"Whatever he does, he'll have to do it quickly," Abivard said. "This letter should reach him before the roads get too gloppy to carry traffic, but not long before. He'll need to hurry if he's going to give any kind of response before winter or maybe even before spring. I'm hoping that by the time he gets around to answering me, so many other things will have happened that he'll have forgotten all about my letter."

"That would be fine," Mikhran repeated. "In fact, maybe you should even arrange for your messenger to take so long that he gets stuck in the mud and makes your letter later still."

"I thought about that," Abivard said. "I've decided I dare not take the risk. I don't know who else has written to the King of Kings and what he or they may have said, but I have to think some of my officers will have complained about the settlement we've made. Sharbaraz needs to have our side of it before him, or he's liable to condemn us out of hand."

The *marzban* considered that, then reluctantly nodded. "I suppose you're right, lord, but I fear this letter will be enough to convict us of disobedience by itself. The Vaspurakaners are not worshiping the God."

"They aren't assassinating *marzbans* and waylaying soldiers, either," Abivard returned. "Sharbaraz will have to decide which carries the greater weight."

There the matter rested. Once the letter was properly signed and sealed, a courier rode off to the west with it. It would pass through the western regions of Vaspurakan and the Thousand Cities before it came to Mashiz—and to Sharbaraz' notice. As far as Abivard could see, he was obviously doing the right thing. But Panteles' magic made him doubt the King of Kings would agree.

Several days after the letter left his hands he wished he had it back again so he could change it—or so he could change his mind and not send it at all. He even started to summon Panteles to try to blank the parchment by sorcery from far away but ended up refraining. If Sharbaraz got a letter with no words from him, he'd wonder why and would keep digging till he found out. Better to give him something tangible on which to center his anger.

Abivard slowly concluded that he would have to give Tzikas something tangible, too. The Videssian turncoat had fought very well in Vaspurakan; how in justice could Abivard deny him a command commensurate with his talent? The plain truth was, he couldn't.

"But oh, how I wish I could," he told Roshnani one morning before a meeting with Tzikas he'd tried but failed to avoid. "He's so—polite." He made a gesture redolent of distaste.

"Sometimes all you can do is make the best of things," Roshnani said. She spoke manifest truth, but that did not make Abivard feel any better about the way Tzikas smiled.

Tzikas bowed low when Abivard approached his pavilion. "I greet you, brother-in-law to the King of Kings, may his days be long and his realm increase. May he and his kingdom both prosper."

"I greet you, eminent sir," Abivard answered in Videssian far more ragged than it had been a few months before. Don't use a language and you will forget it, he'd discovered.

Tzikas responded in Makuraner, whether just for politeness' sake or to emphasize how much he was himself a man of Makuran, Abivard couldn't guess. *Probably both,* he thought, and wondered whether Tzikas himself knew the proportions of the mix. "Brother-in-law to the King of Kings, have I in some way made myself odious to you? Tell me what my sin is and I shall expiate it, if that be in my power. If not, I can do no more than beg forgiveness."

"You have done nothing to offend me, eminent sir." Abivard stubbornly stuck to Videssian. His motives were mixed, too: not only did he need the practice, but by using the language of the Empire he reminded Tzikas that he remained an outsider no matter what services he'd rendered to Makuran.

The Videssian general caught that signal: Tzikas was sometimes so subtle, he imagined signals that weren't there, but not today. He hesitated, then said, "Brother-in-law to the King of Kings, would I make myself more acceptable in your eyes if I cast off the worship of Phos and publicly accepted the God and the Prophets Four?"

Abivard stared at him. "You would do such a thing?"

"I would," Tzikas answered. "I have put Videssos behind me; I have wiped her dust from the soles of my sandals." As if to emphasize his words, he scraped first one foot and then the other against the soil of Vaspurakan. "I shall also turn aside from Phos; the lord with the great and good mind has proved himself no match for the power of the God."

"You are a—" Abivard had to hunt for the word he wanted but found it— "a *flexible* man, eminent sir." He didn't altogether mean it as a compliment; Tzikas' flexibility, his willingness to adhere to any cause that looked advantageous, was what worried Abivard most about him.

But the Videssian renegade nodded. "I am," he declared. "How could I not be when unswerving loyalty to Videssos did not win me the rewards I had earned?"

What Tzikas had was unswerving loyalty to Tzikas. But if that could be transmuted into unswerving loyalty to Makuran ... it would be a miracle worthy of Fraortish eldest of all. Abivard chided himself for letting the nearly blasphemous thought cross his mind. Tzikas was a tool, like a sharp knife, and, like a sharp knife, he would cut your hand if you weren't careful.

Abivard had no trouble seeing that much. What lay beyond it was harder to calculate. One thing did seem likely, though: "Having accepted the God, you dare not let the Videssians lay hands on you again. What do they do to those who leave their faith?"

"Nothing pretty, I assure you," Tzikas answered, "but no worse than what they'd do to a man who tried to slay the Avtokrator but failed."

"Mm, there is that," Abivard said. "Very well, eminent sir. If you accept the God, we shall make of that what we can."

He did not promise Tzikas his regiment. He waited for the renegade to beg for it or demand it or try to wheedle it out of him, all ploys Tzikas had tried before. But Tzikas, for once, did not push. He answered only, "As you say, brother-in-law to the King of Kings, Videssos shall reject me as I have rejected her. And so I accept the God in the hope that Makuran will accept me in return." He bowed and ducked back inside his pavilion.

Abivard stared thoughtfully after him. Tzikas had to know that, no matter how fervently and publicly he worshiped the God, the grandees of Makuran would never stop looking on him as a foreigner. They might one day come to look on him as a foreigner who made a powerful ally, perhaps even as a foreigner to whom one might be wise to marry a daughter. From Tzikas' point of view that would probably constitute acceptance.

Sharbaraz already thought well of Tzikas because of his support for the latest "Hosios Avtokrator." Add the support of the King of Kings to the turncoat's religious conversion and he might even win a daughter of a noble of the Seven Clans as a principal wife. Abivard chuckled. Infusing some Videssian slyness into those bloodlines would undoubtedly improve the stock. As a man who knew a good deal about breeding horses, he approved.

Roshnani laughed when he told her the conceit later that day, but she did not try to convince him he was wrong.

The first blizzard roared into Vaspurakan from out of the northwest without warning. One day the air still smelled sweet with memories of fruit just plucked from trees and vines; the next, the sky turned yellow-gray, the wind howled, and snow poured down. Abivard had thought he knew everything about winter worth knowing, but that sudden onslaught reminded him that he'd never gone through a hard season in mountain country.

"Oh, aye, we lose men, women, families, flocks to avalanches every year," Tatul said when he asked. "The snow gets too thick on the hillsides, and down it comes."

"Can't you do anything to stop that?" Abivard inquired.

The Vaspurakaner shrugged, as Abivard might have had he been asked what he could do about Vek Rud domain's summer heat. "We might pray for less snow," Tatul answered, "but if the lord with the great and good mind chooses to answer that prayer, the rivers will run low the next spring, and crops well away from them will fail for lack of water."

"Nothing is ever simple," Abivard murmured, as much to himself as to the *nakharar*. Tatul nodded; he took the notion for granted.

Abivard made sure all his men had adequate shelter against the cold. He wished he could imitate a bear and curl up in a cave till spring came. It would have made life easier and more pleasant. As things were, though, he remained busy through the winter. Part of that was routine: he drilled the soldiers when weather permitted and staged inspections of their quarters and their horses' stalls when it did not.

And part was anything but routine. Several of his warriors— most of them light cavalry with no family connections, but one a second son of a *dihqan*—fell so deep in love with Vaspurakaner women that nothing less than marriage would satisfy them. Each of those cases required complicated dickering between the servants of the God and the Vaspurakaner priests of Phos to determine which holy men would perform the marriage ceremony.

Some of the soldiers were satisfied with much less than marriage. A fair number of Vaspurakaner women brought claims of rape against his men. Those were hard for him to decide, as they so often came down to conflicting claims about what had really happened. Some of his troopers said the women had consented and were now changing their minds; others denied association of any sort with them.

In the end he dismissed about half the cases. In the other half he sent the women back to their homes with silver—more if their attackers had gotten them with child—and put stripes on the backs of the men who, he was convinced, had violated them.

The *nakharar* Tatul came out from the frowning walls of Shahapivan to watch one of the rapists take his strokes. Encountering Abivard there for the same reason, he bowed and said, "You administer honest justice, brother-in-law to the King of Kings. After Vshnasp's wicked tenure here, this is something we princes note with wonder and joy."

Craack! The lash scored the back of the miscreant. He howled. No doubt about his guilt: he'd choked his victim and left her for dead, but she had not died. Abivard said, "It's a filthy crime. My sister, principal wife to the King of Kings, would not let me look her in the face if I ignored it." *Craack!*

Tatul bowed again. "Your sister is a great lady."

"That she is." Abivard said no more than that. He did not tell Tatul how Denak had let herself be ravished by one of Sharbaraz' guards when the usurper Smerdis had imprisoned the rightful King of Kings in Nalgis Crag stronghold, thereby becoming able to pass messages to and from the prisoner and greatly aiding in his eventual escape. His sister would have had special reason to spurn him had he gone soft here. *Craack!*

After a hundred lashes the prisoner was cut down from the frame. He screamed one last time when a healer splashed warm salt water on his wrecked back to check the bleeding and make the flesh knit faster.

Once all the Vaspurakaner witnesses were gone and the

punished rapist had been dragged off to recover from his whipping, Farrokh-Zad came up to Abivard. Unlike Tatul, Kardarigan's fiery young subordinate did not approve of the sentence Abivard had handed down. "There's a good man who won't be of any use in a fight for months, lord," he grumbled. "Sporting with a foreign slut isn't anything big enough to have stripes laid across your back on account of it."

"I think it is," Abivard answered. "If the Vaspurakaners came to your domain in Makuran and one of their troopers forced your sister's legs apart, what would you want done to him?"

"I'd cut his throat myself," Farrokh-Zad answered promptly.

"Well, then," Abivard said.

But Farrokh-Zad didn't see it even after Abivard spelled it out in letters of fire a foot in front of his nose. As far as Farrokh-Zad was concerned, anyone who wasn't a Makuraner deserved no consideration: whatever happened, happened, and that was all there was to it. The time Abivard had spent in Videssos and Vaspurakan had convinced him that foreigners, despite differences of language and faith, were at bottom far closer to the folk of Makuran than he'd imagined before he had left Vek Rud domain. Plainly, though, not all his countrymen had drawn the same lesson.

Maybe that gloomy thought was what brought on the next spell of gloomy weather. However that was, a new blizzard howled in the next afternoon. Had Abivard scheduled the rapist's chastisement for that day, the fellow might have frozen to death while taking his lashes. Abivard wouldn't have missed him a bit.

With storms like that, you could only stay inside whatever shelter you had, try to keep warm—or not too cold—and wait till the sun came out again. Even then, you wouldn't be comfortable, but at least you could emerge from your lair and move about in a world gone white.

The fall and spring rains stopped all traffic on the roads for weeks at a time. While it was raining, a road was just a stretch of mud that ran in a straight line. You could move about in winter provided that you had the sense to find a house or a caravansaray while the blizzard raged.

During a lull a courier rode into Shahapivan valley from out of the west. He found Abivard's wagon and announced himself, saying, "I bring a dispatch from Sharbaraz King of Kings, may his days be long and his realm increase." He held out a message tube stamped with the lion of Makuran.

Abivard took it with something less than enthusiasm. After undoing the stopper, he drew out the rolled parchment inside and used his thumbnail to break the red wax seal, also impressed with a lion from Sharbaraz' signet, that held the letter closed. Then, having no better choice, he opened it and began to read.

He skipped quickly through the grandiloquent titles with which the King of Kings bedizened the document: he was after meat. He also skipped over several lines' worth of reproaches; he'd heard plenty of those already. At last he came to the sentence giving him his orders: "You are to come before us at once in Mashiz to explain and suffer the consequences for your deliberate defiance of our will in Vaspurakan." He sighed. He'd feared as much.

IV

Mɪᴋʜʀᴀɴ *ᴍᴀʀᴢʙᴀɴ* ᴘᴜᴛ ᴀ ʜᴀɴᴅ ᴏɴ Aʙɪᴠᴀʀᴅ'ꜱ ꜱʜᴏᴜʟᴅᴇʀ. "I should be going with you. You came to my rescue, you promulgated this policy for my benefit, and you, it seems, will have to suffer the consequences alone."

"No, don't be a fool—stay here," Abivard told him. "Not only that: keep on doing as we've been doing till Sharbaraz directly orders you to stop. Keep on then, too, if you dare. If the princes rise up against us, we aren't going to be able to conquer Videssos."

"What— ?" Mikhran hesitated but finished the question: "What do you suppose the King of Kings will do to you?"

"That's what I'm going to find out," Abivard answered. "With luck, he'll shout and fuss and then calm down and let me tell him what we've been doing and why. Without luck—well, I hope I'll have reason to be glad he's married to my sister."

The *marzban* nodded, then asked, "Whom will you leave in command of the army here?"

"It has to be Romezan," Abivard answered regretfully. "He's senior, and he has the prestige among our men from killing Gazrik. I'd give the job to Kardarigan if I could, but I can't."

"He may have more prestige among us, but the princes won't be happy to see him in charge of our warriors," Mikhran said.

"I can't do anything about that, either," Abivard said. "You're in overall command here, remember: over Romezan, over everyone

95

now that I'm not going to be around for a while. Use that power well and the Vaspurakaners won't notice that Romezan leads the army."

"I'll try," Mikhran said. "But I wasn't part of this army, so there's no guarantee they'll heed me as they would one of their own."

"Act so natural about it that they never think to do anything else," Abivard advised him. "One of the secrets to command is never giving the men you're leading any chance to doubt you have the right. That's not a magic Bogorz knows, or Panteles either, but it's nonetheless real even so."

"Vshnasp spoke of that kind of magic, too," Mikhran said, "save that he said that so long as you never seemed to doubt a woman would come to your bed, in the end she would not doubt it, either. I'd sooner not emulate his fate."

"I don't expect you to seduce Romezan—for which I hope you're relieved," Abivard said, drawing a wry chuckle from the *marzban.* "I only want you to keep him under some sort of rein till I return. Is that asking too much?"

"Time will tell," Mikhran replied in tones that did not drip optimism.

Roshnani, understanding why Abivard had been recalled to Mashiz, shared his worries. Like him, she had no idea whether they would be returning to Vaspurakan. Their children, however, went wild with excitement at the news, and Abivard could hardly blame them. Now, at last, they were going back to Makuran, a land that had assumed all but legendary proportions in their minds. Any why not? They'd heard of it but had hardly any memories of seeing it.

When the King of Kings ordered his general to attend him immediately, he got what he desired. The day after his command reached Shahapivan, Pashang got the wagon in which Abivard and his family traveled rattling westward. With them rode an escort of fourscore heavy cavalry, partly to help clear the road at need and partly to persuade bandits that attacking the wagon would not be the best idea they'd ever had.

Past Maragha, the mountains of Vaspurakan began dwindling

down toward hills once more and then to a rolling steppe country that was dry and bleak and cool in the winter, dry and bleak and blazing hot in summertime.

"I don't like this land," Abivard said when they stopped at one of the infrequent streams to water the horses.

"Nor I," Roshnani agreed. "The first time we went through it, after all—oh, south of here, but the same kind of country—was when we were fleeing the Thousand Cities and hoping the Videssians would give us shelter."

"You're right," he exclaimed. "That must be it, for this doesn't look much different from the badlands west of the Dilbat Mountains, the sort of country you'd find between strongholds. And yet the hair stood up on the back of my neck, and I didn't know why."

After a few days of crossing the badlands, days in which the only life they saw outside their own company was a handful of rabbits, a fox, and, high in the sky, a hawk endlessly circling, green glowed on the western horizon, almost as if the sea lay ahead. But Abivard, these past months, had turned his back on the sea. He pointed ahead, asking his children if they knew what the green meant.

Varaz obviously did but looked down on the question as being too easy for him to deign to answer. After a small hesitation Shahin said, "That's the start of the Thousand Cities, isn't it? The land between the rivers, I mean, the, the—" He scowled. He'd forgotten their names.

"The Tutub and the Tib," Varaz said importantly. Then, all at once, he lost some of that importance. "I'm sorry, Papa, but I've forgotten which one is which."

"That's the Tutub just ahead," Abivard answered. "The Tib marks the western boundary of the Thousand Cities."

Actually, the two rivers were not quiet the boundaries of the rich, settled country. The canals that ran out from them were. A couple of the Thousand Cities lay to the east of the Tutub. Where the canals brought their life-giving waters, everything was green and growing, with farmers tending their onions and cucumbers and cress and lettuces and date-palm trees. A few yards beyond the canals the ground lay sere and brown and useless.

Roshnani peered out of the wagon. "Canals always seem so—wasteful," she said. "All that water on top of the ground and open to the thirsty air. *Qanats* would be better."

"You can drive a *qanat* through rock and carry water underground," Abivard said. Then he waved a hand. "Not much rock here. When you get right down to it, the Thousand Cities don't have much but mud and water and people—lots of people."

The wagon and its escort skirted some of the canals on dikes running in the right direction and crossed others on flat, narrow bridges of palm wood. Those were adequate for getting across the irrigation ditches; when they got to the Tutub, something more was needed, for even months away from its spring rising, it remained a formidable river.

It was spanned by a bridge of boats with timbers—real timbers from trees other than date palms—laid across them. Men in rowboats brought the bridge across from the western bank of the Tutub so that Abivard and his companions could cross over it. He knew there were other, similar bridges north and south along the Tutub and along the Tib and on some of their tributaries and some of the chief canals between them. Such crossings were quick to make and easy to maintain.

They were also useful in time of war: if you did not want your foes to cross a stretch of water, all you had to do was make sure the bridge of boats did not extend to the side of the river or canal he held. In the civil war against Smerdis the usurper's henchmen, who controlled most of the Thousand Cities, had greatly hampered Sharbaraz' movements by such means.

The folk who dwelt between the Tutub and the Tib were not of Makuraner blood, though the King of Kings had ruled the Thousand Cities from Mashiz for centuries. The peasants were small and swarthy, with hair so black that it held blue highlights. They wore linen tunics, the women's ankle-length, those of the men reaching down halfway between hip and knee. They would stare at the wagon and its escort of grim-faced fighting men, then shrug and get back to work.

When the wagon stopped at one of the Thousand Cities for the night, Pashang would invariably have to urge the team up a short but steep hill to reach the gate. That puzzled Varaz, who asked, "Why are the towns here always on top of hills? They aren't like that in Videssos. And why aren't there any hills without towns on them? This doesn't look like country where there should be hills. They stick up like warts."

"If it weren't for the people who live between the Tutub and the Tib, there wouldn't be any hills," Abivard answered. "The Thousand Cities are old; I don't think any man of Makuran knows just how old. Maybe they don't know here, either. But when Shippurak—this town here—was first built, it was on the same level as the plain all around; the same with all the other cities, too. But what do they use for building here?"

Varaz looked around. "Mud brick mostly, it looks like."

"That's right. It's what they have: lots of mud, no stone to speak of, and only date palms for timber. And mud brick doesn't last. When a house would start crumbling, they'd knock it down and build a new one on top of the rubble. When they'd been throwing rubbish into the street for so long that they had to step up from inside to get out through their doors, they'd do the same thing—knock the place down and rebuild with the new floor a palm's breadth higher, maybe two palm's breadths higher, than the old one. You do that again and again and again and after enough years go by, you have yourself a hill."

"They're living on top of their own rubbish?" Varaz said. Abivard nodded. His son took another look around, a longer one. "They're living on top of a *lot* of their own rubbish." Abivard nodded once more.

The city governor of Shippurak, a lean black-bearded Makuraner named Kharrad, greeted Abivard and his escort with wary effusiveness, for which Abivard blamed him not at all. He was brother-in-law to the King of Kings and the author of great victories against Videssos, and that accounted for the effusiveness. He was also being recalled to Mashiz under circumstances that Kharrad obviously did not know in detail but that just as obviously meant he had fallen out of favor to some degree. But how much? No wonder the city governor was wary.

He served up tender beans and chickpeas and boiled onions and twisted loaves of bread covered with sesame and poppy seeds. He did not act scandalized when Abivard brought Roshnani to the supper, though his own wife did not appear. When he saw that Roshnani would stay, he spoke quietly to one of his secretaries. The man nodded and hurried off. The entertainment after supper was unusually brief: only a couple of singers and harpers. Abivard wondered if a troupe of naked dancing girls had suddenly been excised from the program.

Kharrad said, "It must be strange returning to the court of the King of Kings, may his years be many and his realm increase, after so long away."

"I look forward to seeing my sister," Abivard answered. Let the city governor make of that what he would.

"Er—yes," Kharrad said, and quickly changed the subject. He didn't want to make anything of it, not where Abivard was listening to him.

Kharrad's reception was matched more or less exactly by other local leaders in the Thousand Cities over the next several days. The only real difference Abivard noted was that a couple of the city governors came from the ranks of the folk they controlled, having been born between the Tutub and the Tib. They did not receive Roshnani as if they were doing her a favor but as a matter of course and had their own wives and sometimes even their daughters join the suppers.

"Most of the time," one of them said after what might have been a cup too many of date wine, "you Makuraners are too stuffy about this. My wife nags me, but what can I do? If I offend her, she nags me. If I offend a man under the eye of the King of Kings, he makes me wish I was never born and maybe hurts my family, too. But you, brother-in-law to the King of Kings, you are not offended. My wife gets to come out and talk like a civilized human being, so she is not offended, either. Everyone is happy. Isn't that the way it ought to be?"

"Of course it is," Roshnani said. "Women's quarters were a mistake from the beginning. I wish Sharbaraz King of Kings, may his days be long and his realm increase, would outlaw them altogether."

"Yes, by the God!" the city governor's wife exclaimed. "May she plant that idea firmly in his Majesty's mind and heart."

A little farther down the low table Turan, the commander of the troopers escorting Abivard and his family, choked on his date wine. "Sweeter than I'm used to," he wheezed, wiping his mouth on the sleeve of his caftan.

That was true; Abivard found the sticky stuff cloying, too. He didn't think it was why Turan had swallowed wrong. Some nobles did ape Sharbaraz and himself and give their principal wives more freedom than upper-crust Makuraner women had customarily enjoyed. Others, though, muttered darkly about degeneration. Abivard did not think he would have to guess twice to figure out into which camp the escort commander fell.

They crossed the Tib on a bridge of boats much like the one they'd used to cross the Tutub and enter the land between the rivers. Only a narrow strip of cultivated land ran along the western bank of the Tib. Canals could not reach far there, for the country soon began to slope up toward the Dilbat Mountains in whose foothills sat Mashiz.

Abivard pointed to the city and the smoke rising from it. "That's where we're going," he said. His children squealed excitedly. To them Mashiz was more nearly a legend than Videssos the city. They'd seen the capital of the Empire of Videssos misted in sea haze on the far side of the Cattle Crossing. Mashiz was new and therefore fascinating.

"That's where we're going," Roshnani agreed quietly. "How we'll come out again is another matter."

To enter Mashiz the cavalrymen escorting Abivard and his family donned their armor and decked their horses out in chamfrons and iron-studded blankets, too. They carried the lances that had stayed bundled in the bed of a wagon since they'd crossed the Tutub. It was a fine warlike display, making Abivard seem to be returning to the capital of his homeland in triumph. He wished reality were a better match for appearance.

People stared at the jingling martial procession that hurried through the streets toward the palace of the King of Kings. Some pointed, some cheered, and some loudly wondered what was being celebrated and why. Even when the horsemen shouted out Abivard's name, not everyone knew who he was. *So much for fame*, he thought with wry amusement.

In the market squares his escort had to slow from a trot to a walk. They fumed, but Abivard took that as a good sign. If so many people were buying and selling things that they crowded the squares, Makuran had to be prosperous.

The palace of the King of Kings was different from its equivalent in Videssos the city, which Abivard had so often watched with longing. The Avtokrator of the Videssians and his court had a good many buildings scattered among lawns and groves. Here in Mashiz, the King of Kings' palace lay all under one roof, with a dark stone wall surrounding it and turning it into a citadel in the heart of the city.

To preserve the outwall's military usefulness, the square around it was bare of buildings for a bowshot. When Smerdis the usurper had held Mashiz, Abivard had fought his way to the palace against soldiers and sorcery. Now, years later, summoned by the man he'd helped place on the throne, he approached with hardly less apprehension.

"Who comes?" called a sentry from above the gates. Oh, he knew, but the forms had to be observed.

"Abivard son of Godarz, returned to Mashiz from Videssos and Vaspurakan at the order of Sharbaraz King of Kings, may his days be long and his realm increase."

"Enter, Abivard son of Godarz, obedient to the command of Sharbaraz King of Kings," the sentry said. He called to the gate crew. With squeaks from hinges that needed oiling, the gates swung open. Abivard entered the palace.

Almost at once an army of servitors swarmed upon and overwhelmed his little army of warriors. Stablemen and grooms vanquished the riders. They waited impatiently for the cavalrymen to dismount so they could lead the horses off to the stables. Their armored riders accompanied them, reduced to near impotence by having to use their own legs to move from one place to another.

Higher-ranking servants saw to Abivard and Roshnani. A

plump eunuch said, "If you will please to come with me, brother-in-law to the King of Kings, yes, with your excellent family, of course. Oh, yes," he went on, answering a question Abivard had been on the point of asking, "your conveyance and your driver will be attended to: you have the word of Sekandar upon it." He preened slightly so they would know he was Sekandar.

"How soon will we be able to see the King of Kings?" Abivard asked as the chamberlain led them into the palace itself.

"That is for the puissant Sharbaraz, may his years be many and his realm increase, to judge," Sekandar answered.

Abivard nodded and kept on following the eunuch but worried down where—he hoped—it did not show. If the King of Kings seldom left the palace and listened to the advice of Sekandar and others like him, how could he have any notion of what was true? Once, Sharbaraz had been a fighting man who led fighting men and took pleasure in their company. Now . . . Would he even acknowledge who Abivard was?

The apartment in which the eunuch installed Abivard and his family was luxurious past anything he had known in Videssos, and it was luxury of a familiar sort, not the icons and hard furniture of the Empire. Carpets into which his feet sank deep lay on the floor; thick, fat cushions were scattered in the corners of the rooms to support one's back while sitting. They had other uses, too; Varaz grabbed one and clouted Shahin with it. Shahin picked up his own, using it first for defense, then for offense.

"They're used to chairs," Abivard said. "They won't know how comfortable this can be till they try it for a while."

Roshnani was speaking to her sons in standard tones of exasperation. "Try not to tear the palace down around our ears *quite* yet, if you please." She seamlessly made a shift in subject to reply to her husband: "No, they won't." As if making a shameful confession, she added, "Nor will I, as a matter of fact. I got to like chairs a good deal. My knee clicks and my back crackles whenever I have to get up from the floor."

"So Videssos corrupted you, too?" Abivard asked, not quite joking.

"Life in the Empire could be very pleasant," his wife answered, as if defying him to deny it. "Our food is better, but they do more with the rest of life than we do."

"Hmm," Abivard said. "My backside starts turning to stone if I sit in a chair too long. I don't know; I think their towns are madhouses myself, far worse than Mashiz or any of the Thousand Cities. They're too fast, too busy, too set on getting ahead even if they have to cheat to do it. Those are all the complaints we've had about Videssians for hundreds of years, and if you ask me, they're all true."

Roshnani didn't seem to feel like arguing the point. She looked at the chambers in which the palace servitors had established them. "We are going nowhere, fast or slow; the God knows we shan't be busy, and the only way we can get ahead is if the King of Kings should will it."

"As is true of anyone in Makuran," Abivard said loudly for the benefit of anyone in Makuran who might be listening. Without seeming to, though, his wife had not only won the argument but pointed out that, palace though this might be for Sharbaraz, for Abivard and his kin it was a prison.

Winter dragged on, one storm following another till it looked as if the world would stay cold and icy forever. With each passing day Abivard came more and more to realize how right Roshnani had been.

He and his family saw only the servants who brought them food, hot water for bathing, and clothes once they had been laundered. He tried to bribe them to carry a note to Turan, the commander of the guard company that had escorted him to Mashiz. They took his money, but he never heard back from the officer. Their apologies sounded sincere but not sincere enough for him to believe them.

But having nothing better to do with his time and no better place to spend his money, he eventually tried getting a note to Denak. His sister never wrote back, either, at least not with a letter that reached his hands. He wondered whether his note or hers had disappeared. His, he suspected. If she knew what Sharbaraz was doing to him, she would make the King of Kings change his ways.

If she could— "Does she still have the influence she did in the early days of her marriage?" Roshnani asked after the Void had swallowed Abivard's letter. "Sharbaraz will have seen—not to put too fine a point on it, will have had—a lot of women in the years between."

"I know," Abivard said glumly. "As I knew him—" The past tense hurt but was true. "—as I knew him, I say, he always acknowledged his debts. But after a while any man could grow resentful, I suppose."

Varaz said, "Why not petition the King of Kings yourself, Father? Any man of Makuran has the right to be heard."

So, no doubt, his pedagogue had taught him. "What you learned and what is real aren't always the same thing, worse luck," Abivard answered. "The King of Kings is angry at me. That's why he would not hear my petition."

"Oh," Varaz said. "You mean the way Shahin won't listen to me after we've had a fight?"

"You're the one who won't listen to me," Shahin put in.

Having the advantage in age, Varaz took the lofty privilege of ignoring his younger brother. "*Is* that what you mean, Papa?" he asked.

"Yes, pretty much," Abivard answered. When you got down to it, the way Sharbaraz was treating him was childish. The idea of the all-powerful King of Kings in the guise of a bad-tempered small boy made him smile. Again, though, he fought shy of mentioning it out loud. You never could tell whose ear might be pressed to a small hole behind one of the tapestries hanging on the wall. If the King of Kings was angry at him, there was no point making things worse by speaking plain and simple truths in the hearing of his servants.

"I don't like this place," Zarmidukh declared. She was too young to worry about what other people thought when she spoke her mind. She said what she thought, whatever that happened to be. "It's boring."

"It's not the most exciting place I've ever been," Abivard said, "but there are worse things than being bored."

"I don't know of any," Zarmidukh said darkly.

"You're lucky," Abivard told her. "I do."

Someone rapped on the door. Abivard looked at Roshnani. It wasn't any of the times the palace servitors usually made an appearance. The knock came again, imperiously—or perhaps he was reading too much into it. "Who can it be?" he said.

With her usual practicality Roshnani answered, "The only way to find out is to open the door."

"Thank you so much for your help," he said. She made a face at him. He got up and went over to the door, his feet sinking deep into the thick carpet as he walked. He took hold of the handle and pulled the door open.

A eunuch with hard, suspicious eyes in a face of almost unearthly beauty looked him up and down as if to say he'd taken much too long getting there. "You are Abivard son of Godarz?" The voice was unearthly, too: very pure and clear but not in a register commonly used by either men or women. When Abivard admitted who he was, the eunuch said, "You will come with me at once," and started down the halls without waiting to see if he followed.

The guards who stood to either side of the doorway did not acknowledge his passing. Not even their eyes shifted as he walked by. Roshnani closed the door. Had she come after him unbidden, the guards would not have seemed as if they were carved from stone.

He did not ask the eunuch where they were going. He didn't think the fellow would tell him and declined to give him the pleasure of refusing. They walked in silence through close to half a farsang's worth of corridors. At last the eunuch stopped. "Go through this doorway," he said imperiously. "I await you here."

"Have a pleasant wait," Abivard said, earning a fresh glare. Pretending he didn't notice it, he opened the door and went in.

"Welcome to Mashiz, brother of mine," Denak said. She nodded when Abivard closed the door after himself. "That is wise. The fewer people who hear what we say, the better."

Abivard pointed to the maidservant who sat against the wall, idly painting her nails one by one from a pot of red dye and examining them with attention more careful than that she seemed to be giving Denak. "And yet you brought another pair of ears here?" he asked.

Denak assumed an exasperated expression, which brought lines to her face. Abivard hadn't seen much of her after Sharbaraz had taken Mashiz. He knew he'd aged in the intervening decade, but realizing that his sister had also aged came hard. She said, "I am principal wife to the King of Kings. It would be most unseemly for any man to see me alone. Most unseemly."

"By the God, I'm your brother!" Abivard said angrily.

"And that is how I managed to arrange to see you at all," Denak answered. "I think it will be all right, or not too bad. Ksorane is about as likely to tell me what Sharbaraz says as the other way around, or so I've found. Isn't that right, dear?" She waved to the girl.

"How could the principal wife to Sharbaraz King of Kings, may his days be long and his realm increase, be wrong?" Ksorane said. She put another layer of paint on the middle finger of her left hand.

Denak's laugh was as sour as vinegar. "Easily enough, by the God. I've found that out many a time and oft." If she'd said one word more, Abivard would have bet any amount any man cared to name that the maidservant, trusted or not, would have taken her remark straight to Sharbaraz. Even as things were, he worried. But Denak seemed oblivious, continuing, "As you have now found for yourself—is it not so, brother of mine?"

In spite of Denak's assurances, Abivard found it hard to speak his mind before someone he did not know. Cautiously, he answered, "Sometimes a man far from the field of action does not have everything he needs to judge whether his best interests are being followed."

Denak laughed again, a little less edgily this time. "You shouldn't be a general, brother of mine; the King of Kings should send you to Videssos the city as ambassador. You'd win from Maniakes with your honeyed words everything our armies haven't managed to take."

"I've spoken with Maniakes, when he came close to Across in

one of the Videssians' cursed dromons," Abivard said. "I wish the God would drop all of those into the Void. We found no agreement. Nor, it seems, does Sharbaraz King of Kings find agreement with what I did in Vaspurakan. I wish he would summon me and say as much himself, so I might answer."

"People don't get everything they wish," Denak answered. "I know all about that, too." Her hopeless anger tore at Abivard. But then she went on, "This once, though, I got at least part of what I want. When the King of Kings heard you'd ignored his orders about Vaspurakan, he didn't only want to take your head from your shoulders—he wanted to give you over to the torturers."

As Abivard had learned after he had taken the Videssian westlands for Sharbaraz, the parents and nursemaids of the Empire used the ferocious talents of Makuraner torturers to frighten naughty children into obeying. He bowed very low. "Sister of mine, I am in your debt. My children are young to be fatherless. I should not complain about being unable to see the King of Kings."

"Of course you should," Denak said. "After him, you are the most powerful man in Makuran. He has no business to treat you so, no right—"

"He has the right: he is the King of Kings," Abivard said. "After the King of Kings, no man in Makuran is powerful. I was the most powerful Makuraner outside Makuran, perhaps." Now his grin came wry. "Once back within it, though . . . he may do with me as he will."

"In your mind you have no power next to Sharbaraz," Denak answered. "Every day courtiers whisper into his ear that you have too much. I can go only so far in making him not listen. He might pay me more heed if—"

If I had a son. Abivard filled in the words his sister would not say. Sharbaraz had several sons by lesser wives, but Denak had given him only girls. If she had a boy, he would become the heir, for she remained Sharbaraz' principal wife. But what were the odds of that? Did he still call her to his bed? Abivard could not ask, but his sister did not sound as if she expected to bear more children.

As if picking that thought from his mind, Denak said, "He treats me with all due honor. As he promised, I am not mewed up in the women's quarters like a hawk dozing with a hood over its eyes. He does remember—everything. But honor alone is not enough for a man and a wife."

She did speak as if Ksorane weren't there. At last Abivard imitated her, saying, "If Sharbaraz remembers all you did for him—and if he does, I credit him—why, by the God, doesn't he remember what I've done and trust my judgment?"

"I'd think that would be easy for you to see," Denak told him. "Come what may, *I* can't steal the throne from him. *You* can."

"I helped put him on the throne," Abivard protested indignantly. "I risked everything I had—I risked everything Vek Rud domain had—to put him on the throne. I don't want it. Till you spoke of it just now, the idea that I would want it never once entered my mind. If it entered his—"

He started to say, *He's mad.* He didn't, and fear of the maidservant's taking his words to Sharbaraz wasn't what stopped him. For the King of Kings was not mad to fear usurpation. After all, he'd been usurped once already.

"He's wrong." That was better. Abivard reminded himself that he was speaking with Sharbaraz' wife as well as his own sister. But Denak *was* his sister, and how much he'd missed her over the years suddenly rose up in him like a choking cloud. "You *know* me, sister of mine. You know I would never do such a thing."

Her face crumpled. Tears made her eyes bright. "I knew you," she said. "I know the brother I knew would be loyal to the rightful King of Kings through ... anything." She held her hands wide apart to show how all-encompassing *anything* was. But then she went on. "I *knew* you. It's been so long ... Time changes people, brother of mine. I know that, too. I should."

"It's been so long," Abivard echoed sadly. "I can't make Sharbaraz' years many; only the God grants years. But since the days of Razmara the Magnificent, who has increased the realm of the King of Kings more than I?"

"No one." Denak's voice was sad. One of the tears ran down her cheek. "And don't you see, brother of mine, every victory you won, every city you brought under the lion of Makuran, gave him one more reason to distrust you."

Abivard hadn't seen that, not with such brutal clarity. But it was clear enough—all too clear—when Denak pointed it out to him. He chewed on the inside of his lower lip. "And when I disobeyed him in Vaspurakan—"

Denak nodded. "Now you understand. When you disobeyed him, he thought it the first step of your rebellion."

"If it was, why did I come here with all my family at his order?" Abivard asked. "Once I did that, shouldn't he have realized he was wrong?"

"So I told him, though not in those words." One corner of his sister's mouth bent up in a rueful, knowing smile. "So many people tell the King of Kings he is right every moment of every waking hour of every day that when he was already inclined to think so himself, he became . . . quite convinced of it."

"I suppose so." Abivard had noted that trait in Sharbaraz even when he was a hunted rebel against Smerdis. After a decade and more on the throne at Mashiz he might well have come to think of himself as infallible. What Abivard wanted to say was, *He's only a man, after all.* But of all the things Ksorane could take back to Sharbaraz from his lips, that one might do the most damage.

Denak said, "I have been trying to get him to see you, brother of mine. So far . . ." She spread her hands again. He knew how much luck she'd had. But he also knew he still kept his head on his shoulder and all his members attached to his body. That was probably his sister's doing.

"Tell the King of Kings I did not mean to anger him," he said wearily. "Tell him I am loyal—why would I be here otherwise? Tell him in Vaspurakan I was doing what I thought best for the realm, for I was closer to the trouble than he. Tell him—" *Tell him to drop into the Void if he's too vain and puffed up with himself to see that on his own.* "Tell him once more what you've already told him. The God willing, he will hear."

"I shall tell him," Denak said. "I have been telling him. But when everyone else tells him the opposite, when Farrokh-Zad and

Tzikas write from Vaspurakan complaining of how mild you were to the priests of Phos—"

"Tzikas wrote from Vaspurakan?" Abivard broke in. "Tzikas wrote *that* from Vaspurakan? If I see the renegade, the traitor, the wretch again, he is a dead man." His lips curled in what looked like a smile. "I know just what I'll do if I see him again, the cursed Videssian schemer. I'll send him as a present for Maniakes behind a shield of truce. We'll see how he likes *that*." Merely contemplating the idea gave him great satisfaction. Whether he'd ever get the chance to do anything about it was, worse luck, another question altogether.

"I'll pray to the God. May she grant your wish," Denak said. She got to her feet. Abivard rose, too. His sister took him in her arms.

Ksorane, about whom Abivard had almost entirely forgotten, let out a startled squeak. "Highness, to touch a man other than the King of Kings is not permitted."

"He is my brother, Ksorane," Denak answered in exasperated tones.

Abivard did not know whether to laugh or cry. He and Denak had criticized Sharbaraz King of Kings almost to, maybe even beyond, the point of lese majesty, and the serving woman had spoken not a word of protest. Indeed, by her manner she might not even have heard. Yet a perfectly innocent embrace drew horrified anger.

"The world is a very strange place," he said. He went back into the hall. If the eunuch had moved while he had been talking with his sister, it could not have been by more than the breadth of a hair. With a cold, hard nod the fellow led him back through the maze of corridors to the chambers where he and his family were confined.

The guards outside the chamber opened his door. The beautiful eunuch, who had said not a word while guiding him to his private prison, disappeared with silent steps. The door closed behind Abivard, and everything was just as it had been before Denak had summoned him.

When Sharbaraz King of Kings did not call him, Abivard grew furious at his sister. Rationally, he knew that was not only pointless but stupid. Denak might plead for him, as she had been pleading for him, but that did not mean that Sharbaraz would have to hear. By everything Abivard knew of the King of Kings, he was very good at not hearing.

Winter dragged on. The children at first grew restive at being cooped up in a small place like so many doves in a cote, then resigned themselves to it. That worried Abivard more than anything else he'd seen since Sharbaraz had ordered him to Mashiz.

Over and over he asked the guards who kept him and his family from leaving their rooms and the servants who fed them and removed the slop jars and brought fuel what was going on in Vaspurakan and Videssos. He rarely got answers, and the ones he did get formed no coherent pattern. Some people claimed there was fighting; others, that peace prevailed.

"Why don't they just say they don't know?" he demanded of Roshnani after yet another rumor—that Maniakes had slain himself in despair—reached his ears.

"You're asking a lot if you expect people to admit how ignorant they are," she answered. She had adapted to captivity better than he had. She worked on embroidery with thread borrowed from the servants and seemed to take so much pleasure from it that Abivard was more than once tempted to get her to teach him the stitches.

"I admit how ignorant I am here," he said. "Otherwise I wouldn't ask so many questions."

Roshnani loosened the hoop that held a circle of linen taut while she worked on it. She shook her head. "You don't understand. The only reason you're ignorant is that you're shut up here. You can't know what you want to find out. Too many people don't want to find out anything and just repeat what they happen to hear without thinking about it."

He thought about that, then slowly nodded. "You're probably right," he admitted. "It doesn't make this easier to bear, though."

In the end he did learn to embroider and concentrated his fury in producing the most hideous dragon he could imagine. He was glad he had only the rudiments of the craft, for if he could have matched Roshnani's skill, he would have given the dragon Sharbaraz' face.

Some of his imaginings along those lines disturbed him. In his mind he formed a picture of his army swarming out of Vaspurakan to rescue him that felt so real, he was shocked and disappointed when no one came battering down the door. As it had a way of doing, hope outran reality.

Among themselves, the servants began to talk of rain rather than snow. Abivard noted that he wasn't feeding the braziers as much charcoal as he had been or sleeping under such great piles of rugs and furs and blankets. Spring was coming. He, on the other hand, had nowhere to go, nothing to do.

"Ask Sharbaraz King of Kings, may his years be many and his realm increase, if he will free my family and let them go back to Vek Rud domain," he told a guard—and whoever might be listening. "If he wants to punish me, that is his privilege, but they have done nothing to deserve his anger."

Sharbaraz' privilege, though, was whatever he chose to make it. If the message got to him, he took no notice of it.

As one dreary day dragged into the next, Abivard began to understand Tzikas better. Unlike the Videssian renegade, he had done nothing to make his sovereign nervous about his loyalty—so he still believed, at any rate. But Sharbaraz had gotten nervous anyhow, and the results—

"How am I supposed to command another Makuraner army after this?" he whispered to Roshnani in the darkness after their children—and, with luck, any lurking listeners—had gone to bed.

"What would you do, husband of mind, if you got another command?" she asked, even more softly than he had spoken. "Would you go over to the Videssians to pay back the King of Kings for what he's done?"

She had been thinking about Tzikas, too, then. Abivard shook his head. "No. I am loyal to Makuran. I would be loyal to Sharbaraz, if he would let me. But even if I had no grievance against him before, I do now. How could he let me lead troops without being afraid that I would try to take the vengeance I deserve?"

"He has to trust you," Roshnani said. "In the end I think he will.

Did not your wizard see you fighting in the land of the Thousand Cities?"

"Bogorz? Yes, he did. But was he looking into the past or the future? I didn't know then, and I don't know now."

Bogorz had seen another image, too: Videssians and ships, soldiers disembarking at an unknown place at an equally unknown time. How much that had to do with the rest of his vision, Abivard could not begin to guess. If the wizard had shown him a piece of the future, it was a useless one.

Roshnani sighed. "Not knowing is hard," she agreed. "The way we're treated here, for instance: by itself, it wouldn't be bad. But since we don't know what will come at the end of it, how can we help but worry?"

"How indeed?" Abivard said. He hadn't told her that Sharbaraz had wanted to take his head—and worse. *What point to that?* he'd asked himself. Had the King of Kings chosen to do it, Roshnani could not have stopped him, and if he hadn't, Abivard would have made her fret without need. He seldom held things back from her but kept that one to himself without the slightest trace of guilt.

She snuggled against him. Though the night was not so chilly as the nights had been, he was glad of her warmth. He wondered if they would still be in this chamber when nights, no less than days, were sweaty torments and skin did nothing but stick to skin. If they were meant to be, they would, he decided. He could do nothing about it one way or the other. Presently he gave up and fell asleep.

The door to the chamber opened. Abivard's children stared. It wasn't the usual time. Abivard stared, too. He'd been shut up so long, he found a change of routine dangerous in and of itself.

Into the room came the beautiful eunuch who had conducted him to Denak. "Come with me," he said in his beautiful, sexless voice.

"Are you taking me to see my sister again?" Abivard asked, climbing to his feet.

"Come with me," the eunuch repeated, as if it were none of

Abivard's business where he was going till he got there, and perhaps not then, either.

Having no choice, Abivard went with him. As he walked out the door, he reflected that things could hardly be worse. He'd thought that before, too, every now and then. Sometimes he'd been wrong, which was something he would rather not have remembered.

He quickly realized that the eunuch was not leading him down the same halls he had traveled to visit Denak. He asked again where they were going, but only stony silence answered him. Though the eunuch said not a word, hatred bubbled up from him like steam from a boiling pot. Abivard wondered if that was hatred for him in particular or for any man lucky enough to have a beard and all parts complete and in good working order.

Several times they passed other people in the hall: some servants, some nobles. Abivard was tempted to ask them if they knew where he was going and what would happen to him when he got there. The only thing holding him back was a certainty that one way or another the eunuch would pay him back for his temerity.

He hadn't been in the palace for years before the summons had come that had led him to become much more intimately acquainted with one small part of it than he'd ever wanted to be. All the same, the corridors through which he was traveling began to look familiar.

"Are we going to—?" he asked, and then stopped with the question incomplete. The way the eunuch's back stiffened told him plainer than words that he'd get no answer. This once, though, it mattered less than it might have under other circumstances. Sooner or later, regardless of what the eunuch told him, he would know.

Without warning, the hallway turned and opened out into a huge chamber whose roof was supported by rows of columns. Those columns and the long expanse of carpet running straight ahead from the entrance guided the eye to the great throne at the far end of the room. "Advance and be recognized," the eunuch told Abivard. "I presume you still recall the observances."

By his tone, he presumed no such thing. Abivard confined

himself to one tight nod. "I remember," he said, and advanced down the carpet toward the throne where Sharbaraz King of Kings sat waiting.

Nobles standing in the shadows stared at him as he strode forward. The walls of the throne room looked different from the way he remembered them. He could not turn his head—not without violating court ritual—but flicked his eyes to the right and the left. Yes, those wall hangings were definitely new. They showed Makuraner triumphs over the armies of Videssos, triumphs where he had commanded the armies of the King of Kings. The irony smote him like a club.

The eunuch stepped aside when the carpet ended. Abivard strode out onto the polished stone beyond the woven wool and prostrated himself before Sharbaraz. He wondered how many thousands of men and women had gone down on their bellies before the King of Kings in the long years since the palace had been built. Enough, certainly, to give a special polish to the patch of stone where their foreheads touched.

Sharbaraz let him stay prostrate longer than he should have. At last, he said, "Rise."

"I obey, Majesty," Abivard said, getting to his feet. Now he was permitted to look upon the august personage of the King of Kings. His first thought was, *He's gone fat and soft.* Sharbaraz had been a lion of a warrior when he and Abivard had campaigned together against Smerdis the usurper. He seemed to have put on a good many more pounds than the intervening time should have made possible.

"We are not well pleased with you, Abivard son of Godarz," he declared. Even his voice sounded higher and more querulous than it had. His face was pale, as if he never saw the sun. Abivard knew he was pale, too, but he'd been imprisoned; Sharbaraz had no such excuse. Though Abivard hadn't seen himself in a mirror any time lately, he would have bet he didn't carry those dark, pouchy circles under his eyes.

He strangled the scorn welling up in him. No matter how Sharbaraz looked, he remained King of Kings. Whatever he decreed, that would be Abivard's fate. *Walk soft*, Abivard reminded himself. *Walk soft.* "I grieve to have displeased you, Majesty," he said. "I never intended to do that."

"We *are* displeased," Sharbaraz said, as if passing sentence. Perhaps he was doing just that; several of the courtiers let out soft sighs. Abivard wondered if the execution would be performed in the throne room for their edification. The King of Kings went on, "We trusted you to obey our commands pertaining to Vaspurakan, as we expect to be obeyed in all things."

In the old days as a rebel against Smerdis he hadn't been so free with the royal *we*. Hearing it from a man with whose humanity and fallibility he was all too intimately acquainted irked Abivard. With a sudden burst of insight he realized that Sharbaraz was trying to overawe him precisely because they had once been intimates: to subsume the remembered man in the present King of Kings. As such ploys often did, it had an effect opposite to the one Sharbaraz had intended.

Abivard said, "I pray your pardon, Majesty. I served Makuran as best I could."

"The affair appears otherwise to us," the King of Kings replied. "In disobeying our orders, you damaged the realm and brought both it and us into disrepute."

"I pray your pardon," Abivard repeated. He might have known—indeed, he had known—Sharbaraz would say that. Disobedience was a failure no ruler could tolerate, and as he and Roshnani had agreed, being right was in a way worse than being wrong.

But Sharbaraz said, "In our judgment you have now been punished enough for your transgressions. We have summoned you hither to inform you that Makuran once more has need of your services."

"Majesty?" Abivard had been half expecting—more than half expecting—the King of Kings to order him sent to the headsman or the torturers. If he'd frightened Sharbaraz, he could expect no better fate. Now, though, with courtiers murmuring approval in the background, the King of Kings had . . . pardoned him? "What do you need of me, Majesty?" Whatever it was, it couldn't be much worse than going off to meet the chopper.

"We begin to see why you had such difficulties in bringing Videssos the city under the lion of Makuran," Sharbaraz answered. It wasn't an apology—not quite—but it was closer to one than Abivard had ever heard from the King of Kings, who went on, not altogether comfortably, "We also see that Maniakes Avtokrator exemplifies in his person the wicked deviousness our lore so often attributes to the men of Videssos."

"In what way, Majesty?" Abivard asked in lieu of screaming, *By the God, what's he gone and done now?* He made himself keep his voice low and calm as he twisted the knife just a little. "As you will remember, I had not had much chance to learn what passes outside Mashiz." He hadn't had much chance to learn what passed outside the chamber in which Sharbaraz had locked him away, but the King of Kings already knew that.

Sharbaraz said, "Our one weakness is in ships. We have come to realize how serious a weakness it is." Abivard had realized that the instant he had seen how Videssian dromons kept his army from getting over the Cattle Crossing; he was glad Sharbaraz had been given a similar revelation, no matter how long delayed it was. The King of Kings went on. "Taking a sizable fleet, Maniakes has sailed with it to Lyssaion in the Videssian westlands and there disembarked an expeditionary force."

"Lyssaion, Majesty?" Abivard frowned, trying to place the town on his mental map of the westlands. At first he had no luck, for he was thinking of the northern coastline, the one on the Videssian Sea and closest to Vaspurakan. Then he said, "Oh, on the southern coast, the one by the Sailor's Sea—the far southwest of the westlands."

He stiffened. He should have realized that at once—after all, hadn't Bozorg shown him Videssians coming ashore somewhere very like there and then heading up through the mountains? He'd had knowledge of Maniakes' plan for most of a year—and much good that had done him.

"Yes," Sharbaraz was saying, his words running parallel to

Abivard's thoughts. "They landed there, as I told you. And they have been pushing northwest ever since—pushing toward the land of the Thousand Cities." He paused, then said what was probably the worst thing he could think of: "Pushing toward Mashiz."

Abivard took that in and blended it with the insight he now had—too late—from Bogorz' scrying. "After Maniakes beat the Kubratoi last year, he was too quiet by half," he said at last. "I kept expecting him to do something against us, especially when I pulled the field force out of the Videssian westlands to fight in Vaspurakan." *I wouldn't have had to do that but for your order to suppress the worship of Phos*—another thing he couldn't tell the King of Kings. "But he never moved. I wondered what he was up to. Now we know."

"Now we know," Sharbaraz agreed. "We never took Videssos the city in war, but the Videssians have sacked Mashiz. We do not intend this to happen again."

Undoubtedly, the King of Kings intended to sound fierce and martial. Undoubtedly, his courtiers would assure him he sounded very fierce and martial, indeed. *He's afraid*, Abivard realized, and a chill ran through him. *He did well enough when the war was far away, but now it's coming here, almost close enough to touch. He's been comfortable too long. He's lost the stomach for that kind of fight. He had it once, but it's gone.*

Aloud, he repeated, "How may I serve you, Majesty?"

"Take up an army." Sharbaraz' words were quick and harsh. "Take it up, I say, and rid the realm of the invader. Makuran's honor demands it. The Videssians must be repulsed."

Does Maniakes know he's putting him in fear? Abivard wondered. *Or is he striking at our vitals tit for tat, as we have struck at his? Command of the sea lets him pick his spots.*

"What force have you for me to use against the imperials, Majesty?" he asked—a highly relevant question. Was Sharbaraz sending him forth in the hope he would be defeated and killed?

"Take up the garrisons from as many of the Thousand Cities as suits you," Sharbaraz answered. "With them to hand, you will far outnumber the foe."

"Yes, Majesty, but—" Contradicting the King of Kings before the whole court would not improve Abivard's standing here. True, if he took up all the garrisons from the Thousand Cities, he would have far more men in the field than Maniakes did. Being able to do anything useful with them was something else again. Almost all of them were foot soldiers. Simply mustering them would take time. Getting them in front of Maniakes' fast-moving horsemen and bringing him to battle would take not only time but great skill— and even greater luck.

Did Sharbaraz understand that? Studying him, Abivard decided he did. It was one of the reasons he was afraid. He'd sent his best troops, his most mobile troops, into Videssos and Vaspurakan and had left himself little with which to resist a counterthrust he hadn't thought Maniakes would be able to make.

"Using the canals between the Tutub and the Tib will also let you delay the enemy and perhaps turn him back altogether," Sharbaraz said. "We remember well how the usurper whom we will not name put them to good use against us in the struggle for the throne."

"That is so, Majesty," Abivard agreed. It was also the first thing the King of Kings had said that made sense. If he could take up the garrisons from the cities between the rivers and put them to work wrecking canals and flooding the countryside, he might get more use from them than he would if he tried to make them fight the Videssians. It still might not net everything Sharbaraz hoped for; the Videssians were skilled engineers and expert at corduroying roads through unspeakable muck. But it would slow them down, and slowing them was worth doing.

"Also," Sharbaraz said, "for cavalry to match the horsemen Maniakes brings against us, we give you leave to recall Tzikas from Vaspurakan. His familiarity with the foe will win many Videssians to our side. Further, you may take Hosios Avtokrator with you when you go forth to confront the foe."

Abivard opened his mouth, then closed it again. Sharbaraz was living in a dream world if he thought any Videssian would abandon Maniakes for his pretender. But then, insulated by the court from reality, in many ways Sharbaraz *was* living in a dream world.

Tzikas was a different matter. Unlike Sharbaraz' puppet, he did have solid connections within the Videssian army. If he got down to the land of the Thousand Cities soon enough, he might help solidify whatever force Abivard had managed to piece together from the local garrisons. Abivard suspected that Sharbaraz didn't know he knew what Tzikas had been saying about him; that meant Denak's maidservant was more reliable than Abivard had thought.

"Speak!" the King of Kings exclaimed. "What say you?"

"May it please you, Majesty, but I would sooner not have the eminent Tzikas—" Abivard gave the title in Videssian to emphasize the turncoat's foreignness. "—under my command." *About the only thing I'd like less would be the God dropping all Makuran into the Void.*

For a wonder, Sharbaraz took the hint. "Perhaps another commander, then," he said. Abivard had feared he'd insist; he didn't know what he would have done then. Arranged for Tzikas to have an accident, maybe. If any man ever deserved an accident, Tzikas was the one.

"Perhaps so, Majesty," Abivard answered. Curse it, how did you tell the King of Kings he'd made a harebrained suggestion? You couldn't, not if you wanted to keep your head on your shoulders. From what he'd seen, the Avtokrator of the Videssians had a similar problem, perhaps in less acute form.

Sharbaraz said, "We are confident you will hold the enemy far away from us and far away from Mashiz, preserving our complete security."

"The God grant it be so," Abivard said. "The men of Makuran have beaten the Videssians many times during your glorious reign." He had led Sharbaraz' troops to a lot of those victories, too. Now the King of Kings suddenly recalled that: he needed one more victory, or maybe more than one. Abivard went on, "I shall do all I can for you and for Makuran. The Videssians, though, I must say, fight with more spirit for Maniakes than they ever did for Genesios."

"We are confident," the King of Kings repeated. "Go forth, Abivard son of Godarz: go forth and defeat the foe. Then return in triumph to the bosom of your wife and family."

Almost, Abivard missed the meaning lurking there. That made the surge of fury all the more ferocious when it came. Sharbaraz was going to hold Roshnani and his children hostage to guarantee he would neither rebel once he had an army under his command again nor go over to the Videssians.

He thinks he is. Abivard said, "Majesty, my wife and children have always taken the field with me, ever since the days when you guested at Vek Rud stronghold."

The days when you were first a prisoner whom I helped rescue and then a rebel against the King of Kings ruling in Mashiz, he meant. From behind him came the faintest of murmurs: Sharbaraz' courtiers took the point. By the way the countenance of the King of Kings darkened, so did he. He tried to put the best face on it that he could: "We think only for their safety. Here in Mashiz all their needs will be met, and they will be in no danger from vicious marauding Videssians."

Abivard looked Sharbaraz in the face. That was not quite a discourtesy, or did not have to be, but the way he held Sharbaraz' eyes certainly was. "If you rely on me to protect you and your capital, Majesty, surely you can rely on me to protect my kin."

The murmur behind him got louder. He wondered how long it had been since someone had defied the King of Kings, no matter how politely, in his own throne room. Generations, probably. By the dazed expression on Sharbaraz' face, it had never happened to him before.

He tried to rally, saying, "Surely we know better than you the proper course in this affair, that which would be most expedient for all Makuran."

Abivard shrugged. "I have enjoyed the company of my wife and children all through the winter. May it please you, Majesty, I would just as soon return to them in the chambers you so generously granted us." *If I don't take them with me, I won't go out.*

"It does not please us," Sharbaraz answered in a hard voice. "We place the good of the realm ahead of that of any one man."

"The good of the realm will not be harmed if I take my family with me." Abivard gave the King of Kings a sidelong look. "I will have one more reason to repel the Videssians if my wife and children are at my side."

"That is not our view of the matter," Sharbaraz said.

The murmurs behind Abivard were almost loud enough now for him to make out individual voices and words. People would speak of this scandal for years. "Perhaps, Majesty, you would be better served with a different general in command of these garrison troops," he said.

"Had we wanted a different general, be sure we should have selected one," the King of Kings replied. "We are aware we have a great many from among whom we may choose. Rest assured you were not picked at random."

You're the one who's done best. That was what he meant. Abivard felt like laughing in his face. If he wanted Abivard and no one else, that limited his choices. He couldn't do anything dreadful to Roshnani or the children, not if he expected Abivard to serve him. What better way to get Abivard to do what he said he would not do and go over to Videssos?

How long had it been since the King of Kings had wanted someone to do something but had not gotten his way? By the frustrated glare on Sharbaraz' face, a long time. "Do you presume to disobey our will?" he demanded.

"No, Majesty," Abivard said. *Yes, Majesty—again.* "Loose me against the Videssians and I will do everything I can to drive them from the realm. So the King of Kings has ordered; so shall it be. My family will watch as I oppose Maniakes with every fiber of my being."

And if my family isn't there to watch—well, it doesn't matter then, anyhow, for I won't be there doing the fighting. Abivard smiled at his brother-in-law. No, Sharbaraz was not giving the orders here. How long would he need to realize as much?

He was not stupid. Arrogant, certainly, and stubborn, and long accustomed to having others leap to fulfill his every wish, but not stupid. "It shall be as you say," he replied at length. "You and your family shall go forth against Maniakes. But as you have set the terms under which you deign to fight, so you have also set for yourself the terms of the fight. We shall look for victory from you, nothing less."

"If you send forth a general expecting him to fail, you've sent forth the wrong general," Abivard answered. A nasty chill of worry ran down his back. Again he wondered if Sharbaraz was setting him up to fail so he could justify eliminating him.

No. Abivard could not believe it. The King of Kings needed no such elaborate justifications. Once Abivard was away from his army and in Mashiz, Sharbaraz could have eliminated him whenever he chose.

The King of Kings gestured brusquely. "We dismiss you, Abivard son of Godarz." It was as abrupt an end to an audience as could be imagined. The hum of talk behind Abivard made him think the courtiers never had imagined anything like it.

He prostrated himself once more, symbolizing the submission he'd subverted. Then he rose and backed away from Sharbaraz' throne until he could turn around without causing a scandal—*a bigger scandal than I've caused already*, he thought, amused by the contrast between ritual and substance.

The beautiful eunuch fell in beside him. They walked out of the throne room together, neither of them saying a word. Once they were in the hallway, though, the eunuch turned blazing eyes on Abivard. "How dare you defy the King of Kings?" he demanded, his voice beautiful no more but cracking with rage.

"How dare I?" Abivard echoed. "I didn't dare leave my family behind in his clutches, that's how." No doubt every word he said would go straight back to Sharbaraz, but he got the idea that words would go back to Sharbaraz whether he said anything or not. If he didn't, the eunuch would invent something.

"He should have given you over to the torturers," the eunuch hissed. "He should have given you over to the torturers when first you came here."

"He needs me," Abivard answered. The beautiful eunuch recoiled, almost physically sickened at the idea that the King of Kings could need anyone. Abivard went on, "He needs me in particular. You can't pick just anyone and order him to go out and win your battles for you. Oh, you could, but you wouldn't care for the results. If people can win battles for you, giving them to the torturers is wasteful."

"Do not puff yourself up like a pig's bladder at me," the eunuch snarled. "All your pretensions are empty and vain, foolish and insane. You shall pay for your presumption; if not now, then in due course."

Abivard did not answer, on the off chance that keeping quiet would prevent the beautiful eunuch from growing more angry at him still. He was even gladder than he had been while facing down Sharbaraz that he'd managed to pry his family out of the palace. If the eunuch was any indication, the servitors to the King of Kings distrusted and feared him even more than Sharbaraz did.

And for what? The only thing he could think of was that he'd been too successful at doing Sharbaraz' bidding. If the King of Kings was lord over all the realm of Makuran, could he afford such successful servants? Evidently he didn't think so.

"I hope you lose," the beautiful eunuch said. "No matter how you boast, Sharbaraz King of Kings, may his years be many and his realm increase, is rash in putting his faith in you. The God grant that the Videssians bewilder you, befuddle you, and beat you."

"An interesting prayer," Abivard answered. "Should the God grant it, I expect Maniakes would be here a few days later to burn Mashiz around your ears. Shall I tell Sharbaraz you wished for that?"

The eunuch glared again. They had come to hallways Abivard knew. In a moment they rounded a last corner and came up to the guarded door behind which Abivard had passed the winter. At the beautiful eunuch's brusque gesture, the guardsmen opened the door. Abivard went in. The door slammed shut.

Roshnani pounced on him. "Well?" she demanded.

"I was summoned before the King of Kings," he told her.

"And?"

"There's more to the world than this suite of rooms," Abivard told her. She hugged him. Their children squealed.

V

In early spring even the parched country between Mashiz and the westernmost tributaries of the Tib bore a thin carpet of green that put Abivard in mind of the hair on top of a balding man's head: you could see the bare land beneath, as you could see the bald man's scalp, and you knew it would soon prevail over the temporary covering.

For the first few farsangs out of the capital, though, such fine distinctions were the last thing on Abivard's mind, or his principal wife's, or those of their children. Breathing fresh air, seeing the horizon farther than a wall away—those were treasures beside which the riches in the storerooms of the King of Kings were pebbles and lumps of brass by comparison.

And happy as they were to escape their confinement, Pashang, their driver, was more joyful yet. They had been confined in genteel captivity: mewed up, certainly, but in comfort and with plenty to eat. Pashang had gone straight to the dungeons under the palace.

"The God only knows how far they go, lord," he told Abivard as the wagon rattled along. "They're getting bigger all the time, too, for Sharbaraz has gangs of Videssian prisoners driving new tunnels through the rock. He uses 'em hard; when one dies, he just throws in another one. I was lucky they didn't put me in one of those gangs, or somebody else would be driving you now."

"We took a lot of Videssian prisoners," Abivard said in a troubled voice. "I'd hoped they were put to better use than that."

Pashang shook his head. "Didn't look so to me, lord. Some of those poor buggers, they'd been down underground so long, they were pale as ghosts, and even the torchlight hurt their eyes. Some of 'em, they didn't even know Maniakes was Avtokrator in Videssos; they were trying to figure out what year of Genesios' reign they were in."

"That's . . . alarming to think about," Abivard said. "I'm glad you're all right, Pashang; I'm sorry I couldn't protect you as I would have liked."

"What could you do, when you were in trouble yourself?" the driver answered. "It could have been worse for me, too. I know that. They just held me in a cell and didn't try to work me to death, till they finally let me out." He glanced down at his hands. "First time in more years'n I can remember I don't have calluses from the reins. I'll blister, I suppose, then get 'em back."

Abivard set a hand on his shoulder. "I'm glad you'll have the chance."

The soldiers who had accompanied him to the capital now accompanied him away from it. Their fate had been milder than his and far milder than Pashang's. They'd been quartered apart from the rest of the troops in Mashiz, as if they carried some loathsome and contagious illness, and they'd been subjected to endless interrogations designed to prove that either they or Abivard was disloyal to the King of Kings. After that failed, they'd been left almost as severely alone as Abivard had.

One of them rode up to him as he was walking back to the wagon from a call of nature. The trooper said, "Lord, if we weren't angry at Sharbaraz before we got into Mashiz, we are now, by the God."

He pretended he hadn't heard. For all he knew, the trooper was an agent of the King of Kings, trying to entrap him into a statement Sharbaraz could construe as treasonous. Abivard hated to think that way, but everything that had happened to him since he had been recalled from Vaspurakan warned him that he'd better.

When he came to Erekhatti, one of the westernmost of the Thousand Cities, he got his next jolt: the sort of men Sharbaraz expected him to forge into an army with which to vanquish Maniakes. The city governor assembled the garrison for his inspection. "They are bold men," the fellow declared. "They will fight like lions."

What they looked like to Abivard was a crowd of tavern toughs or, at best, tavern bouncers: men who would probably be fierce enough facing foes smaller, weaker, and worse armed than themselves but who could be relied on to panic and flee under any serious attack. Though almost all of them wore iron pots on their heads, a good quarter were armed with nothing more lethal than stout truncheons.

Abivard pointed those men out to the city governor. "They may be fine for keeping order here inside the walls, but they won't be enough if we're fighting real soldiers—and we will be."

"We have spears stored somewhere, I think," the governor said doubtfully. After a moment he added, "Lord, garrison troops were never intended to go into battle outside the city walls, you know."

So much for fighting like lions, Abivard thought. "If you know where those spears are, dig them up," he commanded. "These soldiers will do better with them than without."

"Aye, lord, just as you desire, so shall it be done," the governor of Erekhatti promised. When Abivard was ready to move out the next morning with the garrison in tow, the spears had not appeared. He decided to wait till afternoon. There was still no sign of the spears. Angrily, he marched out of Erekhatti. The governor said, "I pray to the God I did not distress you."

"As far as I'm concerned, Maniakes is welcome to this place," Abivard snarled. That got him a hurt look by way of reply.

The next town to which he came was called Iskanshin. Its garrison was no more prepossessing than the one in Erekhatti—less so, in fact, for the city governor of Iskanshin had no idea where to lay his hands on the spears that might have turned his men from bravos into something at least arguably resembling soldiers.

"What am I going to do?" Abivard raved as he left Iskanshin. "I've seen two cities now, and I have exactly as many men as I started out with, though three of those are down with a flux of the bowels and useless in a fight."

"It can't all be this bad," Roshnani said.

"Why not?" he retorted.

"Two reasons," she said. "For one, when we were forced through the Thousand Cities in the war against Smerdis, they defended themselves well enough to hold us out. And second, if they were all as weak as Erekhatti and Iskanshin, Videssos would have taken the land between the Tutub and the Tib away from us hundreds of years ago."

Abivard chewed on that. It made some of his rage go away—some, but not all. "Then why aren't these towns in any condition to meet an attack now?" he demanded not so much of Roshnani as of the world at large.

The world didn't answer. The world, he'd found, never answered. His wife did: "Because Sharbaraz King of Kings, may his years be many and his realm increase, decided the Thousand Cities couldn't possibly be in any danger and so scanted them. And one of the reasons he decided the Thousand Cities were safe for all time was that a certain Abivard son of Godarz had won him a whole great string of victories against Videssos. How could the Videssians hope to trouble us after they'd been beaten again and again?"

"Do you know," Abivard said thoughtfully, "that's not the answerless question it seems to be when you ask it that way. Maniakes has started playing the game by new rules. He's written off the westlands for the time being, which is something I never thought I'd see from an Avtokrator of the Videssians. But the way he's doing it makes a crazy kind of sense. If he can strike a blow at our heart and drive it home, whether we hold the westlands won't matter in the long run, because we'll have to give them up to defend ourselves."

"He's never been foolish," Roshnani said. "We've seen that over the years. If this is how he's fighting the war, it's because he thinks he can win."

"Far be it from me to argue," Abivard exclaimed. "By all I've seen here, I think he can win, too."

But his pessimism was somewhat tempered by his reception at Harpar, just east of the Tib. The city governor there did not seem to regard his position as an invitation to indolence. On the contrary: Tovorg's garrison soldiers, while not the most fearsome men Abivard had ever seen, all carried swords and bows and looked to have some idea what to do with them. If they ever got near horsemen or in among them, they might do some damage, and they might not run in blind panic if enemy troopers moved toward them.

"My compliments, Excellency," Abivard said. "Compared to what I've seen elsewhere, your warriors deserve to be recruited into the personal guard of the King of Kings."

"You are generous beyond my deserts, lord," Tovorg answered, cutting roast mutton with the dagger he wore on his belt. "I try only to do my duty to the realm."

"Too many people are thinking of themselves first and only then of the realm," Abivard said. "To them—note that I name no names—whatever is easiest is best."

"You need name no names," the city governor of Harpar said, a fierce gleam kindling in his eyes. "You come from Mashiz, and I know by which route. Other towns between the rivers are worse than those you have seen."

"You do so ease my mind," Abivard said, to which Tovorg responded with a grin that showed his long white teeth.

He said, "This was of course my first concern, lord." Then he grew more serious. "How many peasants shall I rout out once you have moved on, and how much of the canal system do you think we'll have to destroy?"

"I hope it doesn't come to that, but get ready to rout out as many as you can. Destroying canals will hurt the cropland but not your ability to move grain to the storehouses—is that right?"

"There it might even help," Tovorg said. "We mostly ship by water in these parts, so spreading water over the land won't hurt us much. What we eat next year is another question, though."

"Next year may have to look out for itself," Abivard answered. "If Maniakes gets here, he'll wreck the canals as best he can instead of just opening them here and there to flood the land on either side of the banks. He'll burn the crops he doesn't flood, and he'll burn Harpar, too, if he can get over the walls or through them."

"As we did in the Videssian westlands?" Tovorg shrugged. "The idea, then, is to make sure he doesn't come so far, eh?"

"Yes," Abivard said, wondering as he spoke where he would find the wherewithal to stop Maniakes. Harpar's garrison was a start but no more. And they were infantry. Positioning them so they could block Maniakes' progress would be as hard as he'd warned Sharbaraz.

"I will do everything I can to work with you," Tovorg said. "If the peasants grumble—if they try to do anything more than grumble—I will suppress them. The realm as a whole comes first."

"The realm comes first," Abivard repeated. "You are a man of whom Makuran can be proud." Tovorg hadn't asked about rewards. He hadn't made excuses. He'd just found out what needed doing and promised to do it. If things turned out well afterward, he undoubtedly hoped he would be remembered. And why not? A man was always entitled to hope.

Abivard hoped he would find more city governors like Tovorg.

"There!" A mounted scout pointed to a smoke cloud. "D'you see, lord?"

"Yes, I see it," Abivard answered. "But so what? There are always clouds of smoke on the horizon in the Thousand Cities. More smoke here than I ever remember seeing before."

That wasn't strictly true. He'd seen thicker, blacker smoke rising from Videssian cities when his troops had captured and torched them. But that smoke had lasted only until whatever was burnable inside those cities had burned itself out. Between the Tutub and the Tib smoke was a fact of life, rising from all the Thousand Cities as their inhabitants baked bread, cooked food, fired pots, smelted iron, and did all the countless other things requiring flame and fuel. One more patch of it struck Abivard as nothing out of the ordinary.

But the scout spoke with assurance: "There lies the camp of the Videssians, lord. No more than four or five farsangs from us."

"I've heard prospects that delighted me more," Abivard

said. The scout showed white teeth in a grin of sympathetic understanding.

Abivard had known for some time the direction from which Maniakes was coming. Had the refugees fleeing before the Videssian Avtokrator been mute, their presence alone would have warned him of Maniakes' impending arrival, as a shift in the wind foretells a storm. But the refugees were anything but mute. They were in fact voluble and volubly insistent that Abivard throw back the invader.

"Easy to insist," Abivard muttered. "Telling me how to do it is harder."

The refugees had tried that, too. They'd bombarded him with plans and suggestions till he had tired of talking with them. They were convinced that they had the answers. If he'd had as many horsemen as there were people in all the Thousand Cities put together, the suggestions—or some of them—might have been good ones. Had he even had the mobile force he'd left behind in Vaspurakan, he might have been able to do something with a few of the half-bright schemes. As things were—

"As things are," he said to no one in particular, "I'll be lucky if I don't get overrun and wiped out." Then he called to Turan. The officer who had commanded his escort on the road from Vaspurakan down to Mashiz was now his lieutenant general, for he'd found no man from the garrison forces of the Thousand Cities whom he liked better for the role. He pointed to the smoke from Maniakes' camp, then asked, "What do you make of our chances against the Videssians?"

"With what we've got here?" Turan shook his head. "Not good. I hear the Videssians are better than they used to be, and even if they weren't, it wouldn't much matter. If they hit us a solid blow, we'll shatter. By any reasonable way of looking at things, we don't stand a chance."

"Exactly what I was thinking," Abivard said, "almost word for word. If we can't do anything reasonable to keep Maniakes from rolling over us, we'll just have to try something unreasonable."

"Lord?" Turan stared in blank incomprehension. Abivard took

that as a good sign. If his own lieutenant couldn't figure out what he had in mind, maybe Maniakes wouldn't be able to, either.

The night was cool only by comparison to the day that had just ended. Crickets chirped, sawing away like viol players who knew no tunes and had only one string. Somewhere off in the distance a fox yipped. Rather closer, the horses from Maniakes' army snorted and occasionally whickered on the picket lines where they were tied.

Stars blazed down from the velvety black dome of the sky. Abivard wished the moon were riding with them. Had he been able to see his way here, he wouldn't have fallen down nearly so often. But had the moon been in the sky, Videssian sentries might well have seen him and his comrades, and that would have been disastrous.

He tapped Turan—he hoped it was Turan—on the shoulder. "Get going. You know what to do."

"Aye, lord." The whisper came back in the voice of his lieutenant. That took one weight off his mind, leaving no more than ninety or a hundred.

Turan and the band he led slipped away. To Abivard they seemed to be making an appalling amount of noise. The Videssians not far away—not far away at all—appeared to notice nothing, though. Maybe the crickets were drowning out Turan's racket. *Or maybe,* Abivard thought, *you're wound as tight as a youth going into his first battle, and every little noise is loud in your ears.*

Had he had better officers, he wouldn't have been out here himself, nor would Turan. But if you couldn't trust someone else to do the job properly, you had to take care of it for yourself. Had Abivard been younger and less experienced, he would have found crouching there in the bushes exciting. How often did a commanding general get to lead his own raiding party? *How many times does a commanding general* want *to lead his own raiding party?* he wondered, and came up with no good answer.

He hunkered down, listening to the crickets, smelling the manure—much of it from the farmers themselves—in the fields.

Waiting came hard, as it always did. He was beginning to think Turan had somehow gone astray when a great commotion broke out among the Videssians' tethered horses. Some of the animals whinnied in excitement as the lines holding them were cut; others screamed in pain and panic when swords slashed their sides. Turan and his men ran up and down the line, doing as much harm in as short a time as they could.

Mingled with the cries of the horses were those of the sentries guarding them. Some of those cries were cut off abruptly as Turan's followers cut down the Videssians. But some sentries survived and fought and helped raise the alarm for their fellows in the tents off to the side of the horse lines.

The watch fires burning around those tents showed men bursting forth from them, helms jammed hastily onto heads, sword blades glittering. "Now!" Abivard shouted. The warriors who had stayed behind with him started shooting arrows into the midst of the Videssians. At night and at long range they could hardly aim, but with enough arrows and enough targets, some were bound to strike home. Screams said that some did.

Abivard plucked arrow after arrow from his bow case, shooting as fast as he could. This was a different sort of warfare from the one to which he was accustomed. Normally he hunted with the bow but in battle charged with the lance. Using archery against men felt strange.

Strange or not, he saw Videssians topple and fall. Hurting one's foe was what war was all about, so he stopped worrying about how he was doing it. He also saw more Videssians, urged on by cursing officers, trot out toward him and his men.

He gauged their numbers—many more than he had. "Back, back, back!" he yelled. Most of the soldiers he had with him were men from the city garrisons, not Turan's troopers. They saw nothing shameful about retreat. Very much the reverse; he heard a couple of them grumbling that he'd waited too long to order it.

They ran back toward the rest. Most of them wore only tunics, so Abivard in their midst felt himself surrounded by ghosts. When they'd gotten across the biggest canal between Maniakes' camp and their own, some of them attacked its eastern bank with a mattock. Water poured out onto the fields.

The Makuraners raised a cheer when Abivard and his little band returned after losing only a couple of men. "That was better than a flea bite," he declared. "We've nipped their finger like an ill-mannered lapdog, perhaps. The God willing, we'll do worse when next we meet." His men cheered again more loudly.

"The God willing," Roshnani said when he'd returned to the wagon giddy with triumph and date wine, "you won't feel compelled to lead another raid like that any time soon." Abivard did not argue with her.

Abivard hoped Maniakes would be angry enough at the lapdog nip he'd given him to lunge straight ahead without worrying about the consequences. A couple of years before Maniakes would have been likely to do just that; he'd had a way of leaping before he looked. And if he was heading straight for Mashiz, as Sharbaraz had thought—as Sharbaraz had feared—Abivard's army lay directly across his path. That hadn't been easy to arrange, since it involved maneuvering infantry against cavalry.

But to Abivard's dismay, Maniakes did not try to bull his way straight to Mashiz. Instead, he moved north toward the Mylasa Sea, up into the very heart of the land of the Thousand Cities.

"We have to follow him," Abivard said when a scout brought the unwelcome news that the Avtokrator had broken camp. "If he gets around us, our army might as well fall into the Void for all the help it will be to the realm."

As soon as he put his army on the road, he made another unpleasant discovery. Up till that time his forces had been impeding Maniakes' movements by destroying canals. Now, suddenly, the boot was on the other foot. The floods that spilled out over the fields and gardens of the lands between the rivers meant that he had to move slowly in pursuit of the Videssians.

While his men were struggling with water and mud, a great pillar of smoke rose into the sky ahead of him. "That's not a camp," Abivard said grimly. "That's not the ordinary smoke from a city, either. It's the pyre of a town that's been sacked and burned."

So indeed it proved to be. Just as the sack was beginning, Maniakes had gathered up a couple of servants of the God and sent them back to Abivard with a message. "He said this to us with his own lips and in our tongue so we could not misunderstand," one of the men said. "We were to tell you this is repayment for what Videssos has suffered at the hands of Makuran. We were also to tell you this was only the first coin of the stack."

"Were you?" Abivard said.

The servants of the God nodded together. Abivard's pedagogue had given him a nodding acquaintance with logic and rhetoric and other strange Videssian notions. Years of living inside the Empire and dealing with its people had taught him more. Not so the servants of the God, who didn't know what to do with a rhetorical question.

Sighing, Abivard said, "If that's how Maniakes intends to fight this war, it will be very ugly indeed."

"He said you would say that very thing, lord," one of the servants of the God said, scratching himself through his dirty yellow robe. "He said to tell you, if you did, that to Videssos it was already ugly and that we of Makuran needed to be reminded wars aren't always fought on the other man's soil."

Abivard sighed again. "Did he tell you anything else?"

"He did, lord," the other holy man answered. "He said he would leave the Thousand Cities if the armies of the King of Kings, may his days be long and his realm increase, leave Videssos and Vaspurakan."

"Did he?" Abivard said, and then said no more. He had no idea whether Maniakes meant that as a serious proposal or merely as a ploy to irk him. Irked he was. He had no intention of sending Sharbaraz the Avtokrator's offer. The King of Kings was inflamed enough without it. The servants of the God waited to hear what he would say. He realized he would have to respond. "If we can destroy Maniakes here, he'll be in no position to propose anything."

Destroying Maniakes, though, was beginning to look as hard to

Abivard as stopping the Makuraners formerly had to have looked to the Videssian Emperor.

Up on its mound the city of Khurrembar still smoked. Videssian siege engines had knocked a breach in its mud-brick wall, allowing Maniakes' troopers in to sack it. One of these days the survivors would rebuild. When they did, so much new rubble would lie underfoot that the hill of Khurrembar would rise higher yet above the floodplain.

Surveying the devastation of what had been a prosperous city, Abivard said, "We must have more cavalry or Maniakes won't leave one town between the Tutub and the Tib intact."

"You speak nothing but the truth, lord," Turan answered, "but where will we come by horsemen? The garrisons hereabouts are all infantry. Easy enough to gather together a great lump of them, but once you have it, what do you do with it? By the time you move it *here*, the Videssians have already ridden *there*."

"I'd even take Tzikas' regiment now," Abivard said, a telling measure of his distress.

"Can we pry those men out of Vaspurakan?" Turan asked. "As you say, they'd come in handy now, whoever leads them."

"Can we pry them loose?" Abivard plucked at his beard. He hadn't meant it seriously, but now Turan was forcing him to think of it that way. "The King of Kings was willing—even eager—to give them to me at the start of the campaign. I still despise Tzikas, but I could use his men. Perhaps I'll write to Sharbaraz—and to Mikhran *marzban*, too. The worst they can tell me is no, and how can hearing that make me worse off?"

"Well said, lord," Turan said. "If you don't mind my telling you so, those letters shouldn't wait."

"I'll write them today," Abivard promised. "The next interesting question is, Will Tzikas want to come to the Thousand Cities when I call him? Finding out should be interesting. So should finding out how reliable he proves if he gets here. One more thing to worry about."

Turan corrected him: "Two more."

Abivard laughed and bowed. "You are a model of precision

before which I can only yield." His amusement vanished as quickly as it had appeared. "Now, to keep from having to yield to Maniakes' men—"

"Yield to them?" Turan said. "We can't keep up with them, which is, if you ask me, a worse problem than that. The Videssians, may they fall into the Void, move over the land of the Thousand Cities far faster than we can."

"Over the land of the Thousand Cities—" Abivard suddenly leaned forward and kissed Turan on the cheek, as if to suggest his lieutenant were of higher rank than he. Turan stared till he began to explain.

Abivard laughed out loud. The rafts that now transported his part of the army up a branch of the Tib had carried beans and lentils down to the town where he'd commandeered them. With the current of the river, though, and with little square sails raised, they made a fair clip—certainly as fast as horses went if they alternated walk and trot as they usually did.

"Behold our fleet!" he said, waving to encompass the awkward vessels with which he hoped to steal a march on Maniakes. "We can't match the Videssians dromon for dromon on the sea, but let's see them match us raft for raft here on the rivers of the Thousand Cities."

"No." Roshnani sounded serious. "Let's not see them match us."

"You're right," Abivard admitted. "Like a lot of tricks, this one, I think, is good for only one use. We need to turn it into a victory."

The flat, boring countryside flowed by on either bank of the river. Peasants laboring in the fields that the canals from the stream watered looked up and stared as the soldiers rafted north, then went back to their weeding. Off to the east another one of the Thousand Cities went up in smoke. Abivard hoped Maniakes would spend a good long while there and sack it thoroughly. That would keep him too busy to send scouts to the river to spy this makeshift flotilla. With luck, it would also let Abivard get well ahead of him.

Abivard also hoped Maniakes would continue to take the part of the army still trudging along behind him—now commanded by

Turan—for the whole. If all went perfectly, Abivard would smash the Avtokrator between his hammer and Turan's anvil. If all went well, Abivard's part of the army would be able to meet the Videssians on advantageous terms. If all went not so well, something else would happen. The gamble, though, struck Abivard as worthwhile.

One advantage of the rafts that he hadn't thought of was that they kept moving through the night. The rafters took down the sails but used poles to keep their unwieldy craft away from the banks and from shallow places in the stream. They seemed so intimately acquainted with the river, they hardly needed to see it to know where they were and where the next troublesome stretch lay.

As with sorcery, Abivard admired and used the rafters' abilities without wanting to acquire those abilities himself. Even had he wanted to acquire them, the rafters weren't nearly so articulate as mages were. When Varaz asked one of them how he'd learned to do what he did, the fellow shrugged and answered, "Spend all your years on the water. You learn then. You learn or you drown." That might have been true, but it left Varaz unenlightened.

Abivard's concern was not for the rafts themselves but for the stretch of fertile ground along the eastern bank of the river: he did not want to discover Videssian scouts riding there to take word of what he was doing back to Maniakes.

He did not see any scouts. Whether they were there at some distance, he could not have said. When the rafts came ashore just south of the city of Vepilanu, he acted on the assumption that he had been seen, ordering his soldiers to form a line of battle immediately. He visualized Videssian horsemen thundering down on them, wrecking them before they had so much as a chance to deploy.

Nothing of the sort happened, and he let out a silent sigh of relief where his half-trained troopers couldn't see it. "We'll take our positions along the canal," he told the garrison troops, pointing to the broad ditch that ran east from the river. "If the Videssians want to go any farther north, they'll have to go through us."

The soldiers cheered. They hadn't done any fighting yet; they didn't know what that was like. But they had done considerable foot slogging and then had endured the journey by raft. Those trials had at least begun to forge them into a unit that might prove susceptible to his will . . . provided that he didn't ask too much.

He knew that the field army he had commanded in the Videssian westlands would have smashed his force like a dropped pot. But the field army also had spent a lot of time smashing Videssian forces. What he still did not know was how good an army Maniakes had managed to piece together from the rubble of ten years of almost unbroken defeats.

For two days his soldiers stood to arms when they had to and spent most of the rest of their time trying to spear carp in the canal and slapping at the clouds of mosquitoes, gnats, midges, and flies that buzzed and hovered and darted above it. Some of them soon began to look like raw meat. Some of them came down with fevers, but not too many: most were native to the land and used to the water. Abivard hoped that more of the Videssians would sicken and that the ones who did would sicken worse. The Videssians had better, more skilled healers than his own people had but he didn't think they could stop an epidemic; diseases could be more deadly than a foe to an army.

The Videssian scouts who discovered his army showed no sign of illness. They rode along the southern bank of the canal, looking for a place to cross. Abivard wished he'd given them an obvious one and then tried to ambush Maniakes' forces when they used it. Instead, he'd done his best to make the whole length of the canal seem impassable.

"You can't think of everything all the time," Roshnani consoled him when he complained about that.

"But I have to," he answered. "I feel the weight of the whole realm pressing down on my shoulders." He paused to shake his head and slap at a mosquito. "Now I begin to understand why Maniakes and even Genesios wouldn't treat with me while I was on Videssian soil: they must have felt they were all that stood between me and ruin." His laugh rang bitter. "Maniakes has managed to put that boot on my foot."

Roshnani sounded bitter, too, but for a different reason. Lowering her voice so that only Abivard could hear, she said, "I wonder what Sharbaraz King of Kings feels now. Less than you, or I miss my guess."

"I'm not doing this for Sharbaraz," Abivard said. "I'm doing it for Makuran." But what helped Makuran also helped the King of Kings.

Abivard had not seen the Videssian banner, gold sunburst on blue, flying anywhere in the westlands of the Empire for years. To see that banner now in among the Thousand Cities came as a shock. He peered across the canal at the Videssian force that had come up to challenge his. The first thing that struck him was how small it was. If this was as much of the Videssian army as Maniakes had rebuilt, he was operating on a shoestring. One defeat, maybe two, and he'd have nothing left.

He must have known that, too, but he didn't let on that it bothered him. His troopers rode up and down along the canal as the scouts had the day before, looking for a place to force a crossing and join battle with their Makuraner foes. There weren't many of them, but they did look like good troops. Like Abivard's field force, they had a way of responding to commands instantly and without wasted motion. Abivard judged that they would do the same in battle.

A couple of times the Videssians made as if to cross the canal, but Abivard's men shot swarms of arrows at them, and they desisted. The garrison troops walked tall and puffed out their chests with pride. Abivard was glad of that but did not think the archery was what had thwarted the Videssians. He judged that Maniakes was trying to make him shift troops back and forth either to expose or to create a weakness along his line. Declining to be drawn out, he sat tight, concentrating his men at the fords about which the peasants told him. If Maniakes wanted to come farther, he would have to do it on Abivard's terms.

As the sun set, the Videssians, instead of forcing another attack, made camp. Abivard thought about trying to disrupt them again but decided against it. For one thing, he suspected that Maniakes would have done a better job of posting sentries than he had before. And for another, he did not want to make the Videssians move. He wanted them to stay where they were so he could pin them between the force he had with him and the rest of his army which was still slowly slogging up from the south.

He looked east and west along the canal. As far as his eye could see, the campfires of his own host blazed. That encouraged him; the numbers that had seemed to be useless when he had begun assembling the garrison troops into an army proved valuable after all, in defense if not in attack.

"Will we fight tomorrow?" Roshnani and Varaz asked together. His wife sounded concerned, his elder son excited.

"It's up to Maniakes now," Abivard answered. "If he wants to stay where he is, I'll let him—till the other half of my men come up. If he tries to force a crossing before then, we'll have a battle on our hands."

"We'll beat him," Varaz declared.

"Will we beat him?" Roshnani asked quietly.

"Mother!" Now Varaz sounded indignant. "Of course we'll beat him! The men of Makuran have been beating Videssians for as long as I've been alive, and they've never beaten us, not once, in all that time."

Above his head Abivard and Roshnani exchanged amused looks. Every word he'd said was true, but that truth was worth less than he thought. His life did not reach over a great stretch of time, and Maniakes' army was better and Abivard's worse than had been true in any recent encounters.

"If Maniakes attacks us, we'll give him everything he wants," Abivard promised. "And if he doesn't attack us, we'll give him everything he wants then, too. The only thing is, that will take longer."

When it grew light enough to see across the canal, sentries came shouting to wake Abivard, who'd let exhaustion overwhelm him at a time he gauged by the moon to be well after midnight. Yawning and rubbing sand from his eyes with his knuckles, he stumbled out of his tent—the wagon hadn't gone aboard the raft—and walked down to the edge of the water to see why the guards had summoned him.

Already drawn up in battle array, the Videssian army stood,

impressively silent, impressively dangerous-looking, in the brightening morning light. As he stood watching them, they sat on their horses and stared over the irrigation channel toward him.

Yes, that was Maniakes at their head. He recognized not only the imperial armor but also the man who wore it. To Maniakes he was just another Makuraner in a caftan. He turned away from the canal and called orders. Horns blared. Drums thumped. Men began tumbling out of tents and bedrolls, looking to their weapons.

Abivard ordered archers right up to the bank of the canal to shoot at the Videssians. Here and there an imperial trooper in the front ranks slid off his horse or a horse bounded out of its place in line, squealing as an arrow pierced it.

A return barrage would have hurt Abivard's unarmored infantry worse than their shooting had harmed the Videssians. Instead of staying where he was and getting into a duel of arrows with the Makuraners, though, Maniakes, with much loud signaling from trumpets and pipes, ordered his little army into motion, trotting east along the southern bank of the canal. Abivard's troops cheered to see the Videssians ride off, perhaps thinking they'd driven them away. Abivard knew better.

"Form line of battle facing east!" he called, and the musicians with the army blew great discordant blasts on their horns and thumped the drums with a will. The soldiers responded as best they could: not nearly so fast as Abivard would have expected from trained professionals, not nearly so raggedly as they would have a few weeks before.

Once they had formed up, he marched all of them after Maniakes except for a guard he left behind at the ford. He knew he could not match the speed of cavalry with men afoot but hoped that, if the Videssians forced a crossing, he could meet them at a place of his choosing, not theirs.

He found such a place about half a farsang east of the encampment: rising ground behind a north-south canal flowing into—or perhaps out of—the larger one that ran east-west. There he established himself with the bulk of his force, sending a few men ahead to get word of what was happening farther east. If one of his detachments was battling to keep Maniakes from fording the bigger canal, Abivard would order more troops forward to help. If it was already too late for that . . .

The canal behind which he'd positioned his men was perhaps ten feet wide and hardly more than knee-deep. It would not have stopped advancing infantry; it wouldn't do anything but slow oncoming horses a little. Abivard's foot soldiers stood in line at the crest of their little rise. Some grumbled about having missed breakfast, and others boasted of what they would do when they finally came face to face with Maniakes' men.

That was harmless and, since it helped them build courage, might even have helped. What he feared they would do, on facing soldiers trained in a school harder than garrison duty, was run as if demons like those the Prophets Four had vanquished were after them.

"These are the tools Sharbaraz gave me," Abivard muttered, "and I'm the one he'll blame if they break in my hand." Already, though, he'd drawn Maniakes away from the straight road to Mashiz, and so Sharbaraz, with luck, was breathing easier on his throne.

He shaded his eyes against the sun and peered eastward. Dust didn't rise up from under horses' hooves in this well-irrigated country as it did most places, but the glitter of sun off chain mail was unmistakable. So was the group of men fleeing his way. Maniakes' troopers had found and forced a ford.

Abivard yelled like a man possessed, readying his army against the imminent Videssian attack as best he could. Maniakes' horsemen grew with alarming speed from glints of sun off metal to toy soldiers that somehow moved of their own accord to real warriors. Abivard watched his own men for signs of panic as the Videssians, horns blaring, came up to the canal behind which his force waited.

Water splashed and sprayed upward when the imperials rode into the canal. Just for an instant the Videssians seemed to be wreathed in rainbows. Then, as if tearing a veil, they galloped through them, up onto the rising ground that led to Abivard's position.

"Shoot!" Abivard shouted. His own trumpeters echoed and amplified the command. The archers in his army snatched arrows from their quivers, drew their bows to the ear, and let fly at the oncoming Videssians. The thrum of bowstrings and the hissing drone of arrows through the air put Abivard in mind of horseflies.

Like horseflies, the arrows bit hard. Videssians tumbled from the saddle. Horses crashed to the ground. Other horses behind them could not swerve in time and fell over them, throwing more riders.

But the Videssians did not press their charge with the thundering drumroll of lances Abivard's field force would have used. Instead, their archers returned arrows at long range. Some of their javelin men did ride closer so they could hurl the light spears at the Makuraners. That done, the riders would gallop back out of range.

Except for helmets and wicker shields, Abivard's men had no armor to speak of. When an arrow struck, it wounded. Near Abivard a man moaned and clutched at a shaft protruding from his belly. Blood ran between his fingers. His feet kicked at the ground in agony. The soldiers on either side of him gaped in horror and dismay. No, garrison duty had not prepared them for anything like this.

But they did not run. They dragged their stricken comrade out of the line and then returned to their own places. One of them stuffed the wounded man's arrows into his own bow case and went back to shooting at the Videssians with no more fuss than if he'd just straightened his caftan after making water.

The Videssians wore swords on their belts but did not come close enough to use them. Abivard's spirits rose. He shook his fist at Maniakes, who stayed just out of arrow range. The Avtokrator was finding out that facing Makuraners was a different business from beating barbarians. Where was the dash, the aggressiveness the Videssians had shown against the Kubratoi? Not here, not if they couldn't make a better showing than this against the inexperienced troops Abivard commanded.

Maniakes' one abiding flaw as a commander had been that he thought he could do more than he could. If he couldn't make his men go forward against garrison troops, he'd soon get a rude surprise as the rest of Abivard's army came up to try to cut off his escape. Before this fight began Abivard had had scarcely any hope of accomplishing that. Now, seeing how tentative the Videssians were . . .

It was almost as if Maniakes had no particular interest in winning the fight but merely wanted to keep it going. When that thought crossed Abivard's mind, his head went up like a fox's on catching the scent of rabbit—or, rather, like a rabbit's on catching the scent of fox.

He didn't see anything untoward. There, at the front, the Videssians were keeping up their halfhearted archery duel with his soldiers. Because they were so much better armored than their foes, they were causing more casualties than they suffered. They were not causing nearly enough, though, to force Abivard's men from their position, nor were they trying to bull their way through the line. What exactly *were* they doing?

Abivard peered south, wondering if Maniakes had gotten into a fight here so he could sneak raftloads of Videssians over the large canal and into the Makuraner rear. He saw no sign of it. Had the Avtokrator's sorcerers come up with something new in the line of battle magic? There was no sign of that, either: no cries of alarm from the mages with Abivard's force, no Makuraner soldiers suddenly falling over dead.

A moment before his head would have turned in that direction anyhow, Abivard heard sudden shouts of alarm from the north. The horsemen riding down on his army came behind a banner bearing a gold sunburst on a field of blue. Maniakes' detachment must have crossed the large canal well to the east before his own men had moved so far. They'd trotted right out of his field of view—but they were back now.

"I *thought* Maniakes had more men than that," Abivard said, as much to himself as to anyone else. While he'd been trying to trap the Videssians between the two pieces of his army, they'd been trying to do the same thing to him. The only difference was that they'd managed to spring their trap.

The battle was lost—no help for that now. The only thing left was to save as much as he could from the wreck. "Hold fast!" he shouted to his men. "Hold fast! If you run from them, you're done for."

One advantage of numbers was having reserves to commit. He sent all the men in back of the line up to the north to face the oncoming Videssians squarely; if he'd tried swinging around the troops that already were engaged, he would have lost everything in confusion and in the certainty of being hit from the flank.

Maniakes' Videssians held back no more. The Avtokrator had kept Abivard in play until his detached force could reach the field. Now he pressed forward as aggressively as he had before he'd had the resources to let him get by with a headlong attack. This time, he did.

The Videssians, instead of stopping short and plying Abivard's army with arrows, charged up with drawn swords and got in among the garrison troops, hacking down at them from horseback. Abivard felt a certain somber pride in his men, who performed better than he'd dared hope. They fell—by scores, by hundreds they fell—but they did not break. They did what they could to fight back, stabbing horses and dragging Videssians out of the saddle to grapple with them in the dirt.

On the northern flank the blow fell at about the same time as it did in the east. It fell harder in the north, for the soldiers there had not gotten a taste of fighting but were rushed up to plug a gap. Still, the Videssians did not have it all their own way there, as they might have hoped. They did not—they could not—break through into the rear of the Makuraner line and roll up Abivard's men like a seamstress rolling up a line of yarn.

He rode north, figuring to show himself where he was most needed. He wished he'd had a few hundred men from the field force up in Vaspurakan with him. They would have sent the Videssians reeling off in dismay. No, he wouldn't have minded—well, he didn't think he would have minded—if Tzikas had been at the head of the regiment. The Videssian renegade could hardly have made things worse.

"Hold as firm as you can!" Abivard yelled. Telling his soldiers to yield no ground at all was useless now; they *were* retreating, as any troops caught in a like predicament would have done. But there were retreats and retreats. If you kept facing the foe and hurting him wherever you could, you had a decent chance of coming whole through a lost battle. But if you turned tail and ran, you would be cut down from behind. You couldn't fight back that way.

"Rally on the baggage train!" Abivard commanded. "We won't let them have that, will we, lads?"

That order surely would have made the field army fight harder. All the booty those soldiers had collected in years of triumphant battle traveled in the baggage train; if they lost it, some of them would have lost much of their wealth. The men who had come from the city garrisons were poorer and had not spent years storing up captured money and jewels and weapons. Would they battle to save their supplies of flour and smoked meat?

As things turned out, they did. They used the wagons as small fortresses, fighting from inside them and from the shelter they gave. Abivard had hoped for that but had not ordered it for fear of being disobeyed.

Again and again the Videssians tried to break their tenuous hold on the position, to drive them away from the baggage train so they could be cut down while flying or forced into the big canal and drowned.

The Makuraners would not let themselves be dislodged. The fight raged through the afternoon. Abivard broke his lance and was reduced to clouting Videssians with the stump. Even with its scale mail armor, his horse took several wounds. *He* had an incentive to hold the baggage wagons: his wife and family were sheltering among them.

Maniakes drew his troops back from combat about an hour before sunset. At first Abivard thought nothing of that, but the Avtokrator of the Videssians did not send them forward again. Instead, singing a triumphant hymn to their Phos, they rode off toward the nearest town.

Abivard ordered his horn players to blow the call for pursuit. He had the satisfaction of seeing several Videssians' heads whip around in alarm. But despite the defiant horn calls, he was utterly unable to pursue Maniakes' army, and he knew it. The mounted foes were faster than his own foot soldiers, and despite the protection they'd finally gotten from the wagons of the baggage train, his men had taken a far worse drubbing. He began riding around to see just how bad things were.

A soldier sat stolidly while another one sewed up his wounded shoulder. He nodded to Abivard. "You must be one tough general, lord, if you beat them buggers year in and year out. They can fight some." He laughed at his own understatement.

"You can fight some yourself," Abivard answered. Though beaten, the garrison troops had done themselves proud. Abivard knew that was so and also knew that Sharbaraz King of Kings would not see it the same way. Having done his best to make victory impossible, Sharbaraz now insisted that nothing less would do. If the miracle inexplicably failed to materialize, he would not blame himself—not while he had Abivard.

Weary soldiers began lighting campfires and seeing about supper. Abivard grabbed a lump of hard bread—that better described the misshapen object the cook gave him than would a neutral term such as *loaf*—and a couple of onions and went from fire to fire, talking with his men and praising them for having held their ground as well as they had.

"Aye, well, lord, sorry it didn't work out no better than it did," one of the warriors answered, picking absently at the black blood on the edges of a cut that ran from just below his ear to near the corner of his mouth. "They beat us, is all."

"Maybe next time we beat them," another warrior put in. He drew a dagger from his belt. "Give you a chunk of mutton sausage—" He held it up. "—for half of one of those onions."

"I'll make that trade," Abivard said, and did. Munching, he reflected that the soldier might well be right. If his army got another chance against the Videssians, they might well beat them. Getting that chance would be the hard part. He'd stolen a march on Maniakes once, but how likely was he to be able to do it twice? When you had one throw of the dice and didn't roll the twin twos of the Prophets Four, what did you do next?

He didn't know, not in any large sense of the word, not with the force he had here. On a smaller scale, what you did was keep your men in good spirits if you could so that they wouldn't brood on this defeat and expect another one in the next fight. Most of the men with whom he talked didn't seem unduly downhearted. Most of them in fact seemed happier about the world than he was.

When he finally got back to his tent, he expected to find everyone asleep. As it had the night before, the moon told him it was past midnight. Snores from soldiers exhausted after the day's marching and fighting mingled with the groans of the wounded. Out beyond the circles of light the campfires threw, crickets chirped. Mosquitoes buzzed far from the fires and close by. Every so often someone cursed as he was bitten.

Seeing Pashang beside the fire in front of the tent was not a large surprise, nor was having Roshnani poke her head out when she heard his approaching footsteps. But when Varaz stuck his head out, too, Abivard blinked in startlement.

"I'm angry at you, Papa," his elder son exclaimed. "I wanted to go and fight the Videssians today, but Mama wouldn't let me— she said you said I was too little. I could have hit them with my bow; I know I could."

"Yes, you probably could," Abivard agreed gravely. "But they could have hit you, too, and what would you have done when the fighting got to close quarters? You're learning the sword, but you haven't learned it well enough to hold off a grown man."

"I think I have," Varaz declared.

"When I was your age, I thought the same thing," Abivard told him. "I was wrong, and so are you."

"I don't think I am," Varaz said.

Abivard sighed. "That's what I said to my father, too, and it got me no further with him than you're getting with me. Looking back, though, he was right. A boy can't stand against men, not if he hopes to do anything else afterward. Your time will come—and one fine day, the God willing, you'll worry about keeping your son out of fights he isn't ready for."

Varaz looked eloquently unconvinced. His voice had years to go before it started deepening. His cheeks bore only fine down. To expect him to think of the days when he'd be a father himself was to ask too much. Abivard knew that but preferred argument to breaking his son's spirit by insisting on blind obedience.

There was, however, a time and place for everything. Roshnani cut off the debate, saying, "Quarrel about it tomorrow. You'll get the same answer, Varaz, because it's the only one your parents can give you, but you'll get it after your father has had some rest."

Abivard hadn't let himself think about that. Hearing the word made him realize how worn he was. He said, "If you two don't want my footprints on your robes, you'd best get out of the way."

Before long he was lying in the crowded tent on a blanket under mosquito netting. Then, no matter how his body craved sleep, it would not come. He had to fight the battle over again, first in his own mind and then, softly, aloud for his principal wife.

"You did everything you could," Roshnani assured him.

"I should have realized Maniakes had split his army, too," he said. "I thought it looked small, but I didn't know how many men he really had, and so—"

"Only the God knows all there is to know, and only she acts in perfect rightness on what she does know," Roshnani said. "This once, the Videssians were luckier than we."

Everything she said was true and in perfect accord with Abivard's own thoughts. Somehow that helped not at all. "The King of Kings, may his years be long and his realm increase, entrusted me with this army to—"

"To get you killed or at best ruined," Roshnani broke in quietly but with terrible venom in her voice.

He'd had those thoughts, too. "To defend the realm," he went on, as if she hadn't spoken. "If I don't do that, nothing else I do, no matter how well I do it, matters anymore. Any soldier would say the same. So will Sharbaraz."

Roshnani stirred but did not speak right away. At last she said, "The army still holds together. You'll have your chance at revenge."

"That depends," Abivard said. Roshnani made a questioning noise. He explained: "On what Sharbaraz does when he hears I've lost, I mean."

"Oh," Roshnani said. On that cheerful note they fell asleep.

* * *

When Abivard emerged from the wagon the next morning, Er-Khedur, the town north and east of the battle site, was burning. His mouth twisted into a thin, bitter line. If his army couldn't keep the Videssians in check, why should the part of the garrison of Er-Khedur he'd left behind?

He didn't realize he'd asked the question aloud till Pashang answered it: "They did have a wall to fight from, lord."

That mattered less in opposing the Videssians than it would have against the barbarous Khamorth, perhaps less than it would have in opposing a rival Makuraner army. The Videssians were skillful when it came to siegecraft. Wall or no wall, a handful of half-trained troops would not have been enough to keep them out of the city.

Abivard thought about going right after the imperials and trying to trap them inside Er-Khedur. Reluctantly, he decided not to. They'd just mauled his army once; he wanted to drill his troops before he put them into battle again. And he doubted the Videssians would tamely let themselves be trapped. They had no need to stay and defend Er-Khedur; they could withdraw and ravage some other city instead.

The Videssians didn't have to stay and defend any one point in the Thousand Cities. The chief reason they were there was to do as much damage as they could. That gave them more freedom of movement than Abivard had had when he was conquering the westlands from the Empire. He'd wanted to seize land intact first and destroy it only if he had to. Maniakes operated under no such restraints.

And how were the westlands faring these days? As far as Abivard knew, they remained in the hands of the King of Kings. Dominating the sea as he did, Maniakes hadn't had to think about freeing them before he invaded Makuran. Now each side in the war had forces deep in the other's territory. He wondered if that had happened before in the history of warfare. He knew of no songs that suggested that it had. Groundbreaking was an uncomfortable sport to play, as he'd found out when ending Roshnani's isolation from the world.

If he couldn't chase right after Maniakes, what could he do? One thing that occurred to him was to send messengers south over the canal to find out how close Turan was with the rest of the assembled garrison troops. He could do more with the whole army than he could with this battered piece of it.

The scouts rode back late that afternoon with word that they'd found the host Turan commanded. Abivard thanked them and then went off away from his men to kick at the rich black dirt in frustration. He'd come so close to catching Maniakes between the halves of the Makuraner force; that the Videssians had caught him between the halves of theirs seemed most unfair.

He posted sentries out as far as a farsang from his camp, wanting to be sure Maniakes could not catch him by surprise. He had considerably more respect for the Videssian Avtokrator now than he'd had when his forces had been routing Maniakes' at every turn.

When he said as much, Roshnani raised an eyebrow and remarked, "Amazing what being beaten will do, isn't it?" He opened his mouth, then closed it, discovering himself without any good answer.

Turan's half of the Makuraner army reached the canal a day and a half later. After the officer had crossed over and kissed Abivard's cheek by way of greeting, he said, "Lord, I wish you could have waited before you started your fight."

"Now that you mention it, so do I," Abivard answered. "We don't always have all the choices we'd like, though."

"That's so," Turan admitted. He looked around as if gauging the condition of Abivard's part of the army. "Er—lord, what do we do now?"

"That's a good question," Abivard said politely, and then proceeded not to answer it. Turan's expression was comical, or would have been had the army's plight been less serious. But here, unlike in his conversations with his wife, Abivard understood he would have to make a reply. At last he said, "One way or another we're going to have to get Maniakes out of the land of the Thousand Cities before he smashes it all to bits."

"We just tried that," Turan answered. "It didn't work so well as we'd hoped."

"One way or another, I said," Abivard told him. "There is something we haven't tried in fullness, because as a cure it's almost worse than the sickness of invasion."

"What's that?" Turan asked. Again Abivard didn't answer, letting his lieutenant work it out for himself. After a while Turan did. Snapping his fingers, he said, "You want to do a proper job of flooding the plain."

"No, I don't *want* to do that," Abivard said. "But if it's the only way to get rid of Maniakes, I *will* do it." He laughed wryly. "And if I do, half the Thousand Cities will close their gates to me because they'll think I'm a more deadly plague than Maniakes ever was."

"They're our subjects," Turan said in a that-settles-it tone.

"Yes, and if we push them too far, they'll be our *rebellious* subjects," Abivard said. "When Genesios ruled Videssos, he had a new revolt against him every month, or so it seemed. The same could happen to us."

Now Turan didn't answer at all. Abivard started to try to get him to say something, to say anything, then suddenly stopped. One of the things he was liable to say was that Abivard might lead a revolt himself. Abivard didn't want to hear that. If he did hear it, he would have to figure out what to do about Turan. If he let his lieutenant say it without responding, he would in effect be guilty of treasonous conspiracy. If Turan wanted to take word of that back to Sharbaraz, he could. But if Abivard punished him for saying such a thing, he would cost himself an able officer.

And so, to forestall any response, Abivard changed the subject: "Do your men still have their fighting spirit?"

"They did till they got here and saw bodies out in the sun starting to stink," Turan said. "They did till they saw men down with festering wounds or out of their heads from fever. They're garrison troops. Most of 'em never saw what the aftermath of a battle—especially a lost battle—looks like before. But your men seem to be taking it pretty well."

"Yes, and I'm glad of that," Abivard said. "When we'd beat the

Videssians, they'd go all to pieces and run every which way. I thought my own raw troops would do the same thing, but they haven't, and I'm proud of them for it."

"I can see that, since it would have been your neck, too, if they did fall apart," Turan said judiciously. "But you can fight another battle with 'em, and they're ready to do it, too. My half of the army will be better for seeing that."

"They are ready to fight again," Abivard agreed. "That surprises me, too, maybe more than anything else." He waved toward the northeast, the direction in which Maniakes' army had gone. "The only question is, Will we be able to catch up with the Videssians and bring them to battle again? It's because I have my doubts that I'm thinking so hard of flooding the land between the Tutub and the Tib."

"I understand your reasons, lord," Turan said, "but it strikes me as a counsel of desperation, and there are a lot of city governors it would strike the same way. And if they're not happy—" He broke off once more. They'd already been around to that point on the wheel.

Abivard didn't know how to keep them from going around again, either. But before he had to try, a scout interrupted the circle, crying, "Lord, cavalry approach from out of the north!"

Maybe Maniakes hadn't been satisfied to beat just one piece of the Makuraner army, after all. Maybe he was coming back to see if he could smash the other half, too. Such thoughts ran through Abivard's mind in the couple of heartbeats before he shouted to the trumpeters: "Blow the call for line of battle!"

Martial music rang out. Men grabbed weapons and rushed to their places more smoothly than he would have dared hope a couple of weeks before. If Maniakes was coming back to finish the job, he'd get a warm reception. Abivard was pleased to see how well Turan's troops moved along with his own, who had been blooded. The former squadron commander had done well with as large a body of men.

"Sharbaraz!" roared the Makuraner troops as the onrushing cavalry drew near. A few of them yelled "Abivard!" too, making their leader proud and apprehensive at the same time.

And then they got a better look at the approaching army. They cried out in wonder and delight, for it advanced under the red-lion banner of the King of Kings. And its soldiers also cried Sharbaraz' name, and some few of them the name of their commander as well: "Tzikas!"

VI

ONE OF THE LESSONS ABIVARD'S FATHER, GODARZ, HAD drilled into him was not asking the God for anything he didn't really want, because he was liable to get it anyhow. He'd forgotten that principle on this campaign, and now he was paying for it.

The look on Turan's face probably mirrored the one on his own. His lieutenant asked, "Shall we welcome them, lord, or order the attack?"

"A good question." Abivard shook his head, as much to suppress his own temptation as for any other reason. "Can't do that, I'm afraid. We welcome them. Odds are, Tzikas doesn't know I know he sent those letters complaining of me to Sharbaraz."

If the Videssian renegade did know that, he gave no sign of it. He rode out in front of the ranks of his own horsemen and through the foot soldiers—who parted to give him a path—straight up to Abivard. When he reached him, he dismounted and went down on one knee in what was, by Videssian standards, the next closest thing to an imperial greeting. "Lord, I am here to aid you," he declared in his lisping Makuraner.

Abivard, for his part, spoke in Videssian: "Rise, eminent sir. How many men have you brought with you?" He gauged Tzikas' force. "Three thousand, I'd guess, or maybe a few more."

"Near enough, lord," Tzikas answered, sticking to the language of the land that had adopted him. "You gauge numbers with marvelous keenness."

"You flatter me," Abivard said, still in Videssian; he would not acknowledge Tzikas as a countryman. Then he showed his own fangs, adding, "I wish you had been so generous when you discussed me with Sharbaraz King of Kings, may his days be long and his realm increase."

A Makuraner, thus caught out, would have shown either anger or shame. Tzikas proved himself foreign by merely nodding and saying, "Ah, you found out about that, did you? I wondered if you would."

Abivard wondered what he was supposed to make of that. It sounded as if in some perverse way it was a compliment. However Tzikas meant it, Abivard didn't like it. He growled, "Yes, I found out about it, by the God. It almost cost me my head. Why shouldn't I bind you and give you to Maniakes to do with as he pleases?"

"You could do that." Though Tzikas continued to speak Makuraner, even without his accent Abivard would have had no doubt he was dealing with a Videssian. Instead of bellowing in outrage or bursting into melodramatic tears, the renegade sounded cool, detached, calculating, almost amused. "You could—if you wanted to put the realm in danger or, rather, in more danger than it's in already."

Abivard wanted to hit him, to get behind the calm mask he wore to the man within . . . if there was a man within. But Tzikas, like a rider controlling a restive horse, had known exactly where to flick him with the whip to get him to jump in the desired direction. Abivard tried not to acknowledge that, saying, "Why should removing you from command of your force here have anything to do with how well the troopers fight? You're good in the field, but you're not so good as all that."

"Probably not—not in the field," Tzikas answered, sparring still. "But I am very good at picking the soldiers who go into my force, and, brother-in-law to the King of Kings, I am positively a genius when it comes to picking the officers who serve under me."

Abivard had learned something of the subtle Videssian style of fighting with words while in exile in the Empire and later in treating with his foes. Now he said, "You may be good at picking those who serve under you, eminent sir, but not in picking those under whom you serve. First you betrayed Maniakes, then me. Beware falling between two sides when both hate you."

Tzikas bared his teeth; that had pierced whatever armor he had put around his soul. But he said, "You may insult me, you may revile me, but do you want to work with me to drive Maniakes from the land of the Thousand Cities?"

"An interesting choice, isn't it?" Abivard said, hoping to make Tzikas squirm even more. Tzikas, though, did not squirm but merely waited to see what Abivard would say next—which required Abivard to decide what he *would* say next. "I still think I should take my chances on how your band performs without you."

"Yes, that is what you would be doing," the renegade said. "I've taught them everything I know—everything."

Abivard did not miss the threat there. What Tzikas knew best was how to change sides at just the right—or just the wrong—moment. Would the soldiers he commanded go over to Maniakes if something—even something like Maniakes, if Abivard handed Tzikas to him—happened to him? Or would they simply refuse to fight for Abivard? Would they perhaps do nothing at all except obey their new commander?

Those were all interesting questions. They led to an even more interesting one: *could Abivard afford to find out?*

Reluctantly, he decided he couldn't. He desperately needed that cavalry to repel the Videssians, and Tzikas, if loyal, made a clever, resourceful general. The trouble was, he made a clever, resourceful general even if he wasn't loyal, and that made him more dangerous than an inept traitor. Abivard did his best not to worry about that. His best, he knew, would not be good enough.

Hating every word, he said, "If you keep your station, you do it as my hunting dog. Do you understand, eminent sir? I need not give you to the Avtokrator to be rid of you. If you disobey me, you are a dead man."

"By the God, I understand, lord, and by the God, I swear I will obey your every command." Tzikas made the left-handed gesture every follower of the Prophets Four used. He probably meant it to reassure Abivard. Instead, it only made him more suspicious. He doubted Tzikas' conversion as much as he doubted everything else about the renegade.

But he needed the horsemen Tzikas had led down from Vaspurakan, and he needed whatever connections Tzikas still had inside Maniakes' army. Treachery cut both ways, and Tzikas still hated Maniakes for being Avtokrator in place of someone more deserving—someone, for instance, like Tzikas.

Abivard chuckled mirthlessly. "What amuses you, lord?" Tzikas asked, the picture of polite interest.

"Only that one person, at least, is safe from your machinations," Abivard said. One of Tzikas' disconcertingly mobile eyebrows rose in silent question. With malicious relish Abivard explained: "You may want my post, and you may want Maniakes' post, but Sharbaraz King of Kings, may his years be many and his realm increase, is beyond your reach."

"Oh, indeed," Tzikas said. "The prospect of overthrowing *him* never once entered my mind." By the way he said it and by his actions, the same did not apply to Abivard or Maniakes.

Abivard watched glumly as, off in the distance, another of the Thousand Cities went up in flames. "This is madness," he exclaimed. "When we took Videssian towns, we took them with a view to keeping them intact so they could yield revenue to the King of Kings. A burned city yields no one revenue."

"When we went into Videssos, we went as conquerors," Turan said. "Maniakes isn't out for conquest. He's out for revenge, and that changes the way he fights his war."

"Well put," Abivard said. "I hadn't thought of it in just that way, but you're right, of course. How do we stop him?"

"Beat him and drive him away," his lieutenant answered. "No other way to do it that I can think of."

That was easy to say, but it had proved harder to do. Being uninterested in conquest, Maniakes didn't bother garrisoning the towns he took: he just burned them and moved on. That meant he kept his army intact instead of breaking it up into small packets that Abivard could have hoped to defeat individually.

Because the Videssian force was all mounted, Maniakes moved

through the plain between the Tutub and the Tib faster than Abivard could pursue him with an army still largely made up of infantry. Not only that, he seemed to move through the land of the Thousand Cities faster than Abivard's order to open the canals and flood the plain reached the city governors. Such inundations as did take place were small, hindered Maniakes but little, and were repaired far sooner that they should have been.

Abivard, coming upon the peasants of the town of Nashvar doing everything they could to make a broken canal whole once more, angrily confronted the city governor, a plump little man named Beroshesh. "Am I to have my people starve?" the governor wailed, making as if to rend his garment. His accented speech proclaimed him a local man, not a true Makuraner down from the high plateau to the west.

"Are you to let all the Thousand Cities suffer because you do not do all you can to drive the enemy from our land?" Abivard returned.

Beroshesh stuck out his lower lip, much as Abivard's children did when they were feeling petulant. "I do as much as any of my neighbors, and you cannot deny this, lord. For you to single me out—where is the justice there? Eh? Can you answer?"

"Where is the justice in not rallying to the cause of the King of Kings?" Abivard answered. "Where is the justice in your ignoring the orders that come from me, his servant?"

"In the same place as the justice of the order to do ourselves such great harm," Beroshesh retorted, not retreating by so much as the width of a digit. "If you could by some great magic make all my fellow officials obey to the same degree, this would be another matter. All would bear the harm together, and all equally. But you ask me to take it all on my own head, for the other city governors are lazy and cowardly and will not do any such thing, not unless you stand over them with whips."

"And what would they say of you?" Abivard asked in a mild voice. Beroshesh, obviously convinced he was the soul of virtue, donned an expression that might better have belonged on the face of a bride whose virginity was questioned. Abivard wanted to laugh. "Never mind. You needn't answer that."

Beroshesh did answer, at considerable length. After a while Abivard stopped listening. He wished he had a magic that could make all the city governors in the Thousand Cities obey his commands. If there were such a magic, though, Kings of Kings would have been using it for hundreds of years, and rebellions against them would have been far fewer.

Then he had another thought. He sat up straighter in his chair and took a long pull at the goblet of date wine a serving girl had set before him. The stuff was as revoltingly sweet as it always had been. Abivard hardly noticed. He set down the goblet and pointed a finger at Beroshesh, who reluctantly stopped talking. Quietly, thoughtfully, Abivard said, "Tell me, do your mages do much with the canals?"

"Not mine, no," the city governor answered, disappointing him. Beroshesh went on, "My mages, lord, are like you: they are men of the high country and so do not know much about the way of this land. Some of the wizards of the town, though, do repair work on the banks now and again. Sometimes one of them can do at once what it would take a large crew of men with mattocks and spades days to accomplish. And sometimes, magic being what it is, not. Why do you ask?"

"Because I was wondering whether—" Abivard began.

Beroshesh held up his right hand, palm out. Bombastic he might have been, but he was not stupid. "You want to work a magic to open the canals all at once. Tell me if I am not correct, lord."

"You are right," Abivard answered. "If we gathered wizards from several cities here, all of them, as you say, from the land of the Thousand Cities so they knew the waters and the mud and what to do with them . . ." His voice trailed away. Knowing what one wanted to do and being able to do it were not necessarily identical.

Beroshesh looked thoughtful. "I do not know whether such a thing has ever been essayed. Shall I try to find out, lord?"

"Yes, I think you should," Abivard told him. "If we have here a weapon against the Videssians, don't you think we ought to learn whether we can use it?"

"I shall look into it," Beroshesh said.

"So shall I," Abivard assured him. He'd heard that tone in functionaries' voices before, whenever they made promises they didn't intend to keep. "I will talk to the mages here in town. You find out who the ones in nearby cities are and invite them here. Don't say too much about why or spies will take the word to Maniakes, who may try to foil us."

"I understand, lord," Beroshesh said in a solemn whisper. He looked around nervously. "Even the floors have ears."

Considering how much of the past of any town hereabouts lay right under one's feet, that might have been literally true. Abivard wondered whether those dead ears had ever heard of a scheme like his. Then, more to the point, he wondered whether Maniakes had. The Avtokrator had surprised Makuran and had surprised Abivard himself. Now, maybe, Abivard would return the favor.

Abivard had never before walked into a room that held half a dozen mages. He found the prospect daunting. In his world, with the mundane tools of war, he was a man to be reckoned with. In their world, which was anything but mundane, he held less power to control events than did the humblest foot soldier of his army.

Even so, the wizards reckoned him a man of importance. When he nerved himself and went in to them, they sprang to their feet and bowed very low, showing that they acknowledged he was far higher in rank than they. "We shall serve you, lord," they said, almost in chorus.

"We shall all serve the King of Kings, may his days be long and his realm increase," Abivard said. He waved to the roasted quails, bread and honey, and jars of date wine on the sideboard. "Eat. Drink. Refresh yourselves." By the cups some of the mages were holding, by the gaps in the little loaves of bread, by the bird bones scattered on the floor, they hadn't needed his invitation to take refreshment.

They introduced themselves, sometimes between mouthfuls. Falasham was fat and jolly. Glathpilesh was also fat but looked as if he hated the world and everyone in it. Mefyesh was bald and had the shiniest scalp Abivard had ever seen. His brother, Yeshmef, was almost as bald and almost as shiny but wore his beard in braids tied with yellow ribbons, which gave him the look of a swarthy sunflower. Utpanisht, to whom everyone, even Glathpilesh, deferred, was ancient and wizened; his grandson, Kidinnu, was in the prime of life.

"Why have you summoned us, lord?" Glathpilesh demanded of Abivard in a voice that suggested he had better things to do elsewhere.

"Couldn't you have found that out by magic?" Abivard said, thinking, *If you can't, what are you doing here?*

"I could have, aye, but why waste time and labor?" the wizard returned. "Magic is hard work. Talk is always easy."

"Listening is easier yet," Falasham said so good-naturedly that even dour Glathpilesh could not take offense.

"You know the Videssians have invaded the land of the Thousand Cities," Abivard said. "You may also know they've beaten the army I command. I want to drive them off, if I can find a way."

"Battle magic," Glathpilesh said scornfully. "He wants battle magic to drive off the Videssians. He doesn't want much, does he?" His laugh showed what he thought of what Abivard wanted.

In a creaking voice Utpanisht said, "Suppose we let him tell us what he wants? That might be a better idea than having us tell him." Glathpilesh glared at him and muttered something inaudible but subsided.

"What I want is not battle magic," Abivard said with a grateful nod to Utpanisht. "The passion of those involved will have nothing to do with diluting the power of the spell." He laughed. "And I won't try to explain your own business to you anymore, either. Instead, I'll explain what I do want." He spent the next little while doing just that.

When he was finished, none of the magicians spoke for a moment. Then Falasham burst out with a high, shrill giggle. "This is not a man with small thoughts, whatever else we may say of him," he declared.

"Can you do this thing?" Abivard asked.

"It would not be easy," Glathpilesh growled.

Abivard's hopes soared. If the bad-tempered mage did not

dismiss the notion as impossible out of hand, that might even mean it was easy. Then Yeshmef said, "This magic has never been done, which may well mean this magic cannot be done." All the other wizards nodded solemnly. Mages were conservative men, even more likely to rely on precedent than were servants of the God, judges, and clerks.

But Utpanisht, whom he would have expected to be the most conservative of all, said, "One reason it has not been done is that the land of the Thousand Cities had never faced a foe like this Videssian and his host. Desperate times call out for desperate remedies."

"*Can* call out for them," Mefyesh said. To Abivard's disappointment, Utpanisht did not contradict him.

Kidinnu said, "Grandfather, even if we can work this magic, should we? Will it not cause more harm than whatever the Videssian does?"

"It is not a simple question," Utpanisht said. "The harm from this Maniakes lies not only in what he does now but in what he may do later if we do not check him now. That could be very large indeed. A flood—" He shrugged. "I have seen many floods in my years here. We who live between the rivers know how to deal with floods."

Kidinnu bowed his head in acquiescence to his grandfather's reasoning. Abivard asked his question again: "Can you do this thing?"

This time the wizards did not answer him directly. Instead, they began arguing among themselves, first in the Makuraner language and then, by the sound of things because they didn't find that pungent enough, in the guttural tongue the folk of the Thousand Cities used among themselves. Mefyesh and Yeshmef didn't find even their own language sufficiently satisfying, for after one hot exchange they pulled each other's beards. Abivard wondered if they would yank out knives.

At last, when the wrangling died down, Utpanisht said, "We think we can do this. All of us agree it is possible. We still have not made up our minds about what method we need to use."

"That is because some of these blockheads insist on treating canals as if they were rivers," Glathpilesh said, "when any fool— but not any idiot, evidently—can see they are of two different classes."

Falasham's good nature was fraying at the edges. "They hold flowing water," he snapped. "Spiritually and metaphorically speaking, that makes them rivers. They aren't lakes. They aren't baths. What are they, if not rivers?"

"Canals," Glathpilesh declared, and Yeshmef voiced loud agreement. The row started up anew.

Abivard listened for a little while, then said sharply, "Enough of this!" His intervention made all the wizards, regardless of which side they had been on, gang up against him instead. He'd expected that would happen and was neither disappointed nor angry. "I admit you are all more learned in this matter that I could hope to be—"

"He admits the sun rises in the east," Glathpilesh muttered. "How generous!"

Pretending he hadn't heard that, Abivard plowed ahead: "But how you work this magic is not what's important. That you work it is. And you must work it soon, too, for before long Maniakes will start wondering why I've stopped here at Nashvar and given up on pursuing him." *Before long Sharbaraz King of Kings will start wondering, too, and likely decide I'm a traitor, after all. Or if he doesn't, Tzikas will tell him I am.*

Kidinnu said, "Lord, agreeing on the form this sorcery must take is vital before we actually attempt it."

That made sense; Abivard wasn't keen on the idea of going into battle without a plan. But he said, "I tell you, we have no time to waste. By the time you leave this room, hammer out your differences." All at once, he wished he hadn't asked Beroshesh to set out such a lavish feast for the mages. Empty bellies would have sped consensus.

His uncompromising stand drew more of the wizards' anger. Glathpilesh growled, "Easier for us to agree to turn you into a cockroach than on how to breach the canals."

"No one would pay you to do that to me, though," Abivard

answered easily. Then he thought of Tzikas and then of Sharbaraz. Well, the wizards didn't have to know about them.

Yeshmef threw his hands in the air. "Maybe my moron of a brother is right. It has happened before, though seldom."

Glathpilesh was left all alone. He glared around at the other five wizards from the Thousand Cities. Abivard did not like the look on his face—had being left all alone made him more stubborn? If it had, could the rest of the mages carry on with the conjuration by themselves? Even if they could, it would surely be more difficult without their colleague.

"You are all fools," he snarled at them, "and you, sirrah—" He sent Yeshmef a look that was almost literally murderous."—fit for nothing better than bellwether, for you show yourself to be a shambling sheep without ballocks." He breathed heavily, jowls wobbling; Abivard wondered whether he would suffer an apoplectic fit in his fury.

He also wondered whether the other wizards would want to work with Glathpilesh after his diatribe. There, at least, he soon found relief, for the five seemed more amused than outraged. Falasham said, "Not bad, old fellow." And Yeshmef tugged at his beard as if to show he still had that which enabled him to grow it.

"Bah," Glathpilesh said, sounding angry that he had been unable to anger his comrades. He turned to Abivard and said "Bah" again, perhaps so Abivard would not feel left out of his disapproval. Then he said, "None of you has the wit the God gave a smashed mosquito, but I'll work with you for no better reason than to keep you from going astray without my genius to show you what needs doing."

"Your generosity, as usual, is unsurpassed," Utpanisht said in his rusty-hinge voice.

Glathpilesh spoiled that by swallowing its irony. "I know," he answered. "Now we'll see how much I regret it."

"Not as much as the rest of us, I promise," Mefyesh said.

Falasham boomed laughter. "A band of brothers, the lot of us," he declared, "and we fight like it, too." Remembering the fights he'd had with his own brothers, Abivard felt better about the prospects for the mages' being able to work together than he had since he'd walked into the room.

Having wrangled about how to flood the canals, the wizards spent a couple of more days wrangling over how best to make that approach work. Abivard didn't listen to all those arguments. He did stop in to see the wizards several times a day to make sure they were moving forward rather than around and around.

He also sent Turan out with some of the assembled garrison troops and some of the horsemen Tzikas had brought from Vaspurakan. "I want you to chase Maniakes and to be obvious and obnoxious about doing it," he told his lieutenant. "But by the God, don't catch him, whatever you do, because he'll thrash you."

"I understand," Turan assured him. "You want it to look as if we haven't forgotten about him so he won't spend too much time wondering what we're doing here instead of chasing him."

"That's it," Abivard said, slapping him on the back. He called to a servant for a couple of cups of wine. When he had his, he poured libations to the Prophets Four, then raised the silver goblet high and proclaimed, "Confusion to the Avtokrator! If we can keep him confused for a week, maybe a few days longer, he'll be worse than confused after that."

"If we make it so he can't stay here, he might have a hard time getting back to Videssos, too," Turan said with a predatory gleam in his eye.

"So he might," Abivard said. "That would have been more likely before we had to pull our mobile force out of Videssos and into Vaspurakan last year, but . . ." His voice trailed away. What point was there to protesting orders straight from the King of Kings?

Turan's force set out the next day with horns blowing and banners waving. Abivard watched them from the city wall. They looked impressive; he didn't think Maniakes would be able to ignore them and go on sacking towns. Stopping that would be an added benefit of Turan's sortie.

From up there Abivard could see a long way across the floodplain of the Tutub and the Tib. He shook his head in mild bemusement. How many centuries of accumulated rubbish lay under his feet to give him this vantage point? He was no scholar; he couldn't have begun to guess. But if the answer proved less than the total of his own toes and fingers, he would have been astonished.

The vantage point would have been even more impressive had there been more to see. But the plain was as flat as if a woman had rolled it with a length of dowel before putting it on the griddle to bake—and the climate of the land of the Thousand Cities made that seem possible. Here and there, along a canal or a river, a few lines of date palms rose up above the fields. Most of the country-side, though, was mud and crops growing on top of mud.

Aside from the palms, the only breaks in the monotony were the hillocks on which the cities of the floodplain grew. Abivard could see several of them, each crowned with a habitation. All were as artificial as the one on which he stood. A great many people had lived in the land between the Tutub and the Tib for a long, long time.

He thought of the hill on which Vek Rud stronghold sat. There was nothing man-made about that piece of high ground: the stronghold itself was built of stone quarried from it. Here, all stone, right down to the weights the grain merchants used on their scales, had to be brought in from outside. *Mud*, Abivard thought again. He was sick of mud.

He wondered if he would ever see Vek Rud domain again. He still thought of it as home, though it had scarcely seen him since Genesios had overthrown Likinios and given Sharbaraz both the pretext and the opportunity he had needed to invade Videssos. How were things going up in the far northwest of Makuran? He hadn't heard from his brother, who was administering the domain for him, in years. Did Khamorth raiders still strike south over the Degird River and harass the domain, as they had since Peroz King of Kings had thrown away his life and his army out on the Pardrayan steppe? Abivard didn't know, and throughout his early years he'd expected to live out his whole life within the narrow confines of the domain and to be happy doing it, too.

As he seldom did, he thought about the wives he'd left behind in the women's quarters of Vek Rud stronghold. Guilt pierced him; their confines were far narrower than those he would have known even had he remained a *dihqan* like any other. When he'd left the domain, he'd never thought to be away so long. And yet, many if not most of his wives would have taken a proclamation of divorce as an insult, not as liberation. He shook his head. Life was seldom as simple as you wished it would be.

That thought made him feel kinder toward the wrangling wizards who labored to create a magic that would make the canals of the floodplain between the Tutub and the Tib spill their waters onto the land. Even the little he understood about sorcery convinced him they were undertaking something huge and complex. No wonder, then, if they quarreled as they figured out how to go about it.

Things they would need for the spell kept coming in: sealed jars with water from canals throughout the land of the Thousand Cities, each one neatly labeled to show from which canal it had come; mud from the dikes that kept the canals going as they should; wheat and lettuce and onions nourished by the water in the canals.

All those Abivard instinctively understood—they had to do with the waterways and the land they would inundate. But why the wizards also wanted oddments such as several dozen large quail's eggs, as many poisonous serpents, and enough pitch to coat the inside of a couple of wine jars was beyond him. He knew he'd never make a mage and so didn't spend a lot of time worrying about the nature of the conjuration the wizards would try.

What did worry him was *when* the wizards would try it. Short of lighting a bonfire under their chambers, he didn't know what he could do to make them move faster. They knew how important speed was here, but one day faded into the next without the spell being cast.

As he tried without much luck to hustle the wizards along, a messenger arrived from Mashiz. Abivard received the fellow with something less than joy. He wished the wizards had flooded the land of the Thousand Cities, for that would have kept the messenger from arriving. The timing was right for Sharbaraz King of Kings to have heard of his defeat at Maniakes' hands.

Sure enough, the letter was sealed with the lion of the King of Kings stamped into red wax. Abivard broke the seal, waded through the grandiose titles and epithets with which Sharbaraz bedizened his own name, and got to the meat of the missive: "We are once more displeased that you should take an army and lead it only into defeat. Know that we question your judgment in dividing your force in the face of the foe and that we are given to understand this contravenes every principle of the military art. Know further that any more such disasters associated with your name shall have a destructive and deleterious effect on our hopes and expectations for complete victory over Videssos."

"Is there a reply, lord?" the messenger asked when Abivard had rolled up the parchment and tied it with a bit of twine.

"No," he said absently, "no reply. Just acknowledge that you gave it to me and I read it."

The messenger saluted and left, presumably to make his return to Mashiz. Abivard shrugged. He saw no reason to doubt that the canals would remain unflooded till the man had returned—and maybe for a long time afterward, too.

He undid the twine that bound up Sharbaraz' letter and read it over again. That brought on another shrug. The tone was exactly as he'd expected, with petulance the strongest element. No mention—not even the slightest notion—that any of the recent reverses might have been partly the fault of the King of Kings. Sharbaraz' courtiers were undoubtedly encouraging him to believe he could do no wrong, not that he needed much in the way of encouragement along those lines.

But the letter was as remarkable for what it didn't say as for what it did. In with the usual carping criticism and worries lay not the slightest hint that Sharbaraz was thinking about changing commanders. Abivard had dreaded a letter from the King of Kings not least because he'd looked for Sharbaraz to remove him from his command and replace him, perhaps with Turan, perhaps with Tzikas.

Could he have taken orders from the Videssian renegade? He

didn't know and was glad he didn't have to find out. Did Sharbaraz trust him? Or did the King of Kings merely distrust Tzikas even more? If the latter, it was, in Abivard's opinion, only sensible of his sovereign.

He took the letter to Roshnani to find out whether she could see in it anything he was missing. She read it through, then looked up at him. "It could be worse," she said, as close as she'd come to praising Sharbaraz for some time.

"That's what I thought." Abivard picked up the letter from the table where she'd laid it, then read it again himself. "And if I lose another battle, it *will* be worse. He makes that clear enough."

"All the more reason to hope the wizards do succeed in flooding the plain," his principal wife answered. She cocked her head to one side and studied him. "How are they coming, anyhow? You haven't said much about them lately."

Abivard laughed and gave her a salute as if she were his superior officer. "I should know better than to think being quiet about something is the same as concealing it from you, shouldn't I? If you really want to know what I think, it's this: if Sharbaraz' courtiers were just a little nastier, they'd make pretty good sorcerers."

Roshnani winced. "I hadn't thought it was that bad."

All of Abivard's frustration came boiling out. "Well, it is. If anything, it's worse. I've never seen such backbiting. Yeshmef and Mefyesh ought to have their heads knocked together; that's what my father would have done if I quarreled like that with a brother of mine, anyhow. And as for Glathpilesh, I think he delights in being hateful. He's certainly made all the others hate him. The only ones who seem like good and decent fellows are Utpanisht, who's too old to be as useful as he might be, and his grandson, Kidinnu, who's the youngest of the lot and so not taken seriously—not that Falasham would take anything this side of an outbreak of pestilence seriously."

"And these were the good wizards?" Roshnani asked. At Abivard's nod, she rolled her eyes. "Maybe you should have recruited some bad ones, then."

"Maybe I should have," Abivard agreed. "I'll tell you what I've thought of doing: I've thought of making every mage in this crew shorter by a head and showing the heads to the next lot I recruit. That might get their attention and make them work fast." He regretfully spread his hands. "However tempting that is, though, gathering up a new lot would take too long. For better or worse, I'm stuck with these six."

He supposed it was poetic justice, then, that only a little while after he had called the six mages from the land of the Thousand Cities every name he could think of, they sent him a servant who said, "Lord, the wizards say to tell you they are ready to begin the conjuration. Will you watch?"

Abivard shook his head. "What they do wouldn't mean anything to me. Besides, I don't care how the magic works. I care only that it works. I'll go up on the city wall and look out over the fields to the canals. What I see there will tell the tale one way or the other."

"I shall take your words to the mages, lord, so they will know they may begin without you," the messenger said.

"Yes. Go." Abivard made little impatient brushing motions with his hands, sending the young man on his way. When the fellow had gone, Abivard walked through Nashvar's twisting, crowded streets to the wall. A couple of garrison soldiers stood at the base to keep just anyone from ascending it. Recognizing Abivard, they lowered their spears and stepped aside, bowing as they did so.

He had not climbed more than a third of the mud-brick stairs when he felt the world begin to change around him. It reminded him of the thrum in the ground just before an earthquake, when you could tell it was coming but the world hadn't yet started dancing under your feet.

He climbed faster. He didn't want to miss whatever was about to happen. The feeling of pressure grew until his head felt ready to burst. He waited for others to exclaim over it, but no one did. Up on the wall sentries tramped along, unconcerned. Down on the ground behind him merchants and customers told one another lies that had been passed down from father to son and from mother to daughter for generations uncounted.

Why was he, alone among mankind, privileged to feel the magic build to a peak of power? Maybe, he thought, because he had been the one who had set the sorcery in motion and so had some special affinity for it even if he was no wizard. And maybe, too, he was imagining all this, and nobody else felt it because it wasn't really there.

He couldn't make himself believe that. He looked out over the broad, flat floodplain. It seemed no different from the way it had the last time he'd seen it: fields and date palms and peasants in loincloths down in a perpetual stoop, weeding or manuring or gathering or trying to catch little fish in streams or canals.

Canals . . . Abivard looked out at the long straight channels that endless labor had created and more endless labor now maintained. Some of the fishermen, tiny as ants in the distance, suddenly sprang to their feet. One or two of them, for no apparent reason, looked back toward Abivard up on the city wall of Nashvar. He wondered if they had some tiny share of magical ability, enough at any rate to sense the rising power of the spell.

Would it never stop rising? Abivard thought he would have to start pounding his temples with his fists to let out the pressure inside. And then, all at once, almost like an orgasm, came release. He staggered and nearly fell, feeling as if he'd suddenly been emptied.

And all across the floodplain, as far as he could see, the banks of canals were opening up, spilling water over the land in a broad sheet that sparkled silver as the sunlight glinted off it. Thin in the distance came the cries of fishers and farmers caught unaware by the flood. Some fled. Some splashed in the water. Abivard hoped they could swim.

He wondered how widely through the land of the Thousand Cities canal banks were crumbling and water was pouring out over the land. For all he knew for certain, the flood might have been limited to the narrow area he could see with his own eyes.

But he didn't believe it. The flood *felt* bigger than that. Whatever he'd felt inside himself, whatever had made him feel he was about to explode like a sealed pot in a fire, was too big to be merely a local marvel. He had no way to prove that—not yet—but he would have sworn by the God it was so.

People began running out of Nashvar toward the breached canals. Some carried mattocks, others hoes, others spades. Wherever they could reach a magically broken bank, they started to repair it with no more magic than that engendered by diligent work.

Abivard scowled when he saw that. It made perfect sense—the peasants didn't want to see their crops drowned and all the labor they'd put into them lost—but it took him by surprise all the same. He'd been so intent on covering the floodplain with water, he hadn't stopped to think what the people would do when that happened. He'd realized that they wouldn't be delighted; that they'd immediately try to set things right hadn't occurred to him.

He'd pictured the land between the Tutub and the Tib underwater, with only the Thousand Cities sticking up out of it on their artificial hillocks like islands from the sea. With the certainty that told him the flood stretched farther than his body's eyes could reach, he now saw in his mind's eye men—aye, and probably women, too—pouring out of the cities all across the floodplain to repair what the great conjuration had wrought.

"But don't they want to be rid of the Videssians?" Abivard said out loud, as if someone had challenged him on that very point.

The folk who lived—or had lived—in cities Maniakes and his army had sacked undoubtedly hoped every Videssian ever born would vanish into the Void. But the Videssians had sacked but a handful of the Thousand Cities. In all the other towns, they were no more than a hypothetical danger. Flood was real and immediate—and familiar. The peasants wouldn't know, or care, what had caused it. They would know what to do about it.

That worked against Makuran and for Videssos. The land between the Tutub and the Tib would, Abivard realized, come back to normal faster than he had expected. And, during the time when it wasn't normal, he would have as much trouble moving as Maniakes did. Maybe, though, Turan could strike a blow at some of the Videssians if they'd grown careless and split their forces.

Less happy than he'd thought he'd be, Abivard descended from the wall and walked back toward the city governor's residence. There he found Utpanisht, who looked all but dead from exhaustion, and Glathpilesh, who was methodically working his way through a tray of roasted songbirds stuffed with dates. Fragile bones crunched between his teeth as he chewed.

Swallowing, he grudged Abivard a curt nod. "It is accomplished," he said, and reached for another songbird. More tiny bones crunched.

"So it is, for which I thank you," Abivard answered with a bow. He could not resist adding, "And done well, in spite of its not being done as you first had in mind."

That got him a glare; he would have been disappointed if it hadn't. Utpanisht held up a bony, trembling hand. "Speak not against Glathpilesh, lord," he said in a voice like wind whispering through dry, dry straw. "He served Makuran nobly this day."

"So he did," Abivard admitted. "So did all of you. Sharbaraz King of Kings owes you a debt of gratitude."

Glathpilesh spit out a bone that might have choked him had he swallowed it. "What he owes us and what we'll get from him are liable to be two different things," he said. His shrug made his flabby jowls wobble. "Such is life: what you get is always less than you deserve."

Such a breathtakingly sardonic view of life would have annoyed Abivard most of the time. Now he said only, "Regardless of what Sharbaraz does, I shall reward all six of you as you deserve."

"You are generous, lord," Utpanisht said in that dry, quavering voice.

"Just deserts, eh?" Glathpilesh said with his mouth full. He studied Abivard with eyes that, while not very friendly, were disconcertingly keen. "And will Sharbaraz King of Kings, may his days be long and his realm increase—" He made a mockery of the honorific formula. "—reward you as you deserve?"

Abivard felt his face heat. "That is as the King of Kings wishes. I have no say in the matter."

"Evidently not," Glathpilesh said scornfully.

"I am sorry," Abivard told him, "but your wit is too pointed for me today. I'd better go and find the best way to take advantage of what your flood has done to the Videssians. If we had a great fleet of light boats . . . but I might as well wish for the moon while I'm at it."

"Use well the chance you have," Utpanisht told him, almost as if prophesying. "Its like may be long in coming."

"That I know," Abivard said. "I did not do all I could with our journey by canal. The God will think less of me if I let this chance slip, too. But—" He grimaced. "—it will not be so easy as I thought when I asked you to flood the canals for me."

"When is anything ever as easy as you think it will be?" Glathpilesh demanded. He pointed to the tray of songbirds, which was empty now. "There. You see? As I said, you never get all you want."

"Getting all I want is the least of my worries," Abivard answered. "Getting all I need is another question altogether."

Glathpilesh eyed him with sudden fresh interest and respect. "For one not a mage—and for one not old—to know the difference between those two is less than common. Even for mages, *need* shades into *want* so that we must ever be on our guard against disasters spawned from greed."

To judge from the empty tray in front of him, Glathpilesh was intimately acquainted with greed, perhaps more intimately acquainted than he realized—no one needed to devour so many songbirds, but he'd certainly wanted them. The only disaster to which such gluttony could lead, though, Abivard thought, was choking to death on a bone, or perhaps getting so wide that you couldn't fit through a door.

Utpanisht said, "May the God grant you find a way to use our magic as you had hoped and drive the Videssians and their false god from the land of the Thousand Cities."

"May it be as you say," Abivard agreed. He was less sure it would be that way now than he had been when he had decided to use the flood as a weapon against Maniakes. But no matter what else happened, the Videssians would not be able to move around on the plain between the Tutub and the Tib as freely as they had been doing. That would reduce the amount of damage they could inflict.

"It had better be as Utpanisht says," Glathpilesh said. "Otherwise a lot of time and effort will have gone for nothing."

"A lot of time," Abivard echoed. The wizards, as far as he was concerned, had wasted a good deal of it all by themselves. They, no doubt, would vehemently disagree with that characterization and would claim they had spent time wisely. But whether wasted or spent, time had passed—quite a bit of it. "Not much time is left for this campaigning season. We've held Maniakes away from Mashiz for the year, anyhow."

That was exactly what Sharbaraz King of Kings had sent him out to do. Sharbaraz had expected he'd do it by beating the Videssians, but making them shift their path, making them fight even if he couldn't win, and then using water as a weapon seemed to work as well.

"As harvest nears, the Videssians will leave our land, not so?" Utpanisht said. "They are men; they must harvest like other men."

"The land of the Thousand Cities grows enough for them to stay here and live off the countryside if they want to," Abivard said, "or it did before the flood, at any rate. But if they do stay here, who will bring in the harvests back in their homeland? Their women will go hungry; their children will starve. Can Maniakes make them go on while that happens? I doubt it."

"And I as well," Utpanisht said. "I raised the question to be certain you were aware of it."

"Oh, I'm aware of it," Abivard answered. "Now we have to find out whether Maniakes is—and whether he cares."

With the countryside flooded around them, the Videssians no longer rampaged through the land of the Thousand Cities. Not even their skill at engineering let them do that. Instead, they stayed near the upper reaches of one of the Tutub's tributaries, from which they could either resume the assault they had carried on through the summer or withdraw back into the westlands of their own empire.

Abivard tried to force them to the latter course, marching out and joining up with Turan's force before moving—sometimes single file along causeways that were the only routes through drowned farmlands—against the Videssians. He sent a letter off to Romezan up in Vaspurakan, asking him to use the cavalry of the field force to attack Maniakes once he got back into Videssos. The garrisons holding the towns in the Videssian westlands weren't much better equipped for mobile warfare than were those that had held down the Thousand Cities.

Word came from out of Videssian-held territory that Maniakes' wife, Lysia—who was also his first cousin—not only was with the Avtokrator but had just been delivered of a baby boy. "There—do you see?" Roshnani said when Abivard passed the news to her. "You're not the only one who takes his wife on campaign."

"Maniakes is only a Videssian bound for the Void," Abivard replied, not without irony. "What he does has no bearing on the way a proper Makuraner noblewoman should behave."

Roshnani stuck out her tongue at him. Then she grew serious once more. "What's she like—Lysia, I mean?"

"I don't know," Abivard admitted. "He may take her on campaigns with him, but I've never met her." He paused thoughtfully. "He must think the world of her. For the Videssians, marrying your cousin is as shocking as letting noblewomen out in public is for us."

"I wonder if that's part of the reason he's brought her along," Roshnani mused. "Having her with him might be safer than leaving her back in Videssos the city while he's gone."

"It could be so," Abivard said. "If you really want to know, we can ask Tzikas. He professed to be horrified about Maniakes' incest—that's what he called it—when he came over to us. The only problem is, Tzikas would profess anything if he saw as much as one chance in a hundred that he might get something he wants by doing it."

"If I thought you were wrong, I would tell you," Roshnani said. She thought for a moment, then shook her head. "If finding out about Lysia means asking Tzikas, I'd rather not know."

Abivard gave the Videssian renegade such praise as he could:

"He hasn't done anything to me since he came here from Vaspurakan."

Roshnani tempered even that: "Anything you know of, you mean. But you didn't know everything he was doing to you before, either."

"I'm not saying you're wrong, either, mind you, but I am learning," Abivard answered. "Tzikas doesn't know it, but slipping a few arkets to his orderlies means I read everything he writes before it goes into a courier's message tube."

Roshnani kissed him with great enthusiasm. "You *are* learning," she said.

"I should be clever more often," Abivard said. That made her laugh and, as he'd hoped, kiss him again.

The closer his army drew to Maniakes' force, the more Abivard worried about what he'd do if the Videssians chose battle instead of retreat. Tzikas' regiment of veteran cavalry stiffened the men he already had, and half of those garrison soldiers had fought well even if they had lost in the end. He was still leery of the prospect of battle and suddenly understood why the Videssians had been so hesitant about fighting his army after losing to it a few times. Now he felt the pinch of that sandal on his foot.

In the fields the peasants of the Thousand Cities worked stolidly away at repairing the damage from the breaches in the canals he'd had the wizards make. He wanted to shout at them, try to make them see that in so doing they were also helping to turn Maniakes loose on their land once more. He kept quiet. From long, often unhappy experience, he knew a peasant's horizon seldom reached farther than the crop he was raising. There was some justification for that way of thinking, too: if the crop didn't get raised, nothing else mattered, not to the peasant who stood to starve.

But Abivard saw farther. If Maniakes got loose to rampage over the land between the Tutub and the Tib once more, these particular peasants might escape, but others, probably more, would suffer.

He found himself glancing at the sun more often than usual. Like anyone else, he looked to the sky to find out what time it was. Nowadays, though, he paid more attention to where in the sky the sun was rising and setting. The sooner autumn came, the happier he would be. Maniakes would have to withdraw to his own land then . . . wouldn't he?

If he did intend to withdraw, he gave no sign of it. Instead, he sent out horsemen to harass Abivard's soldiers and slow their already creeping advance even further. With Abivard's reluctant blessing, Tzikas led his cavalry regiment in a counterattack that sent the Videssians back in retreat.

When the renegade tried to push farther still, he barely escaped an ambush Maniakes' troopers set for him. On hearing that, Abivard didn't know whether to be glad or sorry. Seeing Tzikas fall into the hands of the Avtokrator he'd tried to slay by sorcery would have been the perfect revenge on him even if Abivard had decided not to hand him over to Maniakes.

"Why can't you?" Turan asked when Abivard grumbled about that. "I wish you would have after he came down here, no matter what he said about his regiment." He paused thoughtfully. "The cursed Videssian's not a coward in battle, whatever else you want to say about him. Arrange for him to meet about a regiment's worth of Videssians with maybe half a troop of his own at his back. That'll settle him once and for all."

Abivard pondered the idea. It brought a good deal of temptation with it. In the end, though, and rather to his own surprise, he shook his head. "It's what he would do to me were our places reversed."

"All the more reason to do it to him first," Turan said.

"Thank you, but no. If you have to become a villain to beat a villain, the God will drop you into the Void along with him."

"You're too tenderhearted for your own good," Turan said. "Sharbaraz King of Kings, may his days be long and his realm increase, would have done it without blinking an eye, and he wouldn't have needed me to suggest it to him, either."

That was both true and false. Sharbaraz, these days, could be as ruthless as any man ever born when it came to protecting his throne . . . yet he had not put Abivard out of the way when he had had the chance. Maybe that meant a spark of humanity did still lurk within the kingly facade he'd been building over the past decade and more.

Turan looked sly. "If you want to keep your hands clean, lord, I expect I could arrange something or other. You don't even have to ask. I'll take care of it."

Abivard shook his head again, this time in annoyance. If Turan had quietly arranged for Tzikas' untimely demise without telling him about it, that would have been between his lieutenant and the God. But for Turan to do that after Abivard had said he didn't want it done was a different matter. What would have been good service would have turned into villainy.

"You've got more scruples than a druggist," Turan grumbled as he walked off, as disappointed with Abivard as Abivard was with him.

The next day Tzikas returned to camp to give Abivard the details of his skirmish with the Videssians. "The enemy, at least, thought I was a man of Makuran," he said pointedly. " 'There's that cavalry general of theirs, curse him to the ice,' they said. A good many of them have fallen into the Void now, eternal oblivion their fate."

He said all the right things. He'd let his beard grow out so that it made his face seem more rectangular, less pinched in at the jaw and chin. He wore a Makuraner caftan. And he still was, to Abivard, a foreigner, a Videssian, and so not to be trusted because of who he was, let alone because of his letters to Sharbaraz King of Kings.

But he'd done decent service here. Abivard acknowledged that, saying, "I'm glad you beat them back. Knowing a cavalry regiment is here and able to do its job will make Maniakes think twice about getting pushy so late in the year."

"Yes," Tzikas said. "Your magic helped there, too, even if not quite so much as you'd hoped." His lips twisted in a grimace no Makuraner could have matched, an expression of self-reproach that was quintessentially Videssian: he was berating himself for being less underhanded than he would have wanted. "Had the magic I essayed worked even half so well, I, not Maniakes, would be Avtokrator now."

"And I might be trying to figure out how to drive you from the land of the Thousand Cities," Abivard answered. His gaze sharpened. Here was a chance to get a look at the way Tzikas' mind worked. "Or would you have tried such a bold thrust if you had the Videssian throne under your fundament?"

"No, not I," Tzikas said at once. "I would have held on to what I had, strengthened that, and then begun to wrest back what was mine. I would have had no need to hurry, for I could have held out in Videssos the city forever, so long as my fleet kept you from crossing over from the westlands. Once my plans were ripe, I'd have struck and struck hard."

Abivard nodded. It was a sensible, conservative plan. That mirrored the way Tzikas had opposed Makuran back in the days when he'd been the best of the Videssian generals in the westlands—and the one who had paid the most attention to fighting the invaders and the least to the endless rounds of civil war engulfing the Empire after Genesios had murdered his way to the Videssian throne. Only in treachery, it seemed, was Tzikas less than conservative, although by Videssian standards, even that might not have been so.

"But Maniakes has thrown us back on our heels," Abivard argued. "Would your scheme have done so much so soon?"

"Probably not," Tzikas said. "But it would have risked less. Maniakes, whining pup that he is, has a way of overreaching that will bring him down in the end—you mark my words."

"I always mark your words, eminent sir," Abivard answered. Tzikas scowled at his use of the Videssian title. Abivard didn't care. He also didn't think Tzikas was right. Maniakes, unlike a lot of generals, kept getting better at what he did.

"By the God," Tzikas replied, again reminding Abivard that he had bound himself to Makuran for better or for worse—*or until he sees a chance for some new treachery*, Abivard thought— "we should push straight at Maniakes with everything we have and force him out of the land of the Thousand Cities."

"I'd love to," Abivard said. "The only problem with the plan is that everything we have hasn't been enough to force him out of the Thousand Cities."

Tzikas didn't answer, not with words. He simply donned another of those characteristically Videssian expressions, this one saying that, had he been in charge of things, they would have gone better.

Before Abivard could get angry at that, he realized there was another problem with the scheme the Videssian renegade had proposed. Like Tzikas' plan for fighting Makuran had he been Avtokrator, this one lacked imagination; it showed no sense of where the enemy's real weakness lay.

Slowly Abivard said, "Suppose we do force Maniakes away from the Tutub. What happens next? Where does he go?"

"He falls back into the westlands. Where else can he go?" Tzikas said. "Then, I suppose, he makes for the coast, whether north or south I couldn't begin to guess. And then he sails away, and Makuran is rid of him till the spring campaigning season, by which time, the God willing, we shall be better prepared to face him here in the land of the Thousand Cities than we were this year."

"My guess is he'll go south," Abivard said. "To reach the coast of the Videssian Sea, he'd have to skirt Vaspurakan, where we have a force that should be coming out to hunt him anyhow, and he controls none of the ports along that coast. But he's taken Lyssaion, which means he has a gateway out on the coast of the Sailors' Sea."

"Clearly reasoned," Tzikas agreed. From a Videssian that was no small praise. "Yes, I suppose he likely will escape to the south, and we shall be rid of him—and we shall not miss him one bit."

"Do you play the Videssian board game?" Abivard asked, continuing, "I was never very good at it, but I liked it because it leaves nothing to chance but rests everything on the skill of the players."

"Yes, I play it," Tzikas answered. By the predatory look that came into his eyes, he played well. "Perhaps you would honor me with a game one day."

"As I say, you'd mop the floor with me," Abivard said, reflecting that Tzikas would no doubt enjoy mopping the floor with him, too. "But that's not the point. The point is, you can hurt the fellow playing the other side, sometimes hurt him a lot, just by putting one of your pieces between his piece and where it's trying to go."

"And so?" Tzikas said, right at the edge of rudeness. But then his manner changed. "I begin to see, lord, what may be in your mind."

"Good," Abivard told him, less sardonically than he'd intended. "If we can set an army on his road down to Lyssaion, that will cause him all manner of grief. And unless I misremember, delaying him on the road to Lyssaion really matters at this season of the year."

"You remember rightly, lord," Tzikas said. "The Sailors' Sea turns stormy in the fall and stays stormy through the winter. No captain would want to risk taking his Avtokrator and the best soldiers Videssos has back to the capital by sea, not in a few weeks, not when he'd know he was only too likely to lose them all. And that would mean—"

"That would mean Maniakes would have to try to cross the westlands to get home," Abivard said, interrupting not from irritation but from excitement. "He'd have to capture each town along the way if he wanted to encamp in it, and the winter there is hard enough that he'd have to try—he couldn't very well live under canvas till spring came. So if we can get between him and Lyssaion, we don't even have to win a battle—"

"A good thing, too, with these odds and sods under your command," Tzikas broke in. Now he was being rude but not inaccurate.

"And whose fault is it that Sharbaraz King of Kings, may his years be many and his realm increase, wouldn't trust me with better?" Abivard retorted. The prospect of discomfiting Maniakes made him better able to tolerate Tzikas, so that came out as badinage, not rage. He went on, "If you think they're bad now, you should have seen them when I first got them. Eminent sir, they're brave enough, and they are starting to learn their trade."

"I'd cheerfully trade them for a like number of real soldiers nonetheless," Tzikas said, again impolite but again correct.

Abivard said, "It's settled, then. We advance against Maniakes and demonstrate in front of him, with luck making him abandon his base here. And as he moves south, we have a force waiting to engage him. We don't have to win; we simply have to keep him in play till it's too late for him to sail out of Lyssaion."

"That's it," Tzikas said. He bowed to Abivard. "A plan worthy of Stavrakios the Great." The Videssian renegade suddenly suffered a coughing fit; Stavrakios was the Avtokrator who'd smashed every Makuraner army he had faced and had occupied Mashiz. When Tzikas could speak again, he went on: "Worthy of the great heroes of Makuran, I should have said."

"It's all right," Abivard said magnanimously. In a way he was relieved Tzikas had slipped. The cavalry officer did do an alarmingly good job of aping the Makuraners with whom he'd had to cast his lot. It was just as well he'd proved he remained a Videssian at heart.

Abivard wasted no time sending a good part of his army south along the Tutub. Had he seriously intended to defeat Maniakes as the Avtokrator headed for Lyssaion, he would have gone with that force. As things were, he sent it out under the reliable Turan. He commanded the rest of the Makuraner army, the part demonstrating against Maniakes in his lair.

His force included almost all of Tzikas' cavalry regiment. That left him nervous in spite of the accord he seemed to have reached with the Videssian renegade. Having betrayed Maniakes and Abivard both, was he now liable to betray one of them to the other? Abivard didn't want to find out.

But Tzikas stayed in line. His cavalry fought hard against the Videssian horsemen who battled to hold them away from Maniakes' base. He reveled in fighting for his adopted country against the men of his native land and worshiped the God more ostentatiously than did any Makuraner.

Maniakes once more took to breaking canals to keep Abivard's men at bay. Flooding was indeed a two-edged sword. Wearily, Abivard's soldiers and the local peasants worked side by side to repair the damage so the soldiers could go on and the peasants could save something of their crops.

And then, from the northeast, the smoke from a great burning rose into the sky, as it so often had in the land of the Thousand

Cities that summer. More wrecked canals kept Abivard's men from reaching the site of that burning for another couple of days, but Abivard knew what it meant: Maniakes was gone.

VII

ABIVARD GLARED AT THE PEASANT IN SOME EXASPERATION. "You saw the Videssian army leave?" he demanded. The peasant nodded. "And which way did they go? Tell me again," Abivard said.

"That way, lord." The peasant pointed east, as he had before.

Everyone with whom Abivard had spoken had said the same thing. Yes, the Videssians were gone. Yes, the locals were glad—although they seemed less glad to see a Makuraner army arrive to take the invaders' place. And yes, Maniakes and his men had gone east. No one had seen them turn south.

He's being sneaky, Abivard thought. *He'll go out into the scrub country between the Tutub and Videssos and stay there as long as he can, maybe even travel south a long way before he comes back to the river for water.* You could travel a fair distance through that semidesert, especially when the fall rains—the same rains that would be storms on the Sailors' Sea—brought the grass and leaves to brief new life.

But you could not travel all the way down to Lyssaion without returning to the Tutub. Even lush scrub wouldn't support an army's horses indefinitely, and there weren't enough water holes to keep an army of men from perishing of thirst. And when Maniakes came back to the Tutub, Abivard would know exactly where he was.

True, Maniakes' army could move faster than his. But that

army, burdened by a baggage train, could not outrun the scouting detachments Abivard sent galloping southward to check the likely halting places along the Tutub. If the scouts came back, they would bring news of where the Videssians were. And if one detachment did not come back, that would also tell Abivard where the Videssians were.

All the detachments came back. None of them had found Maniakes and his men. Abivard was left scratching his head. "He hasn't vanished into the Void, however much we wish he would," he said. "Can he be mad enough to try crossing the Videssian westlands on horseback?"

"I don't know anything about that, lord," answered the scout to whom he'd put the question. "All I know is I haven't seen him."

Snarling, Abivard dismissed him. The scout hadn't done anything wrong; he'd carried out the orders Abivard had given him, just as his fellows had. Abivard's job was to make what the scouts had seen—and what they hadn't seen—mean something. But what?

"He hasn't gone south," he said to Roshnani that evening. "I don't want to believe that, but I haven't any choice. He can't have chosen to fight his way across the westlands. I *won't* believe that; even if he made it, he'd throw away most of his army in the doing, and he hasn't got enough trained men to use them up so foolishly."

"Maybe he headed into Vaspurakan to try to rouse the princes against our field force again," Roshnani suggested.

"Maybe," Abivard said, unconvinced. "But that would tie him down in long, hard fighting and make him winter in Vaspurakan. I have trouble thinking he'd risk so much with such a distance and so many foes between him and country he controls."

"I'm no general—the God knows that's so—but I can see that what you say makes sense," Roshnani said. "But if he hasn't gone south and he hasn't gone into the Videssian westlands and he hasn't gone to Vaspurakan, where is he? He hasn't gone west, has he?"

Abivard snorted. "No, and that's not his army camped around us, either." He plucked at his beard. "I wonder if he could have gone north, up into the mountains and valleys of Erzerum. He might find friends up there no matter how isolated he was."

"From what the tales say, you can find anything up in Erzerum," Roshnani said.

"The tales speak true," Abivard told her. "Erzerum is the rubbish heap of the world." The mountains that ran from the Mylasa Sea east to the Videssian Sea and the valleys set among them were as perfectly defensible a terrain as had ever sprung from the mind and hand of the God. Because of that, almost every valley there had its own people, its own language, its own religion. Some were native, some survivors whose cause had been lost in the outer world but who had managed to carve out a shelter for themselves and hold it against all comers.

"The folk in some of those valleys worship Phos, don't they?" Roshnani asked.

"So they do," Abivard said. "What I'd like to see is Videssos pushed back into one of those valleys and forgotten about for the rest of time." He laughed. "It won't happen any time soon. And the Videssians would like to see us penned back there for good. That won't happen, either."

"No, of course not," Roshnani said. "The God would never allow such a thing; the very idea would appall her." But she didn't let Abivard distract her, instead continuing with her own train of thought: "Because some of them worship Phos, wouldn't they be likely to help Maniakes?"

"Yes, I suppose so," Abivard agreed. "He might winter up there. I have to say, though, I don't see why he would. He couldn't keep it a secret the winter long, and we'd be waiting for him to try to come back down into the low country when spring came."

"That's so," Roshnani admitted. "I can't argue with a word of it. But if he hasn't gone north, south, east, or west, *where is he?*"

"Underground," Abivard said. But that was too much to hope for.

He made his own arrangements for the winter, billeting his troops in several nearby cities and overcoming the city governors' remarkable lack of enthusiasm for keeping them in supplies. "Fine," he told one such official when the man flatly refused to aid the soldiers. "When the Videssians come back next spring, if they do, we'll stand aside and let them burn your town without even chasing them afterward."

"You couldn't do anything so heartless," the city governor exclaimed.

Abivard looked down his nose at him. "Who says I can't? If you don't help feed the soldiers, sirrah, why should they help protect you?"

The soldiers got all the wheat and vegetables and poultry they needed.

Only a couple of days after Abivard had won that battle a messenger reached him with a letter from Romezan. After the usual greetings the commander of the field forces came straight to the point: "I regret to tell you that the cursed Videssians, may they and their Avtokrator fall into the Void and be lost forever, slipped past my army, which was out hunting them. Following the line of the Rhamnos River, they reached Pityos, on the Videssian Sea, and took it by surprise. With the port in their hands, ships came and carried them away; my guess is that they have returned to Videssos the city by now, having also succeeded in embarrassing us no end. By the God, lord, I shall have my revenge on them."

"Is there a reply, lord?" the messenger asked when Abivard rolled up the message parchment once more.

"No, no reply," Abivard answered. "Now I know where the Videssians disappeared to, and I rather wish I didn't."

Winter in the land of the Thousand Cities meant mild days, cool nights, and occasional rain—no snow to speak of, though there were a couple of days of sleet that made it all but impossible to go outside without falling down. Abivard found that a nuisance, but his children enjoyed it immensely.

Although Maniakes would not be back till the following spring, if then, Abivard did not let his army rest idle. He drilled the foot soldiers every day the ground was dry enough to let them maneuver. The more he worked with them, the happier he grew. They would make decent fighting men once they had enough practice marching and got used to the idea that the enemy could not easily crush them so long as they stood firm.

And then, as the winter solstice approached, Abivard got the message he'd been waiting for and dreading since Sharbaraz had ordered him into the field against Maniakes with a force he knew to be inadequate: a summons to return to Mashiz at once.

He looked west across the floodplain toward the distant Dilbat Mountains. News of the order had spread very fast. Turan, who had rejoined him after Maniakes had escaped, came up beside him and said, "I'm sorry, lord. I don't know what else you could have done to hold the Videssians away from Mashiz."

"Neither do I," Abivard said wearily. "Nothing would have satisfied the King of Kings, I think."

Turan nodded. He couldn't say anything to that. No, there was one thing he could say. But the question, *Why don't you go into rebellion against Sharbaraz?* was not one a person could ask his commander unless that person was sure his answer would be something like, *Yes, why don't I?* Abivard had never let—had been careful never to let—anyone get that impression.

Every now and then he wondered why. These past years he'd generally been happiest when farthest away from Sharbaraz. But he'd helped Sharbaraz cast down one usurper simply because Smerdis had been a usurper. Having done that, how could he think of casting the legitimate King of Kings from a throne rightfully his? The brief answer was that he couldn't, not if he wanted to be able to go on looking at himself in the mirror.

And so, without hope and without fear, he left the army in Turan's hands—better his than Tzikas', Abivard judged—and obeyed Sharbaraz' order. He wanted to leave Roshnani and his children behind, but his principal wife would not hear of it. "Your brother and mine can avenge us if we fall," she said. "Our place is at your side." Glad of her company, Abivard stopped arguing perhaps sooner than he should have.

The journey across the land of the Thousand Cities showed the scars the Videssian incursion had left behind. Several hills were topped by charred ruins, not living towns. Soon, Abivard vowed, those towns would live again. If he had anything to say about it, money and artisans from the Videssian westlands would help make sure they lived again—that appealed to his sense of justice.

Whether he would have anything to say about it remained to be seen. The letter summoning him to Mashiz hadn't been so petulant as some of the missives he'd gotten from Sharbaraz. That might mean the King of Kings was grateful he'd kept Maniakes from sacking the capital. On the other hand, it might also mean Sharbaraz was dissembling and wanted him back in Mashiz before doing whatever dreadful things he would do.

As usual, Roshnani thought along with him. When she asked what he thought awaited them in Mashiz, he shrugged and answered, "No way to judge till we get there." She nodded, if not satisfied, then at least knowing that she knew as much as her husband.

They crossed the Tib on a bridge of boats that the operator dragged back to the western bank of the river after they went over it. That sort of measure was intended to make life difficult for invaders. Abivard doubted it would have thwarted Maniakes long.

After they left the land of the Thousand Cities, they went up into the foothills of the Dilbat Mountains toward Mashiz. Varaz said, "They're not going to lock us up in one suite of rooms through the whole winter again, are they, Father?"

"I hope not," Abivard answered truthfully, "but I don't know for certain."

"They'd better not," Varaz declared, and Shahin nodded.

"I wish they wouldn't, too," Abivard said, "but if they do, what can you do about it—aside from driving everyone crazy, I mean?"

"What we should do," Varaz said, with almost the force of someone having a religious revelation, "is drive the palace servants and the guards crazy, not you and Mother and—" He spoke with the air of one yielding a great concession. "—our sisters."

"If I told you I thought that an excellent plan, I would probably be guilty of lese majesty in some obscure way, and I don't want that," Abivard said, "so of course I won't tell you any such thing." He set a finger alongside his nose and winked. Both his sons laughed conspiratorial laughs.

* * *

There ahead stood the great shrine dedicated to the God. Abivard had seen the High Temple in Videssos the city at a shorter remove, though here no water screened him from reaching the shrine if he so desired. Again, whether Sharbaraz' minions would keep him from the shrine was a different matter.

Away from the army, Abivard was just another traveler entering Mashiz. No one paid any special attention to his wagon, which was but one of many clogging the narrow streets of the city. Drivers whose progress he impeded cursed him with great gusto.

Abivard had studied from afar the palaces in Videssos the city. They sprawled over an entire district, buildings set among trees and lawns and gardens. But then, as he knew all too well, Videssos the city was a fortress, the mightiest fortress in the world. Mashiz was not so lucky, and the palace of the King of Kings had to double as a citadel.

The wheels of the wagon rattled and clattered off the cobbles of the open square surrounding the wall around the palace. As he had the winter before, Abivard identified himself to the guards at the gate. As before, the valves of the gate swung wide to let him and his family come in, then closed with a thud that struck him as ominous.

And as before, and even more ominously, grooms led the horses away from the stables, while a fat eunuch in a caftan shot through with silver threads took charge of Pashang. The wagon driver sent Abivard a look of piteous appeal. "Where are you taking him?" Abivard demanded.

"Where he belongs," the eunuch answered, sexless voice chillier than the cutting breeze that blew dead brown leaves over the cobbles.

"Swear by the God you are not taking him to the dungeon," Abivard said.

"It is no business of yours where he goes," the eunuch told him.

"I choose to make it my business." Abivard set a hand on the hilt of his sword. Even as he made the gesture, he knew how foolish it was. If the eunuch so much as lifted a finger, the palace guards would kill him. Sharbaraz would probably reward them for doing it.

The finger remained unlifted. The eunuch licked his lips; his tongue was very pink against the pale, unweathered flesh of his face. He looked from Abivard to Pashang and back again. At last he said, "Very well. He shall dwell in the stables with your horses. By the God, I swear that to be true; may it drop me into the Void if I lie. There. Are you satisfied?"

"I am satisfied," Abivard answered formally. Men used masculine pronouns when speaking of the God, women feminine; it had never occurred to Abivard that eunuchs would refer to him—for so Abivard conceived of his deity—in the neuter gender. He turned to Pashang. "Make sure they feed you something better than oats."

"The God go with you and keep you safe, lord," Pashang said, and started to prostrate himself as if Abivard were King of Kings. With a snort of disgust the eunuch hauled him to his feet and led him away. Pashang waved clumsily, like a bear trained to do as much in hopes of winning a copper or two.

Another eunuch emerged from the stone fastness of the palace. "You will come with me," he announced to Abivard.

"Will I?" Abivard murmured. But that question had only one possible answer. His family trailing behind him, he did follow the servitor into the beating heart of the kingdom of Makuran.

He knew—knew only too well—every turn and passageway that would lead him to the suite where he and his family had been politely confined the winter before. As soon as the eunuch turned left instead of right, he breathed a long if silent sigh of relief. He glanced over to Roshnani. She was doing the same thing.

The chambers to which the fellow did lead them were in a wing far closer to the throne room than the place they had been before. Abivard would have taken that as a better sign had not two tall, muscular men in mail shirts and plume-crested helms stood in front of the doorway.

"Are we prisoners here?" he demanded of the eunuch.

"No," that worthy replied. "These men are but your guard of honor."

Abivard plucked a hair from his beard as he thought that over. The winter before no one in the palace had pretended he was anything but a prisoner. That had had the virtue of honesty, if no other. Would Sharbaraz lie, though, if he thought it served his purpose? The answer seemed obvious enough.

"Supposed we go in there," Abivard said. "Then suppose we want to come out and walk through the halls of the palace here. What would the guards do? On your oath by the God."

Before answering, the eunuch held a brief, low-voiced colloquy with the soldiers. "They tell me," he said carefully, "that if you came out for a stroll, as you say, one of them would accompany you while the other remained on guard in front of your door. By the God, lord, that is what they say."

The guardsmen nodded and gestured with their left hands to confirm his words. "We have no choice," Roshnani said. She had picked up Gulshahr, who was tired from all the walking she'd done.

"You're right," Abivard said, though there had been that unspoken choice: rebelling rather than coming to Mashiz a second time after what had happened before. But rebellion was no longer possible, not here, not now. Lion trainers, to thrill a crowd, would stick their heads into the mouths of their beasts day after day. But the lions they worked with were tame. One could form a pretty good notion of what they would do from day to day. With Sharbaraz—

"Does it suit you, lord?" the eunuch asked.

"For now it suits me," Abivard said, "but I want an audience with the King of Kings as soon as may be."

Bowing, the eunuch said, "I shall convey your request to those better able than I to make certain it is granted."

Abivard had no trouble translating that for himself. He might gain an audience with Sharbaraz tomorrow, or he might have to wait till next spring. No way to guess which—not yet.

"Please let me or another of the servitors know whatever you may be lacking or what may conduce toward your pleasure," the eunuch said. "Rest assured that if it be within our power, it shall be yours."

Abivard paused thoughtfully. No one had spoken to him like that last winter. Maybe he hadn't been summoned back here in disgrace, after all. Then again, maybe he had. He did his best to find out: "I would like to see my sister Denak, principal wife to the King of Kings as soon as I can, to thank her for her help." Let the eunuch make of that what he would.

Whatever he made of it he concealed, saying as he had before, "I shall take your words to those better able to deal with them than I."

One of the guardsmen in front of the door opened it and gestured for Abivard and his family to go through and enter the suite of rooms set aside for them. Full of misgivings, he went in. The door closed. The rooms had carpets and pillows different from the ones that had been in the suite of the winter before. Other than that, was there any difference from that year to this?

The latch clicked. Abivard opened the door. He stepped out into the corridor. The guards who'd been standing watch when he had gone into the chamber were gone, but the ones who'd taken their place looked enough like them to be their cousins.

He took a couple of steps down the hall. One of the guards came after him; the fellow's mail shirt jingled as he walked. Abivard kept on going. The soldier came after him but did not call him back or try to stop him. It was exactly as the eunuch had said it would be. That left Abivard disconcerted; he wasn't used to having promises from Sharbaraz or his servitors kept.

After a while he turned and asked the guard, "Why are you following me?"

"Because I have orders to follow you," the fellow answered at once. "Don't want you winding up in any mischief, lord, and I don't want you getting lost here, either."

"I can see how I might get lost," Abivard admitted; one palace hallway looked much like another one. "But what sort of mischief am I liable to get into?"

"Don't ask me, lord—I've no idea," the guardsman said with a grin. "I figure anybody can if he tries, though."

"You sound like a man with children," Abivard said, and the

guard laughed and nodded. Seeing the people set to keep an eye on him as ordinary human beings was strange for Abivard.

And then, around a corner, came one who would never have children but who had assuredly gotten Abivard into mischief: the beautiful eunuch who'd escorted him first to his sister and then to Sharbaraz.

He gave Abivard a look of cold indifference. That was one of the friendlier looks Abivard had received from him. Abivard said, "You might thank me."

"Thank you?" The eunuch's voice put Abivard in mind of silver bells. "Whatever for?"

"Because the Videssians didn't burn Mashiz down around your perfect, shell-like ears, for starters," Abivard said.

The beautiful eunuch's skin was swarthy, like that of most Makuraners, but translucent even so; Abivard could watch the tips of those ears turn red. "Had you brought Maniakes' head hither or even sent it on pickled in salt, you might have done something worthy of gratitude," the eunuch said. "As things are, however, I give you—this—as token of my esteem." He turned his back and walked away.

Staring after him, the guard let out a soft whistle. "You put Yeliif's back up—literally, looks like."

"Yeliif?" But Abivard realized who the fellow had to mean. "Is that what his name is? I never knew till now."

"You never knew?" Now the guardsman stared at him. "You made an enemy of Yeliif without knowing what you were doing? Well, the God only knows what you could have managed if you'd really set your mind to it."

"I didn't make him an enemy," Abivard protested. "He made himself an enemy. I never laid eyes on him till the King of Kings summoned me here last winter. If I never lay eyes on him again, I won't be sorry."

"Can't blame you there," the guardsman said, but he dropped his voice as he did it. "Not a drop of human kindness in dear Yeliif, from all I've seen. They say losing their balls makes eunuchs mean. I don't know if that's what bothers him, but mean he is. And it might not matter whether you set eyes on him again or not.

Sooner or later you're going to have to eat some of the food that goes into your room there."

"What?" Abivard said, his wits working more slowly than they should, and then, a moment later, "Oh. Now, that's a cheerful thought."

He didn't think the beautiful eunuch would poison him. Had Yeliif wanted to do that, he could have managed it easily the winter before. Then Sharbaraz probably would have given him anything this side of his stones back for doing the job. Abivard didn't think he was as deeply disgraced now as he had been then. Now the King of Kings might be annoyed rather than relieved at his sudden and untimely demise.

Or, on the other hand, Sharbaraz might not. You never could tell with the King of Kings. Sometimes he was brilliant, sometimes foolish, sometimes both at once—and sorting the one out from the other was never easy. That made living under him . . . interesting.

Someone knocked on the door to the suite in which Abivard and his family were quartered. The winter before that would have produced surprise and alarm, for it was not time for the servants to bring in a meal, being about halfway between luncheon and dinner. Now, though, people visited at odd hours; sometimes Abivard almost managed to convince himself he was a guest, not a prisoner.

He could, for instance, bar the door on the inside. He'd done so the first several days after he'd arrived in Mashiz. After that, though, he gave it up. If Sharbaraz wanted to kill him badly enough to send assassins in after him, he'd presumably send assassins with both the wit and the tools to break down the door. And so, of late, Abivard had left it unbarred. As yet, he also remained unmurdered.

He doubted Sharbaraz would send out a particularly polite assassin, and so he opened the door at the knock with no special qualms. When he discovered Yeliif standing in the hallway, he wondered if he'd made a mistake. But the eunuch was armed with nothing but his tongue—which, while poisonous, was not deadly in and of itself. "For reasons beyond my comprehension and far beyond your desserts," he told Abivard, "you are summoned before Sharbaraz King of Kings, may his days be long and his realm increase."

"I'm coming," Abivard answered, turning to wave quickly to Roshnani. As he closed the door after himself, he asked, "So what are these reasons far beyond your desserts or my comprehension?"

The beautiful eunuch started to answer, stopped, and favored him with a glare every bit as toxic as his usual speech. Without a word, he led Abivard through the maze of hallways toward the throne room.

This time, Abivard not being isolated as if suffering from a deadly and infectious disease, the journey took far less time than it had when he'd finally been summoned into Sharbaraz' presence the winter before. At the entrance to the throne room Yeliif broke his silence, saying, "Dare I hope you remember the required procedure from your last appearance here?"

"Yes, thank you very much, Mother, you may dare," Abivard answered sweetly. If Yeliif was going to hate him no matter what he did, he had no great incentive to stay civil.

Yeliif turned and, back quiveringly straight, stalked down the aisle toward the distant throne on which Sharbaraz sat. Not many nobles attended the King of Kings this day. Those who were there, as best Abivard could guess from their faces, were not anticipating the spectacle of a bloodbath, as the courtiers and nobles emphatically had been the last time Abivard had come before his sovereign.

Yeliif stepped to one side, out of the direct line of approach. Abivard advanced to the paving slab prescribed for prostration and went to his knees and then to his belly to honor Sharbaraz King of Kings. "Majesty," he murmured, his breath fogging the shiny marble of the slab.

"Rise, Abivard son of Godarz," Sharbaraz said. He did not keep Abivard down in a prostration any longer than was customary, as he had in the previous audience. When he spoke again, though, he sounded far from delighted to see his brother-in-law: "We are deeply saddened that you permitted Maniakes and his Videssian bandits not only to inflict grievous damage upon the land of the

Thousand Cities but also, having done so, to escape unharmed, seize one of the towns in the Videssian westlands now under our control, and thence flee by sea to Videssos the city."

He was saddened, was he? Abivard almost said something frank and therefore unforgivable. But Sharbaraz was not going to trap him like that, if such was his aim. Or was he simply blind to mistakes he'd helped make? Would the likes of Yeliif tell him about them? Not likely!

"Majesty, I am also saddened, and I regret my failure," Abivard said. "I rejoice, however, that through the campaigning season Mashiz had no part of danger and remained altogether safe and secure."

Sharbaraz squirmed on the throne. He was vain, but he wasn't stupid. He understood what Abivard didn't say; those unspoken words seemed to echo in the throne room. *You sent me out to find my own ragtag army. You wanted to hold my family hostage while I did it. And now you complain because I didn't bring you Mani- akes weighted down with chains? Be thankful he didn't visit you in spite of everything I did.*

Behind Abivard a faint, almost inaudible hum rose. The court- iers and nobles in the audience could catch those inaudible echoes, too, then.

Sharbaraz said, "When we send a commander out against the foe, we expect him to meet our requirements and expectations in every particular."

"I regret my failure," Abivard repeated. "Your Majesty may of course visit any punishment he pleases upon me to requite that failure."

Go ahead. Are you so blind to honor that you'll torment me for failing to do the impossible? More murmurs said the courtiers had again heard what he had meant along with what he had said. The trouble was, the King of Kings might not have. The only subtleties Sharbaraz was liable to look for were those involving danger to him, which he was apt to see regardless of whether it was real. Kings of Kings often died young, but they always aged quickly.

"We shall on this occasion be clement, given the difficulties with which you were confronted on the campaign," Sharbaraz said. It was as close as he was ever likely to come to admitting he'd been at fault.

"Thank you, Majesty," Abivard said without the cynicism he'd expected to use. Deciding to take advantage of what seemed to be Sharbaraz' good humor, he went on, "Majesty, will you permit me to ask a question?"

"Ask," the King of Kings said. "We are your sovereign; we are not obliged to answer."

"I understand this, Majesty," Abivard said, bowing. "What I would ask is why, if you were not dissatisfied—not too dissatisfied, perhaps I should say—with the way I carried out the campaign in the land of the Thousand Cities this past summer, did you recall me from my army to Mashiz?"

For a moment Sharbaraz did not look like a ruler who used the royal *we* as automatically as he breathed but like an ordinary man taken aback by a question he hadn't looked for. At last he said, "This course was urged upon us by those here at court, that we might examine the reasons behind your failure."

"The chief reason is easy to see," Abivard answered. "We saw it, you and I, when you sent me out against Maniakes last spring: Videssos has a fleet, and we have not. That gives the Avtokrator a great advantage in choosing when and where to strike and in how he can escape. Had we not already known as much, the year's campaign would have shown it."

"Had we had a fleet—" Sharbaraz said longingly.

"Had we had a fleet, Majesty," Abivard interrupted, "I think I should have laid Videssos the city at your feet. Had we had a fleet, I—or Mikhran *marzban*—could have chased Maniakes after he swooped down on Pityos. Had we had a fleet, he might never have made for Pityos, knowing our warships lay between Pityos and the capital. Had we had a fleet—"

"The folk of Makuran are not sailors, though," Sharbaraz said—an obvious truth. "Getting them into a ship is as hard as getting the Videssians out of one, as you no doubt will know better than we."

Abivard's nod was mournful. "Nor do the Videssians leave any ships behind for their fisherfolk to crew for us. They are not fools, the imperials, for they know we would use any ships and sailors against them. Could we but once get soldiers over the Cattle Crossing—" He broke off. He'd sung that song too many times to too many people.

"We have no ships. We are not sailors. Not even our command can make the men of Makuran into what they are not," Sharbaraz said. Abivard dipped his head in agreement. The King of Kings went on. "Somewhere we must find ships." He spoke as if certain his will could conjure them up, all difficulties notwithstanding.

"Majesty, that would be excellent," Abivard said. He'd been saying the same thing since the Makuraner armies had reached the coasts of the Videssian westlands. He'd been saying it loudly since the Makuraner armies had reached the Cattle Crossing, with Videssos the city so temptingly displayed what would have been an easy walk away . . . if men could walk on water, which they couldn't, save in ships. Wanting ships and having them, though, were two different things.

Thinking of ships seemed to make Sharbaraz think of water in other contexts, although he didn't suggest walking on it. He said, "We wish you had not loosed the waters of the canals that cross the land of the Thousand Cities, for the damage the flooding did has reduced the tax revenues we shall be able to gather in this year."

"I regret my failure," Abivard said for the third time. But that wooden repetition of blame stuck in his craw, and he added, "Had I not arranged to open the canals, Maniakes Avtokrator might now be enjoying those extra tax revenues."

Behind him one of the assembled courtiers, against all etiquette, laughed for a moment. In the deep, almost smothering quiet of the throne room that brief burst of mirth was all the more startling. Abivard would not have cared to be the man who had so forgotten himself. Everyone near him would know who he was, and Yeliif would soon learn—his job was to learn of such things, and Abivard had no doubt he was very good at it. When he did . . . Abivard had found out what being out of favor at court was like. He would not have recommended it to his friends.

Sharbaraz' expression was hooded, opaque. "Even if this be

true, you should not say it," he replied at last, and then fell silent again.

Abivard wondered how to take that nearly oracular pronouncement. Did the King of Kings mean he shouldn't publicly acknowledge Videssos' strength? Or did he mean he thought Maniakes would keep whatever Makuraner revenue he got his hands on? Or was he saying that it wasn't true, and even if it was, it wasn't? Abivard couldn't tell.

"I did what I thought best at the time," he said. "I think it did help Maniakes decide he couldn't spend the winter between the Tutub and the Tib. We have till spring to prepare the land of the Thousand Cities against his return, which the God prevent."

"So may it be," Sharbaraz agreed. "My concern is, will he do the same thing twice running?"

"Always a good question, Majesty," Abivard said. "Maniakes has a way of learning from his mistakes that many have said to be unusual."

"So I have heard," Sharbaraz said.

He said nothing about learning from his own mistakes. Was that because he was sure he learned or because he assumed he made no mistakes? Abivard suspected the latter, but some questions not even he had the nerve to put to the King of Kings.

He did press Sharbaraz a little, asking, "Majesty, will you grant me leave to return to the land of the Thousand Cities so I can go back to training the army I raised from the troops you had me gather together last year? I must say I am also anxious at being so far from them when one of my commanders does not enjoy my full confidence."

"What?" Sharbaraz demanded. "Who is that?"

"Tzikas, Majesty—the Videssian," Yeliif answered before Abivard could speak. "The one who helped alert you to unreliability before." *To Abivard's unreliability*, he meant.

Sharbaraz said, "Ah, the Videssian. Yes, I remember now. No, he needs to remain in his place. He is one general who cannot plot against me."

Abivard had had that same thought himself. "As you say, Majesty," he replied. "I do not ask that he be removed. I want only to go and join him and make sure that the cavalry he leads is working well with the infantry from the city garrisons. And just as he keeps an eye on me, I want to keep an eye on him."

"What you want is not my chiefest concern," the King of Kings answered. "I think more of my safety and of the good of Makuran."

In that order, Abivard noted. It wasn't anything he hadn't already understood. In a way, having Sharbaraz come right out and own up to it made things better rather than worse—no pretending now. Abivard said, "Letting the army go soft and its pieces grow apart from each other serves neither of those purposes, Majesty."

Sharbaraz hadn't expected his army to amount to anything. The King of Kings had thrown him and the garrison soldiers at the Videssians in the way a man throws a handful of dirt on a fire when he has no water: in the hope it would do some good, knowing he'd lose little if it didn't. He hadn't expected them to turn into an army, and he hadn't expected the army to seem so important for the battles of the coming campaigning season.

What you expected, though, wasn't always what you got. With Videssian mastery of the sea, Maniakes was liable to land his armies anywhere when spring brought good weather. If he did strike again for the land of the Thousand Cities, that makeshift army Abivard had patched together would be the only force between the Videssians and Mashiz. At that, Sharbaraz would be better off than he had been, for he'd had no shield the year before.

When the King of Kings did not answer right away, Abivard grasped his dilemma. An army worth something as a shield was also worth something as a sword. Sharbaraz did not merely fear Maniakes and the Videssians; he also feared any army Abivard was able to make effective enough to confront the invaders. An army effective enough to do that could threaten Mashiz in its own right.

At last Sharbaraz King of Kings said, "I believe you have officers who know their business. If you did not, you could not have done what you did against the Videssians. They will hold your army together for you until spring comes and the general is needed in the field. So shall it be."

"So shall it be," Abivard echoed, bowing, acquiescing. Sharbaraz still did not trust him as far as he should have, but he did trust him more than he had the winter before. Abivard chose to look on that as progress—not least because looking on it any other way would have made him scream in frustration or despair or rage or maybe all three at once.

He expected the King of Kings to dismiss him after rendering his decision. Instead, after yet another hesitation Sharbaraz said, "Brother-in-law of mine, I am asked by Denak my principal wife—your sister—to tell you that she is with child. Her confinement should come in the spring."

Abivard bowed again, this time in surprise and delight. From what Denak had said, Sharbaraz seldom summoned her to his bedchamber these days. One of those summonses, though, seemed to have borne fruit.

"May she give you a son, Majesty," Abivard said—the usual thing, the polite thing, the customary thing to say.

But nothing was simple, not when he was dealing with Sharbaraz. The King of Kings sent him a hooded look, though what he said—"May the God grant your prayer"—was the appropriate response. Here, for once, Abivard needed no time to figure out how he had erred. The answer was simple: he hadn't.

But Denak's pregnancy complicated Sharbaraz' life. If his principal wife did bear a son, the boy automatically became the heir presumptive. And if Denak bore a boy, Abivard became uncle to the heir presumptive. Should Sharbaraz die, that would make Abivard uncle to the new King of Kings and a very important man, indeed. The prospect of becoming uncle to the new King of Kings might even—probably would in the eyes of the present King of Kings—give Abivard an incentive for wanting Sharbaraz dead.

Almost, Abivard wished Denak would present the King of Kings with another girl. Almost.

Now Sharbaraz dismissed Abivard from the audience. Abivard prostrated himself once more, then withdrew, Yeliif appearing at his side as if by magic as he did so. The beautiful eunuch stayed silent till they left the throne room, and that suited Abivard fine.

Afterward, in the hallway, Yeliif hissed, "You are luckier than you deserve, brother-in-law to the King of Kings." He made Abivard's title, in most men's mouths one of respect, into a reproach.

Abivard had expected nothing better. Bowing politely, he said, "Yeliif, you may blame me for a great many things, and in some of them you will assuredly be right, but that my sister is with child is not my fault."

By the way Yeliif glared at him, everything was his fault. The eunuch said, "It will cause Sharbaraz King of Kings, may his days be long and his realm increase, to forgive too readily your efforts to subvert his position on the throne."

"What efforts?" Abivard demanded. "We went through this last winter, and no one, try as everybody here in Mashiz would, was able to show I've been anything but loyal to the King of Kings, the reason being that I *am* loyal."

"So you say," Yeliif answered venomously. "So you claim."

Abivard wanted to pick him up and smash him against the stone of the wall as if he were an insect to crush underfoot. "Now you listen to me," he snapped, as he might have at a soldier who hesitated to obey orders. "The way you have it set up in your mind is that, if I win victories for the King of Kings, I'm a traitor because I'm too successful and you think the victories are aggrandizing me instead of Sharbaraz, whereas if I lose, I'm a traitor because I've thrown victory away to the enemies of the King of Kings."

"Exactly," Yeliif said. "Precisely."

"Drop me into the Void, then!" Abivard exclaimed. "How am I supposed to do anything right if everything I can possibly do is wrong before I try it?"

"You cannot," the beautiful eunuch said. "The greatest service you could render Sharbaraz King of Kings would be, as you say, to drop into the Void and trouble the realm no more."

"As far as I can tell, the next time I trouble the realm will be the first," Abivard said stubbornly. "And if you ask me, there can be a difference between serving the King of Kings and serving the realm."

"No one asked you," Yeliif said. "That is as well, for you lie."

"Do I?" Such an insult from a whole man would have made Abivard challenge him. Instead, he stopped walking and studied Yeliif. Eunuchs' ages were generally hard to judge, and Yeliif powdered his face, making matters harder yet, but Abivard thought he might be older than he seemed at first glance. Doing his best to sound innocent, he said, "Tell me, were you here in the palace to serve Peroz King of Kings?"

"Yes, I was." Pride rang in Yeliif's voice.

"Ah. How lucky for you." Abivard bowed again. "And tell me, when Smerdis usurped the throne after Peroz died, did you serve him, too, while he held Mashiz and kept Sharbaraz prisoner?"

Yeliif's eyes blazed hatred. He did not reply, which Abivard took to mean he had won the argument. As he realized a moment later, that might have done him more harm than good.

"It's not as bad as it could be," Roshnani said one day about a week after Abivard's audience with the King of Kings.

"No, it's not," Abivard agreed, "although I don't think our children would say that you're right." Even though they could go though the corridors of the palace, the children still felt very much confined. Most of the time that would have been Abivard's chief concern. Now, though, he burst out, "What drives me mad is that it's so useless. Sharbaraz King of Kings, may his years be many and his realm increase—" He generally used the full honorific formula, for the benefit of any unseen listeners. "—has declared his trust in me and admits I did little wrong and much right during the campaigning season just past. I wish he would let me go back to the army I built."

"He trusts you—but he doesn't trust you," Roshnani said with a rueful smile. "That's better than it was, too, but it's not good enough." She raised her voice slightly. "You've shown your loyalty every way a man can." Yes, she, too, was mindful of people who might not even be there but who were noting her words for the King of Kings if they were.

"The only good thing I can see about having to stay here," Abivard said, also pitching his voice to an audience wider than one person, "is that, if the God is kind, I'll get the chance to see my sister and give her my hope for a safe confinement."

"I'd like to see her, too," Roshnani said. "It's been too long, and I didn't get the chance when we were here last winter."

They smiled at each other, absurdly pleased with the game they were playing. It put Abivard in mind of the skits the Videssians performed during their Midwinter's Day festivals, when the players performed not only for themselves but also for the people watching them. Here, though, everything he and his principal wife said was true, only the intonation changing for added effect.

Roshnani went on, "It's not as if I couldn't go through the corridors to see her, either, in the women's quarters or outside them. Thanks to Sharbaraz King of Kings, may his days be long and his realm increase—" No, Roshnani didn't miss a trick, not one. "—women are no longer confined as straitly as they used to be."

Take that, Abivard thought loudly at whatever listeners he and Roshnani had. If there were listeners, they probably would not take it gladly. From all he'd seen, people at the court of the King of Kings hated change of any sort more than anyone else in the world did. Abivard was not enthusiastic about change; what sensible man was? But he recognized that change for the better was possible. Sharbaraz' courtiers rejected that notion out of hand.

"To the Void with them," he muttered, this time so quietly that Roshnani had to lean forward to catch his words. She nodded but said nothing; the unseen audience did not have to know everything that went on between the two principal players.

A couple of days later Yeliif came to the door. To Abivard's surprise, the beautiful eunuch wanted to speak not to him but to Roshnani. As always, Yeliif's manners were flawless, and that made the message he delivered all the more stinging. "Lady," he said, bowing to Roshnani, "for you to be honored by an audience with Denak, principal wife to Sharbaraz King of Kings, is not, cannot be, and shall not be possible, for which reason such requests, being totally useless, should in future be dispensed with."

"And why is that?" Roshnani asked, her voice dangerously calm. "Is it that my sister-in-law does not wish to see me? If she will tell me how I offended her, I will apologize or make any other compensation she requires. I will say, though, that she was not ashamed to stay with me in the women's quarters of Vek Rud domain after Sharbaraz King of Kings made her his principal wife."

That shot went home; Yeliif's jaw tightened. The slight shift of muscle and bone was easily visible beneath his fine, beardless skin. The eunuch answered, "So far as I know, lady, you have not given offense. But we of the court do not deem it fitting for a lady of your quality to expose herself to the stares of the vulgar multitude in her traversal of the peopled corridors of the palace."

Abivard started to explode—he thought Denak and Roshnani had put paid to that attitude, or at least its public expression, years before. But Roshnani's raised hand stopped him before he began. She said, "Am I to understand, then, that my requests to see Denak do not reach her?"

"You may understand whatever you like," Yeliif replied.

"And so may you. Stand aside now, if you please." Roshnani advanced on the beautiful eunuch. Yeliif did stand aside; had he not done so, she would have stamped on his feet and walked over or through him—that was quite plain. She opened the door and started out through it.

"Where are you going?" Yeliif demanded. "What are you doing?" For the first time his voice was less than perfectly controlled.

Roshnani took a step out into the hall, as if she'd decided not to answer. Then, at the last minute, she seemed to change her mind—or maybe, Abivard thought admiringly, she'd planned that hesitation beforehand. She said, "I am going to find Sharbaraz King of Kings, may his years be many and his realm increase, wherever he is, and I am going to put in his ear the tale of how his courtiers seek to play havoc with the new customs for noblewomen he himself, in his wisdom, chose to institute."

"You can't do that!" Now Yeliif sounded not just imperfectly controlled but appalled.

"No? Why can't I? I abide by the customs the King of Kings began; don't you think he'd be interested to learn that you don't?"

"You cannot interrupt him! It is not permitted."

"You cannot keep my messages from reaching Denak, but you do," Roshnani said sweetly. "Why, then, can't I do what cannot be done?"

Yeliif gaped. Abivard felt like snickering. Roshnani's years of living among the Videssians had made her a dab hand at chopping logic into fine bits, as if it were mutton or beef to be made into sausage. The beautiful eunuch wasn't used to argument of that style and plainly had no idea how to respond.

Roshnani gave him little chance, in any case. When she said she would do something, she would do it. She started into the hallway. Yeliif dashed out after her. "Stop her!" he shouted to the guards who were always posted outside the suite of rooms.

Abivard went out into the hall, too. The guards were armored and had spears to his knife. Even so, the only way he would let them lay hands on Roshnani was over his dead body.

But he needn't have worried. One of the soldiers said to Yeliif, "Sir, our orders say she is allowed to go out." He did his best to sound regretful—the eunuch was a powerful figure at court—but couldn't keep amusement from his voice.

Yeliif made as if to grab Roshnani himself but seemed to think better of it at the last minute. That was probably wise on his part; Roshnani made a habit of carrying a small, thin dagger somewhere about her person and might well have taken it into her head to use the knife on him.

He said, "Can we not reach agreement on this, thereby preventing an unseemly display bound to upset the King of Kings?"

Abivard had no trouble reading between the lines there: an unseemly display would leave Yeliif in trouble with Sharbaraz because the eunuch had permitted it to happen. Roshnani saw that, too. She said, "If I am allowed to see Denak today, then very well. If not, I go out searching for the King of Kings tomorrow."

"I accept," Yeliif said at once.

"Don't think to cheat by delaying and getting the guards' orders changed," Roshnani told him, rubbing in her victory. "Do you know what will happen if you try? One way or another I'll manage to get out and go anyway, and when I do, you'll pay double."

The threat was probably idle. The palace was Yeliif's domain, not Roshnani's. Nevertheless, the beautiful eunuch said, "I have made a bargain, and I shall abide by it," and beat a hasty retreat.

Roshnani went back into the chamber. So did Abivard, shutting the door behind him. He did his best to imitate the fanfare horn players blew to salute a general who had won a battle. Roshnani laughed out loud. From the other side of the closed door, so did one of the guardsmen.

"You ground him for flour in the millstones," Abivard said.

"Yes, I did—for today." Roshnani was still laughing, but she also sounded worn. "Will he stay ground, though? What will he do tomorrow? Will I have to go out looking for the King of Kings and humiliate myself if I find him?"

Taking her in his arms, Abivard said, "I don't think so. If you show you're willing to do whatever you have to, very often you end up not needing to do it."

"I hope this is one of those times," Roshnani said. "If the God is kind, she'll grant it be so."

"May he do that," Abivard agreed. "And if not, Sharbaraz King of Kings, may his years be many and his realm increase, will at least have learned that one of his principal servants is a liar and a cheat."

By what Yeliif had said, he'd learned that he and Roshnani did indeed have listeners. With any luck at all, some of them would report straight to the King of Kings.

Abivard had guessed that Yeliif would break his promise, but he didn't. Not long after breakfast the next day he came to the suite of rooms where Abivard and his family were staying and, as warmly as if he and Roshnani had not quarreled the day before, bade her accompany him to see her sister-in-law, "who," he said, "is in her turn anxious to see you."

"Nice to know that," Roshnani said. "If you'd delivered my requests sooner, we might have found out before."

Yeliif stiffened and straightened up, as if a wasp had stung him at the base of the spine. "I thought we might agree to forget yesterday's unpleasantness," he said.

"I may not choose to do anything about it," Roshnani told him, "but I never, ever forget." She smiled sweetly.

The beautiful eunuch grimaced, then shook himself as if using a counterspell against a dangerous sorcery. Maybe that was what he thought he was doing. His manner, which had been warm, froze solid. "If you will come with me, then?" he said.

Roshnani came with condescension that, if it wasn't queenly, would have made a good imitation.

Abivard stayed in the suite and kept his children from injuring themselves and one another. For no visible reason Varaz seemed to have decided Shahin was good for nothing but being punched. Shahin fought back as well as he could, but that often wasn't well enough. Abivard did his best to keep them apart, which wasn't easy. At last he asked Varaz, "How would you like it if I walloped you for no reason at all whenever I felt like it?"

"I don't know what you're talking about," Varaz said. Abivard had heard that tone of voice before. His son meant every word of the indignant proclamation, no matter how unlikely it sounded to Abivard. Varaz wasn't old enough—and was too irked—to be able to put himself in his brother's shoes. But he also knew Abivard would wallop him if he disobeyed, and so desisted.

Worry over Roshnani also made Abivard more likely to wallop Varaz than he would have been were he calm. Abivard, knowing that, tried to hold his temper in check. It wasn't easy, not when he trusted Yeliif not at all. But he could no more have kept Roshnani from going to see Denak than he could have held some impetuous young man out of battle. He sighed, wishing relations between husband and wife could be managed by orders given and received as they were on the battlefield.

Then he wished he hadn't thought of the battlefield. Time seemed elastic now, as it did in the middle of a hot fight. An hour or two seemed to go by; then he looked at a shadow on the floor and realized that only a few minutes had passed. A little later an hour did slide past without his even noticing. Servants startled him when they brought in smoked meats and saffron rice for his luncheon; he'd thought it still midmorning.

Roshnani came back not long after the servitors had cleared

away the dishes. "I wouldn't have minded eating more, though they fed me there," she said, and then, "Ah, they left the wine. Good. Pour me a cup, would you, while I use the pot. Not something you do in the company of the principal wife of the King of Kings, even if she is your sister-in-law." She undid the buckles on her sandals and kicked the shoes across the room, then sighed with pleasure as her toes dug into the rug.

Abivard poured the wine and waited patiently till she got a chance to drink it. Along with wanting to ease herself, she also had to prove to her children that she hadn't fallen off the edge of the world while she had been gone. But finally, wine in hand, she sat down on the floor pillows and got the chance to talk with her husband.

"She looks well," she said at once. "In fact, she looks better than well. She looks smug. The wizards have made the same test with her that Tanshar did with me. They think she'll bear a boy."

"By the God," Abivard said softly, and then, "May it be so."

"May it be so, indeed," Roshnani agreed, "though there are some here at court who would sing a different song. I name no names, mind you."

"Names?" Abivard's voice was the definition of innocence. "I have no idea who you could mean." Off in a corner of the room the children were quarreling again. Instead of shouting for them to keep quiet as he usually would have, Abivard was grateful. He used their racket to cover his own quiet question: "So her bitterness is salved, is it?"

"Some," Roshnani answered. "Not all. She wishes—and who could blame her?—this moment had come years before." She spoke so softly, Abivard had to bend so his head was close to hers.

"No one could blame her," he said as softly. But he had a harder time than usual blaming Sharbaraz here. The King of Kings could pick and choose among the most beautiful women of Makuran. Given that chance, should anyone have been surprised he took advantage of it?

Roshnani might have been thinking along with him, for she said, "The King of Kings needs to get an heir for the realm on his principal wife if he can, just as a *dihqan* needs to get an heir for his domain. Failing in this is neglecting your plain duty."

"It's more enjoyable carrying out some duties than others," Abivard observed, which won him a snort from Roshnani. He went on, "What news besides that of the coming boy?" The wizards' predictions weren't always right, but maybe speaking as if they were would help persuade the God to let this one be.

"Denak notes she will have more influence over the King of Kings for the next few months than she has enjoyed lately," Roshnani said; in her voice Abivard could hear echoes of his sister's weary, disappointed tones. "How long this lasts afterward will depend on how wise the wizards prove to be. May the lady Shivini prove them so."

Now Abivard echoed her: "Aye, may that be so." Then he remembered the six squabbling sorcerers he'd assembled in Nashvar. If he'd needed a curative for the notion that mages were always preternaturally wise and patient, they'd given him one.

Roshnani said, "Your sister thinks Sharbaraz will soon give you leave to go back to your command in the land of the Thousand Cities."

"It's not really the command I want," Abivard said. "I want to be back at the head of the field force and take it into the Videssian westlands again. If we're on the move there, maybe we can keep Maniakes from attacking the Thousand Cities this year." He paused and laughed at himself. "I'm trying to spin moonshine into thread, aren't I? I'll be lucky to have any command at all; getting the one I particularly want is too much to ask."

"You deserve it," Roshnani said, her voice suddenly fierce.

"I know I do," he answered without false modesty. "But that has only so much to do with the price of wine. What does Tzikas deserve? To have his mouth pried open and molten lead poured down his gullet by us and the Videssians both. What will he get? The way to bet is that he'll get to die old and happy and rich, even if nobody on whichever side of the border on which he ends up trusts him as far as I could throw him. Where's the justice there?"

"He will drop into the Void and be gone forever while you spend eternity in the bosom of the God," Roshnani said.

"That's so—or I hope that's so," Abivard said. It did give him some satisfaction, too; the God was as real to him as the pillow on which he sat. But— "I won't see him drop into the Void, and where's the justice *there*, after what he's done to me?"

"That I can't answer," his principal wife said with a smile. She held up a forefinger. "But Denak said to tell you to remember your prophecy whenever you feel too downhearted."

Abivard bowed low as he sat, bending almost double. He would never see a silver shield shining across a narrow sea if he remained commander in the land of the Thousand Cities. "I may have been wrong," he said humbly. "There may be some use to foretelling, after all. Knowing I *will* see what was foretold lets me bear up under insults meanwhile."

"Under some insults, for some time, certainly," Roshnani replied. "But Tanshar didn't say when you would see these things. You're a young man still; it might be thirty years from now."

"It might be," Abivard agreed. "I don't think it is, though. I think it's connected to the war between Makuran and Videssos. That's what everything about it has seemed to mean. When it comes, whatever it ends up meaning, it will decide the war, one way or the other." He held up a hand, palm out. "I don't know that for a fact, but I think it's true even so."

"All right," Roshnani said. "You should also know you're going back to the land of the Thousand Cities for a while, because you didn't see the battle Bogorz' scrying showed you."

"That's true; I didn't," Abivard admitted. "Or I don't think I did, anyhow. I don't remember seeing it." The frown gave way to a sheepish laugh. "Is it a true prophecy if it happens but no one notices?"

"Take that one to the Videssians," Roshnani said. "They'll spend so much time arguing over it, they won't be ready to invade us when the campaigning season starts."

By her tone of voice, she was only half joking. From his time spent among the Videssians, Abivard thoroughly understood that. If a problem admitted of two points of view, some Videssians would take the one and some the other, as far as he could tell for the sake of disputation. And if a problem admitted of only one point of view, some Videssians would take that and some the other, again for the sake of disputation.

Roshnani said, "If we understand the prophecies rightly, you'll beat Maniakes in the land of the Thousand Cities. If you don't beat him there, you won't have the chance to go back into the Videssian westlands and draw near Videssos the city, now, will you?"

"I don't see how I would, anyhow," Abivard said. "But then, I don't see everything there is to see, either."

"Do you see that for once you worry too much?" Roshnani said. "Do you see that?"

Abivard held up his hand again, and she stopped. Genuine curiosity in his voice, he said, "*Could* Sharbaraz have ordered me slain last winter? Could I have died with the prophecies unfulfilled? What would have happened if he'd given the order? Could the headsman have carried it out?"

"There's another question the Videssians would exercise themselves over for years," Roshnani answered. "All I can tell you is that I not only don't know, I'm glad we didn't have to find out. If you have to hope for a miracle to save yourself, you may not get it."

"That's true enough," Abivard said. The children's game broke down in a multisided squabble raucous enough to make him get up and restore order. He kept on wondering, though, all the rest of the day.

VIII

IF YOU WERE GOING TO BE IN THE LAND OF THE THOUSAND Cities, the very beginning of spring was the time to do it. The weather hadn't yet grown unbearably hot, the flies and mosquitoes weren't too bad, and a steady breeze from the northwest helped blow smoke away from the cities instead of letting it accumulate in foglike drifts, as could happen in the still air of summer.

Beroshesh, the city governor of Nashvar, did a magnificent job of concealing his delight at Abivard's return. "Are you going to flood us out again?" he demanded, and then, remembering his manners, added, "Lord?"

"I'll do whatever needs doing to drive the Videssians from the domain of Sharbaraz King of Kings, may his years be many and his realm increase," Abivard answered. Casually, he asked, "Have you heard the news? Sharbaraz' principal wife is with child, and the wizards believe it will be a boy."

"Congratulations are due her, I'm sure, but why do you—?" Beroshesh stopped the rather offhanded question as he remembered who Sharbaraz' principal wife was and what relation she held to Abivard. When he spoke again, his tone was more conciliatory: "Of course, lord, I shall endeavor to conform to any requirements you may have of me."

"I knew you would," Abivard lied politely. Then, finding a truth he could tell, he went on, "Turan and Tzikas both tell me you have done well in keeping the army supplied through the winter."

"Even with the ravages of the Videssians, the land of the Thousand Cities remains rich and fertile," Beroshesh said. "We had no trouble supplying the army's wants."

"So I heard, and as I say, I'm glad of it," Abivard told him. The floodplain was indeed rich and fertile if, even after all the damage it had suffered through the previous year, it still yielded surplus enough to feed the army on top of the peasantry.

"What do you expect Maniakes to do this season?" Beroshesh asked. "Will he come here at all? Will he come from north or south or straight out of the east?"

"Good question," Abivard said enthusiastically, making as if to applaud. "If you should have a good answer for it, please let me know. Whichever way he comes, though, I'll fight him. Of that I'm sure." He hesitated. "Fairly sure." He couldn't know for certain the scrying Bogorz had shown him would come to pass in this campaigning season, but that did seem to be the way to bet.

Beroshesh said, "Lord, you have been fighting this Maniakes for many years. Do you not know in your mind what will be in his?"

That was a legitimate question. In fact, it was better than a legitimate question; it was a downright clever question. Abivard gave it the careful thought it deserved before answering, "My best guess is that he'll do whatever he doesn't think we'll expect him to do. Whether that means setting out from Lyssaion again or picking a new way to get at us, I can't really tell, I fear. Trying to fathom the way Videssians think is like looking into several mirrors reflecting one from another, so that after a while what's reflection and what's real blur together."

"If the God be kind, the barbarians who infest his—southern—frontier, is it?" Beroshesh hesitated.

"Northern frontier," Abivard said, not unkindly. There was no reason for a city governor to have any clear notion of Videssian geography, especially for the lands on the far side of the imperial capital.

"Yes, the northern frontier. Thank you, lord. If they were to attack Maniakes, he could hardly assail us here and defend against them at the same time, could he?"

"It's not something I'd want to try, I'll tell you that," Abivard said. "Yes, the God would be kind if he turned the Kubratoi—that's what the barbarians call themselves—loose on Videssos again. The only trouble is, Maniakes beat them badly enough to make them thoughtful about having another go at him."

"Pity," Beroshesh murmured. He clapped his hands loudly. "How much you know about these distant peoples! Surely you and they must have worked together closely when you forced your way to the very end of the Videssian westlands."

"I wish we would have," Abivard said. No, Beroshesh didn't know much about how the Empire of Videssos was made and how it operated. "But Videssos the city, you see, kept the Kubratoi from crossing over to join us, and the Videssian navy not only kept us from going over the Cattle Crossing to lay siege to the city, it also kept the Kubratoi from going over to the westlands in the boats they make. Together, we might have crushed Videssos, but Maniakes and his forces and fortress held us apart."

"Pity," Beroshesh said again. He pointed to a silver flagon. "More wine?"

It was date wine. "No, thank you," Abivard said. He would drink a cup for politeness' sake but had never been fond of the cloying stuff.

Quite seriously Beroshesh asked, "Could you not put your soldiers on barges and in skin boats and cross this Cattle Crossing without the Videssians' being the wiser till you appeared on the far shore?"

Beroshesh had never seen the sea, never seen a Videssian war galley. Abivard remembered that as he visualized a fleet of those swift, maneuverable, deadly galleys descending on rafts and round skin boats trying to make their way over the Cattle Crossing. He saw in his mind's eye rams sending some of them to the bottom and dart-throwers and fire-throwers wrecking many more. He might get a few men across alive, but even fewer in any condition to fight; he was all too sure of that.

Out of respect for Beroshesh's naïveté, he didn't laugh in the city governor's face. All he said was, "That has been discussed, but no one seems to think it would turn out well."

"Ah," Beroshesh said. "Well, I didn't want to take the chance that you'd overlooked something important."

Abivard sighed.

"Lord!" A member of the city garrison of Nashvar came running up to Abivard. "Lord, a messenger comes with news of the Videssians."

"Thank you," Abivard said. "Bring him to me at once." The guardsman bowed and hurried away.

Waiting for his return, Abivard paced back and forth in the room Beroshesh had returned to him when he had come back to Nashvar. Soon, instead of having to guess, he would know how Maniakes intended to play the game this year and how he would have to respond.

The soldier came back more slowly than he'd hoped, leading the messenger's horse. The messenger probably would have gotten there sooner without the escort, but after so long a wait, a few minutes mattered little, and the member of the garrison got to enjoy his moment in the light.

Bowing low to Abivard, the messenger cried, "Lord, the Videssians come down from the north, from the land of Erzerum, where treacherous local nobles let them land and guided them through the mountains so they could descend on the land of the Thousand Cities!"

"Down from the north," Abivard breathed. Had he bet on which course Maniakes would take, he would have expected the Avtokrator to land in the south and move up from Lyssaion once more. He knew nothing but relief that he'd committed no troops to backing his hunch. He wouldn't have to double back against his foe's move.

"I have only one order for the city governors in the north," he told the messenger, who poised himself to hear and remember it. "That order is, *Stand fast!* We will drive the invaders from our soil."

"Aye, lord!" the messenger said, and dashed off, his face glowing with inspiration at Abivard's ringing declaration. Behind him Abivard stood scratching his head, wondering how he was going to turn that declaration into reality. Words were easy. Deeds mattered more but were harder to produce on the spur of the moment.

The first thing that needed doing was reassembling the army. He sent messengers to the nearby cities where he'd billeted portions of his infantry. The move would undoubtedly delight the governors of those cities and just as undoubtedly dismay Beroshesh, for it would mean Nashvar would have to feed all his forces till they moved against Maniakes.

As the soldiers from the city garrisons whom Abivard had hastily gathered together the spring before began returning to Nashvar, they found ways to let him know they were glad he was back to command them. It wasn't that they obeyed him without grumbling; the next army to do that for its leader would be the first. But whether they grumbled or not, they did everything he asked of them and did it promptly and well.

And they kept bringing tidbits here and tidbits there to the cook who made the meals for him and Roshnani and their children, so that they ended up eating better than they had at the palace in Mashiz. "It's almost embarrassing when they do things like this," Abivard said, using a slender dagger to spear from its shell a snail the cook had delicately seasoned with garlic and ginger.

"They're fond of you," Roshnani said indignantly. "They ought to be fond of you. Before you got hold of them, they were just a bunch of tavern toughs—hardly anything better. You made an army out of them. They know it, and so do you."

"Well, put that way, maybe," Abivard said. A general whom his men hated wouldn't be able to accomplish anything. That much was plain. A general whom his men loved . . . was liable to draw the watchful attention of the King of Kings. Abivard supposed that was less an impediment for him than it might have been for some other marshals of Makuran. He already enjoyed—if that was the word—Sharbaraz' watchful attention.

Seeing how much better at their tasks the soldiers were than they had been the spring before gratified Abivard as much as their affection did. He'd done his job and given them the idea that they could go out and risk maiming and death for the good of a cause they didn't really think about. He sometimes wondered whether to be proud or ashamed of that.

Sooner than he'd hoped, he judged the army ready to use against Maniakes. Sharbaraz King of Kings had been right in thinking the officers Abivard had left behind could keep the men in reasonably good fighting trim. That pleased Abivard and irked him at the same time: was he really necessary?

Turan and Tzikas were getting along well, too. Again, Abivard didn't know what to make of that. Had the Makuraner succumbed to Tzikas' charm? Abivard would have been the last to deny that the Videssian renegade had his full share of that—and then some.

"He's a fine cavalry officer," Turan said enthusiastically after he, Tzikas, and Abivard planned the move they'd be making in a couple of days. "Having commanded a cavalry company myself, I was always keeping an eye on the officers above me, seeing how they did things. Do you know what I mean, lord?" He waited for Abivard to nod, then went on, "And Tzikas, he does everything the way it's supposed to be done."

"Oh, that he does." Abivard's voice was solemn. "He's a wonderful officer to have for a superior. It's only when you're *his* superior that you have to start watching your back."

"Well, yes, there is that," Turan agreed. "I hadn't forgotten about it. Just like you, I made sure I had his secretary in my belt pouch, so a couple of letters never did travel to Mashiz."

"Good," Abivard said. "And good for you, too."

However much Abivard loathed him, Tzikas had done a fine job making the cavalry under his command work alongside the infantry. That wasn't how the men of Makuran usually fought. Light cavalry and heavy horse worked side by side, but infantry was at best a scavenger on the battlefields where it appeared. Those were few and far between; in most fights cavalry faced cavalry.

"I didn't think Videssian practice so different from our own," Abivard remarked after watching the horsemen practice a sweep from the flank of the foot soldiers. "Or to put it another way, you didn't fight against us like this when you were on the other side in the westlands."

"By the God, I am a Makuraner now," Tzikas insisted. But then his pique, if it had been such, faded. "No, Videssians did not fight that way. Cavalry rules their formations no less than ours." He was playing the role of countryman to the hilt, Abivard thought. Thoughtfully, the renegade went on, "I've just been wondering how best to use the two arms together now that you and Turan have made these infantrymen into real soldiers. This is the best answer I found."

Abivard nodded—warily. He heard the flattery there: not laid on as thickly as was the usual Videssian style but perhaps more effective on account of that. Or it would have been more effective had he not suspected everything Tzikas said. Didn't Tzikas understand that? If he did, he concealed it well.

And he had other things on his mind, too, saying, "This year we'll teach Maniakes not to come into Makuran again."

"I hope so," Abivard said; that had the twin virtues of being true and of not committing him to anything.

He moved the army out of Nashvar a few days later. Beroshesh had assembled the artisans and merchants of the town to cheer the soldiers on their way. How many of those were cheers of good luck and how many were cheers of good riddance, Abivard preferred not to try to guess.

Along with the chorus of what might have been support came another, shriller, altogether unofficial chorus of the women and girls of the town, many with visibly bulging bellies. That sort of thing, Abivard thought with a mental sigh, was bound to happen when you quartered soldiers in a town over a winter. Some lemans were accompanying the soldiers as they moved, but others preferred to stay with their families and scream abuse at the men who had helped make those families larger.

Scouts reported that Maniakes and the Videssians were moving southwest from Erzerum toward the Tib River and leaving behind them the same trail of destruction they'd worked the year before. Scouts also reported that Maniakes had more men with him than he'd brought on his first invasion of Makuran.

"I have to act as if they're right and hope they're wrong,"

Abivard said to Roshnani when the army camped for the night. "They often are—wrong, I mean. Take a quick look at an army from a distance and you'll almost always guess it's bigger than it is."

"What do you suppose he plans?" Roshnani asked. "Fighting his way down the Tib till he can strike at Mashiz?"

"If I had to guess, I'd say yes," Abivard answered, "but guessing what he has in mind gets harder every year. Still, though, that would be about the second worst thing I can think of for him to do."

"Ah?" His principal wife raised an eyebrow. "And what would be worse?"

"If he struck down the Tib and at the same time sent envoys across the Pardrayan steppe to stir up the Khamorth tribes against us and send them over the Degird River into the northwest of the realm." Abivard looked grim at the mere prospect. So did Roshnani. Both of them had grown up in the Northwest, not far from the frontier with the steppe. Abivard went on, "Likinios played that game, remember—Videssian gold was what made Peroz King of Kings move into Pardraya, what made him meet his end, what touched off our civil war. Couple that with the Videssian invasion of the land of the Thousand Cities and—"

"Yes, that would be deadly dangerous," Roshnani said. "I see it. We'd have to divide our forces, and we might not have enough to be able to do it."

"Just so," Abivard agreed. "Maniakes doesn't seem to have thought of that ploy, the God be praised. When Likinios used it, he didn't think to invade us himself at the same time. From what I remember of Likinios, he was always happiest when money and other people's soldiers were doing his fighting for him."

"Maniakes isn't like that," Roshnani said.

"No, he'll fight," Abivard said, nodding. "He's not as underhanded as Likinios was, but he's learning there, too. As I say, I'm just glad he hasn't yet learned everything there is to know."

Hurrying west across the floodplain from the Tutub to the Tib brought Abivard's army across the track of devastation Maniakes had left the summer before. In more than one place he found peasants repairing open-air shrines dedicated to the God and the Prophets Four that the Videssians had made a point of wrecking.

"He had some men who spoke Makuraner," one of the rural artisans told Abivard. "He had them tell us he did this because of what Makuran does to the shrines of his stupid, false, senseless god. He pays us back, he says."

"Thank you, Majesty," Abivard murmured under his breath. Once again Sharbaraz' order enforcing worship of the God in Vaspurakan was coming back to haunt Makuran. The peasant stared at Abivard, not following what he meant. If the fellow hoped for an explanation, he was doomed to disappointment.

Tzikas' horsemen rode ahead of the main force, trying to let Abivard know where the Videssians were at any given time. Every so often the cavalry troopers would skirmish with Maniakes' scouts, who were trying to pass to the Avtokrator the same information about Abivard's force.

And then, before too long, smoke on the northern horizon said the Videssians were drawing close. Tzikas' scouts confirmed that they were on the eastern bank of the Tib; they'd been either unwilling or unable to cross the river. Abivard took that as good news. He would, however, have liked it better had he had it from men who owed their allegiance to anyone but Tzikas.

Because Maniakes was staying on the eastern side of the Tib, Abivard sent urgent orders to the men in charge of the bridges of boats across the river to withdraw those bridges to the western bank. He hoped that would help him but did not place sure trust in the success of the ploy: being skilled artificers, the Videssians might not need boats to cross the river.

But Maniakes, who had not gone out of his way to look for a fight the summer before, seemed more aggressive now, out not just to destroy any town in the land of the Thousand Cities but also to collide with the Makuraner army opposing him.

"I think the scouts are right—they do have more men than they did last year," Turan said unhappily. "They wouldn't be pushing so hard if they didn't."

"Whereas we still have what we started last year with—minus casualties, whom I miss, and plus Tzikas' regiment of horse, whom I wouldn't miss if they fell into the Void this minute," Abivard said, Tzikas not being in earshot to overhear. "Now we get to find out whether that will be enough."

"Oh, we can block the Videssians," Turan said, "provided they don't get across to the far side of the river. If they do—"

"They complicate our lives," Abivard finished for him. "Maniakes has been complicating my life for years, so I have no reason to think he'll stop now." He paused thoughtfully. "Come to that, I've been complicating his life for a good many years now, too. But I intend to be the one who comes out on top in the end." After another pause he went on. "The question is, Does he intend to do any serious fighting this year, or is he just raiding to keep us off balance, the way he was last summer? I think he really wants to fight, but I can't be certain—not yet."

"How will we know?" Turan asked.

"If he gets across the river somehow—and he may, because the Videssians have fine engineers—he's out to harass us like last year," Abivard answered. "But if he comes straight at us, he thinks he can beat us with the new army he's put together, and it'll be up to us to show him he's wrong."

Turan glanced at the long files of foot soldiers marching toward the Tib. They were lean, swarthy men, some in helmets, some in baggy cloth caps, a few with mail shirts, most wearing leather vests or quilted tunics to ward off weapons, almost all of them with wicker shields slung over their shoulders, armed with spears or swords or bows or, occasionally, slings. "He's not the only one who's put a new army together," Abivard's lieutenant said quietly.

"Mm, that's so." Abivard studied the soldiers, too. They seemed confident enough, and thinking you could hold off a foe was halfway to doing it. "They've come a long way this past year, haven't they?"

"Aye, lord, they have," Turan said. He looked down at his hands before going on. "They've done well learning to work with cavalry, too."

"Learning to work with Tzikas' cavalry, you mean," Abivard said, and Turan, looking uncomfortable, nodded. Abivard sighed. "It's for the best. If they didn't know what to do, we'd be in a worse position than we are now. If only Tzikas weren't commanding that regiment of horse, I'd be happy."

"He was—harmless enough this past winter," Turan said, giving what praise he could.

"For which the God be praised," Abivard said. "But he's wronged me badly, and he knows it, which might tempt him to betray me to the Videssians. On the other hand, he tried to kill Maniakes, so he wouldn't be welcomed back with open arms, not unless the Avtokrator of the Videssians is stupider than I know he is. How badly would Tzikas have to betray me, do you suppose, to put himself back into Maniakes' good graces?"

"It would have to be something spectacular," Turan said. "I don't think betraying you would be coin enough to do the job, truth to tell. I think he'd have to betray Sharbaraz King of Kings himself, may his years be many and his realm increase, to buy Maniakes' favor once more."

"How would Tzikas betray the King of Kings?" Abivard said, gesturing with his right hand to turn aside the evil omen. Then he held up that hand. "No, don't tell me if you know of a way. I don't want to think about it." He stopped. "No, if you know of a way, you'd better say you do. If you can think of one, without a doubt Tzikas can, too."

"I can't, the God be praised," Turan said. "But that doesn't mean Tzikas can't."

Abivard positioned his men along the Tib, a little north of one of the boat bridges drawn up on the far side of the river. If the Videssians did seek to cross to the other side, he hoped he could either get across himself in time to block them or at least pursue and harass them on the western side.

But Maniakes showed no intention of either crossing to the west bank or swinging east and using the superior speed with which his army could move to get around Abivard's force. His scouts came riding down to look over the position Abivard had established and then, after skirmishing once more with Tzikas' horsemen, went galloping back to give the Videssian Avtokrator the news.

Two days later the whole Videssian army came into sight just after the first light of day. With trumpets and drums urging them to ever greater speed, Abivard's troops formed their battle line. Abivard had Tzikas' horsemen on his right flank and split the infantry in which he had the most confidence in two, stationing half his best foot soldiers in the center and the other half closest to the Tib to anchor the line's left.

For some time the two armies stood watching each other from beyond bowshot. Then, without Abivard's order, one of the warriors from Tzikas' regiment rode out into the space between them. He made his horse rear, then brandished his lance at the Videssians as he shouted something Abivard couldn't quite make out.

But he didn't need to understand the words to know what the warrior was saying. "He's challenging them to single combat!" Abivard exclaimed. "He must have watched that Vaspurakaner who challenged Romezan the winter before last."

"If none of them dares come out or if this fellow wins, we gain," Turan said. "But if he loses—"

"I wish Tzikas hadn't let him go forth," Abivard said. "I—"

He got no further than that, for a great shout arose from the Videssian ranks. A mounted man came galloping toward the Makuraner, who couched his lance and charged in return. The Videssian's mail shirt glittered with gilding. So did his helm, which also, Abivard saw, had a golden circlet set on it.

"That's Maniakes!" he exclaimed in a hoarse voice. "Has he gone mad to risk so much on a throw of the dice?"

The Avtokrator had neither lance nor javelin, being armed instead with bow and arrows and a sword that swung from his belt. He shot at the Makuraner, reached over his shoulder for another arrow, set it in his bow, let fly, and grabbed for yet another shaft. He'd shot four times before his foe came close.

At least two, maybe three, of the shafts went home, piercing the Makuraner champion's armor. The fellow was swaying in the saddle when he tried to spear Maniakes off his horse. The lance stroke missed. The Avtokrator of the Videssians drew his sword and slashed once, twice, three times. His foe slipped off his horse and lay limp on the ground.

Maniakes rode after the Makuraner's mount, caught it by the reins, and began to lead it back toward his own line. Then, almost as an afterthought, he waved toward the Makuraner cavalry and toward the fallen champion. *Pick him up if you like,* he said with gestures.

He spoke the Makuraner tongue. He might have said that to his opponents with words, but his own men were cheering so loudly, no words would have been heard. As he rejoined his soldiers, a couple of Makuraners rode out toward the man who had challenged the Videssian army. The imperials did not attack them. They heaved the beaten man up onto one of their horses and rode slowly back to their position on the right.

"If Maniakes didn't kill that fellow, we ought to take care of the job," Turan said.

"Isn't that the sad and sorry truth?" Abivard agreed. "All right—he was brave. But he couldn't have done us more harm than by challenging and losing, not if he tried to murder you and me both in the middle of the battle. It disheartened us—and listen to the Videssians! If they were still wondering whether they could beat us, they aren't anymore."

He wondered whether Tzikas hadn't set up the whole thing. Could the Videssian renegade, despite his fervent protestations of loyalty and his worship of the God, have urged a warrior forward while sure he would lose, in the hope of regaining favor back in Videssos? The answer was simple: of course he could. But the next question—would he?—required more thought.

He had everything he could want in Makuran—high rank, even the approval of Sharbaraz King of Kings. Why would he throw that away? The only answer that occurred to Abivard was the thrill that had to go with treason successfully brought off. He shook his head. Videssians were connoisseurs of all sorts of subtle refinements, but could one become a connoisseur of treason? He didn't think so. He hoped not.

Abivard got no more time to think about it, for as soon as the cavalrymen had returned with their would-be champion, horns sounded up and down the Videssian line. The imperials rode forward in loose order and began plying the Makuraners with arrows, as they had at the battle by the canal the summer before.

As before, Abivard's men shot back. He waved. Horns rang out on his army's right wing. He had cavalry now. Were they loyal? They were: Tzikas' men thundered at the Videssians.

Maniakes must have been expecting that. After the fact, Abivard realized he'd advertised it in his deployment—but given the position he had had to protect, he'd found himself with little choice.

A regiment of Videssians, armed with their usual bows and javelins, peeled off from the left wing of Maniakes' army and rode to meet the Makuraners. Being less heavily armed and armored than Tzikas' horsemen, the Videssians could not stop their charge in its tracks as a countercharge by a like number of Makuraners might well have done. But they did blunt it, slow it, and keep it from smashing into their comrades on the flank. That let the rest of the Videssians assail Abivard's foot soldiers.

Maniakes' men did not hold back as they had in the battle by the canal. Then they'd wanted to keep the Makuraners in play till their fellows could circle around and hit Abivard's force from an unexpected direction. Now they were coming straight at Abivard and the assembled city garrison troops, plainly confident that no such army could long stand in their way.

Because they wore mail shirts and their foes mostly did not, their archery was more effective than that of Abivard's men. They drew close enough to ply the front ranks of the Makuraners with javelins and hurt them doing it.

"Shall we rush at them, lord?" Turan shouted above the screams and war cries of the fight.

Abivard shook his head. "If we do that, we're liable to open up holes in our line, and if they once pour into holes like that, we're done for. We just have to hope we can stand the pounding."

He wished Maniakes hadn't overthrown the Makuraner champion. That had to have left his own men glum and the Videssians elated. But when you were fighting for your life, weren't you too busy to worry about what had happened a while ago? Abivard hoped so.

When arrows and javelins failed to make the Makuraners break and run, the Videssians drew swords and rode straight into the line Abivard had established. They slashed down at their enemies on foot; some of them tried to use their javelins as the Makuraner heavy horse used lances.

The Makuraners fought back hard not only against Maniakes' men but also against the horses they rode. Those poor beasts were not armored like the ones atop which Tzikas' men sat; they were easy to slash and club and shoot. Their blood splashed on the ground with that of their riders; their screams rose to the sky with those of wounded men on both sides.

Abivard rushed reserves to a dangerously thin point in the line. He had tremendous pride in his troops. This was not a duty they'd expected to have a year before. They were standing up to the Videssians like veterans. Some of them were veterans now; by the end of the battle they'd all be veterans.

"Don't let them through!" Abivard shouted. "Stand your ground!"

Rather to Abivard's surprise, they stood their ground and kept standing it. Maniakes did have more men with him than he'd brought the year before, but Tzikas' cavalry regiment neutralized a good part of his increased numbers. The rest were not enough to force a breakthrough in Abivard's line.

The stalemate left Abivard tempted to attack in turn, allowing openings to develop in his position in the hope of trapping a lot of Videssians. He had little trouble fighting down the temptation. He found it too easy to imagine himself on the other side of the battlefield, looking for an opportunity. If Maniakes spotted one, he'd take full advantage of it. Abivard knew that. Most important, then, was not giving the Avtokrator the chance.

As fights had a way of doing, this one seemed to go on forever. Had the sun not shown him it was but midafternoon, Abivard would have guessed the battle had lasted three or four days. Then, little by little, Videssian pressure eased. Instead of attacking, Maniakes' men broke contact and rode back toward the north, back the way they had come. Tzikas' men made as if to pursue—the foot soldiers could hardly do so against cavalry—but a shower of arrows and a fierce countercharge said the Videssians remained in good order. The pursuit quickly stalled.

"By the God, we threw them back," Turan said in tones of wonder.

"By the God, so we did." Abivard knew he sounded as surprised as his lieutenant. He couldn't help that. He *was* surprised.

Maybe his soldiers were surprised, and maybe they weren't. Surprised or not, they knew what they'd accomplished. Above and through the moans of the wounded and the shriller shrieks of hurt horses rose a buzz that swelled to a great cheer. The cheer had but one word: "Abivard!"

"Why are they shouting my name?" he demanded of Turan. "They're the ones who did it."

His lieutenant looked at him. "Sometimes, lord, you can be too modest."

The soldiers evidently thought so. They swarmed around Abivard, still calling his name. Then they tried to pull him down from his horse, as if he were a Videssian to be overcome. Turan's expression warned him he had better yield to the inevitable. He let his feet slide out of the stirrups. As Turan leaned over and grabbed hold of his horse's reins, he let himself slide down into the mass of celebrating soldiers.

They did not let him fall. Instead, they bore him up so he rode above them on a stormy, choppy sea of hands. He waved and shouted praise the foot soldiers didn't hear because they were all shouting and because they were passing him back and forth so everyone could carry him and have a go at dropping him.

At last he did slip down through the sea of hands. His feet touched solid ground. "Enough!" he cried; being upright somehow put fresh authority in his voice. Still shouting his praises, the soldiers decided to let him keep standing on his own.

"Command us, lord!" they shouted. A man standing near Abivard asked, "Will we go after the Videssians tomorrow?" Somewhere in the fighting a sword had lopped off the fleshy bottom part of his left ear; blood dried black streaked that side of his face. He didn't seem to notice.

Abivard suffered a timely coughing fit. When he did answer, he said, "We have to see what they do. The trouble is, we can't move as fast as they do, so we have to figure out where they're going and get there first."

"You'll do that, lord!" the soldier missing half an ear exclaimed. "You've done it already, lots of times."

Twice, to Abivard's way of thinking, didn't constitute lots of times. But the garrison troops were cheering again and shouting for him to lead them wherever they were supposed to go. Since he'd been trying to figure out how to bring about exactly that effect, he didn't contradict the wounded man. Instead he said, "Maniakes wants Mashiz. Mashiz is what he's wanted all along. Are we going to let him have it?"

"No!" the soldiers yelled in one great voice.

"Then tomorrow we'll move south and cut him off from his goal," Abivard said. The soldiers shouted louder than ever. If he'd told them to march on Mashiz instead of defending it, he thought they would have done just that.

He shoved the idea down into some deep part of his mind where he wouldn't have to think about it. That wasn't hard. The aftermath of battle had given him plenty to think about. They'd fought, the Videssians had retreated, and now his men were going to retreat, too. He wondered if there had ever been a battlefield before where both sides had abandoned it as soon as they could.

The secretary was a plump, fastidious little man named Gyanarspar. More than a bit nervously, he held out a sheet of parchment to Abivard. "This is the latest the regimental commander Tzikas has ordered me to write, lord," he said.

Abivard quickly read through the letter Tzikas had addressed to Sharbaraz King of Kings. It was about what he might have thought Tzikas would say but not what he'd hoped. The Videssian renegade accused him of cowardice for not going after Maniakes' army in the aftermath of the battle by the Tib and suggested that a different leader—coyly unnamed—might have done more.

"Thank you, Gyanarspar," Abivard said. "Draft something innocuous to take the place of this tripe and send it on its way to the King of Kings."

"Of course, lord—as we have been doing." The secretary bowed and hurried out of Abivard's tent.

Behind him Abivard kicked at the dirt. Tzikas made a fine combat soldier. If only he'd been content with that! But no, not Tzikas. Whether in Videssos or in Makuran, he wanted to go straight to the top, and to get there he'd give whoever was ahead of him a good boot in the crotch.

Well, his spiteful bile wasn't going to get to Sharbaraz. Abivard had taken care of that. The silver arkets he lavished on Gyanarspar were money well spent as far as he was concerned. The King of Kings hadn't tried joggling his elbow nearly so much or nearly so hard since Abivard had started making sure the scurrilous things Tzikas said never reached his ear.

Gyanarspar, the God bless him, didn't aspire to reach the top of anything. Some silver on top of his regular pay sufficed to keep him sweet. Abivard suddenly frowned. How was he to know whether Tzikas was also bribing the secretary to let his letters go out as he wrote them? Gyanarspar might think it clever to collect silver from both sides at once.

"If he does, he'll find he's made a mistake," Abivard told the wool wall of the tent. If Sharbaraz all at once started sending him more letters full of caustic complaint, Gyanarspar would have some serious explaining to do.

At the moment, though, Abivard had more things to worry about than the hypothetical treachery of Tzikas' secretary. Maniakes' presence in the land of the Thousand Cities was anything but hypothetical. The Avtokrator hadn't tried circling around Abivard's forces and striking straight for Mashiz, as had been Abivard's greatest worry. Instead, Maniakes had gone back to his tactics of the summer before and was wandering through the land between the Tutub and the Tib, destroying everything he could.

Abivard kicked at the dirt yet again. He couldn't chase Maniakes over the floodplain any more than he could have pursued him after the battle by the Tib. He didn't know what he was supposed to do. Was he to travel back to Nashvar and have the contentious local wizards break the banks of the canals again? He was less convinced than he had been the year before that that would accomplish everything he wanted. He also knew Sharbaraz would not thank him for any diminution in revenue from the land of the Thousand Cities. And two years of flooding in a row were liable to put the peasants in an impossible predicament. They weren't highest on his list of worries, but they were there.

Sitting there and doing nothing did not appeal to him, either. He might be protecting Mashiz where he was, but that didn't do the rest of the realm any good. While he kept Maniakes from falling on the capital with fire and sword, the Avtokrator visited them upon other cities instead. Sharbaraz' realm was being diminished, not increasing, while that happened.

"I can keep Maniakes from breaking past me and driving into Mashiz," Abivard said to Roshnani that night. "I think I can do that, at any rate. But keep him from tearing up the land of the Thousand Cities? How? If I venture out against him, he *will* break around me, and then I'll have to chase his dust back to the capital."

For a moment he was tempted to do just that. If Maniakes put paid to Sharbaraz, the King of Kings wouldn't be able to harass him anymore. Rationally, he knew that wasn't a good enough reason to let the realm fall into the Void, but he was tempted to be irrational.

Roshnani said, "If you can't beat the Videssians with what you have here, can you get what you need to beat them somewhere else?"

"I'm going to have to try to do that, I think," Abivard replied. If his principal wife saw the same possible answer to his question that he saw himself, the chance that answer was right went up a good deal. He went on, "I'm going to send a letter to Romezan, asking him to move the field force out of Videssos and Vaspurakan and to bring it back here so we can drive Maniakes away. I hate to do that—I know it's what Maniakes wants me to do—but I don't see that I have any choice."

"I think you're right." Roshnani hesitated, then asked the question that had to be asked: "What will Sharbaraz think, though?"

Abivard grimaced. "I'll have to find out, won't I? I don't intend to ask him for permission to recall Romezan; I'm going to do that on my own. But I will write him and let him know what I've done.

If he wants to badly enough, he can countermand my order. I know just what I'll do if he does that."

"What?" Roshnani asked.

"I'll lay down my command and go back to Vek Rud domain, by the God," Abivard declared. "If the King of Kings isn't satisfied with the way I defend him, let him choose someone who does satisfy him: Tzikas, maybe, or Yeliif. I'll go back to the Northwest and live out my days as a rustic *dihqan*. No matter how far Maniakes goes into Makuran, he'll never, ever reach the Vek Rud River."

He waited with some anxiety to see how Roshnani would take that. To his surprise and relief, she shoved aside the plates off which they'd eaten supper so she could lean over on the carpet they shared and give him a kiss. "Good for you!" she exclaimed. "I wish you would have done that years ago, when we were in the Videssian westlands and he kept carping because you couldn't cross to attack Videssos the city."

"I felt as bad about that as he did," Abivard said. "But it's only gotten worse since then. Sooner or later everyone has a breaking point, and I've found mine."

"Good," Roshnani said again. "It would be fine to get back to the Northwest, wouldn't it? And even finer to get out from under a master who's abused you too long."

"He'd still be my sovereign," Abivard said. But that wasn't what Roshnani had meant, and he knew it. He wondered how well his resolve would hold up if Sharbaraz put it to the test.

The letters went out the next day. Abivard thought about delaying the one to Sharbaraz, to present the King of Kings with troop movements too far along for him to prevent when he learned of them. In the end Abivard decided not to take that chance. It would give Yeliif and everyone else at court who was not well inclined toward him a chance to say he was secretly gathering forces for a move of his own against Mashiz. If Sharbaraz thought that and tried to recall him, it might force him to move against Mashiz, which he did not want to do. As far as he was concerned, beating Videssos was more important.

"All I want," he murmured, "is to ride my horse into the High

Temple in Videssos the city and to see the expression on the patriarch's face when I do."

When he'd spent a couple of years in Across, staring over the Cattle Crossing at the Videssian capital, that dream had seemed almost within his grasp. Now here he was with his back against the Tib, doing his best to keep Maniakes Avtokrator from storming Mashiz. War was a business full of reversals, but going from the capital of the Empire of Videssos to that of Makuran in the space of a couple of years felt more like an upheaval.

"Ships," he said, turning the word into a vile curse. Had he had some, he would long since have ridden in triumph into Videssos the city. Had Makuran had any, Maniakes would not have been able to leap the length of the Videssian westlands and bring the war home to the land of the Thousand Cities. And after a moment's reflection, he found yet another reason to regret Makuran's lack of a navy: "If I had a ship, I could put Tzikas on it and order it sunk."

That bit of whimsy kept him happy for an hour, until Gyanarspar came into his tent with a parchment in his hand and a worried expression on his face. "Lord, you need to see this and decide what to do with it," he said.

"Do I?" If Abivard felt any enthusiasm for the proposition, he concealed it even from himself. But he held out his hand, and Gyanarspar put the parchment into it. He read Tzikas' latest missive to the King of Kings with incredulity that grew from one sentence to the next. "By the God!" he exclaimed when he was through. "About the only thing he doesn't accuse me of is buggering the sheep in the flock of the King of Kings."

"Aye, lord," Gyanarspar said unhappily.

After a bit of reflection Abivard said, "I think I know what brought this on. Before, his letters to Sharbaraz King of Kings, may his days be long and his realm increase, got action—action against me. This year, though, the letters haven't been getting through to Sharbaraz. Tzikas must think that they have—and that the King of Kings is ignoring them. And so he decided to come up with something a little stronger." He held his nose. This letter, as far as he was concerned, was strong in the sense of stale fish.

"What shall we do about it, lord?" Gyanarspar asked.

"Make it disappear, by all means," Abivard said. "Now, if we could only make Tzikas disappear, too."

Gyanarspar bowed and left. Abivard plucked at his beard. Maybe he could sink Tzikas even without a ship. He hadn't wanted to before, when the idea had been proposed to him. Now— Now he sent a servant to summon Turan.

When his lieutenant stepped into the tent, he greeted him with, "How would you like to help make the eminent Tzikas a hero of Makuran?"

Turan was not the swiftest man in the world, but he was a long way from the slowest. After a couple of heartbeats of blank surprise his eyes lit up. "I'd love to, lord. What have you got in mind?"

"That scheme you had a while ago still strikes me as better than most: finding a way to send him out with a troop of horsemen against a Videssian regiment. When it's over, I'll be very embarrassed I used such poor military judgment."

Turan's predatory smile said all that needed saying there. But then the officer asked, "What changed your mind, lord? When I suggested this before, you wouldn't hear me. Now you like the idea."

"Let's just say Tzikas has been making a little too free with his opinions," Abivard answered, at which Turan nodded in grim amusement. Abivard turned practical: "We'll need to set this up with the Videssians. When we need to, we can get a message to them, isn't that right?"

"Aye, lord, it is," Turan said. "If we want to exchange captives, things like that, we can get them to hear us." He smiled again. "For the chance of getting their hands on Tzikas, after what he tried to do to Maniakes, I think they'll hear us, as a matter of fact."

"Good," Abivard said. "So do I. Oh, yes, very good indeed. You will know and I will know and our messenger will know, and a few Videssians, too."

"I don't think they'd give us away, lord," Turan said. "If things were a little different, they might, but I think they hate Tzikas worse than you do. If they can get their hands on him, they'll keep quiet about hows and whys."

"I think so, too," Abivard said. "But there is one other person I'd want to know before the end."

"Who's that?" Turan sounded worried. "The more people who know about a plot like this, the better the chance it'll go wrong."

" 'Before the end,' I said," Abivard replied. "Don't you think it would be fitting if Tzikas figured out how he'd ended up in his predicament?"

Turan smiled.

After swinging away from the Tib to rampage through the floodplain, Maniakes' army turned back toward the west, as if deciding it would attack Mashiz after all. Abivard spread his own force out along the river to make sure the Videssians could not force a crossing without his knowing about it.

He spread his cavalry particularly wide, sending the horsemen out not only to scout against the Videssians but also to nip at them with raids. Tzikas was like a whirlwind, now here, now there, always striking stinging blows against the countrymen he'd abandoned.

"He *can* fight," Abivard said grudgingly one evening after the Videssian had come in with a couple of dozen of Maniakes' men as prisoners. "I wonder if I really should—"

Roshnani interrupted him, her voice very firm: "Of course you should. Yes, he can fight. Think of all the other delightful things he can do, too."

His resolve thus stiffened, Abivard went on setting up the trap that would give Tzikas back to the Videssians. Turan had been right: once his messenger met Maniakes', the Avtokrator proved eager for the chance to get his hands on the man who had nearly toppled him from his throne.

When the arrangements were complete, Abivard sent most of Tzikas' cavalry force under a lieutenant against a large, ostentatious Videssian demonstration to the northeast. "That should have been my mission to command," Tzikas said angrily. "After all this time and all this war against the Videssians, you still don't trust me not to betray you."

"On the contrary, eminent sir," Abivard replied. "I trust you completely."

Against a Makuraner that would have been a safe reply. Tzikas, schooled in Videssian irony, gave Abivard a sharp look. Abivard was still kicking himself when, as if on cue in a Videssian Midwinter's Day mime show, a messenger rushed up, calling, "Lords, the imperials are breaking canals less than a farsang from here!" He pointed southeast, though a low rise obscured the Videssians from sight.

"By the God," Tzikas declared, "I shall attend to this." Without paying Abivard any more attention, he hurried away. A few minutes later, leading the couple of hundred heavy horsemen left in camp, he rode off, the red-lion banner of Makuran fluttering at the head of his force.

Abivard watched him go with mingled hope and guilt. He still wasn't altogether pleased at the idea of getting rid of Tzikas this way, no matter how necessary he found it. And he knew Makuraners would suffer in the trap Maniakes was setting. He hoped they would make the Videssians pay dearly for every one of them they brought down.

But most of all he hoped the scheme would work.

Only a remnant of the cavalry troop came back later that afternoon. A good many of the warriors who did return were wounded. One of the troopers, seeing Abivard, cried out, "We were ambushed, lord! As we engaged the Videssians who were wrecking the waterway, a great host of them burst out of the ruins of a village nearby. They cut us off and, I fear, had their way with us."

"I don't see Tzikas," Abivard said after a quick glance up and down the battered column. "What happened to him? Does he live?"

"The Videssian? I don't know for certain, lord," the soldier answered. "He led a handful of men on a charge straight into the heart of the foe's force. I didn't see him after that, but I fear the worst."

"May the God have given him a fate he deserved," Abivard

said, a double-edged wish if ever there was one. He wondered if Tzikas had attacked the Videssians so fiercely to try to make them kill him instead of taking him captive. Had he done to Maniakes what Tzikas had done, he wouldn't have wanted the Avtokrator to capture him.

The next day Tzikas' Makuraner lieutenant, a hot-blooded young hellion named Sanatruq, returned with most of the cavalry regiment after having beaten back the large Videssian movement. He was very proud of himself. Abivard was proud of him, too, but rather less so: he knew Maniakes had made the movement to draw out most of the Makuraner cavalry so that, when Tzikas led out the rest, he would face overwhelming odds.

"He was overwhelmed?" Sanatruq said in dismay. "Our lord? It is sad—no, it is tragic! How shall we carry on without him?" He reached down to the ground, pinched up some dust, and rubbed it on his face in mourning.

"I give the regiment to you for now," Abivard said. "Should the God grant that Tzikas return, you'll have to turn it over to him, but I fear that's not likely."

"I shall avenge his loss!" Sanatruq cried. "He was a brave leader, a bold leader, a man who fought always at the fore, in the days when he was against us and even more after he was with us."

"True enough," Abivard said; it was likely to be the best memorial Tzikas got. Abivard wondered what Maniakes was having to say to the man who'd tried to murder him with magic. He suspected it was something Tzikas would remember for the rest of his life, however long—or short—that turned out to be.

Whatever Maniakes was saying to Tzikas, he wasn't staying around the Tib to do it. He went back into the central region of the land of the Thousand Cities, doing his best to make Abivard's life miserable in the process. Abivard had had a vague hope that the cooperation between the Avtokrator and himself over Tzikas might make a broader truce come about, but that didn't happen. Both he and the Avtokrator had wanted to be rid of the Videssian renegade, and that had let them work together in ways they couldn't anywhere else.

Sanatruq proved to have all the energy Tzikas had had as a

cavalry commander but less luck. The Videssians beat back his raids several times in a row, till Abivard almost wished he had Tzikas back again.

"Don't say that!" Roshnani exclaimed one day when he was irked enough to complain out loud. Her hand moved in a gesture designed to turn aside evil omens. "You know you'd go for his throat if he chanced to walk in here right now."

"Well, so I would," Abivard said. "All right, then, I don't wish Tzikas to come walking into the tent right now."

That was true enough. He did want to find out what had happened to the Videssian renegade, though. Had he fallen in the fight where he'd unexpectedly been so outnumbered, or had he fallen into Maniakes' hands instead? If he was a captive, what was Maniakes doing with—or to—him now?

When the Videssians had invaded the land of the Thousand Cities, they hadn't brought all the laborers and servants they'd needed. Instead, as armies will, they'd taken men from the cities to do their work for them and rewarded those men with not enough food and even less money. They'd also ended up with the usual number of camp followers.

Laborers and camp followers were not permanent parts of an army, though. They came and went—or sometimes they stayed behind as the army came and went. Abivard ordered his men to bring in some of them so he could try to learn Tzikas' fate.

And so, a few days later, he found himself questioning a small, swarthy woman in a small, thin shift that clung to her wherever she would sweat—and in summer in the land of the Thousand Cities, there were very few places a woman or even a man would not sweat.

"You say you saw them bring him into the Videssian camp?" Abivard asked. He put the question in Videssian first and only afterward in Makuraner. The woman, whose name was Eshkinni, had learned a fair amount of the language of the Empire (and who could say what else?) in her time in the invaders' camp but used the tongue of the floodplain, of which Abivard knew a bare handful of words, in preference to Makuraner.

Eshkinni tossed her head, making the fancy bronze earrings she wore clatter softly. She had a necklace of gaudy glass beads and more bronze bangles on her arms. "I to see him, that right," she said. "They to drag him, they to curse him with their god, they to say Avtokrator to do to him something bad."

"You are sure this was Tzikas?" Abivard persisted. "Did you hear them say the name?"

She frowned, trying to remember. "I to think maybe," she said. She wiggled a little and stuck out her backside, perhaps hoping to distract him from her imperfect memory. By the knowing look in her eye, some time as a camp follower probably hadn't taught her much she hadn't already known.

Abivard, however, cared nothing for the charms she so calculatingly flaunted. "Did Maniakes come out and see this captive, whatever his name was?"

"Avtokrator? Yes, he to see him," Eshkinni said. "Avtokrator, I to think Avtokrator old man. But he not old . . . not too old. Old like you, maybe."

"Thank you so much," Abivard said. Eshkinni nodded as if his gratitude had been genuine. He couldn't be properly sardonic in a language not his own, even if Videssian was made for shades of irony. And he thought she had seen Maniakes; the Avtokrator and Abivard really were about of an age. He tried another question: "What did Maniakes say to the captive?"

"He to say he to give him what he have to come to him," Eshkinni answered. Abivard frowned, struggling through the freshet of pronouns and infinitives, and then nodded. Had he had Tzikas in front of him, he would have said very much the same thing, though he probably would have elaborated on it a good deal. For that matter, Maniakes might well have elaborated on it; Abivard realized that Eshkinni wasn't giving him a literal translation.

He asked, "Did Maniakes say what he thought Tzikas had coming to him?" He itched to know, an itch partly gleeful, partly guilty.

But Eshkinni shook her head. Her earrings clinked again. Her lip curled; she was plainly bored with this whole proceeding. She tugged at her shift not to get rid of the places where it clung to her but to emphasize them. "You to want?" she asked, twitching her hip to leave no possible doubt about what she was offering.

"No, thank you," Abivard said politely, though he felt like exclaiming, *By the God, no!* Polite still, he offered an explanation: "My wife is traveling with me."

"So?" Eshkinni stared at him as if that had nothing to do with anything. In her eyes and in her experience, it probably didn't. She went on. "Why for big fancy man to have only one wife?" She sniffed as an answer occurred to her. "To be same reason you no to want me, I to bet. You no to have beard, I to wonder if you a—" She couldn't come up with the Videssian word for *eunuch* but made crotch-level cutting motions to show what she meant.

"No," Abivard said, sharply now. But she had done him a service, so he reached into a pouch he wore on his belt and drew from it twenty silver arkets, which he gave her. Her mood improved on the instant; it was far more than she would have hoped to realize by opening her legs for him.

"You to need to know any more things," she declared, "you to ask me. I to find out for you, you to best believe I to do." When she saw Abivard had nothing more to ask her then, she walked off, rolling her haunches. Abivard remained unstirred by the charms thus advertised, but several of his troopers appreciatively followed Eshkinni with their eyes. He suspected she might enlarge upon her earnings.

Later that day he asked Turan, "What would you do if you had Tzikas in your clutches?"

His lieutenant gave a pragmatic answer: "Cast him in irons so he couldn't escape, then get drunk to celebrate."

Abivard snorted. "Aside from that, I mean."

"If I found a pretty girl, I might want to get laid, too," Turan said, and then, grudgingly, seeing the warning on Abivard's face, "I suppose you mean after that. If I were Maniakes, the next thing I'd do would be to squeeze him dry about whatever he'd done while he was here. After that I'd get rid of him, fast if he'd done a good job of singing, slow if he hadn't—or maybe slow on general principles."

"Yes, that sounds reasonable," Abivard agreed. "I suspect I'd do much the same myself. Tzikas has it coming, by the God." He thought for a minute or so. "Now we have to tell Sharbaraz what happened without letting him know we made it happen. Life is never dull."

He learned how true that was a few days later, when one of his cavalry patrols came across a westbound rider dressed in the light tunic of a man from the land of the Thousand Cities. "He didn't sit his horse quite the way most of the other folk here do, so we thought we'd look him over," the soldier in charge of the patrol said. "And we found—this." He held out a leather message tube.

"Did you?" Abivard turned to the captured courier, asking in Videssian, "And what is—this?"

"I don't know," the courier answered in the same language; he was one of Maniakes' men, sure enough. "All I know is that I was supposed to get through your lines and carry it to Mashiz, then bring back Sharbaraz' answer if he had one."

"Were you?" Abivard opened the tube. Save for being stamped with the sunburst of Videssos rather than Makuran's lion, it seemed ordinary enough. The rolled-up parchment inside was sealed with scarlet wax, an imperial prerogative. Abivard broke the seal with his thumbnail.

He read Videssian, but haltingly; he moved his lips, sounding out every word. "Maniakes Avtokrator to Sharbaraz King of Kings: Greetings," the letter began. A string of florid salutations and boasts followed, showing that the Videssians could match the men of Makuran in such excess as well as in war.

After that, though, Maniakes got down to cases faster than most Makuraners would have. In his own hand—which Abivard recognized—he wrote, "I have the honor to inform you that I am holding as a captive and condemned criminal a certain Tzikas, a renegade formerly in your service, whom I had previously condemned. For the capture of this wretch I am indebted to your general Abivard son of Godarz, who, being as vexed by Tzikas' treacheries as I have been myself, arranged to have me capture him and dispose of him. He shall not be missed when he goes, I assure you. He—"

Maniakes went on at some length to explain Tzikas' iniquities.

Abivard didn't read all of them; he knew them too well. He crumpled up the parchment and threw it on the ground, then stared at it in genuine, if grudging, admiration. Maniakes had more gall than even he'd expected. The Avtokrator had used him to help get rid of Tzikas and now was using Sharbaraz to help get rid of him because of Tzikas! If that wasn't effrontery, Abivard didn't know what was.

And only luck had kept the plan from working or at least had delayed it. If the Videssian courier had ridden more like a local—

Abivard picked up the sheet of parchment, unfolded it as well as he could, and summoned Turan. He translated the Videssian for his lieutenant, who did not read the language. When he was through, Turan scowled and said, "May he fall into the Void! What a sneaky thing to do! He—"

"Is Avtokrator of the Videssians," Abivard interrupted. "If he weren't sneaky, he wouldn't have the job. My father could go on for hours at a time about how devious and underhanded the Videssians were, and he—" He stopped and began to laugh. "Do you know, I can't say whether he ever had anything more to do with them than skirmishing against them. But however he knew or heard, he was right. You can't trust the Videssians when your eye's not on them, nor sometimes when it is."

"You're too right there." Now Turan laughed, though hardly in a way that showed much mirth. "I wish Maniakes were out of the land of the Thousand Cities. Then my eye wouldn't be on him."

Later that evening Roshnani found a new question to ask: "Did Maniakes' letter to the King of Kings actually come out and say he was going to put Tzikas to death?"

"It said he wouldn't be missed when he went," Abivard answered after a little thought. "If that doesn't mean the Avtokrator is going to kill him, I don't know what it does mean."

"You're right about that," Roshnani admitted, sounding for all the world like Turan. "The only trouble is, I keep remembering the Videssian board game."

"What has that got to do with—?" Abivard stopped. While he'd liked that game well enough during the time he had lived in Across, he'd hardly thought of it since leaving Videssian soil. One salient feature—a feature that made the game far more complex and difficult than it would have been otherwise—was that captured pieces could return to the board, fighting under the banner of the player who had taken them.

Abivard had used Tzikas exactly as if he were a board-game piece. For as long as the Videssian renegade had been useful to Makuran after failing to assassinate Maniakes, Abivard had hurled him against the Empire he'd once served. Once Tzikas was no longer useful, Abivard had not only acquiesced in but arranged his capture. But that didn't necessarily mean he was gone for good, only that Videssos had recaptured him.

"You don't suppose," Abivard said uneasily, "Maniakes would give him a chance to redeem himself, do you? He'd have to be crazy, not just foolish, to take a chance like that."

"So he would," Roshnani said. "Which doesn't mean he wouldn't try it if he thought he could put sand in the axles of our wagon."

"If Tzikas does fight us, he'll fight as if he thinks the Void is a short step behind him—and he'll be right," Abivard said. "If he's not useful to Maniakes, he's dead." He rubbed his chin. "I'm still more worried about Sharbaraz."

IX

"LORD," THE MESSENGER SAID WITH A BOW AS HE PRESENTED the message tube, "I bring you a letter from Sharbaraz King of Kings, may his years be many and his realm increase."

"Thank you," Abivard lied, taking the tube. As he opened it, he reflected on what he'd said to Roshnani a few days before. When you were more worried about what your own sovereign would do to hamstring your campaign than you were about the enemy, things weren't going as you had hoped when you'd embarked on that campaign.

He broke the seal, unrolled the parchment, and began to read. The familiar characters and turns of phrase of his own language were a pleasant relief after struggling through the Videssian intricacies of the dispatch from Maniakes he'd intercepted before it could get to Sharbaraz.

He waded through the list of Sharbaraz' titles and pretensions with amused resignation. With every letter, the list got longer and the pretensions more pretentious. He wondered when the King of Kings would simply declare he was the God come down to earth and let it go at that. It would save parchment, if nothing else.

After the bombast Sharbaraz got down to the meat: "Know that we are displeased you have presumed to summon our good and loyal servant Romezan from his appointed duties so that he might serve under you in the campaign against the usurper Maniakes. Know further that we have sent under our seal orders to Romezan, commanding him in no way to heed your summons but to continue on the duties upon which he had been engaged prior to your illegal, rash, and foolish communication."

"Is there a reply, lord?" the messenger asked when Abivard looked up from the parchment.

"Hmm? Oh." Abivard shook his head. "Not yet, anyhow. I have the feeling Sharbaraz King of Kings has a good deal more to say to me than I can answer right at this moment."

He read on. The next chunk of the letter complained about his failure to drive the Videssians out of the land of the Thousand Cities and keep them from ravaging the floodplain between the Tutub and the Tib. He wished he were in a building of brick or sturdy stone, not a tent. That would have let him pound his head against a wall. Sharbaraz didn't care for what was going on now but didn't want him to do anything about it, either. *Lovely*, he thought. *No matter what I do, I end up getting blamed.* He'd seen that before, too, more times than he cared to remember.

"Know also," Sharbaraz wrote, "that we are informed you not only let the general Tzikas fall into the hands of the foe but also connived at, aided, and abetted his capture. We deem this an act both wretched and contemptible and one for which only a single justification and extenuation may be claimed: which is to say, your success against the Videssians without Tzikas where you failed with him. Absent such success during this campaigning season, you shall be judged most harshly for your base act of betrayal."

Abivard let out a sour laugh there. He was being blamed for betraying Tzikas, oh yes, but had Tzikas ever been blamed for betraying him? On the contrary—Tzikas had found nothing but favor with the King of Kings. And Sharbaraz had ordered him to go out and win victories or face the consequences, all without releasing Romezan's men, who might have made such victory possible.

"Have you a reply, lord?" the messenger asked again.

The one that came to mind was scatological. Abivard suppressed it. With Maniakes in the field against him, he had no time for fueling a feud with the King of Kings, especially since in such a feud he was automatically the loser unless he rebelled, and if he started a civil war in Makuran, he handed not only the land of the Thousand Cities but also Vaspurakan to the Empire of Videssos. He understood that from direct experience: Makuran held the Videssian westlands because of the Empire's descent into civil war during Genesios' reign.

"Lord?" the messenger repeated.

"Yes, I do have a reply," Abivard said. He called for a servant to fetch parchment, pen, and ink. When he got them, he wrote his own name and Sharbaraz', then meticulously copied all the titles with which the King of Kings adorned himself—he didn't want Yeliif or someone like him imputing disloyalty because of disrespect. When that was finally done, halfway down the sheet, he got to his real message: *Majesty, I will give you the victory you desire even if you do not give me the tools I need to make it.* He signed his name, rolled up the message, and stuffed it into the tube. He did not care whether the messenger read it.

When the fellow had ridden off, Abivard turned and looked west toward the Dilbat Mountains and Mashiz. Half of him wished he had the letter back; he knew he'd promised more than he could deliver and knew he would be punished for failing to deliver. But the other half of him did not care. The promise aside, he'd told Sharbaraz nothing but the truth, a rarity in the palace at Mashiz. He wondered if the King of Kings would recognize it when he heard it.

He told Roshnani what he'd done. She said, "It's not enough. You said you would resign your command if Sharbaraz countermanded your order to Romezan. He has." She cocked her head to one side and waited to hear how he would answer.

"I know what I said." He didn't want to meet her eye. "Now that it's happened, though . . . I can't. I wish I could, but I can't. Talking of it was easy. Doing it—" Now he waited for the storm to burst on his head.

Roshnani sighed. "I was afraid you would find that was so." She smiled wryly. "To tell you the truth, I thought you would find that was so. I wish you hadn't. You have to beat Maniakes once to make the King of Kings shut up, and that won't be easy. But you have to do it anyway, so I don't see you've made yourself any worse off in Mashiz than you were already."

"That's what I thought," Abivard said, grateful that his wife was accepting his change of heart with no more than private disappointment. "That's what I hoped, at any rate. Now I have to figure out how to give myself the best chance of making my boast come true."

Maniakes seemed to have given up on the notion of assaulting Mashiz and was going through the land of the Thousand Cities as he had the year before, burning and destroying. Flooding the plain between the Tutub and the Tib had proved less effective than Abivard had hoped. If he was going to stop the Videssians, he'd have to move against them and fight them where he could.

He left the encampment along the Tib with a certain amount of trepidation, sure that Sharbaraz would interpret his move as leaving Mashiz uncovered. He was, though, so used to being in the bad graces of the King of Kings that making matters a little worse no longer worried him as much as it once had.

He wished he had more cavalry. His one effort to use Tzikas' regiment as a major force in its own right had been at best a qualified success. If he tried it again, Maniakes was all too likely to anticipate his move and pinch off and destroy the regiment.

"You can't do the same thing to Maniakes twice running," he told Turan, as if his lieutenant had disagreed with him. "If you do, he'll punish you for it. Why, if we had another traitor to feed him, we'd have to do it a different way this time, because he'd suspect a trap if we didn't."

"As you say, lord," Turan answered. "And what new stratagem will you use to surprise and dazzle him?"

"That's a good question," Abivard said. "I wish I had a good answer to give you. Right now the best I can think of is to close with him—if he'll let us close with him—and see what sorts of chances we get."

To make sure the Videssians did not take him by surprise, he decided to use his cavalry not so much as an attacking force but as screens and scouts, sending riders much farther out ahead of his main body of foot soldiers than usual. Sometimes he thought more of them were galloping back and forth with news and orders than were actually keeping track of Maniakes' army, but he found he had no trouble staying informed about where the Videssians were going and even, after he'd been watching them for a while, guessing what they were liable to do next. He vowed to shadow his foes more closely in future fights, too.

Maniakes' force did not move as quickly as it might have. Every day Abivard drew closer. Maniakes did not turn and offer battle but made no move to avoid it, either. He might have been saying, *If you're sure this is what you want, I'll give it to you.* Abivard still wondered that the Videssians had such confidence; he was used to imperial armies that fled before his men.

The only exception to that rule, he remembered with painful irony, had been the men under Tzikas' command. But the army Abivard commanded now, he silently admitted, was only a shadow of the striking force he'd once led. And the Videssians had gotten used to the idea that they could win battles. He knew how much difference that made.

He began putting his horsemen into larger bands to skirmish with the Videssians. If Maniakes would accept battle, he intended to give it to the Avtokrator. His foot soldiers, having stood up to Maniakes' cavalry twice, were loudly certain they could do it again. He would let them have their chance. If he didn't fight the Videssians, he had no hope of beating them.

After a few days of small-scale clashes he drew his army up in a battle line on gently rising ground not far from Zadabak, one of the Thousand Cities, inviting an attack if Maniakes cared to make it. And Maniakes, sure enough, brought the Videssians up close to look over the Makuraner position and camped for the night close enough to make it clear he intended to fight when morning came.

Abivard spent much of the night exhorting his soldiers and making final dispositions for the battle to come. His own disposition was somewhere between hopeful and resigned. He was going to make the effort to drive the Videssians from the land of the Thousand Cities. If the God favored him, he would succeed. If not, he would have done everything he could with the force Sharbaraz had allowed him. The King of Kings might blame him but would have trouble doing so justly.

When morning came, Abivard scowled as his troops rose from their bedrolls and went back into line. They faced east, into the rising sun, which meant the Videssians had the advantage of the light, being able to see his forces clearly instead of having to squint against glare. If the fight quickly went against the Makuraners, that would be an error over which Sharbaraz would have every right to tax him.

He summoned Sanatruq and said, "We have to delay the general engagement till the sun is higher in the sky."

The cavalry commander gauged the light and nodded. "You want me to do something about that, I take it."

"Your men can move about the field faster than the foot soldiers, and they're lancers, not archers; the sun won't bother them so much," Abivard answered. "I hate to ask you to make a sacrifice like that—I feel almost as if I'm ... betraying you." He'd almost said *treating you as I did Tzikas.* But Sanatruq didn't know about that, and Abivard didn't want him to learn. "I wish we had more cavalry, too."

"So do I, lord," Sanatruq said feelingly. "For that matter, I wish we had more infantry." He waved toward the slowly forming line, which was not so long as it might have been. "But we do what we can with what we have. If you want me to throw my men at the Videssians, I'll do it."

"The God bless you for your generous spirit," Abivard said, "and may you—may we all—come through safe so you can enjoy the praise you will have earned."

Sanatruq saluted and rode off to what was left of his regiment. Moments later they trotted toward the ranks of the Videssians. As they drew near, they lowered their lances and went from trot up to thunderous gallop. The Videssians' response was not so swift as it might have been; perhaps Maniakes did not believe the small force would attack his own till the charge began.

Whatever the reason, the Makuraner heavy horse penetrated deep into the ranks of the Videssians. For a few shining moments Abivard, who was peering into the sun, dared to hope that the surprise assault would throw his enemies into such disorder that they would withdraw or at least be too shaken to carry out the assault they'd obviously intended.

A couple of years before he probably would have been right, but no more. The Videssians took advantage of their superior numbers to neutralize the advantage the Makuraners had in armor for men and horses and in sheer weight of metal. The imperials did not shrink from the fight but carried on with a businesslike competence that put Abivard in mind of the army Maniakes' father had led to the aid of Sharbaraz King of Kings during the last years of the reign of the able but unlucky and unloved Avtokrator Likinios.

Sanatruq must have known, or at least quickly seen, that he had no hope of defeating the Videssians. He fought on for some time after that had to have become obvious, buying the foot soldiers in Abivard's truncated battle line the time needed so that the archers would no longer be hampered by shooting straight into the sun.

When at last the choice was continuing the unequal struggle to the point of destruction or pulling back and saving what he could of his force, the cavalry commander did pull back, but more toward the north than to the west, so that if Maniakes chose to pursue, he could do so only by pulling men away from the force with which he wanted to assail Abivard's line of infantrymen.

To Abivard's disappointment, Maniakes did not divide his force in that way. The Avtokrator had learned the trick or acquired the wisdom of concentrating on what he really wanted and not frittering away his chances of gaining it by going after three other things at the same time. Abivard wished his foe would have proved more flighty.

Horns blaring, the Videssians moved across the plain and up the gently sloping ground against Abivard's men. The horsemen plied Abivard's soldiers with arrows, raising their shields to ward themselves from the Makuraners' reply. Here and there a Videssian or a horse would go down, but only here and there. More lightly armed infantrymen were pierced than their opponents.

Some Videssians, brandishing javelins, rode out ahead of their main force. They pelted Abivard's men with the throwing spears from close range. He itched to order his troops forward against them but deliberately restrained himself. Infantry charging cavalry opened gaps into which the horsemen could force their way, and if they did that, they could break his whole army to pieces in the same way a wedge, well driven home, would split a large, thick piece of wood.

He suspected that Maniakes was trying to provoke him into a charge for that very reason. The javelin men stayed out there in front of his own army, temptingly close, as if itching to be assailed. "Hold fast!" Abivard shouted, over and over. "If they want us so badly, let them come and get us."

Had he ever imagined that the Videssians lacked the stomach for close combat, their response when they saw their foes refusing to be lured out of their position would have disabused him of the notion forever. Maniakes' men drew their swords and rode forward against the Makuraners. If Abivard would not hand them a breach in the Makuraner line, they'd manufacture one for themselves.

The Makuraners thrust with spears at their horses, used big wicker shields to turn aside their slashes, and hit back with clubs and knives and some swords of their own. Men on both sides cursed and gasped and prayed and shrieked. Though not Makuraner heavy cavalry, the Videssians used the weight of their horses to force Abivard's line to sag back in the center like a bent bow.

He rode to where the battle raged most fiercely, not only to fight but to let the soldiers from the garrisons of the Thousand Cities, men who up till the summer before had never expected to do any serious fighting, know he was with them. "We can do it!" he called to them. "We can hold the imperials back and drive them away."

Hold the Makuraners did, and well enough to keep the Videssians from smashing through their line. Maniakes sent a party to try to outflank Abivard's relatively short line but had little luck there. The ground at the unanchored end was soft and wet, and his horsemen bogged down. His whole attack bogged down not far from victory. He kept feeding men into the fight till he was heavily engaged all along the line.

"Now!" Abivard said, and a messenger galloped away. The fight went on, for *now* did not translate to *immediately*. He wished he'd arranged some special signal, but he hadn't, and he would just have to wait till the messenger got where he was going.

He also had to worry about whether he'd waited too long before releasing the rider. If the battle was lost here before he could put his scheme into play, what point was there to having had the idea in the first place?

Actually, the battle didn't look as if it would be lost or won any time soon. It was a melee, a slugging match, neither side willing to go back, neither able to force its way forward. Abivard had not expected the Videssians to make that kind of fight. Perhaps Maniakes had not expected the Makuraners, the former garrison troops, to withstand it if he did.

If he hadn't, he found himself mistaken. His men hewed and cursed at Makuraners who hewed and cursed back, the two armies locked together as tightly as lovers. And with them locked together thus, Zadabak's gates came open and a great column of foot soldiers, all yelling like fiends, rushed down the artificial hill and across the gently sloping flatlands below toward the Videssians.

Maniakes' men yelled, too, in surprise and alarm. Now, instead of trying to fight their way forward against the Makuraners, they found themselves taken in the flank and forced to a sudden, desperate defense. The horns directing their movements blared urgent orders that often were impossible to fulfill.

"Let's see how you like it!" Abivard shouted at the Videssians. He'd had a year and a half of having to react to Maniakes' moves and hadn't liked it a bit. As men will, he'd conveniently forgotten that for some years before he'd driven the Videssians back across the length of the westlands. "Let's see!" he yelled again. "What are you made of? Have you got ballocks, or are you just the bunch of prancing, mincing eunuchs I think you are?"

If word of that taunt ever got back to Yeliif, he was in trouble. But then, he was in trouble with the beautiful eunuch no matter what he said or did, so what did one taunt matter? Along with his soldiers, he screamed more abuse at the Videssians.

To his surprise and disappointment Maniakes' men did not break at the new challenge. Instead, they turned to meet it, the soldiers on their left facing outward to defend themselves against the Makuraner onslaught. Romezan's veterans might have done better, but not much. Instead of the Videssians' having their line rolled up, they only had it bent in, as Abivard's had been not long before.

The Videssian horns blared anew. Now, as best they could, the imperials did break off combat with their foes, disengaging, pulling back. They had the advantage there; even moving backward, they were quicker than their foes. They regrouped out of bowshot, shaken but not broken.

Abivard cursed. Just as his men had proved better and steadier than Maniakes had thought, so the Videssians had outdone what he had thought they could manage. The end result of that was a great many men on both sides dead or maimed for no better reason than that each commander had underestimated the courage of his opponents.

"We rocked them!" Turan shouted to Abivard.

"Aye," Abivard said. But he'd needed to do more than rock the Videssians. He'd needed to wreck them. That hadn't happened. As before up at the canal, he'd come up with a clever stratagem and one that hadn't failed, not truly . . . but one that hadn't succeeded to the extent he'd hoped, either.

And now, as then, Maniakes enjoyed the initiative once more. If he wanted, he could ride away from the battle. Abivard's men would not be able to keep up with his. Or, if he wanted, he could renew the attack on the battered Makuraner line in the place and manner he chose.

For the moment he did neither, simply waiting with his force, perhaps savoring the lull as much as Abivard was. Then the Videssian ranks parted and a single rider approached the Makuraners, tossing a javelin up into the air and catching it as it came down again. He rode up and down between the armies before shouting in accented Makuraner: "Abivard! Come out and fight, Abivard!"

At first Abivard thought of the challenge only as a reversal of the one his men had hurled at Maniakes before the fight by the Tib. Then he realized it was a reversal in more ways than one, for the warrior offering single combat was none other than Tzikas.

He wasted a moment admiring the elegance of Maniakes' scheme. If Tzikas slew him, the Avtokrator profited by it—and could still dispose of Tzikas at his leisure. If, on the other hand, he slew Tzikas, Maniakes would still be rid of a traitor but would not suffer the onus of putting Tzikas to death himself. No matter what happened, Maniakes couldn't lose.

Admiration, calculation—they did not last long. There rode Tzikas, coming out from the enemy army, a legitimate target at last. If he killed the renegade—the double renegade—now, the only thing Sharbaraz could do would be to congratulate him. And since he wanted nothing so much as to stretch Tzikas' body lifeless in the dirt, he spurred his horse forward, shouting, "Make way, curse you!" to the foot soldiers standing between him and his intended prey.

But the sight of Tzikas back serving the Videssians once more after renouncing not only them but their god inflamed the members of the Makuraner cavalry regiment that had fought so long and well under his command. Before Abivard could charge the man who had betrayed Maniakes and him both, a double handful of horsemen were thundering at the Videssian. Tzikas had shown himself no coward, but he'd also shown himself no fool. He galloped back to the protection of the Videssian line.

All the Makuraner cavalrymen screamed abuse at their former leader, reviling him in the foulest ways they knew. Abivard started to join them but in the end kept silent, savoring a more subtle revenge: Tzikas had failed in the purpose to which Maniakes had set him. What was the Avtokrator of the Videssians likely to do with—or to—him now? Abivard didn't know but enjoyed letting his imagination run free.

He did not get to enjoy such speculation long. Videssian horns squalled again. Shouting Maniakes' name—conspicuously not shouting Tzikas' name—the Videssian army rode forward again. Fewer arrows flew from their bows, and fewer from those of the Makuraners as well. A lot of quivers were empty. Picking up shafts from the ground was not the same as being able to refill those quivers.

"Stand fast!" Abivard called. He had never seen a Videssian force come into battle with such grim determination. Maniakes' men were out to finish the fight one way or the other. His own foot soldiers seemed steady enough, but how much more pounding could they take before they broke? In a moment he'd find out.

Swords slashing, the Videssians rode up against the Makuraner line. Abivard hurried along the line to the place that looked most threatening. Trading strokes with several Videssians, he acquired a cut—luckily a small one—on the back of his sword hand, a dent in his helmet, and a ringing in the ear by the dent. He thought he dealt out more damage than that, but in combat, with what he saw constantly shifting, he had trouble being sure.

Peering up and down the line, he saw the Videssians steadily forcing his men back despite all they could do. He bit his lip. If the Makuraners did not hold steady, the line would break somewhere. When that happened, Maniakes' riders would pour through and cut up his force from in front and behind. That was a recipe for disaster.

Forcing the enemy back seemed beyond his men's ability now that his stratagem had proved imperfectly successful. What did that leave him? He thought for a moment of retreating back into Zadabak, but then glanced over toward the walled city atop its mound of ancient rubbish. Retreating uphill and into the city was liable to be a nightmare worse than a Videssian breakthrough down here on the flatlands.

Which left . . . nothing. The God did not grant man's every prayer. Sometimes, even for the most pious, even for the most virtuous, things went wrong. He had done everything he knew how to do here to beat the Videssians and had proved to know not quite enough. He wondered if he would be able to retreat on the flat without tearing the army to pieces. He didn't think so but had the bad feeling he would have to try it anyhow before long.

Messengers rode and ran up to him, reporting pressure on the right, pressure on the left, pressure in the center. He had a last few hundred reserves left and fed them into the fight more in the spirit of leaving nothing undone than with any serious expectation that they would turn the tide. They didn't, which left him facing the same dilemma less than half an hour later, this time without any palliative to apply.

If he drew back with his left, he pulled away from the swamp anchoring that end of the line and gave the Videssians a free road into his rear. If he drew back with his right, he pulled away from Zadabak and its hillock. He decided to try that rather than the other plan, hoping the Videssians would fear a trap and hesitate to push between his army and the town.

A few years before the ploy might have given Maniakes pause, but no more. Without wasted motion or time he sent horsemen galloping into the gap Abivard had created for him. Abivard's heart sank. Whenever he'd been beaten before, here in the land of the Thousand Cities, he'd managed to keep his army intact, ready to fight another day. For the life of him, he didn't see how he was going to manage that this time.

More Videssian horn calls rang out. Abivard knew those calls as well as he knew his own. As people often do, though, at first he heard what he expected to hear, not what the trumpeters blew. When his mind as well as his ear recognized the notes, he stared in disbelief.

"That's *retreat*," Turan said, sounding as dazed as Abivard felt.

"I know it is," Abivard answered. "By the God, though, I don't know why. We were helpless before them, and Maniakes surely knew it."

But the flankers who should have gotten around to Abivard's rear and started the destruction of the Makuraner army instead reined in and, obedient to the Avtokrator's command, returned to their own main body. And then that main body disengaged from Abivard's force and rode rapidly off toward the southeast, leaving Abivard in possession of the field.

"I don't believe it," he said. He'd said it several times by then. "He had us. By the God, he *had* us. And he let us get away. No, he didn't just let us get away. He ran from us even though we couldn't make him run."

"If battle magic worked, it would work like that," Turan said.

"But battle magic doesn't work or works so seldom that it's not worth the effort. Did he up and go mad all of a sudden?"

"Too much to hope for," Abivard said, to which his lieutenant could only numbly nod. He went on, "Besides, he knew what he was doing, or thought he did. He handled that retreat as smoothly as any other part of the battle. It's only that he didn't need to make it . . . did he?"

Turan did not answer that. Turan could not answer that any more than Abivard could. They waited and exclaimed and scratched their heads but came to no conclusions.

In any other country they would have understood sooner than they could on the floodplain between the Tutub and the Tib. On the Pardrayan steppe, on the high plateau of Makuran, in the Videssian westlands, an army on the move kicked up a great cloud of dust. But the rich soil hereabouts was kept so moist, little dust rose from it. They did not know the army was approaching till they saw the first outriders off to the northeast.

Spying them gave rise to the next interesting question: whose army were they? "They can't be Videssians, or Maniakes wouldn't have run from them," Abivard said. "They can't be our men, because these are our men." He waved to his battered host.

"They can't be Vaspurakaners or men of Erzerum, either, or Khamorth from off the steppe," Turan said. "If they were any of those folk Maniakes would have welcomed them with open arms."

"True. Every word of it true," Abivard agreed. "That leaves nobody, near as I can see. By the kind of logic the Videssians love so well, then, that army there doesn't exist." His shaky laugh said what such logic was worth.

He did his best to make his army ready to fight at need. Seeing the state his men were in, he knew how forlorn that best was. The army from which Maniakes had fled drew closer. Now Abivard could make out the banners that army flew. As with the Videssian horn calls, recognition and understanding did not go together.

"They're *our* men," he said. "Makuraners, flying the red lion."

"But they can't be," Turan said. "We don't have any cavalry

force closer than Vaspurakan or the Videssian westlands. I wish we did, but we don't."

"I know," Abivard said. "I wrote to Romezan, asking him to come to our aid, but the King of Kings, in his wisdom, countermanded me."

Still wondering, he rode out toward the approaching horsemen. He took a good-sized detachment of his surviving cavalry with him, still unsure this wasn't some kind of trap or trick—though why Maniakes, with a won battle, would have needed to resort to tricks was beyond him.

A party to match his separated itself from the main body of the mysterious army. "By the God," Turan said softly.

"By the God," Abivard echoed. That burly, great-mustached man in the gilded armor— Now, at last, Abivard rode out ahead of his escort. He raised his voice: "Romezan, is it really you?"

The commander of the Makuraner mobile force shouted back: "No, it's just someone who looks like me." Roaring laughter, he spurred his horse, too, so that he and Abivard met alone between their men.

When they clasped hands, Romezan's remembered strength made every bone in Abivard's right hand ache. "Welcome, welcome, three times welcome," Abivard said most sincerely, and then, lowering his voice though no one save Romezan was in earshot, "Welcome indeed, but didn't Sharbaraz King of Kings, may his days be long and his realm increase, order you to stay in the westlands?"

"He certainly did," Romezan boomed, careless of who heard him, "and so here I am."

Abivard stared. "You got the order—and you disobeyed it?"

"That's what I did, all right," Romezan said cheerfully. "From what you said in your letter, you needed help, and a lot of it. Sharbaraz didn't know what was happening here as well as you did. That's what I thought, anyhow."

"What will he do when he finds out, do you think?" Abivard asked.

"Nothing much—there are times when being of the Seven

Clans works for you," Romezan answered. "If the King of Kings gives us too hard a time, we rise up, and he knows it."

He spoke with the calm confidence of a man born into the high nobility, a man for whom Sharbaraz was undoubtedly a superior but not a figure one step—and that a short one—removed from the God. Although Abivard's sister was married to the King of Kings, he still retained much of the awe for the office, if not for the man who held it for the moment, that had been inculcated in him since childhood. When he thought it through, he knew how little sense that made, but he didn't—he couldn't—always pause to think it through.

Romezan said, "Besides, how angry can Sharbaraz be once he finds out we've made Maniakes run off with his tail between his legs?"

"How angry?" Abivard pursed his lips. "That depends. If he decides you came here to join forces with me, not so you could go after Maniakes, he's liable to be very angry indeed."

"Why on earth would he think that?" Romezan boomed laughter. "What does he expect the two of us would do together, move on Mashiz instead of twisting Maniakes' tail again?"

"Isn't this a pleasant afternoon?" Abivard said, "I don't know that I've seen the sun so bright in the sky since, oh, maybe yesterday."

Romezan stared at him, the beginning of a scowl on his face. "What *are* you talking about?" he demanded. Fierce as fire in a fight, he wasn't the fastest man Abivard had ever seen in pursuit of an idea. But he wasn't a fool, either; he did eventually get where he was going. After a couple of heartbeats the scowl vanished. His eyes widened. "He truly is liable to think that? Why, by the God?"

For all his blithe talk a little while before about going into rebellion, Romezan drew back when confronted with the actual possibility. Having drawn back himself, Abivard did not think less of him for that. He said, "Maybe he thinks I'm too good at what I do."

"How can a general be too good?" Romezan asked. "There's no such thing as winning too many battles."

His faith touched Abivard. Somehow Romezan had managed

to live for years in the Videssian westlands without acquiring a bit of subtlety. "A general who is too good, a general who wins all his battles," Abivard said, almost as if explaining things to Varaz, "has no more foes to beat, true, but if he looks toward the throne on which his sovereign sits . . ."

"Ah," Romezan said, his voice serious now. Yes, talking of rebellion had been easy when it had been nothing but talk. But he went on, "The King of Kings suspects *you*, lord? If you're not loyal to him, who is?"

"If you knew how many times I've put that same question to him." Abivard sighed. "The answer, as best I can see, is that the King of Kings suspects everyone and doesn't think anyone is loyal to him, me included."

"If he truly does think that way, he'll prove himself right one of these days," Romezan said, tongue wagging looser than was perfectly wise.

Wise tongue or not, Abivard basked in his words like a lizard in the sun. For so long everyone around him had spoken nothing but fulsome praises of the King of Kings—oh, not Roshnani, but her thought and his were twin mirrors. To hear one of Sharbaraz' generals acknowledge that he could be less than wise and less than charitable was like wine after long thirst.

Romezan was looking over the field. "I don't see Tzikas anywhere," he remarked.

"No, you wouldn't," Abivard agreed. "He had the misfortune to be captured by the Videssians not so long ago." His voice was as bland as barley porridge without salt: how could anyone imagine *he'd* had anything to do with such a misfortune? "And, having been captured, the redoubtable Tzikas threw in his lot with his former folk and was most definitely seen not more than a couple of hours ago, fighting on Maniakes' side again." That probably wasn't fair to the unhappy Tzikas, who had problems of his own—a good many of them self-inflicted—but Abivard couldn't have cared less.

"The sooner he falls into the Void, the better for everybody," Romezan growled. "Never did like him, never did trust him. The idea that a Videssian could ape Makuraner manners—and to think we'd think he was one of us . . . not right, not natural. How come Maniakes didn't just up and kill him after he caught him? He owes him a big one, eh?"

"I think he was more interested in hurting us than in hurting Tzikas, worse luck," Abivard said, and Romezan nodded. Abivard went on, "But we'll hurt him worse than the other way around. I've been so desperately low in cavalry till you got here, I couldn't take the war to Maniakes. I had to let him choose his moves and then respond."

"We'll go after him." Romezan looked over the field once more. "You took him on with just foot soldiers, pretty much, didn't you?" Abivard nodded. Romezan let out a shrill little whistle. "I wouldn't like to try that, not with infantry alone. But your men seem to have given the misbelievers everything they wanted. How did you ever get infantry to fight so well?"

"I trained them hard, and I fought them the same way," Abivard said. "I had no choice: it was use infantry or go under. When they have confidence in what they're doing, they make decent troops. Better than decent troops, as a matter of fact."

"Who would have thought it?" Romezan said. "You must be a wizard to work miracles no one else could hope to match. Well, the days of needing to work miracles are done. You have proper soldiers again, so you can stop wasting your time on infantrymen."

"I suppose so." Oddly, the thought saddened Abivard. Of course cavalry was more valuable than infantry, but he felt a pang over letting the foot soldiers he'd trained slip back into being nothing more than garrison troops once more. It seemed a waste of what he'd made them. Well, they'd be *good* garrison troops, anyhow, and he could still get some use out of them in this campaign.

Romezan said, "Let's clean up this field here, patch up your wounded, and then we'll go chase ourselves some Videssians."

Abivard didn't need to hear that notion twice to like it. He hadn't been able to chase the Videssians in all his campaigning through the land of the Thousand Cities. He'd put himself where they would be a couple times, and he'd lured them into coming to

him, too. But to go after them, knowing he could catch them . . .
"Aye," he said. "Let's."

Maniakes very quickly made it clear that he did not intend to be
brought to bay. He went back to the old routine of wrecking canals
and levees behind him to slow the Makuraner pursuit. Even with
that, though, not all was as it had been before Romezan had come
to the land of the Thousand Cities. The Videssians did not enjoy
the luxury of leisure to destroy cities. They had to content themselves with burning crops and riding through fields to trample
down grain: wreckage, yes, but of a lesser sort.

Abivard wrote a letter to Sharbaraz, announcing his victory
over Maniakes. Romezan also wrote one with Abivard looking
over his shoulder as he drafted it and offering helpful suggestions.
It apologized for disobeying the orders he'd gotten from the King
of Kings and promised that if forgiven, he'd never again make
such a heinous blunder. After reading it, Abivard felt as if he'd
eaten too much fruit that had been too sweet to begin with and
then had been candied in honey.

Romezan shook his head as he stamped his signet—a wild boar
with great tushes—into the hot wax holding the letter closed. "If
someone sent me a letter like this, I'd throw up."

"So would I," Abivard said. "But it's the sort of thing Sharbaraz
likes to get. We've both seen that: tell the truth straight out and
you're in trouble, load up your letter with this nonsense and you
get what you want."

The same courier carried both letters off toward the west,
toward a Mashiz no longer in danger from the Videssian army,
toward a King of Kings who was likely to care less about that than
about his orders, no matter how foolish, being obeyed. Abivard
wondered what sort of letter would come out of the west, out of
the shadows of the Dilbat Mountains, out of the shadows of a
court life only distantly connected to the real world.

He also wondered when he would hear that Tzikas had been put
to death. When he did not hear of the renegade's premature—
though not, to his way of thinking, untimely—demise, he won-

dered when he would hear of Tzikas' leading the rear guard against his own men.

That did not happen, either. The longer either of those things took to come about, the more unhappy he got. He'd handed Tzikas over to Maniakes in the confident expectation—which Maniakes had fostered—that the Avtokrator would put him to death. Now Maniakes was instead holding on to him: to Abivard it seemed unfair.

But he knew better than to complain. If the Avtokrator had managed to trick him, that was his own fault, no one else's. Maybe he'd get the chance to pay Maniakes back one day soon. And maybe he wouldn't have to rely on trickery. Maybe he'd run the Videssians to earth as if they were a herd of wild asses and ride them down. Amazing, the thoughts to which the arrival of a real cavalry force could give rise.

Sharbaraz King of Kings did not delay in replying to the letters he'd gotten from Abivard and Romezan. When Abivard received a messenger from the King of Kings, he did so with all the enthusiasm he would have shown going off to get a rotting tooth pulled from his head.

By the same token, the leather message tube the fellow handed him might as well have been a venomous serpent. He opened it, broke the seal on the parchment, and unrolled it with no small trepidation. As usual, Sharbaraz had made his scribe waste several lines with his titles, his accomplishments, and his hopes. He seemed to take forever to get to the gist . . .

"We are, as we have said, angered that you should presume to summon to your aid the army commanded by Romezan son of Bizhan, which we had purposed using for other tasks during this campaigning season. We are further vexed with the aforesaid Romezan son of Bizhan for hearkening to your summons rather than ignoring it, as was our command, the aforesaid Romezan being separately admonished in a letter directed specifically to him.

"Only one possible circumstance can mitigate the disobedience the two of you have demonstrated both individually and collectively, the aforementioned circumstance being complete and overwhelming victory against the Videssians violating the land of the Thousand Cities. We own ourselves delighted one such victory has been gained and look forward either to Maniakes' extermination or to his ignominious retreat. The God grant that you soon have the opportunity to inform me of one or the other of these happy results."

As messengers did, this one asked Abivard, "Is there a reply, lord?"

"Wait a bit," Abivard answered. He read the letter again from top to bottom. It was no more vituperative in the second reading than it had been in the first. Abivard stepped out of the tent and spotted Pashang coming by, swigging on a jug of date wine. "Go find Romezan and fetch him to me," he told the driver.

"Aye, lord," Pashang said, and went off for Romezan. His pace was slower than Abivard would have desired; Abivard wondered how much of the wine he'd had.

But he did find Romezan and bring him back. The Makuraner general was waving a parchment as he approached; Abivard assumed that that was because he'd just gotten his letter from the King of Kings, too. And so it proved. Romezan called, "There, you see? I told you that you worry too much."

"So you did," Abivard admitted. By the way Romezan was acting, his letter wasn't actively painful, either. Turning to the messenger, Abivard said, "Please tell Sharbaraz King of Kings we'll do everything we can to obey him." Romezan nodded vigorously.

The messenger bowed. "It shall be as you say, lords." To him Abivard and Romezan were figures almost as mighty as Sharbaraz himself: the one brother-in-law to the King of Kings, the other a great noble of the Seven Clans. Abivard clicked his tongue between his teeth. It all depended on how, and from what station, you looked at life.

When the fellow was gone, Abivard turned to Romezan in some bemusement. "I had expected the King of Kings to be angry at us," he said.

"I told you," Romezan answered. "Victory atones for any number of sins."

"It's not that simple," Abivard insisted to Roshnani over stewed kid that night. "The more victories I won in the Videssian westlands, the more suspicious of me Sharbaraz got. And then here, in the land of the Thousand Cities, I couldn't satisfy him no matter what I did. If I lost, I was a bungling idiot. But if I won, I was setting myself up to rebel against him. And if I begged for some help to give me a chance to win, why then I was obviously plotting to raise up an army against him."

"Until now," his principal wife said.

"Until now," Abivard echoed. "He didn't fall on Romezan like an avalanche, either, and Romezan flat disobeyed his orders. Till now he's screamed at me even though I've done everything he told me to do. I don't understand this. What's wrong with him?" The incongruity of the question made him laugh as soon as it had passed his lips, but he'd meant it, too.

Roshnani said, "Maybe he's finally come to see you really do want to do what's best for him and for Makuran. The years pile up on him the same as they do on everyone else; maybe they're getting through."

"I wish I could believe that—that's he's grown up at last, I mean," Abivard said. "But if he has, it's very sudden. I think something else is going on, but for the life of me I have no idea what."

"Well, let's see if we can figure it out," Roshnani said, logical as a Videssian. "Why is he ignoring things that would have made him angry if he were acting the way he usually does?"

"The first thing I thought of is that he's trying to lull Romezan and me into feeling all calm and easy when he really does intend to fall on us like an avalanche," Abivard said. "But if that's so, we'll have to look out for people trying to separate us from the army in the next few days, either that or people trying to murder us right in the middle of it. That could be, I suppose. We'll have to keep an eye out."

"Yes, that certainly is possible," Roshnani agreed. "But again, it's not the way he's been in the habit of behaving. Maybe he really is pleased with you."

"That would be even more out of character," Abivard said, his voice bitter. "He hasn't been, not for years."

"He was . . . better this past winter than the one before," Roshnani said. Odd for her to be defending the King of Kings and for Abivard to be assailing him. "Maybe he's warming up to you again. And then—" She paused before going on thoughtfully. "And then, your sister is drawing nearer to her time every day. Maybe he remembers the family connection."

"Maybe." Abivard sounded imperfectly convinced, even to himself. "And maybe he remembers that, if he does have a boy, all he has to do is die for me to become uncle and maybe regent to the new King of Kings."

"Absent assassins, that doesn't add up," Roshnani said, to which Abivard had to nod. His principal wife sighed. "Day by day we'll see what happens."

"So we will," Abivard said. "One of the things that will happen, by the God, is that I'll drive Maniakes out of the land of the Thousand Cities."

With Romezan's cavalry added to the infantry he'd trained, Abivard knew he had a telling advantage over the force Maniakes had operating between the Tutub and the Tib. Making the telling advantage actually tell was another matter altogether. Maniakes proved an annoyingly adroit defender.

What irked Abivard most was the Avtokrator's mutability. When Maniakes had had the edge in numbers and mobility, he'd pressed it hard. Now that his foes enjoyed it, he was doing everything he could to keep them from getting the most out of it.

Wrecked canals, little skirmishes, nighttime raids on Abivard's camp—much as Abivard had raided him the year before—all added up to an opponent who might have smeared butter over his body to make himself too slippery to be gripped. And whenever Maniakes got the chance, he would storm another town on the floodplain; another funeral pyre rising from an artificial hillock marked a success for him, a failure for Makuran.

"Never have liked campaigning in this country," Romezan said. "I remember it from the days when Sharbaraz was fighting Smerdis. Too may things can go wrong here."

"Oh, yes, I remember that, too," Abivard said. "And, no doubt, so docs Maniakes. He's giving us as much grief as we can handle, isn't he?"

"That he is," the cavalry general said. "He doesn't care about proper battle, does he, not so long as he can have a good time raiding?"

"That's what he's here for," Abivard agreed. "It's worked, too, hasn't it? You're not fighting him in the Videssian westlands, and I'm not sitting in Across going mad trying to figure out how to get to Videssos the city."

"You're right, lord," Romezan said, using the title as one of mild, perhaps even amused, respect. "I wish you'd found a way, too; I'd be lying if I said anything else."

"We haven't got any ships, curse it," Abivard said. "We can't get any ships. Our mages couldn't conjure up the number of ships we'd need. Even if they could, it would be battle magic and liable to fall apart when we needed it most. And even if it didn't, the Videssians are a hundred times the sailors we are. They could sink magical ships the same as any others, I fear."

"You're probably right," Romezan admitted. "What we really need—"

"What we really need," Abivard interrupted, "is a mage who could make a giant silvery bridge over the Cattle Crossing into Videssos the city so our warriors could cross dryshod and not have to worry about Videssians in ships. The only trouble with that is—"

"The only trouble with that is," Romezan said, interrupting in turn, "a mage who could bring off that kind of conjuration wouldn't be interested in helping the King of Kings. He'd want to be King of Kings himself or, more likely, king of the world. So it's a good thing there's no such mage."

"So it is," Abivard said with a laugh. "Or it's mostly a good thing, anyhow. But it does mean we'll have to do more of the work ourselves—no, all of the work ourselves, or as near as makes no difference."

A couple of days later a scout brought back a piece of news he'd been dreading and hoping for at the same time: at the head of a troop of Videssian cavalry Tzikas had delivered a formidable attack against Romezan's horsemen. As long as Tzikas stayed in his role, he made a formidable opponent to whichever side he didn't happen to be on at the moment. Since he refused to stay in his role for long, odds were good he wouldn't stay on that particular side forever.

When Abivard passed the news on to Roshnani, she asked, "What are you going to do if he wants to serve Makuran again one day?"

"By the God!" He clapped a hand to his forehead. "You're a step ahead of me there. He probably will want to come back to us one day, won't he?"

"Sooner rather than later," Roshnani guessed. "He's only defamed you, and you don't rule Makuran. He's tried to murder the Avtokrator, and he's renounced Videssos' god for ours. He has to be biding his time in that camp; he can't be happy or comfortable there."

"He's probably renounced the God again for Phos," Abivard said, "or maybe for Skotos, the Videssians' dark god. When he does finally die, I expect there'll be a war in the heavens over whether to torment his soul forever in Skotos' snow and ice or drop it into the Void and make it as if it had never been." The idea struck him as deliciously blasphemous.

At the urging of both Romezan and Turan, Abivard dealt with Tzikas' reappearance in the field by ordering his men to try to kill the renegade whenever they saw him, regardless of what that meant to the rest of the fight. The command struck him as safe enough: Tzikas would not be commanding any vital part of whatever forces were engaged, for Maniakes would not be so stupid as to trust him with anything vital. Abivard remained disappointed that Maniakes had allowed Tzikas to keep breathing, but the Avtokrator must have decided to squeeze whatever use against Makuran he could from the traitor.

Abivard would have loved to squeeze Tzikas—by the neck, if at all possible. Doing that, though, meant catching up to the Videssians. His army, despite the addition of Romezan's cavalry, still moved more slowly than did Maniakes'.

And then the Avtokrator halted on the east side of a large canal that ran north and south through the land of the Thousand Cities. He kept cavalry patrols along the bank of the canal in strength enough to stop Abivard from getting a detachment across it or gaining control of a big enough stretch of bank to let his whole army cross. The Videssians not on patrol resumed the depredations that had grown too familiar over the past couple of campaigning seasons.

Abivard moved more forces forward, expecting to make Maniakes withdraw from the line of the canal; he could not hope to hold it against several simultaneous strong crossings. But Maniakes did not withdraw. Nor did he bring the whole of his army back to the canal to fight the Makuraners once they crossed. He went on about the business of plunder and rapine as if Abivard and his men had fallen ino the Void.

"He's making a mistake," Abivard said in glad surprise at a council of war. "How best do we make him pay?"

"Get across the water, smash his patrols, hammer the rest of his army," Romezan said. Abivard looked to his other officers. Sanatruq, who had commanded the cavalry till Romezan had arrived, nodded. So did Turan. So, in the end, did Abivard. Romezan was never going to be accused of subtlety, but you didn't need to be subtle all the time. Sometimes you just had to get in there and do what needed doing. This looked to be one of those times.

As best he could, Abivard readied his host to cross with overwhelming strength and speed. The canal was half a bowshot wide and, peasants said, better than waist-deep everywhere. The Videssians could make getting over it expensive. But instead of concentrating against his force, they rode back and forth, back and forth, along the eastern bank of the canal.

He chose a late-afternoon attack: let the Videssians fight with the sun in their faces for a change. He formed his army with the infantry in the center and the cavalry on both wings. He commanded the right, Romezan the left, and Turan the foot soldiers in the center.

Horns blared. Standard-bearers waved the red-lion banners of Makuran and the smaller flags and streamers marking regiments and companies. Shouting Sharbaraz' name, the army moved forward and splashed down into the canal.

The muddy water was just the temperature of blood. The muck on the bottom had not been stirred up since the last time the canal had been dredged out, however many years before that might have been. When hooves and feet roiled it, a horrible stench rose. Choking a little, Abivard rode farther out into the canal.

He looked back over his shoulder. The rest of the horsemen on the right were following him into the water, shouting abuse at the Videssians on the far bank as they came. Maniakes' men quietly sat their horses and waited for the onslaught. Had they been Abivard's, he would have had them doing more: if nothing else, riding up to the edge of the canal and plying their foes with arrows. But they simply waited and watched. Maybe the might of the Makuraner force had paralyzed them with dread, he thought.

His head swam. He shook it and sent a curse down to the stinking muck that surely made every man who had to endure it reel in the saddle. If the God was kind, he would grant that no one would get woozy enough to fall off his horse and drown in the dirty water.

Here came the bank of the canal after what seemed like much too long in it. Abivard hoped no leeches were clinging to him or to his horse. He spurred the animal up onto solid ground once more. The red disk of the sinking sun glared into his face.

For a moment he simply accepted that, as one does with any report from the eyes. Then he gave a great cry of amazement and alarm, echoed by the more alert among the soldiers he led. They had ridden into the canal with the sun at their backs. Here they were, coming out with it in their eyes.

Abivard looked back over his shoulder again. Here came the whole army up out of the canal. There, on the far bank, the Videssians still sat on their horses, quietly, calmly, as if nothing in the least out of the ordinary had happened. No, not quite like that:

a couple of them were sketching circles over the left side of their chests, the gesture they used when invoking their god.

Seeing that made Abivard's wits, stunned till then, begin to work once more: Whether well or poorly he could not guess, but thought started replacing the blank emptiness between his ears. He shouted the first word that came into his mind: "Magic!" A moment later he amplified it: "The Videssians have used magic to keep us from crossing the canal and giving them what they deserve!"

"Aye!" Hundreds, then thousands of voices took up that cry and others like it. Like sunshine burning away fog, fury ousted fear. That did Abivard's heart good. The angrier his men were, the less likely whatever crafty spell the Videssians had used was to seize and hold them. Passion weakened sorcery. That was why both battle magic and love philters failed more often than they succeeded.

"Are we going to let them get away with this outrage?" Abivard shouted. "Are we going to let them blind us with treacherous battle magic?"

"No!" the troopers roared back. "No, by the God! We'll pay them back for the affront!" someone shouted. Had Abivard known who, he would cheerfully have paid the fellow a pound of silver; a paid shill could have done no better.

"Battle magic fails!" Abivard cried. "Battle magic fades! Battle magic feeds on fears. Angry men don't let themselves be seduced. Now that we know what we're up against, we'll show the Videssians their charms and spells are useless. And when we've crossed the canal, we'll punish them doubly for seeking to befool us with their wizards' games."

His men roared approval at him. The cavalrymen brandished their lances. Foot soldiers waved clubs and swung swords. Encouraged by their fury, he booted his horse in its armored flanks and urged it toward the canal once more.

The animal went willingly. Whatever the wizards of Videssos had done, it didn't disturb the beasts. The horse snorted a little as its hooves stirred up the muck on the bottom of the canal, but that was only because new noxious bubbles rose to the surface and burst foully and flatulently.

There, straight ahead, were the same Videssians who had watched Abivard cross the canal—or, rather, try to cross the canal—before. This time, the battle magic having been spotted for what it was, he would ride upon them and spear them out of the saddle one after another. Not normally a man who delighted in battle for its own sake, he wanted to fight now, to purge the rage coursing through him at Maniakes' trickery.

Closer and closer to the Videssians he came. Here was the bank of the canal. Here was his horse setting foot on the bank. He couched his lance, ready to charge hard at the first Videssian he saw.

Here was ... the setting sun, almost touching the western horizon, shining straight into his face.

Once more he led his army up onto the bank of the canal from which they'd departed. Once more he had no recollection of turning around. Once more he didn't think he *had* turned around. By the shouts and oaths coming from his men, they didn't think they'd turned around, either. But here they were. And there, on the far—the indisputably eastern—bank of the canal the Videssian cavalry patrols trotted back and forth or simply waited, staring into the sunset—the sunset that should have blinded them in the fighting—at the Makuraners who could not reach them.

Abivard gauged that treacherous sun. If he made another try, it would be in darkness. If the Videssians had one magic working, maybe they had more than one. He decided he dared not take the chance. "We camp here tonight," he declared. A moment later he sent messengers to seek Turan and Romezan and order them to his tent.

The first thing he wanted to find out was whether his officers had experienced anything different from his own mystifying trips into and out of the canal. They looked at each other and shook their heads.

"Not me, lord," Turan said. "I was in the canal. I was moving forward all the time. I never turned around—by the God, I didn't! But when I came up onto dry land, it was the same dry land I'd left. I don't know how and I don't know why, but that's what it was."

"And I the same, lord," Romezan said heavily. "I was in the canal. There, ahead, the Videssians sat their horses, waiting for me to spit them like a man putting meat and onions on a skewer to roast in the fire. I spurred my own mount ahead, eager to slaughter them—ahead, not back, I tell you. I came up onto the bank, and it was this bank. As Turan said, how or why I do not know—I am but a poor, stupid fighting man—but it was." He bowed to Abivard. "Honor to your courage, lord. My bowels turned to jelly within me at the magic. I would never have been so brave as to lead our men into the canal that second time. And they followed you—I followed you—too." He bowed again.

"I don't think I believed it the first time, not all the way through," Abivard said. "And I thought an aroused army would be plenty to beat down Videssian battle magic." He laughed ruefully. "Only shows what I know, doesn't it?"

"What do our own brilliant mages have to say about this?" Turan asked. "I put the question to a couple of the wizards with the infantry: men from the Thousand Cities of the same sort as the ones who worked your canal magic last year, and all they do is gape and mumble. They're as baffled as we are."

Abivard turned to Romezan. "Till now we've had so little need of magic since you arrived, I haven't even thought to ask what sorts of sorcerers you have with you. Are Bozorg and Panteles still attached to the field force?"

"Aye, they are." Romezan hesitated, then said, "Lord, would you trust a Videssian to explain—more, to fight back against—Videssian sorcery? I've kept Panteles with us, but I've hesitated to use him."

"I can see that," Abivard agreed, "but I'd still like to find out what he has to say, and Bozorg, too. And Bozorg should be able to tell if he's lying. If we do decide to use him to try to fight the spell, Bozorg should be able to tell us if he's making an honest effort, too."

Romezan bowed. "This is wisdom. I know it when I hear it." He stepped out of the tent and bawled for a messenger. The man's sandals rapidly pattered away. Romezan came back in and folded broad arms across his chest. "They have been summoned."

Waiting gnawed at Abivard. He'd done too much of it, first in Across, then in the King of Kings' palace, to feel happy standing around doing nothing. He wanted to charge into the canal again—but if he came out once more on the bank from which he started, he feared he'd go mad.

The messenger needed a while to find the wizards in the confusion of a camp Abivard hadn't expected to have to make. At last, though, the fellow returned with them, each warily eyeing the other. They both bowed low to Abivard, acknowledging his rank as far superior to theirs.

"Lord," Bozorg said in Makuraner.

"Eminent sir," Panteles echoed in Videssian, putting Abivard in mind of Tzikas, who presented a problem of which he did not want to be reminded at the moment.

"I think the two of you may have some idea why I've called you here tonight," Abivard said, his voice dry.

Both wizards nodded. They looked at each other, respect mixed with rivalry. Bozorg spoke first: "Lord, whatever this spell may be, it is not battle magic."

"I figured that much out for myself," Abivard answered even more dryly. "If it had been, we would have gotten over on the second try. But if it's not battle magic, what is it?"

"If it were battle magic, it would have been aimed at your soldiers, and their attitude would indeed have influenced the spell," Bozorg said. "Since their attitude did not influence it, I conclude it pertains to the canal, whose emotional state is not subject to flux."

Panteles nodded. Romezan snorted. Turan grinned. Abivard said, "A cogent point, the next question being, What do we do about it?"

The wizards looked at each other again. Again Bozorg spoke for them: "As things stand now, lord, we do not know." Panteles nodded once more.

Romezan snorted again, on an entirely different note. "Glad to have you along, mages; glad to have you along." Panteles looked down at the ground. Bozorg, who had served at the palace of the King of Kings, glared.

Abivard sighed and waved to dismiss both mages. "Bend all your efforts to finding out what Maniakes' wizards have done. When you know—no, when you have even a glimmer—come to me. I don't care what I may be doing; I don't care what hour of the day or night it may be. With you or without you, I intend to keep trying to cross that canal. Come—do you understand?"

Both wizards solemnly nodded.

X

WHEN THE SUN ROSE THE NEXT MORNING, ABIVARD PROVED AS good as his word. He mustered his army, admiring the way the men held their spirit and discipline in the face of the frightening unknown. *Maybe,* he thought, *things will be different this time. The sun is in our face already. Videssian magic often has a lot to do with the sun. If we're already moving toward it, maybe they won't be able to shift us away.*

He thought about spreading that idea among the soldiers but in the end decided against it. Had he been more confident he was right, he might have chosen differently. He knew too well, though, that he was only guessing.

"Forward!" he shouted, raising a hand to his eyes to peer into the morning glare to try to see what the Videssians on the eastern bank of the canal were doing. The answer seemed to be, *Not much.* Maniakes did not have his army drawn up in battle array to meet the Makuraners. A few squadrons of cavalry trotted back and forth; that was all.

"Forward!" Abivard shouted again, and urged his horse down into the muddy water of the canal.

He kept his eye on the sun. *As long as I ride straight toward it, everything should be all right,* he told himself. The canal wasn't that wide. Surely he and his followers could not reverse themselves and go back up onto the bank from which they'd started: not without noticing. No, they couldn't do that . . . could they?

Closer and closer came the eastern bank. The day, like all summer days in the land of the Thousand Cities, promised to be scorchingly hot. Already the sun glared balefully into Abivard's face. He blinked. Yes, the far bank was very close now. But the bank up onto which his dripping horse floundered was the western one, with the sun now unaccountably at his back.

And here came his army after him, storming up to overwhelm the place they'd just left. Their shouts of amazement and anger and despair said everything that needed saying. No, almost everything: the other thing that needed saying was that he and his army weren't going to be able to cross that cursed canal—the canal that might as well have been literally cursed—till they figured out and overcame whatever sorcery Maniakes was using to thwart them.

Glumly, Abivard ordered the army to reestablish the camp it had just struck. He spent the next couple of hours pacing through it, doing his best to lift the soldiers' sagging spirits. He knew that best would have been better had his own spirits been anywhere but at the bottom of the sea. But he did not have to show the men that, and he didn't.

At last he went back to his own pavilion. He didn't know exactly what he'd do there: getting drunk seemed as good a plan as any, since he couldn't come to grips with the Videssians. But when he got to the tent, he found Bozorg and Panteles waiting for him.

"I think I have the answer, eminent sir!" Panteles exclaimed in high excitement.

"I think this Videssian is out of his mind, lord: utterly mad," Bozorg declared, folding his arms across his chest. "I think he wants only to waste your time, to deceive you, and to give the victory to Maniakes."

"I think you are as jealous as an ugly girl watching her betrothed talking to her pretty sister," Panteles retorted—not a comparison a Makuraner was likely to use, not in a land of sequestered women, but a telling one even so.

"I think I'm going to knock your heads together," Abivard said judiciously. "Tell me whatever you have to tell me, Panteles. I'll judge whether it's trickery. If it is, I'll do as I think best."

Panteles bowed. "As you say, eminent sir. Here." He displayed a length of leather about as long as Abivard's forearm: most likely a piece cut from a belt. Joining the ends, he held them together with thumb and forefinger, then pointed to the resulting circle with his other hand. "How many sides does the strap have, eminent sir?"

"How many sides?" Abivard frowned. "What foolishness is this?" Maybe Bozorg had known what he was talking about. "It has two, of course: an inside and an outside."

"And a strap across the Videssian's backside," Bozorg added.

But Panteles seemed unperturbed. "Just so," he agreed. "You can trace it with your finger if you like." He held the leather circle out so Abivard could do just that. Abivard dutifully did, hoping against hope Panteles wasn't talking to hear himself talk, as Videssians often did. "Now—" Panteles said.

Bozorg broke in: "Now, lord, he shows you idiotic nonsense. By the God, he should be made to answer for his foolishness with the lash!"

Anything that could so anger the Makuraner mage was either idiotic nonsense, as he'd said, or exactly the opposite. "As I said, I will judge," Abivard told Bozorg. He turned to Panteles. "Go on. Show me this great discovery of yours, or whatever it is, and explain how it ties up all our troubles like a length of twine around a stack of cured hides."

"It's not my discovery, and I don't know if it ties up our troubles or not," Panteles said. Oddly, Abivard liked him more for that, not less. The more spectacular a claim, the less likely it was to be justified.

Panteles held up the length of leather once more and again shaped it into a continuous band. This time, though, he gave it a half twist before joining the two ends together between his thumb and index finger. Bozorg gestured as if to ward off the evil eye, hissing, "Trickery."

Panteles took no notice either of him or of Abivard's hand upraised in warning. The Videssian wizard said, "This was discovered in the Sorcerers' Collegium in Videssos the city some years ago by a certain Voimios. I don't know whether it's magic or not in any formal sense of the word. Maybe it's only trickery, as the learned Bozorg claims." Like any Videssian worth his salt, he used irony as a stiletto. "Whatever it is, it's interesting. How many sides does the strap have now?" He held it up so Abivard could trace out his answer as he had before.

"What do you mean, how many sides does it have?" Abruptly, Abivard regretted doubting Bozorg. "It has to have two sides, the same as it did before."

"Does it?" Panteles' smile was mild, benign. "Show me with your finger, eminent sir, if you'd be so kind."

With the air of someone humoring a madman, Abivard ran his finger around the outside of the strap. A moment later, he would run it around the inside, and a moment after that he would give Panteles what he deserved for making him the butt of what had to be a foolish joke.

But in tracing the length of leather with his finger, he somehow found himself back where he'd begun after having touched every finger's breadth of it. "Wait a moment," he said sharply. "Let me try that again." This time he paid closer attention to his work. But paying closer attention didn't seem to matter. Again he traced the entire length of leather and returned to his starting point.

"Do you see, eminent sir?" Panteles said as Abivard stared down at his own finger as if it had betrayed him. "Voimios' strap—that's the name it took on at the Sorcerers' Collegium— has only one side, not two."

"That's impossible," Abivard said. Then he looked at his finger again. It looked as if it knew better.

"You just made a continuous line from your starting point back to your starting point," Panteles said politely. "How could you do that if you went from one side to another? You just got there backward and were taken by surprise."

As Panteles had doubtless meant them to, the words hung in the air. "Wait," Abivard said. "Let me think. You're trying to tell me Maniakes' wizards have turned the canal into a strap of Voimios—is that what you called it?"

"Close enough, eminent sir," Panteles said.

"Drivel!" Bozorg said. He snatched the leather strap out of

Panteles' hand and threw it to the ground. "It's a fraud, a fake, a trick. There's no magic whatever to it, only deception."

"What do you have to say to that?" Abivard asked Panteles.

"Eminent sir, I never claimed there was any magic in Voimios' strap," the Videssian wizard answered. "I offered it as analogy, not proof. Besides—" He stooped and picked up the length of leather Bozorg had thrown down. "—this is a flat thing. To twist it so it has only one side, all you need do is this." He gave it the deft half twist that turned it baffling. "But if you were going to make it so that something with length and width and height turned back on itself the same way, the only twist I can imagine to do such a thing is a magical one."

Trying again and again to cross the canal and failing had already done more strange things to Abivard's imagination than he'd ever wanted. He turned to Bozorg. "Have *you* got a different idea how the Videssians could have turned us back on ourselves?"

"No, lord," Bozorg admitted. "But the one this Videssian puts forward is ridiculous on the face of it. His precious Voimios probably got some of his horse's harness on poorly, then spent the next twenty years cadging cups of wine on the strength of it."

"Are you denying what Panteles says is true, or are you only disparaging it?" Abivard asked pointedly.

The question had sharp teeth. Bozorg might have been furious, but he was no fool. He said, "What he said about the strap may be true, I suppose, no matter how absurd it sounds. But how could anyone take seriously this nonsense about twisting a canal back on itself?"

"I'd say some thousands of soldiers take the notion seriously, or would if they heard it," Panteles shot back. "It happened to them, after all."

"So it did," Abivard said. "I was one of them, and thinking of it still makes me shiver." He looked from Panteles to Bozorg and back again. "Do you think the two of you, working together—" He put special stress on those words. "—can find out whether what happened to the canal is the magical equivalent of a Voimios strap?"

Panteles nodded. A moment later, more grudgingly, Bozorg

did, too. Panteles said, "Making a magic of this sort cannot have been easy for Maniakes' wizards. If the traces of the sorcery linger on this plane, we shall find them."

"And if you do?" Abivard asked. "What then?"

"Untwisting the canal should be easier for us than twisting it was for them—if that's what they did," Panteles answered. "Restoring a natural condition takes far less sorcery than changing away from what is natural."

"Mm, I can see the sense in that," Abivard said. "How soon will you be able to find out if Maniakes has turned the canal into a strap of Voimios?"

Bozorg stirred. Abivard looked his way. He said, "Lord, do you feel easy about using a Videssian to fight the Videssians?"

Abivard had been wrestling with that question since he had realized magic was holding him away from Maniakes' army. He'd worried about it less since Panteles had started his elaborate theoretical explanation: any man dedicated enough to put so much effort into figuring out what might have gone into a spell wouldn't be content unless he could have a hand in unraveling it, too . . . would he?

"How say you, Panteles?" Abivard asked.

"Eminent sir, I say I never imagined turning a Voimios strap from an amusement into a piece of creative sorcery," Panteles answered. "To understand how that's done and then to figure out a spell to counter it—I'm lucky to be living in such exciting times, when anything seems possible."

His eyes gleamed. Abivard recognized the expression on his pinched, narrow face. Soldiers with that exalted look would ride to their deaths without flinching; minstrels who had it crafted songs that lived for generations. Panteles would go where knowledge and energy and inspiration took him and would pursue his target with the eagerness of a bridegroom going to his bride.

"I think it will be all right," Abivard said to Bozorg. "And if it isn't all right, I trust your skill to hold disaster away from us."

"Lord, you may honor me beyond my worth," the Makuraner mage murmured.

"I don't think so," Abivard said heartily. "And as I've told you,

I expect you to work with him. If his idea turns out to be wrong-headed after all, I'll need to hear that from you so we can figure out what to try next."

He hoped with all his heart that Panteles and Bozorg would be able to find a way around—or through—Maniakes' magic. If they could, the sorcery would be a one-time wonder: if not, every time Makuraners tried to clash with Videssians, they would find themselves going back the way from which they had come. That would be a worse disaster than defeat in battle.

"What one mage has done, another may undo," Panteles declared. To that Bozorg assented with a cautious nod.

"Finding out what the mage has done can be interesting, though," Abivard remarked.

"Truth, eminent sir. I do not know if I have proposed the correct explanation, either," Panteles said. "One of the many things I need to learn—"

"Don't just stand there." Abivard realized he was being unfair, but urgency counted for more. "Go find out what you can by whatever means you can. I intend to send riders up and down the canal—provided they don't think they're riding north when they're riding south or the other way around. If we can force a crossing somewhere else—"

"Then the notion of the Voimios strap becomes moot," Panteles interrupted.

Abivard shook his head. "Not quite. Oh, we might be able to get around it this one time, but it would keep on being a trick Maniakes has and we don't. He could use it again, say, in a mountain pass where we didn't have any choice about how we tried to get at him. If we can, I want us to have a way to beat this spell so it doesn't stay in the Avtokrator's arsenal, if you take my meaning."

Both Panteles and Bozorg bowed as if to say they not only understood but agreed. Abivard waved them off to begin their investigation. At his shouted orders, horsemen did gather to ride off up and down the canal. But before they set out, one of them asked, "Uh, lord, how are we to know whether the spell still holds?"

Abivard wished he hadn't asked that. Sighing, he answered,

"The only way I can think of is to ride out into the canal and try to cross it. If you do, you've passed the point where the Videssians' magic works. If you don't—"

One of the riders committed the enormity of interrupting the army commander: "If we don't—if we come back where we started from—and we haven't gone crazy before then, that's when we know."

The other horsemen nodded. The fellow had made a pretty fair joke, or what would have been a pretty fair joke under other circumstances, but none of them laughed or even smiled. Neither did Abivard; nor did he stand on his dignity or rank. He said, "That magic is plenty to drive anyone mad, so my best guess is that we've all gone mad already, and getting bitten by it one more time won't do any harm."

"You have a good way of looking at things, lord," said the fellow who had interrupted him. He rode south along the canal. Some men followed him; others headed north.

Was it a good way of looking at things? Abivard didn't know. If Maniakes' magic extended a good distance up and down the canal, some of those men were liable to have to endure having their world twisted several times, not once alone. You could grow used to almost anything . . . but to *that*?

Something else occurred to him: was the canal folded back on itself for the Videssians, too? If they tried to cross from east to west to attack him, what would happen? Would they make it over to his side of the canal, or would they, too, end up riding out onto the bank from which they'd departed? The question was so intriguing, he almost summoned Bozorg and Panteles so he could ask it. All that restrained him was the thought that they already had enough to worry about.

And so did he. The riders he'd sent north along the canal came back perhaps sooner than he'd expected with the news that the spell, whether it was some larger version of Voimios' strap or not, extended in that direction as far as they'd traveled. They hadn't traveled so far as he'd hoped, but the fear on their faces said they'd gone into the canal as often as they could stand.

Men who'd ridden south began coming back to Abivard's

camp, too, not all at once like those who'd gone the other way but a few at a time, some going back into the canal after others could bear it no more. Whether they came soon or late, they had the same news as the men who had traveled north: when they tried to go east over the canal, they found themselves unable.

Last of all to return was the fellow who had suggested that going into the canal would make a man crazy. By the time he came back, the sun was setting in the west. Abivard had begun to wonder whether he'd gone into the canal and never come out.

He shook his fist at the sun, saying, "I've seen that thing too many times—may it drop into the Void. I tried to ride away from it a dozen times, maybe more, this afternoon, and I ended up coming right back at it every one of them. Sorry lord; that spell goes on a long way south."

"No cause for you to be sorry," Abivard answered. "I'd call you a hero for braving the canal more than anyone else did."

"A hero?" The rider shook his head. "I'll tell you what I'd call me, and that's a bloody fool. By your leave, lord, I'll go off and polish my armor—keep it from rusting as best I can, eh?" Abivard nodded permission. Sketching a salute, the soldier strode off.

Abivard muttered something foul under his breath. Maniakes' mages could certainly hold the spell in place for half a day's ride, or perhaps a bit less, to either side of his own position. That meant that shifting camp wasn't likely to do much good, because the Videssians were liable either to move or to extend the spell to his new position.

If he couldn't go around the twisted canal, he'd have to go through it. Going through it meant beating Maniakes' magic. Between them, Bozorg and Panteles would have to come up with some answers.

Summoning them to his tent, Abivard said, "Can you cut through the spell and let us cross?"

"Cutting a Voimios strap is less easy than it sounds, eminent sir," Panteles said. "When you do cut one lengthwise, do you know what you get?"

"I was going to say two thinner ones, but that would be too simple and obvious, wouldn't it?" Abivard said, and Panteles nodded. "All right, what do you get?" Abivard asked. "A bowl of oxtail soup? Three arkets and a couple of coppers? A bad case of the itch?"

Panteles gave him a reproachful look; maybe mighty Makuraner marshals, to his way of thinking, weren't allowed to be absurd. He reached into a pouch he wore on his belt and pulled out a Voimios strap made from thin leather and sewn together at the ends so he didn't need to hold them between his long, thin, agile thumb and forefinger. "See for yourself, eminent sir, and you will better understand the difficulty we face."

"All right, I will." Abivard drew a sharp dagger, poked it through the leather, and began to cut. He worked slowly, carefully, methodically; a pair of shears would have been better for the job, but he had none. When he got the sharp strap cut nearly all the way around, he thought Panteles had been lying to him, for it did look as if it might split in two, as a simple ring would have. But then he made the last cut, and exclaimed in surprise: he still had one twisted strap, but twice as long and half as wide as it had been before.

"This shows some of the complications we face," Panteles said. "Some means of countering the magic are caught up in its twists and prove to be of no use against it."

"Yes, I see," Abivard said "This is what happens when you cut *with* the spell But when you do this—" He cut the strap across instead of lengthwise. "—things look easier." He handed Panteles the simple length of leather.

The wizard took it and looked at it thoughtfully. "Yes, eminent sir, that is the effect we are trying to create. I shall do everything in my power to imitate the elegance of your solution." He rolled up the strap into a tight little cylinder, put it back in his belt pouch, and went away.

Abivard awaited results with growing impatience. Every day he and his army stayed stuck on the western side of the canal was another day in which Maniakes had free rein in the east. Maniakes had done enough—too much—damage even when Abivard had opposed him. Without opposition . . .

* * *

For a wonder, both Panteles and Bozorg looked pleased with themselves. "We can break this spell, lord," Bozorg said to Abivard.

Panteles shook his head. "No, eminent sir," he said. "Breaking it is the wrong way to express what we do. But we can, I think, cut across it as you did with the Voimios strap a few days ago. That will produce the desired effect, or so we believe."

"I say breaking is a better way to describe what we do," Bozorg said. He and Panteles glared at each other.

"I don't care what you call it or how you describe it," Abivard said. "So long as your spell—or whatever it is—works, names don't matter. Argue all you like about them—later."

A few Videssian horsemen still patrolled the eastern bank of the canal—not so many now, for Maniakes must have concluded that his spell was keeping Abivard trapped on the other side. At first the Avtokrator's disposition of his army had been cautious, but now he went about the business of destruction as if Abivard and his men were no longer anywhere near.

Maybe we'll give him a surprise, Abivard thought. *Or maybe we'll just end up here again, where we started. Have to find out, though. That's the worst thing that can happen, and how are we worse off if it does?*

Panteles and Bozorg began to chant, the one in Videssian and the other in the Makuraner language. Bozorg sprinkled sparkling crystals into a bowl of water, which turned bright yellow. Abivard looked out to the canal. The water there did not turn bright yellow but remained muddy brown.

Panteles, chanting still, held a knife over a small fire of fragrant wood till the blade glowed red. Then he plunged it into the bowl of yellow water. A hiss and a puff of strong-smelling steam rose from the water. Still holding the blade in his right hand, he took from his belt pouch a Voimios strap like the one he had given to Abivard to cut lengthwise.

He called on Phos. At the same time, either to complement or to confound his invocation, Bozorg called on the God through the Prophets Four. Panteles took the knife and cut the twisted strap of leather with it—cut it clean across, as Abivard had done, so that it became a plain strap once more, not one with the peculiar properties the Voimios strap displayed.

Abivard looked out toward the canal again. He didn't know what he would see. He didn't know if he would see anything. Maybe the spell would produce no visible effect. Maybe it wouldn't work—that was always possible, too.

Bozorg and Panteles stood as if they didn't know whether the spell was working, either. Watching them, Abivard forgot about the canal for a moment. When Panteles gave a sharp gasp, he stared at the Videssian, not at the muddy ditch. Then the Videssian mage pointed to it.

The surface of the canal roiled and bubbled. That was how it began. Slowly, slowly, over minutes, the water in the canal pulled away from itself: that was how Abivard described it to himself afterward. When the process was done, the muddy bottom of the canal lay exposed to the sun—it was as if someone had taken a knife to the waterway and cut it in two.

"The law of similarity," Panteles said in Videssian.

"Like yields like," Bozorg said in the Makuraner tongue—two ways of putting the same thought into words.

"Come on!" Abivard shouted to his warriors, who gaped at the gap in the canal. "Now we can reach the Videssians. Now we can make them pay for turning us the wrong way time after time." He sprang onto his horse. "Are we going to let them get away with what they did to us, or are we going to punish them?"

"Punish!" the Makuraner soldiers howled, savage as a pack of wolves on a cold winter night. Abivard had to boot his horse hard to make sure he entered the canal first. The going was slow, for the mud was thick and slimy and pulled at the horse's legs. But the beast went on.

In the water piled up to either side of the muddy, stinking canal bottom, Abivard saw a fish. It stared out at him, mouth opening and closing, as if it were a stupid old man. He wondered what it thought of him and then whether it thought at all.

Up toward the eastern bank of the canal he rode. Despite the magic of Panteles and Bozorg, he still feared he would somehow end up back on the west side of the canal again. But he didn't.

Floundering and then gaining steadiness, his horse carried him up onto the eastern side at last.

Had the Videssian soldiers there wanted to make a fight of it, they might well have prevented his army from gaining a lodgment. The opening the two mages had made in the canal was not very wide, and only a few horses could get through it at any one time. A determined stand might have held up the whole Makuraner force.

But the Videssians, who had seemed taken aback by the wizards' success in breaking or breaking through their spell, also seemed startled that the Makuraners were exploiting that success so vigorously. Instead of staying and trying to hold back Abivard and his men, they rode off as fast as their horses would carry them. Maybe they were taking Maniakes the news of what had just happened. Had Abivard been Maniakes, he would have been less than delighted to see them come. As things were, he was delighted to see them go.

Later, he wished he had sent men straight after them. At the moment he was just glad he and his followers wouldn't have to fight them. Instead of pursuit, what he thought about was getting as many men across the canal as he could before either the sorcery Bozorg and Panteles had cobbled together or the two men themselves collapsed.

The bulk of the army did get across before Panteles, who had been swaying like a tree in a high wind, toppled to the ground. As he did, the suspended water in the canal came together with a wet slap. Some of the foot soldiers who were caught in it drowned; more, though, struggled forward and crawled out onto the eastern bank, wet and dripping but alive.

At first Abivard and his companions were so busy helping them to dry land, he had no time for thought. Then he realized the soldiers were reaching the eastern bank, not being thrown back to the west. The spell the Videssian and Makuraner mages had used, though vanished now, had left the canal permanently untwisted. It was, in short, as it had been before Maniakes' wizards had begun meddling with it.

By then Bozorg and some of the other men still on the western bank of the canal had flipped water into Panteles' face. Free of the burden of having to maintain the spell, the Videssian wizard managed to stay on his feet and even rejoin Abivard on the eastern side of the waterway.

"Well done!" Abivard greeted him.

"For which I thank you, eminent sir," Panteles answered. "The relationship between the Voimios strap and the nature of the spell laid on the canal did indeed prove to be close to that which I had envisioned. This conformation between theory and practice is particularly satisfying on those rare occasions when it may be observed."

"You were right," Bozorg said. "You were right, you were right, you were right. By the Prophets Four, I admit it." He spoke as a man might when publicly paying off a bet.

Panteles peered around. Now that the Makuraner army had reached it, the eastern bank of the canal seemed little different from the western: flat, muddy land with a lot of soldiers scattered across it. The Videssian wizard turned to Abivard. "Having gained this side of the canal, eminent sir, what will you do next?"

It was a good question and not one Abivard could answer on the spur of the moment. For the past several days getting across the canal had so consumed him, he'd lost track of the reasons for which he'd sought to do so. One thing, however, remained clear: "I am going to hunt Maniakes down and fight him when I do."

Romezan had never let that escape his mind. Already, with the last of the soldiers across the canal, still muddy and soaked, he was shouting, "Form up, the God curse you. Don't stand around there wasting time. The Videssian patrols rode off to the southeast. You think they went that way by accident? In a horse's pizzle they did! If that's not where we'll find Maniakes, I'll eat my scabbard, metal fittings and all."

Abivard thought he was right. Maniakes hadn't quite taken for granted the Makuraners' inability to cross the canal, but he had left behind a force too small to fight their whole army, especially after failing to fight when Abivard and the first few men following him had floundered up onto the bank the Videssians had been holding without effort. If they weren't going to fight, the only useful service they could perform was warning the Avtokrator. To do that, they'd have to go where he was. Abivard's army would follow them there.

He raised his voice, adding his outcry to Romezan's relentless shouts. The soldiers responded more slowly than he would have wanted but not, he supposed, more slowly than was to be expected after the trouble they'd had reaching the eastern bank of the canal.

And as the men shook themselves out into a line of march, excitement gradually began to seep into them. They cheered Abivard when he rode up and down the line. "Wasn't for you, lord, we'd *still* be stuck over there," somebody called. That made the cheers come louder.

Abivard wondered if Maniakes knew his magic had been defeated even before soldiers had ridden to him with the news. He would have a wizard—more likely wizards—with him. Breaking the Videssian spell probably would have produced a quiver of some sort in the world, a quiver a wizard could sense.

Because of that suspicion, Abivard reinforced what would have been his normal vanguard with picked fighting men who did not usually move at the very fore. He also spread his net of scouts and outriders farther around the army than he normally might have. If trouble threatened, he wanted warning as soon as he could get it.

"Be particularly careful and alert," he warned the scouts. "Tzikas is liable to be commanding the Videssian rear guard. If he is, you'll have to look for something nasty and underhanded. I wish I could guess what, but I can't. All I can tell you is, keep your eyes open."

For the first day after crossing the canal he wondered if Maniakes had bothered with a rear guard. His own army surged forward without resistance. They made so much progress, he almost felt as if they'd made up for all the time they'd spent trapped on the far side of the canal.

When he said that to Roshnani after they'd finally camped for the night, she gave him the look she reserved for times when he'd been especially foolish. "Don't be absurd," she said. "You can't make up that much time in one day, and you know it."

"Well, yes, so I do," he admitted, and gave her a look of his own. "I'd bet none of the great minstrels ever had a wife like you." His voice went falsetto: "No, you can't say his sword sang, dear. Swords don't sing. And was his armor really too heavy for ten ordinary men to lift, let alone wear? That doesn't sound very likely to me. Why don't you change it?"

Roshnani made as if to pick up the pot of saffron rice and black cherries that sat between them and dump it over his head. But she was laughing, too. "Wicked man," she said.

"Thank you," he said, making both of them laugh some more. But he quickly grew serious again. "If the magic this morning had failed, I don't know what I would have done. I don't know what the army would have done."

"The worst you could have done would have been to lay down your command and go back to Vek Rud domain. There are still times I wish you'd done it after Sharbaraz refused to let you summon Romezan."

"That worked out well in spite of Sharbaraz," Abivard answered. "Romezan is like me: he sees what the realm needs and goes ahead and takes care of it no matter what the King of Kings may think of the matter."

Roshnani sniffed. "The King of Kings is supposed to see what the realm needs and take care of it himself. He shouldn't need to rely on others to do that for him. If he can't do it, why is he the one to rule Makuran?"

She spoke in a low voice and looked around before the words left her mouth to make sure no servant—or even her children—could hear. Abivard understood that; unlike Romezan, he found the idea of criticizing the King of Kings daunting at best. And Roshnani wasn't just criticizing. She was suggesting Sharbaraz didn't belong on the throne if he didn't do a better job. And if he didn't belong on that throne, who did?

Abivard answered in a voice as soft as the one his principal wife had used: "I don't want to rebel against Sharbaraz King of Kings. Can you imagine me trying to lord it over the eunuchs in the palace? I only wish Sharbaraz would tend to ruling the realm and let all of us who serve him tend to our own soup without his always sticking his finger in and giving it a stir."

"He *is* the King of Kings, and he knows it," Roshnani said with a wintry sigh. "He knows it too well, maybe. Whenever he can stick his finger in, he feels he has to, as if he wouldn't be ruling if he didn't."

"I've spent a good part of the past ten years and more hoping—wishing—you were wrong," Abivard said, sighing, too. "I'm beginning to think you're right. Pound me on the head with a hammer often enough and ideas do sometimes get in. From brief acquaintance with his father, it's in his blood."

"It might not have been so bad if he hadn't had the throne stolen from him once," Roshnani said.

Abivard gulped down his wine. "It might not have been so bad," he said, spacing his words out to emphasize them, "if Smerdis had kept on being King of Kings and no one had ever found out Sharbaraz was hidden away in Nalgis Crag stronghold."

When the words were out of his mouth, he realized he'd spoken treason—retroactive treason, since Smerdis the usurper was long dead, but treason nonetheless. He waited to hear how Roshnani would react to it. Calmly, she said, "Had matters turned out so, you wouldn't be brother-in-law to the King of Kings, you know."

"Do you think I care?" he returned. "I don't think my sister would have been less happy if she'd stayed married to Pradtak of Nalgis Crag domain than she is married to Sharbaraz of Makuran. No more happy, maybe, but not less." He sighed again. "You can't tell about such things, though. Smerdis was busy paying the Khamorth tribute, if you'll remember. That would have touched off a revolt in the Northwest sooner or later. As well, maybe, that we had a proper King of Kings to head it."

"Maybe." Roshnani emptied her wine cup, too. "All these might-have-beens can make you dizzier than wine if you spend too much time thinking about them."

"Everything is simple now," Abivard said. "All we have to do is beat Maniakes."

First they had to come to grips with Maniakes. As Abivard had already discovered, that wasn't easy, not when Maniakes didn't care to be gripped. But having defeated the Avtokrator's best sorcery—or what he sincerely hoped was the Avtokrator's best sorcery—he pursued him with more confidence than he would have shown before.

In case his sincere hopes proved mistaken, he stopped ignoring Bozorg and Panteles and had the two wizards ride together in a wagon near his own. Sometimes they got on as well as a couple of brothers. Sometimes they quarreled—also like a couple of brothers. As long as they weren't working magic to do away with each other, Abivard pretended not to see.

He sent his part of cavalry out in a wide sweep, first to find Maniakes' army and then to slow it down so he could come up with the main body of his army and fight the Videssians. "This is what we couldn't do before," he said enthusiastically, riding along with Turan. "We can move horsemen out ahead and make the Videssians turn and fight, hold them in place long enough for the rest of us to come forward and smash them."

"If all goes well, we can," Turan said. "Their rear guard has been fighting hard, though, to keep us from getting hold of the main force Maniakes is leading."

"They can only do that for so long, though," Abivard said. "The land between the Tutub and the Tib isn't like the Pardrayan steppe: it doesn't go on forever. After a while you get pushed off the floodplain and out into the scrub country. You can't keep an army alive out there."

"We talked about that last winter," his lieutenant answered. "Maniakes didn't even try then. He just crossed the Videssian westlands till he came to a port, then sailed away, no doubt laughing at us. He could do the same again, every bit as easily."

"Yes, I suppose he could," Abivard said. "He could go on to Serrhes, too, in the interior, the way Sharbaraz did all those years ago. I don't think he'll do either one, though. When he came into the land of the Thousand Cities last year, he had doubts. He was tentative; he wasn't sure at first that his soldiers were reliable. He's not worried about that anymore. He knows his men can fight. If he sees a spot he likes, he'll give battle there. He aimed to wreck us when he came back this year."

"He almost did it a couple of times, too," Turan agreed. "And then, when that didn't work, he tried to drive us mad with the magic his wizards put on the canal." He chuckled. "That was such a twisted scheme, I wonder if Tzikas was the one who thought of it."

Abivard started to answer seriously before realizing Turan was joking. Joke or not, it wasn't the most unlikely notion Abivard had ever heard. As he'd learned from painful experience, Tzikas was devious enough to have done exactly what Turan had said.

Abivard soon had reason to pride himself on his own predictive powers. Not far from the headwaters of the Tutub, where the stream still flowed swift and foamy over stones before taking a generally calmer course, Maniakes chose a stretch of high ground and made it very plain to his pursuers that he intended to be pursued no more.

"We'll smash him!" Romezan shouted. "We'll smash him and be rid of him once and for all." After a moment he added, "Won't miss him a bit once he's gone, either."

"That would be very fine," Abivard agreed. "The longer I look at that position, though, the more I think we'll come out of it like lamb's meat chopped up for the spit if we're not careful."

"They're only Videssians," Romezan said. "It's not as if they're going to come charging down at us while we're advancing on them."

"No, I suppose not," Abivard said. "But an uphill charge—and it would be a long uphill charge—doesn't strike with so much force as one on level ground. And if I know anything about Maniakes, it's that he doesn't intend just to sit up there and await our charge. He'll do something to break it up and keep it from hitting as hard as it should."

"What can he do?" Romezan demanded.

"I don't know," Abivard said. "I wish I did."

"And I wish you wouldn't shy at shadows," Romezan said. "Maniakes is only a man, and soldier for soldier our horsemen are better than his. He can make a river flip—or he could till we figured out how to stop him—but he can't make his whole cursed army leap up in the air and land in our rear and on both flanks at the same time, now, can he?"

"No," Abivard admitted.

"Well, then," Romezan said triumphantly, as if he'd proved his point. Maybe he thought he had; he was as straightforward and aggressive in argument as he was in leading his cavalry into action.

Abivard shook his head. "Go straight into battle against the Videssians and you're asking to come to grief. And not all fields are as open and tempting as they look. Remember how Peroz King of Kings died, leading the flower of the soldiery of Makuran against the Khamorth across what looked like an ordinary stretch of steppe. If my horse hadn't stepped in a hole and broken a leg at the very start of that charge, I expect I would have died there, too, along with my father and my brother and three half brothers."

Romezan scowled but had no quick comeback. Every Makuraner noble family, whether from the Seven Clans or from the lesser nobility, had suffered grievous loss out on the Pardrayan steppe. After that fight how could you argue for a headlong charge and against at least a little caution?

Sanatruq remained impetuous even after Abivard's blunt warning. "What are we going to do, then, lord?" he demanded. "Did we find a way across the canal only to decide we needn't have bothered? If we're not going to fight the Videssians, we might as well have stayed where we were."

"I never said we weren't going to fight them," Abivard said. "But don't you think doing it on our terms instead of theirs matters?"

The argument should have been telling. The argument in fact was telling—to Abivard. Romezan let out a sigh. "I should have stayed in the Videssian westlands and sent Kardarigan to you with this part of the field army. The two of you would have got on better than you and I do, both of you being . . . cautious. But I thought a cautious man better there, where there were towns to guard, and a fighter better here, where there were battles to wage. Maybe I was wrong."

That hurt. Abivard turned away so Romezan wouldn't see him wince. And had Romezan not been intrepid enough to leave the westlands and disobey Sharbaraz' order against doing it, to say nothing of being intrepid enough to pitch right into the Videssians when he found them, Abivard would have been in no condition to hold this conversation now. Still—

"A baker thinks bread is the answer to every question," he said, "while a farrier is sure it's horseshoes. No wonder a battler wants to go straight into the fray. But I don't merely want to fight Maniakes—I want to crush him if we can. If thinking things over instead of wading straight in will help us do that, I'd sooner think."

Romezan's bow was anything but submissive. "There he is," he said, pointing toward the banner with a gold sunburst on blue that marked the Avtokrator's position. "He's got water right behind him, enough to keep him from getting thirsty but not enough to keep him from going over it if he has to. He's got the high ground. If he doesn't have plenty of food, I'll be amazed and so will you. He's got no reason to move, in other words. If we want him, we have to go at him. He's not going to come to us."

All those comments were true. Abivard had been studying the ground and said, "Don't you think the slope is less there on his right—our left?"

"If you say so, lord," Romezan answered, prepared to be magnanimous now that he scented victory. "Do you want the attack to go in on our left? We can do that, of course."

Abivard shook his head, and that made Romezan and Sanatruq look suspicious again. He said, "I want to make it seem as if the main attack is going in on our left. I want Maniakes to think that and to shift his forces to meet it. But once he's gone for the feint, I want the true attack to come from the right."

Romezan toyed with one spiky, waxed mustache tip. "Aye, lord, that's good," he said at last. "We give them something they don't expect that way."

"And you'll want the foot to hold the center, the way you've been doing lately?" Turan asked.

"Just so," Abivard agreed. As Romezan was in the habit of doing, the noble from the Seven Clans looked down his considerable nose at the mere mention of infantry. Before taking over the city garrisons Abivard would have done the same thing. He knew what these men were worth, though. They would fight and fight hard. He slapped Turan on the shoulder. "Get them ready."

"Aye, lord." His lieutenant hurried away.

Something else occurred to Abivard. "When we move against the Videssians, Romezan, I will command on the left and you on the right."

Romezan stared at him. "Lord . . . you would give me the honor of leading the chief attack? I am in your debt, but are you certain you do not damage your own honor with this generosity?"

"The realm comes first," Abivard said firmly. "Maniakes will see me there on the left. He'll recognize my banners, and he'll likely recognize me, too. When he sees me there, that will make him more certain the division of the army I command will be the one to try to smash him. He will reason as you do, Romezan: how could I give up the place of honor to another? But honor lies in victory, and for victory over the Videssians I gladly give up this superficial honor."

Romezan bowed very low, as if Abivard were far superior to him in rank. "Lord, you could do worse than instructing the Seven Clans on the nature of honor."

"To the Void with that. If they want instruction, we've sent them enough Videssian slaves to serve them as pedagogues for the next hundred years. What we have now is a battle to fight." Abivard stared over toward the distant banners of Videssos that marked the Avtokrator's position. Outwitting Maniakes got trickier every time he tried it, but he'd managed to come up with something new. Like a boy with a new toy, he could hardly wait to try it.

"Let me understand you, lord," Romezan said. "You will want my men to hang back somewhat and not show their true courage—they should act as if the steepness of the ground troubles them."

"That's what I have in mind," Abivard agreed, his earlier quarrel with Romezan almost forgotten. "I'll press the attack on my flank as hard as I can and do everything I know how to do to draw as many Videssians to me as will come. Meanwhile, you, poor fellow, will be having all sorts of trouble—till the right moment comes."

"I won't be too soon, lord," Romezan promised. "And you can bet I won't be too late, either." He sounded very sure of himself.

For the first time since his recall from Across Abivard had a proper Makuraner army, not some slapped-together makeshift, to lead into battle against the Videssians. Since Likinios' overthrow, he'd won whenever he had led a proper army against them. Indeed, they'd fled before him time after time. He eyed his men. They seemed full of quiet confidence. They were used to beating the Videssians, too.

He rode to the front of the left wing. On this field he wanted his presence widely advertised. Banners blazoned with the red lion of Makuran fluttered all around him. *Here I am, the commander of this host,* they shouted to the Videssians up on their low rise. *I'm going to lead the main attack—of course I am. Pay me plenty of attention.*

Maniakes, by his own banners, led from the center of his army, the most common Videssian practice. He'd invited battle, which meant he felt confident, too. He'd beaten the Kubrati barbarians. He'd beaten Abivard more often than not—when Abivard had been leading a patchwork force. Did that really make him think he could beat the Makuraner field army? If it did, Abivard intended to show him he was wrong.

Abivard nodded to the horn players. "Sound the advance," he said, and pointed up the slope toward the Videssians. Martial music blared forth. Abivard booted his horse in the ribs. It started forward.

He had to sacrifice a little of the full fury of a Makuraner charge because he was going uphill at the Videssians. He also had to be careful to make sure the horse archers he'd placed to link the heavy cavalry contingents he and Romezan commanded to Turan's infantry kept on linking the different units and didn't go rushing off on some brainstorm of their own. That might open gaps the Videssians could exploit.

Horn calls rang out along the Videssian line, too. Peering over the chain mail veil of his helmet, Abivard watched Maniakes' men ride forward to meet his. Whatever else they intended, the Videssians didn't aim to stand solely on the defensive.

Their archers started shooting at the oncoming Makuraner heavy cavalry. Here and there a man slid from his mount or a horse stumbled and went down, and as often as not, other horses would trip over those in the first ranks that had fallen. Had the Videssians done more damage with their archery, they might have disrupted the Makuraner charge.

But the riders of Makuran were armored in iron from head to foot. Their horses wore iron scales, too, sewn into or mounted in pockets on the blankets that covered their backs and sides, while iron chamfrons protected their heads and necks. Arrows found lodging places far less often than they would have against lightly warded men and animals.

No one now rode out between the armies with a challenge to single combat. In principle, such duels were honorable, even if Tzikas' attempts to use them both for and against Makuran had all but driven Abivard mad. But showy displays of honor had given way—on both sides, apparently—to a hard desire to fight things out to the end as soon as possible.

Lowering his lance, Abivard picked the Videssian he wanted to spear out of the saddle. The imperial saw him coming, saw the stroke was going to be unavoidable, and twisted in the saddle to try to turn the lance head with his small, round shield.

He gauged the angle well. Sparks spit as the iron point skidded across the iron facing of his shield. That deflection kept the point from his vitals. But the force of the blow still all but unhorsed him and meant his answering sword cut came closer to lopping off one of his mount's ears than to doing Abivard any harm.

"Sharbaraz!" Abivard shouted. He spurred his horse forward, using speed and weight against the Videssian. As the man—he *was* a good horseman and as game as they came—righted himself in the saddle, Abivard clouted him on the side of the head with the shaft of his lance. The blow caught the Videssian by surprise; it was one a Makuraner was far likelier to make with a broken lance than with a whole one, the point being so much more deadly than the shaft.

But Abivard knew from painful experience how much damage a blow to the head could do even if it didn't cave in a skull. The Videssian reeled. He held on to the sword but looked at it as if he hadn't the slightest idea what it was good for.

His opponent stunned, Abivard had the moment he needed to draw the lance back and slam it into the fellow's throat. Blood sprayed out, then gushed as he yanked the point free. The Videssian clutched at the shaft of the lance, but his grip had no strength to it. His hands slipped away, and he crumpled to the ground.

Another Videssian slashed at Abivard. Awkwardly, he blocked the blow with his lance. The imperial's blade bit into the wood. The soldier cursed horribly as he worked it free; his face was twisted with fear lest he be assailed while he could not use his weapon. He did manage to clear it before another Makuraner attacked him. What happened to him after that, Abivard never knew. As was often the way of battle, they were swept apart.

Abivard had plenty of fighting nonetheless. Because he had made no secret of his rank, the Videssians swarmed against him, trying to cut him down. He did eventually break his lance over the head of one of those Videssians. That blow didn't merely stun the man—it broke his neck. He slid off his horse like a sack of rice after a strap broke.

Throwing the stump of the lance at the nearest Videssian, Abivard yanked his sword free of the scabbard. He slashed an imperial's unarmored horse. The animal screamed and bucked. The soldier aboard it had all he could do to stay on. For the next little while he couldn't fight. Abivard counted that a gain.

Fighting in the first rank himself, he had less sight of the battlefield as a whole than he'd grown used to enjoying. Whenever he looked around to get a picture of what was happening, some Videssian was generally inconsiderate enough to try to take advantage of his lack of attention by puncturing or otherwise maiming him.

One thing he did discover: in Maniakes the Videssians now had a commander who could make them stand and fight. Throughout Genesios' reign the imperials had fled before the Makuraner field army. They'd fled through the early years of Maniakes' reign, too, but they fled no more.

Abivard, doing everything he could against them, felt their confidence, their cockiness. Whenever his men managed to hew their way a few feet forward, the Videssians, instead of panicking, rallied and pushed them back. Yes, the imperials had the advantage of terrain, but an advantage of that sort meant little unless the soldiers who enjoyed it were prepared to exploit it. The Videssians were.

"Here, come on!" one of their officers called, waving men forward. "Got to plug the holes, boys, or the wine dribbles out of the jar." Having learned Videssian, Abivard had often used his knowledge of the language to gain an edge on his foes. Now, overhearing that calm, matter-of-fact reaction to trouble, he began to worry. Warriors who didn't let themselves get fearful and flustered when things went wrong were hard to beat.

He listened for the Videssian horn calls, gauging how many of the enemy were being drawn from Maniakes' left to help deal with the trouble he was causing here. A fair number, he judged. Enough to let Romezan strike a telling blow on that flank? He'd find out.

Turan's foot soldiers poured volleys of arrows into the ranks of the Videssians. Maniakes' men shot back. Groans rose from the ranks of the infantry as one soldier after another fell. As usual, the Videssians suffered fewer casualties than they inflicted on their foes. Abivard thought kindly of the garrison troops he'd turned into real soldiers. If he'd left them in their cities, though, how many men who had died would still be alive today?

He knew no way to answer that question. He did know that a good many men and women in the Thousand Cities—and probably in Mashiz, too—who lived now would almost certainly have been dead had he not gathered the garrisons together and made the swaggering town toughs warriors instead.

As if struck by the same idea at the same time, Turan's soldiers rushed up at Maniakes' men while a couple of troops of imperials detached themselves from the main Videssian mass and rode down against their tormentors. Neither side, then, got what it wanted. The Makuraners who advanced kept the Videssians from getting in among their fellows, while the surge of the Makuraners upslope kept the imperials from galloping down on them and perhaps slashing their way through them.

And over on the right—what was happening over on the right? From where Abivard had placed himself, with so much of Maniakes' army between him and the division Romezan led, he could not tell. He was sure Romezan hadn't yet charged home with all the strength he had. Had he done so, Videssian horn calls—the God willing, dismayed Videssian horn calls—would have alerted Abivard as they summoned more imperials.

Romezan was still holding back, still waiting for Abivard, by the ferocity of his attack, to convince Maniakes that this was where the supreme Makuraner effort lay, that this was where the Videssians would have to bring all their strength if they were going to survive, that the other wing, without the presence of a supreme commander, could not deliver—could not imagine delivering—a strong blow of its own.

Abivard was the one who had to do the convincing, and the Avtokrator was a much more discriminating audience than he had been before. If you were going to act a part, it was best to do it to the hilt. Waving his sword, Abivard shouted to his men, "Press them hard! We'll bring Maniakes back to Mashiz in chains and throw him down at Sharbaraz' feet!"

He got a cheer from his soldiers, who did press the Videssians harder. As he slashed at an imperial with a heavy-featured, swarthy face that argued for Vaspurakaner blood, he felt the irony of the war cry he had just loosed. He wanted to give Maniakes to the King of Kings, but what had Sharbaraz given him lately? Humiliation, mistrust, suspicion—if Romezan hadn't disobeyed Sharbaraz, Abivard would not have been commanding these men.

But to the soldiers Sharbaraz King of Kings might as well have been Makuran incarnate. They knew little of Abivard's difficulties with him and cared less. When they shouted Sharbaraz' name, they shouted it from the bottoms of their hearts. Absurdly, Abivard felt almost guilty for inspiring them with a leader who was, were the truth known, something less than inspiring.

He shook his head, making the chain mail veil he wore clink and clatter. Inspiration and truth barely spoke to each other. Men picked up pieces of things they thought they knew and sewed them together into bright, shining patterns, patching thin spots and holes with hopes and dreams. And the patterns somehow glowed even if the bits of truth in them were invisibly small.

He was trying to make Maniakes see a pattern, too, a pattern like that of many past Makuraner attacks. It was a point of honor for a Makuraner commander to lead the chief assault of his army. Here was Abivard, commanding the army and ostentatiously leading an assault against the Videssians. If you brought over enough good troops to contain the force he led, you won the battle, didn't you? By the pattern of battles past, you did.

"Here I am," Abivard panted, slashing at an imperial soldier. The fellow took the blow on his shield. The tides of battle swept him away from Abivard before he could return a cut. "Here I am," Abivard repeated. "You have to pay attention to me, don't you, Maniakes?"

When would the big attack on the right go in? Romezan's instinct was to hit as hard as he could as soon as he could. Abivard marveled that he'd managed to restrain himself so long. The next thing to worry about was, would Romezan, restraining himself from striking too early, restrain himself so thoroughly that he struck too late? He'd said not, back when Abivard had given him his orders, but . . .

In the press of fighting—Videssians ahead of him, Makuraners behind him trying to move forward to get at the Videssians—Abivard found himself unable to send a messenger to Romezan. It was a disadvantage of leading from the front he hadn't anticipated. He had to rely on Romezan's good judgment—he had to hope Romezan had good judgment.

The longer the fight went on, the more he doubted that. Over here, on the left, his force and the Videssians facing them were locked together as tightly as two lovers in an embrace that went on and on and on. In the center Turan's foot soldiers, keeping their ranks tight, were doing a good job of holding and harassing their mounted foes. And over on the right—

"Something had better happen over on the right," Abivard said, "or the Videssians will beat us over here before we can beat them over there."

Nobody paid the least bit of attention to him. Most likely nobody heard him, not with the clangor of combat all around and the iron veil he wore over his mouth muffling his words. He didn't care. He was doing his best to make patterns, too, even if they weren't the ones he would have preferred to see.

"Come on, Romezan," he said. Nobody heard that, either. What he feared was that Romezan was among the multitude who didn't hear.

Then, when he'd all but given up hope for the attack from the noble of the Seven Clans, the Videssian horns that ordered the movements of imperial troops abruptly blared out a complicated series of new, urgent commands. The pressure against Abivard and his comrades eased. Even above the din of the field shouts of alarm and triumphant cries rang out on the right.

A great weight suddenly seemed to drop from Abivard. For one brief moment battle seemed as splendid, as glorious, as exciting as he'd imagined before he went to war. He wasn't tired, he forgot he was bathed in sweat, he no longer needed to climb down from his horse and empty his bladder. He'd made Maniakes bar the front door—and then had kicked the back door down.

"Come on!" he shouted to the men around him, who were suddenly moving forward again now that Maniakes had thinned his line to rush troops back to the other side to stem Romezan's advance. "If we drive them, they all perish!"

That was how it looked, anyhow. If the Makuraners kept up the pressure from both wings and the center at the same time, how could the Videssian invaders hope to withstand them?

Over the next couple of hours Abivard found out how. He began to think Maniakes should have been not the Avtokrator but a juggler. No traveling mountebank could have done a neater job of keeping so many sets of soldiers flying this way and that to prevent the Makuraners from turning an advantage into a rout.

Oh, the Videssians yielded ground, especially where Romezan had crumpled them on the right. But they didn't break and flee as they had in so many fights over the years, and they didn't quite let either Romezan's men or Abivard's find a hole in their line, tear through, and cut off part of their army. Whenever that looked like it would happen, Maniakes would find some reserves—or soldiers in a different part of the fight who weren't so heavily pressed—to throw into the opening and delay the Makuraners just long enough to let the Videssians contract and re-form their line.

Abivard tried to send men from his own force around to his left to see if he could get into the Videssians' rear by outflanking them if he couldn't bull his way through. That didn't work, either. For once, the lighter armor the Videssians wore worked to their advantage. Carrying less weight, their horses moved faster than those of Abivard's men, and, even starting later, they were able to block and forestall his force.

"All right, then," he cried, gathering the men together once more. "A last good push and we'll have them!"

He didn't know whether that was true; under Maniakes the Videssians fought as they hadn't since the days of Likinios Avtokrator. He did know that one more push was all his army had time to make. The sun was going down; darkness would be coming soon. He booted his horse forward. "This time, by the God, we take them!" he shouted.

And for a while he thought his army would take them. Back went the Videssians, back and back again, their ranks thinning, thinning, and no more reserves behind them to plug the gap. And then, with victory in Abivard's grasp, close enough for him to reach out and touch it, a hard-riding regiment of imperials came up and hurled themselves at his men, not only halting them but throwing them back. "Maniakes!" the last-minute rescuers and their commander cried. "Phos and Maniakes!"

Abivard's head came up when he heard that commander shout. He had to keep fighting for all he was worth to ensure that the Videssians didn't gain too great an advantage in their turn. But he looked this way and that . . . surely he'd recognized that voice.

Yes! There! "Tzikas!" he cried.

The renegade stared at him. "Abivard!" he said, and then, scornfully, "Eminent sir!"

"Traitor!" they roared together, and rode toward each other.

XI

Abivard slashed at Tzikas with more fury than science. The Videssian renegade—or possibly by now rerenegade—parried the blow with his own sword. Sparks flew as the iron blades belled off each other. Tzikas gave back a cut that Abivard blocked. They struck more sparks.

"You sent me to my death!" Tzikas screamed.

"You slandered me to the King of Kings," Abivard retorted. "You told nothing but lies about me and everything I did. I gave you what you deserved, and I waited too long to do it."

"You never gave me the credit I deserve," Tzikas said.

"You never give anyone around you anything but a kick in the balls, whether he deserves it or not," Abivard said.

As they spoke, they kept cutting at each other. Neither could get through the other's defense. Abivard looked around the field. To his dismay, to his disgust, the same held true of the Makuraners and the Videssians. Tzikas' ferocious counterattack had blunted his last chance for a breakthrough.

"You just saved the fight for a man you tried to murder by magic," Abivard said. If he couldn't slay Tzikas with his sword, he might at least wound him with words.

The renegade's face contorted. "Life doesn't always turn out to be what we think it will, by the God," he said, but at the same time he named the God he also sketched Phos' sun-circle above his

313

heart. Abivard got the idea that Tzikas had no idea which side he belonged on, save only—and always—his own.

A couple of other Videssians rode toward Abivard. He drew back. Wary of a trap, Tzikas did not press him. For once Abivard had no trap waiting. But were he Tzikas, he would have been wary, too. He heartily thanked the God he was not Tzikas, and he did not make Phos' sun-sign as he did so.

He looked over the field again in the fading light to see if he had any hope left of turning victory into rout. Try as he would, he saw none. Here were his banners, and there were those of the Videssians. Horsemen and foot soldiers still hewed at one another, but he did not think anything they did would change the outcome now. Instead of a battlefield, the fight looked more like a picture of a battle on a tapestry or wall painting.

Abivard frowned. That was an odd thought. He stiffened. No, not a picture of a battle—an image of a battle, an image he had seen before. This was the fight Panteles had shown him. He hadn't known, when he had seen it, whether he was looking on past or future. Now, too late to do him any good—as was often true of prophecy—he had the answer.

The Videssians withdrew toward their camp. They kept good order and plainly had plenty of fight left in them. After a last couple of attacks, as twilight began to fall, Abivard let them go.

From his right someone rode up calling his name. His hand tightened on the hilt of his sword. After a clash with Tzikas, he suspected everyone. The approaching horseman wore the full armor of the Makuraner heavy cavalry and rode an armored horse as well. Abivard remained cautious. Armor could be captured, and horses, too. And the chain mail veil the rider wore would disguise a Videssian in Makuraner clothing.

That veil also had the effect of disguising the voice. Not until the rider drew very close did Abivard recognize Romezan. "By the God," he exclaimed, "I wouldn't have known you from your gear. You look as if you've had a smith pounding on you."

If anything, that was an understatement. A sword stroke had sheared the bright, tufted crest from atop Romezan's helm. His surcoat had been cut to ribbons. Somewhere in the fighting he'd lost not only his lance but also his shield. Through the rents in his surcoat Abivard could see the dents in his armor. He had an arrow sticking out of his left shoulder, but by the way he moved his arm, it must have lodged in the padding he wore beneath his lamellar armor, not in his flesh.

"I *feel* as if a smith's been pounding on me," he said. "I've got bruises all over; three days from now I'll look like a sunset the court poets would sing about for years." He hung his head. "Lord, I fear I held off on the charge till too late. If I'd loosed my men at the Videssians sooner, we'd have had so much more time in which to finish the job of beating them."

"It's done," Abivard said; he was also battered and bruised and, as usual after a battle, deathly tired. He thought Romezan had held off till too late, too, but what good would screaming about it do now? "We hold the field where we fought; we can claim the victory."

"It's not enough," Romezan insisted, as hard on himself as he was on the foe. "You wanted to smash them, not just push them back. We could have done it, too, if I'd moved faster. I have to say, though, I didn't think Videssians could fight that well."

"If it makes you feel any better, neither did I," Abivard said. "For as long as I've been warring against them, when we send in the heavy cavalry, they give way. But not today."

"No, not today." Romezan twisted in the saddle, trying to find a way to make the armor fit more comfortably on his sore carcass. "You were right, lord, and I own it. They can be very dangerous to us."

"Right at the end I thought we would break through here on the left," Abivard said. "They threw the last of their reserves in to stop us, and they did. You'll never guess who was leading those reserves."

"No, eh?" All Abivard could see of Romezan was his eyes. They widened. "Not Tzikas?"

"The very same. Somehow Maniakes has found a way to keep him alive and keep him tame, at least for now, because he fought like a demon."

For the next considerable while Romezan spoke with pungent

ingenuity. The gist of what he said boiled down to *how very unfortunate*, but he put it rather more vividly than that. When he'd calmed down to the point where he no longer seemed to be imitating a kettle boiling over, he said, "We may be sorry, but Maniakes also will be. Tzikas is more dangerous to the side he's on than to the one he isn't on, because you never know when he's going to go over to the other one."

"I've had the same notion," Abivard said. "But while he's being good for Maniakes, he knows he has to be very good indeed or the Avtokrator will stake him out for the crows and buzzards."

"If it were me, I'd do it whether he was being very good indeed or not," Romezan said.

"So would I," Abivard agreed. "And next time I get the chance—and there's likely to be a next time—I will . . . unless I don't."

"Do we pick up the fight tomorrow, lord?" Romezan asked. "If it were up to me, I would, but it isn't up to me."

"I won't say yes or no till morning," Abivard answered. "We'll see what sort of shape the army is in then and see what the Videssians are doing, too." He yawned. "I'm so tired now, I might as well be drunk. My head will be clearer come morning, too."

"Ha!" Romezan said in a voice so full of doubt, a Videssian would have been proud to claim it. "I know you better than that, lord. You'll have scouts wake you half a dozen times in the night to tell you what they can see of the Videssian camp."

"After most fights I'd do just that," Abivard said. "Not tonight."

"Ha!" Romezan said again. Abivard maintained a dignified silence.

As things worked out, scouts woke Abivard only four times during the night. He couldn't decide whether that demolished Romezan's point or proved it.

The news the scouts brought back was so utterly predictable, so utterly normal, that Abivard could have neglected to send them out and still have had almost as good a notion of what the

Videssians were doing. The foe kept a great many fires going through the first watch of the night, fewer in the second, and only those near their guard positions for the third. Maniakes' men would have done the same had they not just fought a great murdering battle. They gave the Makuraners no clue to their intentions.

But when morning came, all that lay on the Videssian campsite were the remains of the fires and a few tents, enough to create the impression in dim light that many more were there. Maniakes and his men had decamped at some unknown hour of the night.

Following them was anything but hard. An army of some thousands of men could hardly slip without a trace through the grass like an archer gliding ever closer to a deer. Thousands of men rode thousands of horses, which left tracks and other reminders of their presence.

And in retreat an army often discarded things its men would keep if they were advancing. The more things soldiers threw away, the likelier their retreat was to be a desperate one.

By that standard the Videssians did not strike Abivard as desperate. Yes, they were running away from Abivard and his men. But they were a long way from jettisoning everything that kept them from running faster.

Abivard did some jettisoning of his own: not without regret, he let Turan's foot soldiers fall behind. "The Videssians are all mounted," he told his lieutenant. "If you stay with us, we can't move fast enough to catch up with them. You follow behind. If it looks as if Maniakes is turning to offer battle again, we'll wait till you catch up to start fighting if we can."

"Meanwhile, we eat your dust," Turan said. A couple of years campaigning as an infantry officer seemed to have made him forget he'd served for years as a horseman before. But, however reluctantly, he nodded. "I see the need, lord, no matter how little I like it. I aim to surprise you, though, with how fast we can march."

"I hope you do," Abivard said. Then he summoned Sanatruq, having a use for an intrepid, aggressive young officer. "I am going to put the lightly armed cavalry in your hands. I want you to course ahead of the heavy horse, the way the hounds course ahead of the hunters when we're after antelope. Bring the Videssians to bay for me. Harass them every way you can think of."

Sanatruq's eyes glowed. "Just as you say, lord. And if Tzikas is still heading up Maniakes' rear guard, I have a small matter or two to discuss with him as well."

"We all have a small matter or two to discuss with Tzikas," Abivard said. He drew his sword. "I've been honing my arguments, you might say." Sanatruq grinned and nodded. He rode off, shouting to the Makuraner horse archers to stop whatever they were doing and get busy doing what he told them.

Be careful, Abivard thought as the light cavalry went trotting out ahead of the more heavily armored riders. Tzikas was liable to be trouble no matter how careful you were; that was why so many people had so much to discuss with him.

Almost as an afterthought, Abivard dashed off a quick letter to Sharbaraz, detailing not only the victory he had won over the imperials but also Tzikas' role in making that victory less than it should have been. *Let's see the cursed renegade try to get back into the good graces of the King of Kings after that,* he thought with considerable satisfaction.

The farther south Maniakes rode, the closer to the source of the Tutub he drew. The land rose. In administrative terms it was still part of the land of the Thousand Cities, but it was unlike the floodplain on which those cities perched. For one thing, the hills here were natural, not the end product of countless years of rubble and garbage. For another, none of the Thousand Cities was anywhere close by. A few farmers lived by the narrow stream of the Tutub and the even narrower tributaries feeding it. A few hunters roamed the wooded hills. For the most part, though, the land seemed empty, deserted.

Abivard wondered what Maniakes had in mind in such unpromising country. He understood why this part of the region remained unfamiliar to him: it wasn't worth visiting. He wished the Videssians joy of it. At an officers' council he said, "If they try to stay here, they'll starve, and in short order, too. If they try to leave, they'll have to cross a fair stretch of country worse than this before they come to any that's better."

Sanatruq said, "If they leave, we'll have driven them out of the land of the Thousand Cities. That was what Sharbaraz King of Kings, may his years be many and his realm increase, set us to do at the start of the campaigning season. I'm not sure anyone thought we could do it, but we've done it."

"We had a certain amount of expert help, for which I'm grateful," Abivard said to Romezan.

"You wanted to force battle," the noble of the Seven Clans said. "You were forcing battle when I rode up and found you. Anyone who goes out and fights the enemy deserves to win, so I was glad to give whatever little help I could." *Get in there and fight and worry later about what's supposed to happen next* should have been blazoned on Romezan's surcoat and painted in big letters on the front of his armor.

"Looks to me like good country for scouring with light cavalry," Abivard said, nodding to Sanatruq. "The rest of us can follow after they've developed whatever positions the Videssians are holding."

"What do you think the Videssians *are* doing here, lord?" Romezan asked. "Are they really finished for this campaigning season, or do they aim to give us one more boot in the crotch if we let 'em?"

"From what I know of Maniakes, I'd say he wants to hit us again if he finds the chance," Abivard said. "But I admit that's only a guess." He grinned at the noble of the Seven Clans. "You asked me just to hear me guess so you can twit me for it if I turn out to be wrong."

"Ha!" Romezan said. "I can figure you for foolish without getting as complicated as that."

Abivard waited till his subordinates were done laughing, then said, "We'll go ahead as if we're certain Maniakes is lying in wait for us. Better to worry and be wrong than not to worry—and be wrong." Not even Romezan could argue with him there.

Up close, the ground was worse than it appeared. The road through the highlands from which the Tutub sprang wound into little rocky valleys and over hillsides so packed with thorny, spiky scrub plants that going off it cut your speed not in half but to a quarter of what it was on the track.

No, that wasn't true. Going out into the scrub cut your speed to a quarter of what it would have been if the road had been unobstructed. The road, however, was anything but. The Videssians had thoughtfully sown it with caltrops, the exact equivalent for this terrain of breaking canals in the floodplain. Abivard's men had to slow down to clear the spikes, which let Maniakes' force increase its lead.

And to complicate things further, every so often the Videssians would post archers in the undergrowth by the side of the road and try to pot a few of the Makuraners who were picking up the caltrops. That meant Abivard had to send men after them, and that meant he lost still more time.

Seeing Maniakes getting ever farther ahead ate at him. He wanted to keep moving through the night. That made even Romezan raise an eyebrow. "In this wretched country," he rumbled, "it's hard enough to move during the day. At night—"

If Romezan didn't think it could be done, it couldn't. "But Maniakes is going to get away from us," Abivard said. "We haven't been able to slow him down no matter how we've tried. And if he can travel two or three more days, he'll strike the river that runs south and east to Lyssaion, and he'll have ships waiting there. Ships." As he often had of late, he made the word a curse.

"If we take Lyssaion, he may have ships, but he won't have anywhere they can land," Romezan said.

Abivard shook his head with real regret. "Too late in the year to besiege the place," he said, "and we haven't got the supplies with us to undertake a siege, anyhow." He waited to see whether Romezan would argue with that. The noble from the Seven Clans looked unhappy but kept quiet. Abivard went on, "We have driven him out of the land of the Thousand Cities. At the start of the campaigning season I would have been happy to settle for that."

"Generals who are happy to settle for less than the most they can get mostly don't end up with much," Romezan observed. That made Abivard bite his lip, for it was true.

Coming to a town in the middle of that rugged country was a

surprise. The Videssians had burned the place in passing, but it had been little more than a village even before they had put it to the torch. They'd dumped dead animals into the wells that were probably the town's reason for being, too. After that, though, they seemed to have relented, for they stopped leaving caltrops in the roadway. That might, of course, have indicated a dearth of caltrops rather than a sudden surge in goodwill.

"Now we can make better time," Romezan said, noting the absence of the freestanding spiked obstructions. He shouted for the vanguard to speed up, then turned to Abivard, saying, "We'll catch the bastards yet; see if we don't."

"Maybe we will," Abivard replied. "The God grant we do." He scratched his head. "It's not like the Videssians to make things easy for us, though."

"They can't do everything right all the time," Romezan grunted. "When they squat over a slit trench, it's not rose petals that come out." He shouted again for more speed. Abivard pondered his analogy.

As the day went on, Abivard began to think the noble from the Seven Clans might have had a point. The army hadn't moved so fast since it had gotten into the uplands, and the Videssians couldn't be very far ahead. One more engagement and Maniakes might not be able to get his army back to Lyssaion.

And then, not long before Abivard was going to order his forces out of their column and into a line of battle despite the rugged terrain, a rider came galloping up the path from the southeast, from the Videssian force toward the Makuraners. He was shouting something in the Makuraner tongue as he drew near. Before long Abivard, who was riding at the front of the column, could make out what it was: "Stop! Hold up! It's a trap!"

Abivard turned to the horn players. "Blow halt," he commanded. "We have to find out what this means."

As the call rang out and the horsemen obediently reined in, Abivard studied the approaching horseman, who kept yelling at the top of his lungs. Because the fellow was bawling so hoarsely,

Abivard needed longer than he should have to realize he recognized that voice. His jaw fell.

Before he could speak the name, Romezan beat him to it: "That's Tzikas. It can't be, but it is."

"It really is," Abivard breathed. By then he could see the renegade's face; Videssians usually didn't go in for chain mail veils. "What is he doing here? Did he try killing Maniakes one more time and botch it again? If he did kill him, he'd do us a favor, but if he killed him, he'd be back with the Videssian army, not coming up to ours."

Tzikas rode straight up to Abivard, as he had in battle a few days before. This time, though, he did not draw the sword that hung on his hip. "The God be praised," he said in his lisping Videssian accent. "I've gotten to you before you rode into the trap." The gelding on which he was mounted was blowing and foam-flecked; he'd come at a horse-killing pace.

"What are you talking about, Tzikas?" Abivard ground out. Nothing would have pleased him more than slaying the renegade. No one could stop him now, not with Tzikas coming alone to him in the midst of his army. But the Videssian never would have done such a thing without a pressing reason. Until Abivard found out what that reason was, Tzikas would keep breathing.

Tzikas wasn't breathing well now; gasping was more like it. "Trap," he said, pointing over his shoulder. "Magic. Back there."

"Why should I believe you?" Abivard said. "Why should I ever believe you?" He turned to the men of the vanguard, who were gaping at Tzikas as if he were a ghost walking among men. "Seize him! Drag him off his horse. Disarm him. The God alone knows what mischief he's plotting."

"You're mad!" Tzikas shouted as the Makuraners carried out Abivard's orders. "Why would I stick my head in the lion's mouth if I didn't wish you and the King of Kings well?"

"Escaping from Maniakes comes to mind," Abivard replied. "So does looking for another chance to drag my name through the dirt for Sharbaraz King of Kings, may his days be long and his realm increase." For a despised foreigner like Tzikas, he appended Sharbaraz' honorific formula.

"Why should I want to escape Maniakes when you're just as eager to do me in?" Tzikas asked bitterly. "He gloated about that—by the God, how he gloated about it."

"He gloated so hard and made you hate him so much that you commanded his rear guard, you rode out to challenge me to single combat, and your counterattack wrecked our last chance of beating him," Abivard said. "You were swearing by Phos then, or at least your hand was, though your mouth didn't tell it everything. By the God, Tzikas—" He put into the oath all the contempt he had in him. "—what would you have done if you'd decided you *liked* the Avtokrator?"

"My hand? I don't know what you're talking about," Tzikas said sullenly. It might even have been true. He went on, "Go ahead—mock me, slay me, however you please. And go ahead, run right after the Videssian army. Maniakes will give you a kiss on the cheek for helping him along. See if he doesn't."

He had, if not all the answers, enough of them to make Abivard doubt himself and his purpose. But then, Tzikas usually had a great store of answers, plenty to make you doubt yourself. Videssians bounced truth and lies back and forth, as if in mirrors, till you couldn't tell what you were seeing. Abivard sometimes wondered whether the imperials themselves could keep track.

One thing at a time, then. "What sort of magic is it, Tzikas?"

"I don't know," the renegade answered. "Maniakes didn't tell me. All I know is, I saw his wizards hard at work back there after he and his wife—his cousin who is his wife—had been closeted with them for a couple of hours before they started doing whatever they were doing. I didn't think it was for your health and well-being. I was commanding the rear guard—he'd come to trust me that far again. When I saw my chance, I galloped here. And look at the thanks you give me for it, too."

"You can check this, lord," Romezan rumbled. He'd listened to Tzikas with the same mixture of fascination and doubt Abivard felt.

"I know I can. I intend to," Abivard said. He turned to his men and said to one of them, "Fetch Bozorg and Panteles up here. If there's any magic up ahead, they'll sniff it out. And if there's not,

Tzikas here will wish he'd stayed to suffer Maniakes' tender mercy when he finds out what we end up doing to him." As the soldier hurried off, Abivard shifted to the Videssian to ask a mocking question: "Do you follow that, eminent sir?"

"Perfectly well, thank you." Tzikas had sangfroid, no two ways about it. But then, a man would hardly arrive at a position where he could commit treason—let alone repeated treason—without a goodly helping of sangfroid.

Abivard fretted and stewed. While he waited, Maniakes and his army were getting farther away every moment. After what seemed an interminable delay, Bozorg and Panteles came trotting up behind the soldier Abivard had sent to bring them. He watched Tzikas watching the Videssian in his service and made up his mind not to let the two of them be alone together if he could help it.

No time to worry about that, though. Abivard spoke to the two mages: "This, as you know, is the famous and versatile Tzikas of the Videssian army, our army, the Videssians again, and now—maybe—ours once more."

"One of those transfers was involuntary on my part," Tzikas said. Yes, he had sangfroid and to spare.

As if he hadn't spoken, as if Bozorg and Panteles weren't staring wide-eyed at the famous and versatile Tzikas, whom they could not have expected to find returned to allegiance to the King of Kings—if he had returned to allegiance to the King of Kings— Abivard went on, "Tzikas says the Videssians are planning something unpleasantly sorcerous for us up ahead. I want you to find out whether that's so. If it is, I suppose Tzikas may have earned his life. If not, I promise he will keep it longer than he wants to but not long."

"Aye, lord," Bozorg said.

"It shall be as you say, eminent sir," Panteles added in Videssian. Abivard wished he hadn't done that. The soldiers of the vanguard, from the lowliest trooper up through Romezan, looked from him to Tzikas and back again, tarring both of them with the same brush. Abivard didn't want Panteles getting any ideas, from any source, about disloyalty.

The two wizards worked together smoothly enough, more smoothly than they had when they had been trying to cross the canal, when Bozorg had reckoned the Voimios strap only a figment of Panteles' imagination and a twisted figment at that. Now, sometimes chanting antiphonally, sometimes pointing and gesturing down the road in the direction from which Tzikas had come, sometimes roiling the dust with their spells, they probed what lay ahead.

At last Bozorg reported, "Some sort of sorcerous barrier does lie ahead, lord. What may hide behind it I cannot say: it serves only to mask the sorceries on the farther side. But it is there."

"That's so," Panteles agreed. "No possible argument. There's a sorcerous fog bank, so to speak, dead ahead of us."

Abivard glanced over at Tzikas. The renegade affected not to notice that he was being watched. *I've told the truth,* his posture said. *I've always told the truth.* Abivard wondered if he really grasped the difference between the posture of truth and truth itself.

For the time being that was beside the point. He asked Bozorg, "Can you penetrate the fog bank to see what lies behind it?"

"Can we? Perhaps, lord," Bozorg said. "In fact, it is likely, as penetrating it tends toward a restoration of a natural state. The question of whether we should, however, remains."

"Drop me into the Void if I can see why," Abivard said. "It's there, and we need to find out what's on the other side of it before we send the army into what's liable to be danger. That's plain enough, isn't it?"

"Oh, it's plain enough," Bozorg agreed, "but is it wise? For all we know, trying to penetrate the sorcerous fog, or succeeding in penetrating it, may be the signal for the truly fearsome charm it conceals to spring to life."

"I hadn't thought of that." Abivard was certain his face looked as if he'd been sucking on a lemon. His stomach was as sour as if he'd been sucking on a lemon, too. "What are we supposed to do, then? Sit around here quivering and wait for the sorcerous fog bank to roll away? We're all liable to die of old age before that happens. If I were Maniakes, I'd make sure my wizards gave it a good long life, anyhow."

Neither Bozorg or Panteles argued with him. Neither of them sprang into action to break down the sorcerous fog, either. When Abivard glared at them, Panteles said, "Eminent sir, we have here risks in going ahead and also risks in doing nothing. Weighing these risks is not easy."

Abivard glanced over, not at Tzikas this time but at Romezan. The noble of the Seven Clans would have had only one answer: when in doubt, go ahead, and worry afterward about what happens afterward. Romezan reckoned Abivard a man of excessive caution. This time the two of them were likely to be thinking along the same lines.

"If you can pierce that fog, pierce it," Abivard told the two wizards. "The longer we stay stuck here, the farther ahead of us Maniakes gets. If he gets too far ahead, he escapes. We don't want that."

Panteles bowed, a gesture of respect the Videssians gave to any superior. Bozorg didn't. It wasn't that he minded acknowledging Abivard as being far superior to him in rank; he'd done that before. But to do it now would have been to acknowledge that he thought Abivard was right, and he clearly didn't.

Whether he thought him right or not, though, he obeyed. As at the twisted canal, Panteles took the lead in the answering magic; being a Videssian, he was likely to be more familiar with the sort of sorcery Maniakes' mages employed than Bozorg was.

"We bless thee, Phos, lord with the great and good mind, by thy grace our protector," Panteles intoned, "watchful beforehand that the great test of life may be decided in our favor."

Along with the other Makuraners who understood the Videssian god's creed, Abivard bristled at hearing it. Panteles said, "We have a fog ahead. We need Phos' holy light to pierce it."

Since Bozorg kept quiet, Abivard made himself stay calm, too. Panteles incanted steadily and then, with a word of command that might not have been Videssian at all—that hardly sounded like any human language—stabbed out his finger at what lay ahead. Abivard expected something splendid and showy, perhaps a ray of scarlet light shooting from his fingertip. Nothing of the sort happened, so it seemed the sort of gesture a father might have used to send an unruly son to his room after the boy had misbehaved.

Then Bozorg grunted and staggered as if someone had struck him a heavy blow, though no one stood near him. "No, by the God!" he exclaimed, and gestured with his left hand. "Fraortish eldest of all, lady Shivini, Gimillu, Narseh—come to my aid!"

He straightened and steadied. Panteles repeated Phos' creed. The two wizards shouted together, both crying out the same word that was not Videssian—it might not have been a word at all, not in the grammarians' sense of the term.

Abivard was watching Tzikas. The renegade started to sketch Phos' sun-circle but checked himself with the motion barely begun. Instead, his left hand twisted in the gesture Bozorg had used. *Almost forgot whose camp you were in, didn't you?* Abivard thought.

But Tzikas' return to the Makuraner fold did not seem to have been a trap or a snare. He'd warned of magic ahead, and magic ahead there had been. He'd done Abivard a service the general could hardly ignore. The last time they'd seen each other, Tzikas had done his best to kill him. That had been a more honest expression, no doubt, of how the renegade felt—not that Abivard had any great and abiding love for him, either.

The wizards, meanwhile, continued their magic. At length Abivard felt a sharp snap somewhere right in the middle of his head. By the way the soldiers around him exclaimed, he wasn't the only one. Afterward the world seemed a little clearer, a little brighter.

"We have pierced the sorcerous fog, revealing it for the phantasm it is," Panteles declared.

"And what lies behind it?" Abivard demanded. "What other magic was it concealing?"

Panteles and Bozorg looked surprised. In defeating the first magic, they'd forgotten for a moment what came next. More hasty incanting followed. In a voice that suggested he had trouble believing what he was saying, Bozorg answered, "It does not seem to be concealing any other magic."

"Bluff!" Romezan boomed. "All bluff."

"A bluff that worked, too," Abivard said unhappily. "We've wasted a lot of time trying to break through that screen of theirs. We were almost on their heels, but we're not, not anymore."

"Let's go after them, then," Romezan said. "The longer we stand around jabbering here, the farther away they get."

"That's so," Abivard said. "You don't suppose—" He glanced over at Tzikas, then shook his head. The renegade would not have come to the Makuraner army Abivard commanded for the sole purpose of delaying it. Maniakes could not have forced that from Tzikas, not when he knew Abivard was as eager as the Avtokrator to dispose of him . . . could he?

Romezan's gaze swung to Tzikas, too. "What do we do about him now?"

"Drop me into the Void if I know. He said there was magic being worked, and there was. He's no wizard or he would have tried to murder Maniakes himself instead of hiring someone to do it for him." That made Tzikas bite his lip. Abivard ignored him, continuing: "He had no way to know the magic wasn't worse than what it turned out to be, and so he warned us. That counts for something."

"Far as I'm concerned, it means we don't torture him—just hew off his head and have done," Romezan said.

"Your generosity is remarkable," Tzikas told him.

"What do you think we should do with you?" Abivard asked, curious to hear what the renegade would say.

Without hesitation Tzikas replied, "Give me back my cavalry command. I did nothing to give anyone the idea I don't deserve it."

"Nothing except slander me to Sharbaraz King of Kings, may his years be many and his realm increase," Abivard said. "Nothing except offer to slay me in single combat. Nothing except blunt my troops in battle and keep Maniakes from being wrecked. Nothing except—"

"I did what I had to do," Tzikas said.

How slandering Abivard to Sharbaraz counted as something he had had to do, he did not explain. Abivard wondered if he knew. The most likely explanation was that aggrandizing Tzikas was indeed something Tzikas had to do. Whatever the explanation, though, it was beside the point at the moment. "You will not lead cavalry in my army," Abivard said. "Until such time as I know you can be trusted, you are a prisoner, and you may thank the God or Phos or whomever you're worshiping on any particular day that I don't take Romezan's suggestion, which would without a doubt make my life easier."

"I find no justice anywhere," Tzikas said, melodrama throbbing in his voice.

"If you found justice, you *would* be short a head," Abivard retorted. "If you're going to whine because you don't find as much mercy as you think you deserve, too bad." He turned to some of his soldiers. "Seize him. Strip him and take away whatever weapons you find. Search carefully, search thoroughly, to make sure you find them all. Hold him. Do him no harm unless he tries to escape. If he tries, kill him."

"Aye, lord," the warriors said enthusiastically, and proceeded to give the command the most literal obedience imaginable, stripping Tzikas not only of his mail shirt but also, their pattings not satisfying them, of his undertunic and drawers as well, so that he stood before them clad in nothing more than irate dignity Abivard groped for a word to describe his expression and finally found one in Videssian, for the imperials did more reveling in suffering for the sake of their faith than did Makuraners. Tzikas, now—Tzikas looked *martyred.*

For all their enthusiasm, the searchers found nothing out of the ordinary and suffered him to dress once more. Seeing that Tzikas was not immediately dangerous—save with his tongue, a weapon Abivard would have loved to cut out of him—the bulk of the army rode off in pursuit of Maniakes' force.

The Videssians, though, had used well the time their sorcerous smoke screen had bought them. "We aren't going to catch them," Abivard said, bringing his horse up to trot beside Romezan's. "They're going to make their way down to Lyssaion and get away to fight next spring."

He hoped Romezan would disagree with him. The noble from the Seven Clans was relentlessly optimistic, often believing something could be done long after a more staid man would have given up hope—and often being right, too. But now the wild boar of Makuran nodded. "I fear you're right, lord," he said. "These cursed Videssians are getting to be harder to step on for good and all than so many cockroaches. They'll be back to bother us again."

"We have driven them clean out of the land of the Thousand Cities," Abivard said, as he had before. "That's something. Even the King of Kings will have to admit that's something."

"The King of Kings won't have to do any such thing, and you know it as well as I do," Romezan retorted, tossing his head so that his waxed mustaches flipped back and slapped against his cheeks. "He *may*, if his mood is good and the wind blows from the proper quarter, but to have to? Don't be stupid . . . lord."

That came uncomfortably close to Abivard's own thoughts, so close that he took no offense at Romezan's blunt suggestion. It also sparked another thought in him: "My sister should long since have had her baby by now, and I should have had word, whatever the word was."

Now Romezan sounded reassuring: "Had anything bad happened, lord, which the God forbid, rest assured you would have heard of that."

"I won't say you're wrong," Abivard answered. "Sharbaraz by now probably would be glad to get shut of any family ties to me. But if Denak had another girl—" If, despite the wizards' predictions, she'd had another girl, she would not get another chance for a boy.

Romezan's hand twisted in a gesture intended to turn aside an evil omen. That touched Abivard. The noble of the Seven Clans might well have resented his low birth and Denak's and not wanted the heir of the King of Kings to spring from their line. Abivard was glad none of that seemed to bother him.

"All right, if we can't catch up to the Videssians, what do we do?" Romezan asked.

"Return in triumph to Mashiz, of course," Abivard said, and laughed at the expression on Romezan's face. "What we really need to do is pull back out of this rough country into the floodplain, where we'll have plenty of supplies. Not much to be gathered here."

"That's so," Romezan agreed. "Won't be so much down on the flat as there usually is, either, thanks to Maniakes. But you're right: more than here. One more question and then I shut up: have we won enough of a victory to satisfy the King of Kings?"

Sharbaraz had said that nothing less than complete and overwhelming defeat of the Videssians would be acceptable. Together, Abivard and Romezan had given him . . . something less than that. On the other hand, giving him the complete and overwhelming defeat of Maniakes probably would have frightened him. A general who could completely and overwhelmingly defeat a foreign foe might also, should the matter ever cross his mind, contemplate completely and overwhelmingly defeating the King of Kings. Maniakes had abandoned the land of the Thousand Cities under pressure from Abivard and Romezan. Would that satisfy Sharbaraz?

"We'll find out," Abivard said without hope and without fear.

The messenger from Mashiz reached the army as it was coming down from the high ground in which the Tutub originated. Abivard was still marching as to war, with scouts well out ahead of his force. There was no telling for certain that Maniakes hadn't tried circling around through the semidesert scrub country for another go at the land of the Thousand Cities. Abivard didn't think the Avtokrator would attempt anything so foolhardy, but one thing he'd become sure of was that you never could tell with Maniakes.

Instead of a horde of Phos-worshiping Videssians, though, the scouts brought back the messenger, a skinny little pockmarked man mounted on a gelding much more handsome than he was. "Lord, I give you the words of Sharbaraz King of Kings, may his years be many and his realm increase," he said.

"For which I thank you," Abivard replied, not wanting to say in public that the words of Sharbaraz King of Kings were nothing he looked forward to receiving.

With a flourish the messenger handed him the waterproof leather message tube. He popped it open. The sheet of parchment within was sealed with the lion of Makuran stamped into blood-red wax: Sharbaraz' insigne, sure enough. Abivard broke the seal with his thumbnail, let the fragments of wax fall to the ground, and unrolled the parchment.

As usual, Sharbaraz' titulature used up a good part of the sheet. The scribe who had taken down the words of the King of Kings had a large, round hand that made the titles seem all the more impressive. Abivard skipped over them just the same, running a finger down the lines of fine calligraphy till he came to words that actually said something instead of serving no other function than advertising the magnificence of the King of Kings.

"Know that we have received your letter detailing the joint action you and Romezan son of Bizhan fought against the Videssian usurper Maniakes in the land of the Thousand Cities, the aforesaid Romezan having joined you in defiance of our orders," Sharbaraz wrote. Abivard sighed. Once Sharbaraz got an idea, he never let go of it. Thus, Maniakes was still a usurper even though he was still solidly on the Videssian throne. Thus, too, the King of Kings was never going to forget—or let anyone else forget—that Romezan had disobeyed him.

"Know further that we are glad your common effort met with at least a modicum of success and grieved to learn that Tzikas, with his inborn Videssian treachery, presumed to challenge you to single combat, you having benefited him after his defection to our side," Sharbaraz continued.

Abivard looked down at the parchment in pleased surprise. Had the King of Kings sounded so reasonable more often, he would have been a better ruler to serve.

He went on, "And know also we are happy you succeeded in defeating the vile Videssian sorcery applied to the canal in the aforementioned land of the Thousand Cities and that we desire full details of the said sorcery forwarded to Mashiz so that all our wizards may gain familiarity with it." Abivard blinked. That wasn't just reasonable—it was downright sensible. He wondered if Sharbaraz was well.

"Having crossed the canal in despite of the said sorcery, you and Romezan son of Bizhan did well to defeat the usurper Maniakes in the subsequent battle, the traitor Tzikas again establishing himself as a vile Videssian dog biting the hand of those who nourished them upon his defection and making himself liable to ruthless, unhesitating extermination upon his recapture, should the aforementioned recapture occur."

Abivard was tempted to summon Tzikas and read him that part of the letter just to watch his face. But the Videssian had again muddied the waters by warning of Maniakes' sorcery, even if it had been no more than a smoke screen.

"Know further," Sharbaraz wrote, "that it is our desire to see the Videssians defeated or crushed or, those failing, at the very least driven from the land of the Thousand Cities so that they no longer infest the said land, ravaging and destroying both commerce and agriculture. Failure to accomplish this will result in our severest displeasure."

It is *accomplished,* Abivard thought. He had, for once, done everything the King of Kings had demanded of him. He reveled in the sensation, knowing it was unlikely to recur any time soon. And even doing anything Sharbaraz demanded of him wouldn't keep his sovereign satisfied: if he could do that, who knew what else, what other enormities, he might be capable of?

Sharbaraz went on with more instructions, exhortations, and warnings. At the bottom of the sheet of parchment, almost as an afterthought, the King of Kings added, "Know also that the God has granted us a son, whom we have named Peroz in memory of our father, Peroz King of Kings, who was born to us of our principal wife, Denak: your sister. Child and mother both appear healthy; the God grant that this should continue. Rejoicing reigns throughout the palace."

Abivard read through the last few lines several times. They still said what they had the first time he'd read them. Had Sharbaraz King of Kings had any true familial feelings for him, he would have put that news at the head of the letter and let all the rest wait. Had he followed the advice of Yeliif and those like him, though, he probably wouldn't have let Abivard know of his unclehood at all. It was a compromise, then—not a good one, as far as Abivard was concerned, but not the worst, either.

Sharbaraz' messenger, who had ridden along with him while he read the letter from the King of Kings, now asked him, as messengers were trained to do, "Is there a reply, lord? If you write it, I will deliver it to the King of Kings; if you tell it to me, he will have it as you speak it."

"Yes, there is a reply. I will speak it, if you don't mind," Abivard said. The messenger nodded and looked attentive. "Tell Sharbaraz King of Kings, may his days be long and his realm increase, I have driven Maniakes from the land of the Thousand Cities. And tell him I thank him for the other news as well." He fumbled in his belt pouch, pulled out a Videssian goldpiece with Likinios Avtokrator's face on it, and handed it to the messenger. "You men get blamed too often for the bad news you bring, so here is a reward for good news."

"Thank you, lord, and the God bless you for your kindness," the messenger said. He repeated Abivard's message to make sure he had it right, then kicked his horse up into a trot and headed back toward Mashiz with the reply.

For his part, Abivard wheeled his horse and rode to the wagons that traveled with the army. When he saw Pashang, he waved. Abivard then called for Roshnani. When she came out of the covered rear area and sat beside Pashang, Abivard handed the letter to her.

She read through it rapidly. He could tell when she came to the last few sentences, because she took one hand off the parchment, made a fist, and slammed it down on her leg. "That's the best news we've had in years!" she exclaimed. "In years, I tell you."

"What news is this, mistress?" Pashang asked. Roshnani told him of the birth of the new Peroz. The driver beamed. "That *is* good news." He nodded to Abivard. "Congratulations, lord—or should I say uncle to the King of Kings to be?"

"Don't say that," Abivard answered earnestly. "Don't even think it. If you do, Sharbaraz will get wind of it, and then we'll get to enjoy another winter at the palace, packed as full of delight and good times as the last two we had in Mashiz."

Pashang's hand twisted in the gesture Makuraners used to turn aside evil omens. "I'll not say it again any time soon, lord, I promise you that." He repeated the gesture; that first winter in Makuran had been far harder on him than on Abivard and his family.

Roshnani held out the letter to Abivard, who took it back from her. "The rest of this isn't so bad, either," she said.

"I know," he said, and lowering his voice so that only she and Pashang could hear, he added, "It's so good, in fact, I almost wonder whether Sharbaraz truly wrote it."

His principal wife and the driver both smiled and nodded, as if they'd been thinking the same thing. Roshnani said, "Having a son and heir come into the world is liable to do wonders for anyone's disposition. I remember how you were after Varaz was born, for instance."

"Oh?" Abivard said in a tone that might have sounded ominous to anyone who didn't know him and Roshnani well. "And how was I?"

"Dazed and pleased," she answered; looking back on it, he decided she was probably right. Pointing to the parchment, she went on, "The man who wrote that letter is about as dazed and pleased as Sharbaraz King of Kings, may his days be long and his realm increase, ever lets himself get."

"You're right," Abivard said in some surprise; he hadn't looked at it like that. *Poor bastard,* he thought. He would have said that to Roshnani, but he didn't want Pashang to hear it, so he kept quiet.

Peasants in loincloths labored in the fields around the Thousand Cities, some of them bringing in the crops, others busy repairing the canals the Videssians had wrecked. Abivard wondered, with a curiosity slightly greater than idle, how the peasants would have gone about repairing the half twist Maniakes' mages had given that one canal.

No one in the land of the Thousand Cities came rushing out from the cities or in from the fields to clasp his hand and congratulate him for what he had done. He hadn't expected anyone to do that, so he wasn't disappointed. Armies got no credit from the people in whose land they fought.

Khimillu, city governor of Qostabash, the leading town the

Videssians had not sacked in the area, turned red under his swarthy skin when Abivard proposed garrisoning troops there for the winter. "This is an outrage!" he thundered in a fine, deep voice. "What with the war, we are poor. How are we to support these men gobbling our food and fondling our women?"

However impressive Khimillu's voice, he was a short, plump man, a native of the Thousand Cities. That let Abivard look down his nose at him. "If you don't want to feed them, I suppose they'll just have to go away," he said, using a ploy that had proved effective in the land of the Thousand Cities. "Then, next winter, you can explain to Maniakes why you don't feel like feeding his troopers—if he hasn't burned this town down around your ears by then."

But Khimillu, unlike some other city governors, was made of stern stuff despite his unprepossessing appearance. "You will not do such a thing. You cannot do such a thing," he declared. Again unlike other city governors, he sounded unbluffably certain.

That being so, Abivard did not try to bluff him. Instead he said, "Maybe not. Here is what I can do, though: I can write to my brother-in-law, Sharbaraz King of Kings, may his years be many and his realm increase, and tell him exactly how you are obstructing my purpose here. Have one of your scribes bring me pen and ink and parchment; the letter can be on its way inside the hour. Does that suit you better, Khimillu?"

If the city governor had gone red before, he went white now. Abivard would not have had the stomach to endanger all of Qostabash because of his obstinacy. Getting rid of an obstreperous official, though, wouldn't affect the rest of the town at all. "Very well, lord," Khimillu said, suddenly remembering—or at least acknowledging—Abivard outranked him. "It shall be as you say, of course. I merely wanted to be certain you understood the predicament you face here."

"Of course you did," Abivard said. In another tone of voice that would have been polite agreement. As things were, he had all but called Khimillu a liar to his face. With some thousands of men at his back, he did not need to appease a city governor who cared nothing for those men once they had done him the services he had expected of them.

Blood rose once more to Khimillu's face. Red, white, red—he might have done for the colors of Makuran. Abivard wondered whether he should hire a taster to check his meals for as long as he stayed in Qostabash. In a tight voice the city governor said, "You could spread your men around through more cities hereabouts if the Videssians hadn't burned so many."

"We don't work miracles," Abivard answered. "All we do is the best we can. Your town is intact, and the Videssians have been driven away."

"Small thanks to you," Khimillu said. "For a very long time the Videssians were near, and you far away. Had they stretched out their hands toward Qostabash, it would have fallen like a date from a tree."

"It may yet fall like a date from a tree," Abivard said. The city governor's complaint had just enough truth in it to sting. Abivard had done his best to be everywhere at once between the Tutub and the Tib, but his best had not always been good enough. Still— "We *are* going to garrison soldiers here this winter, the better to carry on the war against Videssos when spring comes. If you try to keep us from doing that, I promise: you and this city will have cause to regret it."

"That is an outrage!" Khimillu said, which was probably true. "I shall write to Sharbaraz King of Kings, may his days be long and his realm increase, and inform him of what . . ."

His voice faded. Complaining to the King of Kings about what one of his generals was doing stood some chance of getting a city governor relief. Complaining to the King of Kings about what his brother-in-law was doing stood an excellent chance of getting a city governor transferred to some tiny village on the far side of the Sea of Salt, to the sort of place where no one cared if the taxes were five years in arrears because five years worth of taxes from it wouldn't have bought three mugs of wine at a decent tavern.

With the poorest of poor graces, Khimillu said, "Very well. Since I have no choice in the matter, let it be as you say."

"The troops do have to stay somewhere," Abivard said reasonably, "and Qostabash is the city that's suffered least in these parts."

"And thus we shall suffer on account of your troops," the governor returned. "I have trouble seeing the justice in that." He threw his hands in the air, defeated. "But you are too strong for me. Aye, it shall be as you desire in all things, lord."

Abivard rapidly discovered what he meant by that: not the wholehearted cooperation the words implied nor, really, cooperation of any sort. What Khimillu and the officials loyal to him did was stand aside and refrain from actively interfering with Abivard. Beyond that they did their best to pretend that neither he nor the soldiers existed. If that was how they viewed granting his desires in all things, he shuddered to think what would have happened had they opposed him.

"We should have loosed Khimillu against the Videssians," Abivard told Roshnani after they and their children had been installed in some small, not very comfortable rooms a good distance from the city governor's palatial residence. "He would have made them flee by irking them too much for them to stay." He chuckled at his own conceit.

"They've been irksome themselves lately," she said, thumping at a lumpy cushion to try to beat it into some semblance of comfort. When she leaned back against it, she frowned and punched it some more. At last satisfied, she went on, "And speaking of irksome, what do you aim to do about Tzikas?"

"Drop me into the Void if I know what to do with him," Abivard said, adding, "Or what to do to him," a moment later. "That last letter from the King of Kings seems to give me free rein, but if the traitor hadn't escaped from Maniakes and come to us, who knows how long we might have been entangled with the Videssians' magic? I do need to remember that, I suppose."

"But the Videssians' magic was only that screen, with nothing behind it," Roshnani said.

"Tzikas couldn't have known that . . . I don't think." Abivard drummed his fingers on his thigh. "The trouble is, if I leave Tzikas to his own devices, in two weeks' time he'll be writing to Sharbaraz, telling him what a wretch I am. Khimillu has a sense of restraint; Tzikas has never heard of one."

"I can't say you're wrong about that, and I wouldn't try," his principal wife said. "You still haven't answered my question: what are you going to do about him?"

"I don't know," Abivard admitted. "On the one hand, I'd like to be rid of him once for all so I wouldn't have to worry about him anymore. But I keep thinking he might be useful against Maniakes, and so I hold off from killing him."

"Maniakes evidently thought the same thing in reverse, or he would have killed Tzikas after you arranged to give him to the Avtokrator," Roshnani said.

"Maniakes got some use out of the traitor," Abivard said resentfully. "If it hadn't been for Tzikas, we would have crushed the Videssians in the battle on the ridge." He checked himself. "But to be honest, we got a couple of years of decent use out of him before he decided to try to convince the King of Kings he could do everything better than I can."

"And the Videssians got good use from him before that, when he sat at Amorion and held us away from the Arandos valley," Roshnani said.

"But he was doing that for himself more than for Genesios or Maniakes." Abivard laughed. "Tzikas has done more for—and to—both sides here than anyone else in the whole war. Nobody can possibly trust him now, but that doesn't mean he has no value."

"If you're going to use him against the Videssians, how do you propose to go about it?" Roshnani asked.

"I don't know that, either, not right now," Abivard admitted. "All I aim to do is keep him alive—however much I don't like the idea—keep him under my control, and wait and see what sorts of chances I get, if I get any. In my place, what would you do?"

"Kill him," Roshnani said at once. "Kill him now and then write to tell the King of Kings what you've done. If Sharbaraz likes it—and after his latest letter he might—fine. If he doesn't like it, well, not even the King of Kings can order a man back from the dead."

That was so. Abivard's chuckle came out wry. "I wonder what

Maniakes would say if he found out the chief marshal of Makuran had a wife who was more ruthless than he."

Roshnani smiled. "He might not be surprised. The Videssians give their women freer rein in more things than we do—why not in ruthlessness, too?" She looked thoughtful. "For that matter, who's to say Maniakes' wife who is also his cousin isn't more ruthless than he ever dreamed of being?"

"Now, there's an interesting idea," Abivard said. "Maybe one day, if we're ever at peace with Videssos and if Maniakes is still on his throne, you and his Lysia can sit down and compare what the two of you did to make each other's lives miserable during the war."

"Maybe we can," Roshnani replied. Abivard had meant it as a joke, but she took him seriously. After a moment he decided she had—or might have had—reason to do so. She went on, "Speaking of ruthlessness, I meant what I said about the Videssian traitor. I'd sooner find a scorpion in my shoe than him on my side."

Abivard spoke in sudden decision. "You're right, by the God. He's stung me too often, too. I've held back because I've thought of the use I could get from him, but I'll never feel safe with him still around to cook up schemes against me."

"Checking you at the battle where you should have crushed Maniakes should weigh in the scales, too," Roshnani said.

"Checking me? He came too close to killing me," Abivard said. "That's the last time he'll thwart me, though, by the God." He went to the door of the apartment and ordered the sentry to summon a couple of soldiers who had distinguished themselves in the summer's fighting. When they arrived, he gave them their orders. Their smiles were all glowing eyes and sharp teeth. They drew their swords and hurried away.

He had a servant fetch a jar of wine, with which he intended to celebrate Tzikas' premature but not untimely demise. But when the soldiers returned to give him their report, they had the look of dogs that had seen a meaty bone between the boards of a fence but hadn't been able to squeeze through and seize the morsel. One of them said, "We found out he has leave to go walking through the streets of Qostabash so long as he returns to his quarters by sunset. He's not quite an ordinary prisoner, the guards told me." His expression said more clearly than words what he thought of that.

"The guard is right, and the fault is mine," Abivard said. "I give you leave to look for him in the city and kill him wherever you happen to find him. Or if that doesn't suit you, wait till sunset and put an end to him then."

"If it's all the same to you, lord, we'll do that," the soldier said. "I'm just a farm boy and not used to having so many people around all the time. I might kill the wrong one by mistake, and that would be a shame." His comrade nodded. Abivard shrugged.

But Tzikas did not return to his quarters when the sun went down. When he didn't, Abivard sent soldiers—farm boys and others—through the bazaars and brothels of Qostabash looking for him. They did not find him. They did find a horse dealer who had sold him—or at least had sold someone who spoke the Makuraner language with a lisping accent—a horse.

"Drop me into the Void!" Abivard shouted when that news reached him. "The rascal saw his head going down on the block, and now he's gone and absconded—and he has most of the day's start on us, too."

Romezan was there to hear the report, too. "Don't take it too hard, lord," he said. "We'll run the son of a whore to earth; you see if we don't. Besides, where is he going to go?"

That was a good question. As Abivard thought about it, he began to calm down. "He can't very well run off to Maniakes' army, now, can he? Not anymore he can't, not with the Videssians gone to Lyssaion and probably back to Videssos the city by sea already. And if he doesn't run off to the Videssians, we'll hunt him down."

"You see?" Romezan said. "It's not so bad." He paused and fiddled with one spike of his mustache. "Pretty slick piece of work, though, wasn't it? Him figuring out the exact right time to slide away, I mean."

"Slick is right," Abivard said, angry at himself. "He never should have had the chance . . . but I did trust him, oh, a quarter of the way, because the warning he gave us was a real one." He paused. "Or I thought it was a real one. Still, the magical screen the Videssians had set up was just that—a screen, nothing more. But it delayed us almost as much as it would have if it had had deadly sorcery concealed behind it. We always thought Tzikas didn't know it was only a screen. But what if he did? What if Maniakes sent him out to make us waste as much time as he possibly could and help the Videssian army get away?"

"If he did that," Romezan said, "if he did anything like that, we don't handle him ourselves when we catch him. We send him back to Mashiz in chains, under heavy guard, and let Sharbaraz' torturers take care of him a little at a time. That's what he pays them for."

"Most of the time I'd fight shy of giving anyone over to the torturers," Abivard said. "For Tzikas, especially if he did that, I'd make an exception."

"I should hope so," Romezan replied. "You're too soft sometimes, if you don't mind my saying so. If I had to bet, I'd say it came from hauling a woman all over the landscape. She probably thinks it's a shame to see blood spilled, doesn't she?"

Abivard didn't answer, convincing Romezan of his own rightness. The reason Abivard didn't answer, though, was that he was having to do everything he could to keep from laughing in his lieutenant's face. Romezan's preconceptions had led him to a conclusion exactly opposite the truth.

But that wouldn't matter, either. However Abivard had reached his decision, he wanted Tzikas dead now. He offered a good-sized reward for the return of the renegade alive and an even larger one for his head, so long as it was in recognizable condition.

When morning came, he sent riders out to the south and east after Tzikas. He also had dogs brought into the Videssian's quarters to take his scent and then turned loose to hunt him down wherever he might be. The dogs, however, lost the trail after the time when Tzikas bought his horse; not enough of his scent had clung to the ground for them to follow it.

The human hunters had no better luck. "Why couldn't you have turned bloodthirsty a day earlier than you did?" Abivard demanded of Roshnani.

"Why couldn't you?" she returned, effectively shutting him up.

Every day that went by the searchers spread their nets wider. Tzikas did not get caught in those nets, though. Abivard hoped he'd perished from bandits or robbers or the rigor of his flight. If he ever did turn up in Videssos again, he was certain to be trouble.

XII

MASHIZ GREW NEARER WITH EVERY CLOP OF THE HORSES' hooves, with every squealing revolution of the wagon's wheels. "Summoned to the capital," Abivard said to Roshnani. "Nice to hear that without fearing it's going to mean the end of your freedom, maybe the end of your life."

"About time you've been summoned back to Mashiz to be praised for all the good things you've done, not blamed for things that mostly weren't your fault," Roshnani said, loyal as a principal wife should be.

"Anything that goes wrong is your fault. Anything that goes right is credited to the King of Kings." Abivard held up a hand. "I'm not saying a word against Sharbaraz."

"I'll say a word. I'll say several words," Roshnani replied.

He shook his head. "Don't. As much as I've complained about it, that's not his fault ... well, not altogether his fault. It comes with being King of Kings. If someone besides the ruler gets too much credit, too much applause, the man on the throne feels he'll be thrown off it. It's been like that in Makuran for a long, long time, and it's like that in Videssos, too, though maybe not so bad."

"It isn't right," Roshnani insisted.

"I didn't say it was right. I said it was real. There's a difference," Abivard said. Because Roshnani still looked mutinous, he added, "I expect you'll agree with me that it's not right to lock up noblemen's wives in the women's quarters of a stronghold. But the custom of doing that is real. You can't pretend it's not there and expect all those wives to come out at once, can you?"

"No," Roshnani said unwillingly. "But it's so much easier and more enjoyable to dislike Sharbaraz the man doing as he pleases than Sharbaraz the King of Kings acting like a King of Kings."

"So it is," Abivard said. "Don't get me wrong: I'm not happy with him. But I'm not as angry as I was, either. The God approves of giving those who wrong you the benefit of the doubt."

"Like Tzikas?" Roshnani asked, and Abivard winced. She went on, "The God also approves of revenge when those who wrong you won't change their ways. She understands there will be times when you have to protect yourself."

"He'd better understand that," Abivard answered. They both smiled, as Makuraners often did when crossing genders of the God.

With the wind coming off the Dilbat Mountains from the west, Mashiz announced itself to the nose as well as to the eye. Abivard had grown thoroughly familiar with the city stink of latrines, smoke, horses, and unwashed humanity. It was the same coming from the capital of Makuran as it was in the land of the Thousand Cities and the same there as in Videssos.

For that matter, it was the same in Vek Rud stronghold and the town at the base of the high ground atop which the stronghold sat. Whenever people gathered together, other people downwind knew about it.

Once the wagon got into Mashiz, Pashang drove it through the city market on the way to the palace of the King of Kings. The going was slow in the market district. Hawkers and customers clogged the square, shouting and arguing and calling one another names. They cursed Pashang with great panache for driving past without buying anything.

"Madness," Abivard said to Roshnani. "So many strangers, all packed together and trying to cheat other strangers. I wonder how many of them have ever before seen the people from whom they buy and how many will ever see them again."

His principal wife nodded. "There are advantages to living in a stronghold," she said. "You know everyone around you. It can get poisonous sometimes—the God knows that's so—but it's for the good, too. A lot of people who would cheat a stranger in a heartbeat will go out of their way to do something nice for someone they know."

They rode through the open square surrounding the walls of the palace of the King of Kings. The courtiers within those walls led lives as ingrown in their own way as those of the inhabitants of the most isolated stronghold of Makuran. And very few of them, Abivard thought, were likely to go out of their way to do anything nice for anyone they knew.

The guards at the gate saluted Abivard and threw wide the valves to let him and his family come inside. Servitors took charge of the wagon—and of Pashang. The driver went with them with less fear and hesitation that he'd shown the winter before. Abivard was glad to see that, though he still wondered what sort of reception he himself was likely to get.

His heart sank when Yeliif came out to greet him; the only people he would have been less glad to see in the palace were, for different reasons, Tzikas and Maniakes. But the beautiful eunuch remained so civil, Abivard wondered whether something was wrong with him, saying only, "Welcome, Abivard son of Godarz, in the name of Sharbaraz King of Kings, may his days be long and his realm increase. Come with me and I shall show you to the quarters you have been assigned. If they prove unsatisfactory in any way, by all means tell me, that I may arrange a replacement."

He'd never said anything like that the past couple of years. Then Abivard's stays in the palace had been in essence house arrest. Now, as he and his family walked through the hallways of the palace, servants bowed low before them. So did most nobles he saw, acknowledging his rank as being far higher than theirs. A few high nobles from the Seven Clans kissed him on the cheek, claiming status only a little lower than his. He accepted that. Had he not done what he'd done, he would have been the one bowing before them.

No. Had he not done what he'd done, the nobles from the Seven Clans would either have fled up into the plateau country west of the Dilbat Mountains or would be trying to figure out what rank they had among Maniakes' courtiers. He'd earned their respect.

The suite of rooms to which Yeliif led him had two great advantages over those in which he'd stayed in the past two years. First was their size and luxury. Second, and better by far, was the complete absence of sentries, guards, keepers, what have you in front of the door.

"Sharbaraz King of Kings, may his days be long and his realm increase, will allow us to come and go as we please and to receive visitors likewise?" Abivard asked. Only after he'd spoken did he realize how great a capacity for irony he'd acquired in his years in Videssos.

Yeliif had never been to Videssos but was formidably armored against irony. "Of course," he replied, his limpid black eyes as wide and candid as if Abivard had enjoyed those privileges on his previous visits to the palace ... and as if he had never urged drastic punishment for the disloyalty of which Sharbaraz so often suspected Abivard.

Abivard's tone swung from sardonic to bland: "Perhaps you could help me arrange a meeting with my sister Denak and even arrange for me to see my nephew, Peroz son of Sharbaraz."

"I shall bend every effort toward achieving your desire in that regard," the beautiful eunuch said, sounding as if he meant it. Abivard studied him in some bemusement; cooperation from Yeliif was so new and strange, he had trouble taking the idea seriously. And then, as politely as ever but with a certain amount of relish nonetheless, the eunuch asked, "And would you also like me to arrange for you a meeting with Tzikas?"

Abivard stared at him. So did Roshnani. So even did Varaz. Yeliif's small smile exposed white, even, sharply pointed teeth. "Tzikas is here—in the palace?" Abivard asked.

"Indeed he is. He arrived a fortnight before you," Yeliif answered. "Would you like me to arrange a meeting?"

"Not right now, thank you," Abivard said. If Tzikas had been there two weeks and had still kept his head on his shoulders, he was liable to keep it a good deal longer. Somehow or other he'd managed to talk Sharbaraz out of giving him over to the torturers.

That meant he'd be getting ready to give Abivard another riding boot between the legs the first chance he saw.

Yeliif said, "The King of Kings was inclined toward severity in the matter of Tzikas until the Videssian enlightened him as to how, after a daring escape from Maniakes' forces, he saved your entire army from destruction at the hands of vicious Videssian sorcery."

"Did he?" Abivard said, unsure whether he meant Tzikas' "enlightenment" of Sharbaraz or his alleged salvation of the Makuraner force. The more he thought about it, the more he wondered whether Maniakes hadn't known perfectly well that Tzikas would flee back to the Makuraners and thus had given him something juicy with which to flee. Maybe the magical preparations had looked worse than they were, to impress the renegade, just as the sorcerous "fog bank" had impressed Abivard's wizards till they had discovered that nothing lay behind it.

And maybe, too, Tzikas had known perfectly well that the Videssians' magecraft was harmless and had gone back with the specific intention of delaying Abivard's army as long as he could and giving Maniakes a chance to get away. He'd certainly done that whether he had intended to or not. And Tzikas, from what Abivard had seen, seldom did things inadvertently.

"These quarters *are* satisfactory?" Yeliif asked.

"Satisfactory in every way," Abivard told him, that being the closest he could come to applauding the lack of keepers. Roshnani nodded. So did their children, who would have more room now than they had enjoyed in some time. Of course, after slow travel in the wagon, any chamber larger than belt-pouch size felt commodious to them.

"Excellent," the beautiful eunuch said, and bowed low, the first such acknowledgment of superiority he'd ever granted Abivard. "And rest assured I shall not forget to make arrangements for you to see your sister and nephew." He slipped from the suite and was gone.

Abivard stared after him. "Was that really the Yeliif we've known and loathed the past couple of years?" he said to no one in particular.

"It really was," Roshnani said, sounding as dazed as he was. "Do you know what I wish we could borrow right now?"

"What's that?" Abivard asked.

"Sharbaraz' food taster, if he has one," his principal wife answered. "And he probably does." Abivard thought about that, then nodded, agreeing with both the need and the likelihood.

Yeliif used a suave and tasteful gesture to point out the door through which Abivard was to enter. "Denak and young Peroz await you within," he said. "I shall await you here in the hall and return with you to your chamber."

"I can probably find my way back by myself," Abivard said.

"It is the custom," the eunuch answered, a sentence from which there could be no possible appeal.

Shrugging, Abivard opened the door and went inside. He didn't shut it in Yeliif's face, as he would have done before. Since the beautiful eunuch was not actively hostile, Abivard didn't want to turn him that way.

Inside the room waited not only his sister and her new baby but also the woman Ksorane. Not even her brother could be alone with the principal wife of the King of Kings, and tiny Peroz didn't count in such matters.

"Congratulations," he said to Denak. He wanted to run to his sister and take her in his arms but knew the serving woman would interpret that as uncouth familiarity no matter how closely they were related. He did the next best thing by adding, "Let me see the baby, please."

Denak smiled and nodded, but even that proved complicated. She could not simply hand Peroz to Abivard, for the two of them would touch each other if she did. Instead, she gave the baby to Ksorane, who in turn passed him to Abivard, asking as she did so, "You know how to hold them?"

"Oh, yes," he assured her. "My eldest will start sprouting his beard before many years go by." She nodded, satisfied. Abivard held Peroz in the crook of his elbow, making sure he kept the baby's head well supported. His nephew stared up at him with the confused look babies so often give the large, confusing world.

Their eyes met. Peroz' blank stare was swallowed by a large, enthusiastic, toothless smile. Abivard smiled back, and that made the baby's smile get even wider. Peroz jerked and waved his arms around, not seeming quite sure they belonged to him.

"Don't let him grab your beard," Denak warned. "He's already pulled my hair a couple of times."

"I know about that, too," Abivard said. He held the baby for a while, then handed it back to the serving woman, who returned it to his sister. "An heir to the throne," he murmured, adding for Ksorane's benefit, "Though I hope Sharbaraz keeps it for many years to come." He remained unsure whether the woman's first loyalty lay with Denak or with the King of Kings.

"As do I, of course," Denak said; maybe she wasn't perfectly sure, either. But then she went on, "Yes, now I've had my foal. And now I'm put back in the stable again and forgotten." She did not bother to disguise her bitterness.

"I'm sure the King of Kings gives you every honor," Abivard said.

"Honor? Yes, though I'd be worse than forgotten if Peroz had turned out to be a girl." Denak's mouth twisted. "I have everything I want—except about three quarters of my freedom." She held up a hand to keep Abivard from saying anything. "I know, I know. If I'd stayed married to Pradtak, I'd still be stuck away in the women's quarters, but I would rule his domain in spite of that. Here I can go about more freely, which looks well, but no one listens to me—no one." The lines new on her face these past few years grew deep and harsh.

"Do you want freedom," Abivard asked, "or do you want influence?"

"Both," Denak answered at once. "Why shouldn't I have both? If I were a man, I could easily have both. Because I'm not, I'm supposed to be amazed to have one. That's not the way I work."

Abivard knew as much. It had never been the way his sister worked. He pointed to Peroz, who was falling asleep in her arms. "You have influence there—and you'll have more as time goes by."

"Influence because I'm his mother," Denak said, looking down at the baby. "Not influence because I am who I am. Influence through a baby, influence through a man. It's not cnough. I have wit cnough to be a counselor to the King of Kings or even to rule in my own right. Will I ever have the chance? You know the answer as well as I do."

"What would you have me do?" Abivard said. "Shall I ask the God to remake the world so it pleases you better?"

"I've asked her that myself often enough," Denak said, "but I don't think she'll ever grant my prayer. Maybe, in spite of what we women call her, the God is a man, after all. Otherwise, how could she treat women so badly?"

Sitting off in a corner of the room, the serving woman yawned. Denak's complaints meant nothing to her. In some ways she was freer than the principal wife of the King of Kings.

Changing the subject seemed a good idea to Abivard. "What did Sharbaraz say when he learned you'd had a son?" he asked.

"He said all the right things," Denak answered: "that hc was glad, that he was proud of me, that Peroz was a splendid little fellow and hung like a horse, to boot." She laughed at the expression on Abivard's face. "It was true at the time."

"Yes, I suppose it would have been," Abivard agreed, remembering how the genitals of his newborn sons had been disproportionately large for the first few days of their lives. "It surprised me."

"It certainly did—you should have seen your jaw drop," Denak said. She went on, "And how have you been? How has life been outside the walls of this palace?"

"I've been fairly well—not perfect but fairly well. We even beat the Videssians this year, not so thoroughly as I would have liked, but we beat them." Abivard shrugged. "That's how life works. You don't get everything you want. If you can get most of it, you're ahead of the game. Maybe Sharbaraz is starting to see that, too: I didn't know how he'd take it when we beat the Videssians without smashing them to bits, but he hardly complained about that."

"He has some sort of scheme afoot," Denak answered. "I don't know what it is." The set of her jaw said what she thought about not knowing. "Whatever it is, he thought it up himself, and he's doubly proud of it on account of that. When he turns it loose, he says, Videssos the city will tremble and fall."

"That would be wonderful," Abivard answered. "For a while there a couple of springs ago, I was afraid Mashiz would tremble and fall."

"He says he's taken a lesson from the Videssians," Denak added, "and they'll pay for having taught him."

"What's that supposed to mean?" Abivard asked.

"I don't know," Denak told him. "That's all he's said to me; that's all he will say to me." Her thinned lips showed how much she cared for her husband's silence. "When he talks about this lesson, whatever it is, he has the look on his face he puts on when he thinks he's been clever."

"Does he?" Abivard said. "All right." He wouldn't say more with Ksorane listening. Sharbaraz was not stupid. He knew that. Sometimes the schemes the King of Kings thought up were very clever indeed. And sometimes the only person Sharbaraz' schemes fooled was Sharbaraz himself. Worst of all was the impossibility of figuring out in advance which was which.

"I'm glad he's—content with you," Denak said. "That's much better than the way things have been."

"Isn't it?" Abivard agreed. He smiled at his sister. "And I'm glad for you—and for little Peroz there."

She looked down at the baby. Her expression softened. "I do love him," she said quietly. "Babies are a lot of fun, especially with so many servants around to help when they're cranky or sick. But . . . it's hard sometimes to think of him as just a baby and not as a new piece of the palace puzzle, if you know what I mean. And that takes away from letting myself enjoy him."

"Nothing is simple," Abivard said with great conviction. "Nothing is ever simple. If living up by the nomads hadn't taught me that, the civil war would have, that or living among Videssians for a while." He rolled his eyes. "You live among Videssians for a while, by the end of that time you'll have trouble remembering your own name, let alone anything else."

Ksorane began to fidget. Abivard took that as a sign that he'd spent about as much time with his sister as had been allotted to him. He said his good-byes. The serving woman got up and served as a conduit so Denak could pass him Peroz once more and he, after holding the baby for a little while, could pass it back again. He reached out his arms toward Denak, and she stretched the one not holding Peroz out to him. They couldn't touch. Custom forbade it. Custom was very hard. He felt defeated as he went out into the corridor.

Yeliif was waiting for him. *Custom again,* he thought—the beautiful eunuch had said as much. Abivard could have walked back alone, but having Yeliif with him now was more a mark of his status than a sign that he was something close to a prisoner.

As the two of them fell into stride, Abivard asked quite casually, "What sort of lessons has Sharbaraz King of Kings, may his years be many and his realm increase, taken from the Videssians?"

"Ah, you heard about that, did you?" Yeliif said. "From the lady your sister, no doubt."

"No doubt," Abivard agreed. They walked on a few steps, neither of them saying anything. Abivard poked a little harder: "You do know the answer?"

"Yes, I know it," the beautiful eunuch said, and said no more.

"Well?"

Yeliif didn't answer right away. Abivard had the pleasure of seeing him highly uncomfortable. At last the beautiful eunuch said, "While I do know the answer, I do not know whether I should be the one to reveal it to you. The King of Kings would be better in that role, I believe."

"Ah." They walked along a little farther. By way of experiment Abivard shifted into Videssian: "Does the eminent Tzikas know this answer, whatever it may be?"

"No, I don't believe he does," Yeliif answered in the same tongue, and then glared at him for being found out.

"That's something, anyhow," Abivard said in relief.

"Sharbaraz King of Kings, may his days be long and his realm increase, considered it, but I dissuaded him," Yeliif said.

"Did you? Good for you," Abivard said; the beautiful eunuch's action met with his complete approval. Something else occurred to Abivard: "Did he by any chance tell Hosios Avtokrator?" He kept all irony from his voice, as one had to do when speaking of "Hosios"; though the King of Kings had gone through several puppet Avtokrators of the Videssians without finding any of them effective in bringing Videssians over to Makuran, he kept on trying.

Or he had kept on trying, anyhow. Matching Abivard in keeping emotion from his voice, Yeliif said, "Hosios Avtokrator—" He did not say, *the most recent Hosios Avtokrator*, either. "—had the misfortune of suddenly departing this world late this past summer. The King of Kings ordered him mourned and buried with the pomp and circumstances he deserved."

"Died suddenly, you say?" Abivard murmured, and Yeliif nodded a bland nod in return. "How unfortunate." Yeliif nodded again. Abivard wondered whether the latest "Hosios," like at least one of his predecessors, had shown an unwonted and unwanted independence that had worried Sharbaraz or whether the King of Kings had simply decided to give up serving as puppet-master.

Then a really horrid thought struck him. "The King of Kings isn't planning on naming Tzikas Avtokrator if we ever do conquer Videssos the city, is he? Please tell me no." For once he spoke to the beautiful eunuch with complete sincerity.

"If he is, I have no knowledge of it," Yeliif answered. That relieved Abivard, but less than he would have liked. The eunuch said, "Myself, I do not believe that policy would yield good results." His doelike black eyes widened as he realized he'd agreed with Abivard.

"When can I hope for an audience with the King of Kings?" Abivard asked, hoping to take advantage of such unusual amiability from Yeliif.

"I do not know," the beautiful eunuch answered. "I shall pass on your request to him. It should not be an excessively long period. Better he should talk to you than to the Videssian."

"When I came to Mashiz, didn't you mock me with the news that Tzikas had gotten here first?" Abivard said.

"So I did," Yeliif admitted. "Well, we all make mistakes. Next

to Tzikas, you are a pillar supporting Sharbaraz' every enterprise."
He glanced toward Abivard. Those black eyes suddenly were not
doelike but cold and hard and shiny as polished jet. "This should
by no means be construed as a compliment, you understand."

"Oh, yes, I understand that," Abivard said, his voice as dry as
the summer wind that blew dust into Vek Rud stronghold. "You
loathe me as much as you ever did; it's just that you've discovered
you loathe Tzikas even more."

"Precisely," the eunuch said. As far as Abivard could tell, he
loathed everyone to some degree, save perhaps the King of Kings.
Did that mean he loathed himself, too? No sooner had the question
crossed Abivard's mind than he realized it was foolish. Being
what he was, any hope of manhood taken from him by a knife,
how could Yeliif help loathing himself? And from that, no doubt,
all else sprang.

Abivard said, "If I were a danger to Sharbaraz, I would have
shown as much a long time ago, wouldn't I? Tzikas, now . . ." A
mutual loathing was as good a reason for an alliance as any, he
thought, and better than most.

Yeliif eyed him with a look as close to approval as he'd ever
won from him. "Those last two words, I believe, with their accompanying ellipsis, are the first sensible thing I have ever heard you
say."

As compliments went, it wasn't much. Abivard was glad of it
all the same.

Courtiers with elaborately curled hair and beards, with rouged
cheeks, with caftans bound by heavy gold belts and shot through
with gold and silver thread drew down their eyebrows—those
whose eyebrows were gray or white had a way of drawing them
down harder than did those whose brows remained dark—when
Abivard and Roshnani came into the banquet hall arm in arm.

Custom died hard. Sharbaraz King of Kings had kept his word
about allowing Denak to leave the women's quarters, a liberty the
wives of nobles had not enjoyed till then. And for a while a good
many nobles had followed their sovereign's lead. Evidently,
though, the old ways were reasserting themselves, for only a

couple of other women besides Roshnani were in the hall. Abivard looked around to see if his sister was among them. He didn't see her, but then, Sharbaraz hadn't yet entered, so that didn't signify anything.

He stiffened. Denak wasn't there, and neither was Sharbaraz, but there sat Tzikas, talking amiably with a Makuraner noble from the Seven Clans. To look at the Videssian renegade, he hadn't a care in the world. His gestured were animated; his face showed nothing but sincerity. Abivard knew, to his cost, how much that sincerity was worth. The noble, though, seemed altogether entranced. Abivard had seen that before, too.

To his dismay, the servant who led Roshnani and him to their places seated them not far from Tzikas. Brawling in the palace was unseemly, so Abivard ignored the Videssian renegade. He poured wine first for Roshnani, then for himself.

Sharbaraz came into the hall. Everyone rose and bowed low. The King of Kings entered alone. Sadness smote Abivard. He hoped Denak was not at Sharbaraz' side because little Peroz needed her. He doubted it, though. The King of Kings had given his principal wife more freedom than was customary, but custom pulled even on him. If he wasn't wholehearted about keeping such changes alive, they would perish.

Roshnani noted Denak's absence, too. "I would have liked to see my sister-in-law without having to go into the women's quarters to do it," she said. She didn't raise her voice but didn't go to any trouble to keep it down, either. A couple of courtiers gave her sidelong looks. She looked back unabashed, which seemed to disconcert them. They muttered back and forth to each other but did not turn their eyes her way again.

A soup of meatballs and pomegranate seeds started the feast. For amusement Abivard and Roshnani counted the seeds in their bowl; pomegranate seeds were supposed to bring good luck. When they both turned out to have seventeen, they laughed: neither one got to tease the other.

After the soup came a salad of beets in yogurt enlivened with mint. Abivard had never been fond of beets. They were far more tolerable here than in most of the dishes where they appeared.

Rice gorgeously stained and flavored with sour cherries and saffron followed the beets. Accompanying it was mutton cooked with onions and raisins. Roshnani mixed hers together with the rice. Abivard, who preferred to savor flavors separately, didn't.

The food, as usual in the palace, was splendid. He gave it less attention than was his habit, and he was moderate with his wine, calling for quince and rhubarb sherbets more often than he did for the captured Videssian vintages Sharbaraz served his grandees. He directed more attention to his ears than to his tongue, trying to catch what Tzikas was saying behind his back.

Tzikas had been saying things behind his back since not long after the Videssian had fled the Avtokrator he had formerly served. He hadn't thought Abivard knew about that—and indeed, Abivard hadn't known about it till almost too late. Now, though, he had to think Abivard would hear him, and that, to Abivard's way of thinking, would have been the best possible reason for him to keep his mouth shut.

Maybe Tzikas didn't know how to keep his mouth shut. Maybe he could no more stop intriguing than he could stop breathing: he might claim to worship the God, but he remained Videssian to the core. Or maybe he just did not really believe Abivard could overhear. Whatever the reason, his tongue rolled on without the least hesitation.

Abivard could not make out everything he said, but what he caught was plenty: "—my victory over Maniakes by the banks of the Tib —" Tzikas was saying to someone who hadn't been there and couldn't contradict him. He sounded most convincing, but then, he always did.

When Abivard turned toward Tzikas, Roshnani set a warning hand on his arm. He usually took her warnings more seriously than he did now. Smiling a smile that had little to do with amiability, he said, "When you came to Mashiz, Tzikas, you should have set up shop in the bazaar, not the palace."

"Oh?" Tzikas said, staring at him as if he'd just crawled out from under a flat stone. "And why is that?" No matter how he aped Makuraner ways, the renegade kept all his Videssian arrogance, remaining convinced that he was and had to be the cleverest man around.

Smiling, Abivard sank his barb: "Because then you could have sold your lies wholesale instead of doling them out one by one the way you do here."

Tzikas glowered at him. "I am not the one who handed my subordinate to the enemy," he said.

"True enough—you don't do things like that," Abivard agreed. "Your subordinates are safe from you. It's your superiors who have to have eyes in the backs of their heads. What would you have done if you had killed Maniakes by magic and made yourself Avtokrator of the Videssians?"

"Beaten you," Tzikas said. Yes, he had his own full measure and to spare of the overweening pride that singularly failed to endear the imperials to the men of Makuran.

But when Abivard said "I doubt it," that didn't merely spring from his angry reaction to the renegade's words. However skilled an intriguer Tzikas was, Abivard was convinced he had his measure in the field. Lightly, casually, he went on, "That wasn't what I meant, anyhow."

"What *did* you mean?" Now Tzikas sounded ominous, beginning to realize Abivard was scoring off him.

Abivard scored again: "I meant you'd be bored sitting on the throne with no one in Videssos to betray."

Tzikas glared at him; that had gotten to the renegade, even though the odds were good that it wasn't true. An intriguer would hardly stop intriguing because he'd schemed his way to the top. He'd sit up there and scheme against all those—and there would surely be some—who'd try to follow him and pull him down. And even if he saw no one who looked dangerous, he would probably destroy a courtier every now and then for the sport of it and to keep rivals wary.

"If you want me to prove what sort of liar you are, I will meet you when and where you like, with the weapons you like," Tzikas said.

Abivard beamed at him. "The first generous offer you've made! We've tried to kill each other before; now I can do it properly."

"It is forbidden," Yeliif said. Abivard and Tzikas both stared in startlement at the beautiful eunuch. Yeliif went on, "Sharbaraz King of Kings, may his years be many and his realm increase, has let me know he requires both of you for the enterprise he contemplates beginning next spring."

"What *is* this fabled enterprise?" Tzikas demanded. *Good,* Abivard thought. *Yeliif wasn't lying to me—Tzikas doesn't know, either.* He would have been offended to the core had Sharbaraz enlightened the Videssian renegade while leaving him in the dark.

Yeliif sniffed. "When the proper time for you to gain that knowledge comes, rest assured it shall be provided to you. Until such time cherish the fact that you will be preserved alive to acquire the knowledge when the time comes."

"He certainly doesn't deserve to live to find out," Abivard said.

"At one time or another a good many have expressed the opinion that you yourself did not merit remaining among the living," the beautiful eunuch replied coldly. Abivard knew full well he had been among the leaders of those expressing that opinion.

Injustice still stung him. "Some people thought I was too successful, and so I had to be a traitor on account of that. But everyone knows Tzikas is a traitor. He doesn't even bother pretending not to be."

"So he doesn't," Yeliif said, favoring Tzikas with a glance as icy as any with which he had ever chilled Abivard. "But a known traitor has his uses, provided he is watched at all times. The King of Kings intends to get such use as he can from the renegade."

Abivard nodded. Where Tzikas was concerned, Sharbaraz had less to worry about than did Maniakes. Tzikas had already tried to steal the Videssian throne. Whatever else he might do, he could not set himself up as King of Kings of Makuran.

That didn't mean he could not aspire to any number of lesser but still prominent offices in Makuran, such as the one Abivard had. He'd already aspired to that office and done his best to throw Abivard out of it. He'd do the same again if he saw a chance and thought Sharbaraz would look the other way.

Abivard made a solemn resolution: regardless of whether

Sharbaraz intended using Tzikas in this grand scheme of his, whatever it was, he was going to take out the Videssian renegade if he saw even the slightest chance of doing so. He could always apologize to the King of Kings afterward, and had no intention of granting Tzikas the same chance.

Winter dragged on. The children got to go out into the courtyard now, as they hadn't in years gone by. Even Gulshahr was old enough now to pack snow into a ball and throw it at her brothers. Doing that left her squealing with glee.

Videssian captives tutored Varaz and Shahin. Abivard's sons took to lessons with the same enthusiasm they would have shown taking poison. He walloped them on the backside and kept them at it.

"We already know how to speak Videssian," Varaz protested. "Why do we have to know how to make speeches in it?"

"And all these numbers, too," Shahin added. "It's like they're all pieces of a puzzle, and they're all scrambled up, and the Videssians expect us to be able to put them together as easy as anything." He stuck out his lower lip. "It's not fair." That was the worst condemnation he could give to anything not to his liking.

"Being able to count past ten without having to take off your shoes won't kill you," Abivard said. He rounded on Varaz. "You'll be dealing with Videssians your whole life, most likely. Knowing how to impress them when you talk won't do you any lasting harm."

"When you first went into Videssos, did you know how to speak the language there?" Varaz asked.

"Not so you'd notice," Abivard answered. "But remember, I grew up in the far Northwest, and I never expected to go into Videssos at all, except maybe as a soldier in an invading army." He folded his arms across his chest. "You'll keep on with your lessons," he declared as firmly as Sharbaraz promulgating a decree. The King of Kings could make the whole of Makuran heed him. Abivard's authority was less than that but did extend to his two boys.

They studied more than mathematics and rhetoric. They rode

ponies, shot bows suited to their strength, and began to learn swordplay. They would acquire a Videssian veneer—Abivard was convinced it would prove useful—but beneath it would have the accomplishments of a proper Makuraner noble.

"The more different things you know how to do, the better off you'll be," Abivard told them.

The man that thought called to mind, unfortunately, was Tzikas. The Videssian renegade knew not only his own tongue but that of Makuran as well. He could tell convincing stories in either one. He was a talented soldier to boot. If he'd been only a little luckier, he would have been Avtokrator of the Videssians or perhaps commander of the Makuraner field army. No one had ever come closer to meeting both of those seemingly incompatible goals.

He was missing one thing, though. Abivard wasn't sure it had a name. *Steadfastness* was as close as he could come, that or *integrity*. Neither word felt quite right. Without the quality, though, Tzikas' manifold talents brought him less than they might have otherwise.

Yeliif said the same thing a different way a few days later. "He is a Videssian," the beautiful eunuch intoned, as if to say that alone irremediably spoiled Tzikas.

Abivard eyed Yeliif with speculation of a sort different from that which he usually gave the eunuch. In the matter of Tzikas, for once, they shared an interest. "I'd be happier if we never had to speak of him again," Abivard said, an oblique message but not so oblique that the beautiful eunuch couldn't follow up on it if he so desired.

Yeliif also looked thoughtful. If the notion of being on the same side as Abivard pleased him, he didn't let his face know about it. After a little while he said, "Didn't you tell me Tzikas has wavered back and forth between the God and the false faith of Phos?"

"I did. He has," Abivard answered. "In the next world he will surely fall into the Void and be forgotten. I wish he would be forgotten here and now, too."

"I wonder," Yeliif said in musing tones, "yes, I wonder what the Mobedhan Mobedh would say on hearing that Tzikas has wavered between the true faith and the false."

"That is an . . . intriguing question," Abivard answered after a moment's pause to weigh just how intriguing it was. "Sharbaraz has forbidden the two of us to quarrel, but if the chief servant of the God comes to him with a complaint that Tzikas is an apostate, he may have to listen."

"So he may," Yeliif agreed. "On the other hand, he may not. Dhegmussa is his servant in all things. But a man who will not notice his servants is less than perfectly wise."

Not a word passed Abivard's lips. For all he knew, the beautiful eunuch was playing a game different from the one that showed on the surface of his words. He might be hoping to get Abivard to call the King of Kings a fool and then report what Abivard had said to Sharbaraz. Abivard did think the King of Kings a fool, but he himself was not so foolish as to say so where any potential foe could hear him.

But Yeliif's idea was far from the worst he'd ever heard. Maybe Dhegmussa wouldn't be able to do anything; the Mobedhan Mobedh was far more the creature of the King of Kings than the Videssians' ecumenical patriarch was the Avtokrator's creature. Apostasy, though, was nothing to take lightly. And making Tzikas sweat was nearly as good as making him suffer.

"I'll talk with Dhegmussa," Abivard said. Something glinted in Yeliif's black, black eyes. Was it approval? Abivard hadn't seen it there often enough to be sure he recognized it.

The shrine in which Dhegmussa, chief servant of the God, performed his duties was the most splendid of its kind in all Makuran. That said, it was nowhere near so fine as several of the temples to Phos Abivard had seen in Videssian provincial towns and not worth mentioning in the same breath as the High Temple in Videssos the city. The Makuraners said, *The God lives in your heart, not on the wall.*

Dhegmussa lived in a small home next to the shrine, a home like that which a moderately successful shoemaker might have inhabited: whitewashed mud bricks forming an unimpressive facade but a fair amount of comfort inside.

"You honor me, marshal of Makuran," the Mobedhan Mobedh said, leading Abivard along a dim, gloomy hall at the end of which light from the courtyard shone. When they got there, Dhegmussa waved a regretful hand. "You must imagine how it looks in spring and summer, all green and full of sweet-smelling, bright-colored flowers. This brown, dreary mess is not what it should be."

"Of course not," Abivard said soothingly. Dhegmussa guided him across the court to a room heated by a couple of charcoal braziers. A servant brought wine and sweet cakes. Abivard studied the Mobedhan Mobedh as they refreshed themselves. Dhegmussa was about sixty, with a closely trimmed gray beard and a loud voice that suggested he was a trifle deaf.

He waited till Abivard had eaten and drunk, then left off the polite small talk and asked, "How may I serve you, marshal of Makuran?"

"We have a problem, holy one, with a man who, while claiming to worship the God, abandoned in time of danger the faith he had professed, only to return to it when that seemed safer than the worship for which he had given it up," Abivard answered.

"This sounds dolorous indeed," Dhegmussa said. "A man who blows whichever way the winds of expediency take him is not one to hold a position of trust nor one who has any great hope of escaping the Void once his life on earth is done."

"I have feared as much myself, holy one," Abivard said, calling up a sadness he did not truly feel.

They went back and forth a while longer. The servant brought more cakes, more wine. At last the Mobedhan Mobedh put the question he had studiously avoided up till then: "Who is this man for whose spiritual well-being you so justly fear?"

"I speak of Tzikas, the Videssian renegade," Abivard said, a reply that could not have surprised Dhegmussa in the least by then. "Can any man who dons and doffs religions as if they were caftans possibly be a reliable servant to Sharbaraz King of Kings, may his years be many and his realm increase?"

"It seems difficult," Dhegmussa said, and then said no more for a time.

When he remained silent, Abivard pressed the matter: "Can a man who chooses whether to swear by the God or by false Phos by who is listening to him at any given moment be believed when he swears by either one?"

"It seems difficult," Dhegmussa said again.

That was as far as he would go on his own. Abivard prodded him to go further: "Would you want such a man close to the King of Kings? He might corrupt him with his own heedlessness, or, on the other hand, failing to corrupt the King of Kings, he might be moved to violence against him."

"Fraortish eldest of all, prevent it," the Mobedhan Mobedh said, his fingers twisting in a sign to avert the evil omen. Abivard imitated the gesture. But then, to his disappointment, Dhegmussa went on: "But surely the King of Kings is aware of the risks entailed in having this Videssian close by him."

"There are risks, holy one, and then there are risks," Abivard said. "You do know, of course, that Tzikas once tried to murder the Videssian Avtokrator by magic." One of the advantages of telling the truth was the casual ease with which he could bring out such horrors.

Dhegmussa suffered a coughing fit. When he could finally speak again, he said, "I had heard such a thing, yes, but discounted it as a scurrilous rumor put about by his enemies." He looked sidelong at Abivard, who was certainly no friend to Tzikas.

"It certainly is scurrilous," Abivard agreed cheerfully, "but rumor it is not. I was the one who received him in Across after he fled in a rowboat over the strait called the Cattle Crossing after his conjuration couldn't kill Maniakes. If he'd stayed in Videssos the city another hour, Maniakes' men would have had him." *And that would have made life simpler for both the Avtokrator and me,* Abivard thought. Ever since he'd rescued Sharbaraz from Nalgis Crag stronghold, though, it had become more and more obvious that his life, whatever else it might hold, would not contain much simplicity.

"You swear this to me?" Dhegmussa asked.

"By the God and the Prophets Four," Abivard declared, raising first the thumb and then the fingers of his left hand.

Still Dhegmussa hesitated. Abivard wanted to kick him to see if direct stimulation would make his wits work faster. The only reason he could conceive for Sharbaraz' having named this man Mobedhan Mobedh was the assurance of having an amiable nonentity in the position. So long as everything went well, having a nonentity in an important place held advantages, chief among them that he was not likely to be dangerous to the King of Kings. But sometimes a man who would not or could not act was more dangerous than one who could and would.

Trying to avoid action, Dhegmussa repeated, "Surely Sharbaraz is familiar with the problems the Videssian represents."

"The problems, yes," Abivard said. "My concern is that he has not fully thought through the religious import of all these things. That's why I came to you, holy one." *Do I have to color the picture as well as draw it?*

Maybe he didn't. Dhegmussa said, "I shall suggest to the King of Kings the possible consequences of keeping near his person a man of such, ah, ambiguous qualities and the benefits to be gained by removing him from a position where he might influence not only the affairs of Makuran but also the spiritual life of the King of Kings."

That was less than Abivard had hoped to get from the Mobedhan Mobedh. He'd wanted Dhegmussa to rear up on his hind legs and bellow something like *Get rid of this man or put your soul in peril of falling into the Void.*

Abivard chuckled. Any Videssian priest who deserved his blue robe would have said something like that, or else something worse. The Videssian patriarch had come out and publicly condemned Maniakes for marrying his own first cousin. That wasn't so offensive to Makuraner morality as it was in Videssos, but even if it had been, the Mobedhan Mobedh would not—could not—have taken such an active role in opposing it. A Mobedhan Mobedh who criticized his sovereign too vigorously wasn't just packed off to a monastery. He was liable to be a dead man.

Mild reproof, then, Abivard supposed, was as much as he could reasonably have expected to get. He bowed and said, "Thank you, holy one." The novelty of having Dhegmussa express anything but complete and glowing approval of everything Sharbaraz did might make the King of Kings sit up and take notice.

If it didn't . . . Abivard had tried direct methods of getting rid of Tzikas before. He'd been too late the last time. If he had to try again, he wouldn't be.

This winter a knock on the door to Abivard's suite of rooms did not provoke the alarm it had the past two years, even if it came at an hour when Abivard wasn't particularly looking for visitors. But when he opened the door and found Yeliif standing there, a memory of that alarm stirred in him. The beautiful eunuch might join him in despising Tzikas, but that did not make him a friend.

Ceremony nonetheless had to be observed. Abivard offered his cheek for the eunuch to kiss: Yeliif had influence but, because of his mutilation, not rank. Then Abivard stepped aside, saying, "Enter. Use these my rooms as your own while you are here."

"You are gracious," Yeliif said without sardonic overtones but also without warmth. "I have the honor to bring you a message from Sharbaraz King of Kings, may his years be many and his realm increase."

"I am always glad to bask in the wisdom of the King of Kings," Abivard answered. "What clever thought would he impart to me today?"

"The same thought he imparted to me not long ago," Yeliif said; by his expression, he would sooner not have had that thought, whatever it was, thus imparted.

"Enlighten me, then, by all means," Abivard said. He glanced over to Roshnani, who was sitting cross-legged on the floor by a window, quietly embroidering. Had she raised an eyebrow, he would have know he'd sounded sarcastic. Since she didn't, he supposed he'd gotten by with that.

"Very well," the beautiful eunuch said. "Sharbaraz King of Kings, may his days be long and his realm increase, bade me tell you—and incidentally bade me bear in mind myself—that he requires Tzikas' service in the enterprise he has planned for the next campaigning season and that he forbids you either to harm Tzikas' person or to seek the Videssian's condemnation for any of the malfeasances he either has committed or may commit in future."

"Of course I obey the King of Kings," Abivard replied. *Better than he deserves, too.* "But Tzikas' obedience in such matters must be questionable at best. If he attacks me, am I to ignore it?"

"If he attacks you, his head shall answer for it," Yeliif said. "So the King of Kings has ordered. So shall it be."

"So shall it be," Abivard echoed. If Sharbaraz really meant that—more to the point, if Sharbaraz convinced Tzikas he really meant that—all would be well. If not, the Videssian was already trying to find a way out of the order. Abivard would have bet on the latter.

"The King of Kings is most determined in this matter," the eunuch said, perhaps thinking along with him, "and has made his determination perfectly clear to Tzikas."

"Tzikas listens to Tzikas, no one else." Abivard held up his hand before Yeliif could reply. "Never mind. He hasn't managed to kill me yet, no matter how often he's betrayed me. I expect I can survive him a while longer. What seems to matter here, though, is why Sharbaraz is insisting we both stay alive and don't try to do each other in. You've said you know."

"I do," Yeliif agreed. "And as I have also said before, it is not my place to enlighten you as to the intentions of the King of Kings. He shall do that himself when he judges the time ripe. Since I have delivered his message and been assured you understand it, I shall take my leave." He did exactly that, sliding away as gracefully as an eel.

Abivard closed the door after him and turned to Roshnani. "So much for Dhegmussa," he said with a shrug.

"Yeliif was right: the idea was worth trying," she answered. They both paused in some surprise at the idea of admitting that the beautiful eunuch had been right about anything. Roshnani went on: "I wonder as much as you do about what's important enough to be worth keeping Tzikas alive. I can't think of anything that important."

"This side of taking Videssos the city, neither can I," Abivard said.

"If you couldn't take Videssos the city, Sharbaraz has to be mad to think Tzikas will be able to do it," Roshnani said indignantly. Abivard pointed to the walls of their suite and then to the ceiling. He didn't know if Sharbaraz had placed listeners by the suite, but the King of Kings surely had done that the past two winters, so taking chances was foolish. Roshnani nodded, following what he'd meant. She went on, "The Videssians hate Tzikas, too, though, so I don't see how he'd be a help in taking their capital."

"Neither do I," Abivard said. Even if Sharbaraz wouldn't listen to Dhegmussa, his spies were going to get an earful of what Abivard thought of the renegade. Sooner or later, he kept telling himself, some dirt would have to stick to Tzikas. "They'd sooner kill him than me. I'm just an enemy, while he's a traitor."

"A traitor to them, a traitor to us, a traitor to them again," Roshnani said, getting into the spirit of the game. "I wonder when he'll betray us again."

"First chance he gets, or I miss my bet," Abivard answered. "Or maybe not—who knows? Maybe he'll wait till he can do us the most harm instead."

They spent the next little while contentedly running down Tzikas. If the listeners in the walls were paying any attention, they could have brought Sharbaraz enough dirt for him to order Tzikas executed five or six times over. After a while, though, Abivard gave up. No matter what the listeners told Sharbaraz, he wasn't going to send Tzikas to the chopping block. He already had all the dirt he needed to order Tzikas executed. The trouble was, the King of Kings wanted the renegade alive so he could figure in his scheme, whatever it was.

Abivard sat down beside Roshnani and slipped an arm around her. He liked that for its own sake. It also gave him the chance to put his head close to hers and whisper, "Whatever plan Sharbaraz has, if it's for taking Videssos the city, it won't work. He can't make ships sprout from thin air, and he can't make Makuraners into sailors, either."

"You don't need to tell me that," she answered, also whispering. "Do you think you were the only one who looked out over the Cattle Crossing from Across at the city—" She dropped into Videssian for those words; to the imperials, their capital was *the* city, incomparably grander than all others. "—on the far side?"

"I never caught you doing that," he said.

She smiled. "Women do all sorts of things their husbands don't catch them doing. Maybe it comes from having spent so much time in the women's quarters—they're as much for breeding secrets as for breeding babies."

"You've been out of the women's quarters since not long after we wed," he said. "You needn't blame that for being sneaky."

"I didn't intend 'blaming' it on anything," Roshnani answered. "I'm proud of it. It's saved us a good deal of trouble over the years."

"That's true." Abivard lowered his voice even further. "If it weren't for you, Sharbaraz wouldn't be King of Kings now. He never would have thought of taking refuge in Videssos for himself—his pride ran too deep for that, even so long ago."

"I know." Roshnani let out a small, almost silent sigh. "Did I save us trouble there or cost us trouble?" The listeners, if there were any, could not have heard her; Abivard scarcely heard her himself, and his ear was close to her mouth. And having heard her, he had no idea what the answer to her question was. Time would tell, he supposed.

Sharbaraz King of Kings had enjoined Abivard from trying to dispose of Tzikas. From what Yeliif had said, Sharbaraz had also enjoined Tzikas from trying to get rid of him. He wouldn't have given a counterfeit copper for the strength of that last prohibition, though.

After that one near disaster at the feast the palace servitors did their best to ensure that Abivard and Tzikas did not come close to occupying the same space at the same time. Insofar as that meant keeping them far apart at ceremonial meals, the servitors' diligence was rewarded. But Abivard was free to roam the corridors of the palace. And so, however regrettable Abivard found the prospect, was Tzikas.

They bumped into each other three or four days after Yeliif had delivered the message from Sharbaraz ordering Abivard not to run down the Videssian renegade. Message or not, that was almost literally what happened. Abivard was hurrying down a passageway not far from his suite of rooms when Tzikas crossed his path. He stopped in a hurry. "I'm sor—" Tzikas began, and then recognized him. "You!"

"Yes, me." Abivard's hand fell, as if of its own accord, to the hilt of his sword.

Tzikas did not flinch from him and was also armed. No one had ever accused the Videssian of cowardice in battle. Plenty of other things had been charged against him, but never that one. He said, "A lot of men have lodged accusations against me—all lies, of course. Not one of those men came to a good end."

"Oh, I don't know," Abivard answered. "Maniakes still seems to be flourishing nicely, however much I wish he weren't."

"His time approaches." For a man who had been condemned to death by both sides, who switched gods as readily as a stylish woman switched necklaces, his confidence was infuriating. "For that matter, so does yours."

Abivard's sword leapt halfway out of its scabbard. "Whatever else happens, I'll outlive you. By the God I swear it—and he's likely to remember me, because I worship him all the time."

Videssian skin being fairer than the Makuraner norm, Tzikas' flush was quite visible to Abivard, who skinned his lips back from his teeth, pleased at having made a hit. The renegade said, "My heart knows where the truth lies."

He was speaking the Makuraner tongue; he wouldn't have given Abivard that kind of opening in Videssian. And Abivard took advantage of it, saying, "Your heart knows all about lies, doesn't it, Tzikas?"

Now the Videssian snarled. His graying beard gave him the aspect of an angry wolf. He said, "Jeer all you like. I am a constant man."

"I should say so—you're false all the time." Abivard pointed rudely at Tzikas' face. "Even your beard is changeable. When you first fled to us, you wore it trimmed close, the way most

Videssians do. Then you grew it out to look more like a Maku-raner. But when I fought you down in the land of the Thousand Cities, after Maniakes got hold of you, you'd cut it short and shaved around the edges again. And now it's getting longer and bushier."

Tzikas brought a hand up to his chin. Maybe he hadn't noticed what he was doing with his beard, or maybe he was angry someone else had noticed. "After Maniakes got hold of me, you say?" His voice went ugly. "You gave me to him, intending that he kill me."

"He has even better reason to love you than I do," Abivard replied, "but I have to say I'm gaining on him fast. You're like a sock, Tzikas—you fit either foot. But whoever made you wove you with a dye that burns like fire. Whatever you touch goes up in flames."

"I'll send you up in flames—or down to the ice," Tzikas said, and snatched out his sword.

Abivard's sword cleared the scabbard at about the same instant. The clash of metal on metal brought shouts from around corners—people knew what that sound was even if they couldn't tell whence it came. Abivard knew what it was, too: the answer to his prayers. Tzikas had drawn on him first. He could kill the renegade and truthfully claim self-defense.

He was bigger and younger than Tzikas. All he had to do, he thought, was cut the Videssian down. He soon discovered it wouldn't be so easy. For one thing, Tzikas was smooth and strong and quick. For another, the corridor was narrow and the ceiling low, cutting into his size advantage: He had no room to make the full-armed cuts that might have beaten their way through Tzikas' guard. And for a third, neither he nor the renegade was used to fighting on foot in any surroundings, let alone such cramped ones. They were both horsemen by choice and by experience.

Tzikas had a strong wrist and tried to twist the sword out of Abivard's hand. Abivard held on to his blade and cut at his foe's head. Tzikas got his sword up in time to block the blow. As they had been on horseback, they were well matched here.

"Stop this at once!" someone shouted from behind Abivard. He took no notice; had he taken any notice, he would have been spitted the next instant. Nor did Tzikas show any signs of trusting him to show restraint—and the renegade had reason, for once two enemies began to fight, getting them to stop before one was bleeding or dead was among the hardest things for individuals and empires both.

A servant behind Tzikas shouted for him to give over. He kept slashing away at Abivard nonetheless, his fencing style afoot taking on more and more of the manner in which he would have fought while horsed as he went on battling his foe. Abivard found himself making more thrusts than cuts, doing his best to adapt to the different circumstances in which he now found himself. But whatever he did, Tzikas kept beating aside his blade. Whatever else anyone said about the Videssian, he could fight.

None of the palace servitors was so unwise as to try to break up the fight by grabbing one of the contestants. If someone did try tackling Tzikas, Abivard was ready to run the renegade through, however unsporting that was. He had no doubt Tzikas would give him the same treatment if he got the chance.

One thing that would stop two parties from fighting each other was overwhelming outside force directed at them both. A shout of "Drop your sword or neither one of you comes out alive!" got Abivard's undivided attention. A squadron of palace guards, bows drawn, were rushing up behind Tzikas.

Abivard sprang back from Tzikas and lowered his sword, though he did not drop it. He hoped Tzikas might pursue the fight without checking and thus get himself pincushioned. To his disappointment, the Videssian looked over his shoulder instead. He also let his arm drop but still kept hold of his sword. "I'll kill you yet," he told Abivard.

"Only in your dreams," Abivard retorted, and started to raise his blade again.

By then, though, the guardsmen had gotten between them. "That will be enough of that," the squadron leader said as if talking to a couple of fractious boys rather than a pair of men far outranking him.

Very much like a fractious boy, Tzikas said, "He started it."

"Liar!" Abivard snapped.

The squadron leader held up a hand. "I don't care who started it. All I know is that Sharbaraz King of Kings, may his days be long and his realm increase, doesn't want the two of you brawling, no matter what. I'm going to split my men in two. Half of them will take one of you back to his lodging; the other half will take the other noble gentleman back to his. That way nothing can go wrong."

"Hold!" That ringing voice could have belonged to only one man—or, rather, not quite man—in the palace. Yeliif strode through the guards, disgust manifest not only on his face but in every line of his body. He looked from Abivard to Tzikas. His eyes flashed contempt. "You fools," he said, making it sound like a revelation from the God.

"But—" Abivard and Tzikas said in the same breath. They glared at each other, angry at agreeing even in protest.

"Fools," Ycliif repeated. He shook his head. "How the King of Kings expects to accomplish anything working through such tools as you is beyond me, but he does, so long as you do not break each other before he can take you in hand."

Abivard pointed at Tzikas. "That tool will cut his hand if he tries to wield it."

"You know not whereof you speak," the beautiful eunuch snapped. "Now more than ever the King of Kings prepares to gather the fruits of what his wisdom long ago set in motion, and you seek in your ignorance to trifle with his design? You do not understand, either one of you. All is changed now. The ambassadors have returned."

XIII

ABIVARD SCRATCHED HIS HEAD. HE HADN'T KNOWN OF ANY embassies going out, let alone any coming back. "What ambassadors?" he asked. "Ambassadors to Videssos? Do we have peace with the Empire, then?" That made no sense. If Sharbaraz had made peace with Videssos, what need had he for either a marshal or a Videssian traitor?

Yeliif rolled his eyes in theatrical scorn. "Since you seem intent on making a display of your ignorance, I shall merely confirm it, noting that you do not in fact know everything there is to know and noting further that the glorious vision of Sharbaraz King of Kings, may his years be many and his realm increase, vastly outranges your own."

"To the ice—uh, to the Void—with me if I know what you're talking about," Tzikas told the eunuch.

"Nor does that surprise me." Yeliif looked at the renegade as if he were something pallid and slimy that lived in the mud under flat stones by the bank of a creek that did not run clean. Abivard loathed Tzikas with a loathing both pure and hot, but that stare made him feel a moment's sympathy for the Videssian. "Your function is solely to serve the King of Kings, not to be privy to his plans."

"If we're going to be part of his plans, we ought to have some idea of what those plans are," Abivard said, and found Tzikas nodding along with him. Accusingly, he went on, "You've known for some time. Why haven't we gained the same knowledge?"

"Until the return of the ambassadors, the King of Kings judged the time unripe," Yeliif answered. Abivard found the hand that wasn't on his sword tightening into a fist. Yeliif knew the answers, while he didn't even know the questions. Until moments before he hadn't known there were any questions. It all struck him as most unfair.

"Now that the ambassadors are back, will the King of Kings let us know what they were doing while they were away?" Tzikas sounded as if he didn't care for having been left in the dark, either.

Not that that mattered to Yeliif. "In his own good time the King of Kings *will* inform you," he said. "It is, then, your task—and I speak to each of you in this instance—to be here to be informed at the time of the King of Kings' choosing and not to eliminate each other before that time. Do you understand?"

He sought to shame them, to make them feel like brawling boys. In no small measure he succeeded. Nevertheless, Abivard knew a stir of anger at being considered only insofar as he fit into Sharbaraz' plans. He said, "I do hope the King of Kings will let us know what he intends us to do before we have to do it, not afterward."

"He will do as he chooses, not as you seek to impose upon—" The perfect apologist for the King of Kings, Yeliif started to defend him before hearing everything Abivard had had to say. When he realized he'd made himself look foolish, the eunuch bared small, white, even teeth in something closer to a snarl than to a smile. "I don't know why you want to kill this Videssian," he said, pointing at Tzikas. "Living among his folk for so long has taught you to play meaningless games with words, just as they do."

"You insult me," Abivard said.

"No, you insult *me*," Tzikas insisted. "Twice, in fact. First you call me a Videssian when I am one no longer, and second you call *him*—" He pointed at Abivard. "—one when he manifestly is not. Were I a Videssian yet, I'd not want him as one."

"He didn't call me a Videssian," Abivard said, "and if he had, he would have insulted me, not you, by doing so."

Tzikas started to raise his sword. The palace guards made ready to pincushion him and Abivard both if they started fighting again. Coldly, Yeliif said, "Do not be more stupid than you can help. I have told you that you and Abivard are required in the future plans of the King of Kings. When those plans are accomplished, you may fight if you so desire. Until then you are his. Remember it and comport yourselves accordingly." He swept away, the hem of his caftan brushing the floor.

"Put up your swords," the guards' leader said as he had before. Abivard and Tzikas reluctantly obeyed. The guard went on, "Now, I'm gonna do like I said before, split my men in half and take you noble gentlemen back where you belong."

"*You* wouldn't know about these ambassadors, would you?" Abivard asked him as they walked down the hallway.

"Who, me?" The fellow shook his head. "I don't know anything. That's not what I'm here for, knowing things. What I'm here for is to keep people from killing other people they're not supposed to kill. You know what I mean?"

"I suppose so," Abivard said, wondering where Sharbaraz had found such a magnificently phlegmatic man. A court officer who did not want to know things surely ranked as a freak of nature.

When Abivard walked into the suite of rooms, the soldiers stayed out in the hallway, presumably to make certain he did not go out hunting Tzikas. Roshnani stared at them till he shut the door after himself; too often in the past couple of years soldiers had stood in the hallways outside their rooms. She pointed past Abivard to the guards and asked, "What are they in aid of?"

"Nothing of any great consequence," he answered airily. "Tzikas and I had a go at settling our differences, that's all."

"Settling your—" Roshnani scrambled to her feet and took great care in inspecting him from all sides. At last, having satisfied herself almost against her will, she said, "You're not bleeding anywhere."

"No, I'm not. Neither is Tzikas, worse luck," Abivard said.

"And if we go after each other again, we face the displeasure of the King of Kings—so I've been told, at any rate." He lowered his voice. "That and a silver arket will make me care an arket's worth."

Roshnani nodded. "Sharbaraz would have done better to take Tzikas' head himself." She tossed her own head in long-standing exasperation. "No plan of his could possibly be clever enough to justify keeping the renegade alive."

"If you expect me to argue with you, you'll be disappointed," Abivard said, to which they both laughed. He grew thoughtful. "Do you know anything about ambassadors returning?"

"I didn't know any ambassadors were out," his principal wife answered, "so I could hardly know they've come back." That was logical enough to satisfy the most exacting, finicky Videssian. Roshnani went on, "Where did you hear about them?"

"From Yeliif, after the guardsmen kept me from giving Tzikas everything he deserved. Whoever they are, wherever they went, however they came back here, they have something to do with Sharbaraz' precious plan."

"Whatever that may be," Roshnani said.

"Whatever that may be," Abivard echoed.

"Whatever it is, when will you find out about it?" Roshnani asked.

"Whenever Sharbaraz King of Kings, may his days be long and his realm increase, finds a day long enough for him to have the time to give to me," Abivard answered. "Maybe tomorrow, maybe next spring." On that cheerful note conversation flagged.

Nine days after Abivard and Tzikas tried to kill each other, Yeliif knocked on the door to Abivard's suite. When Abivard opened the door to let him in, he stuck his head out and looked up and down the hall. The guardsmen had been gone for a couple of days. "How may I help you?" Abivard asked warily; Yeliif as anything other than inimical still struck him as curious.

The beautiful eunuch said, "You are bidden to an audience with

Sharbaraz King of Kings, may his days be long and his realm increase. You shall come with me this moment."

"I'm ready," Abivard said, though he wasn't, not really. It was, he thought sadly, typical of the King of Kings to leave him on a shelf, as it were, for weeks at a time and then, when wanting him, to want him on the instant.

"I am also bidden to tell you that Tzikas shall be there," Yeliif said. When Abivard did nothing more than nod, the eunuch also nodded thoughtfully, as if he'd passed a test. He said, "I *can* tell you—" Not *I am bidden to tell you,* Abivard noted. "—that Tus and Piran are attending the King of Kings."

"I'm sorry, but I don't know those names nor the men attached to them," Abivard said.

"They are the ambassadors whose recent return has provoked this audience," Yeliif answered.

"Are they?" Abivard said, interest quickening in his voice. Now, at last, he would get to find out just how harebrained Sharbaraz' grandiose plan, whatever it was, would turn out to be. He had no great expectations for it, only the small one of having his curiosity satisfied. In aid of which . . . "Ambassadors to whom?" he asked. "I didn't know we'd sent an embassy to Maniakes, even if he has been closer to Mashiz lately than he usually gets." He also remembered the Videssian ambassador Sharbaraz had imprisoned and let die but did not find mentioning him politic.

If Yeliif hadn't been born smiling that knowing, superior smile, he'd spent a lot of time practicing it, perhaps in front of a mirror of polished silver. "All will be made clear to you in due course," he said, and would say no more. Abivard felt like booting him in the backside as they walked down the corridor.

Tzikas had indeed been bidden to the audience: he stood waiting at the rear of the throne room. Someone—very likely Yeliif—had taken the sensible precaution of posting some palace guards back there. Their dour expressions were as well schooled as Yeliif's smile.

Abivard glared at Tzikas but, with the guards there, did no more. Tzikas glared back. Yeliif said, "The two of you shall accompany me to the throne together and prostrate yourselves before the King of Kings at the same time. No lapses shall be tolerated, if I make myself clear."

Without waiting to find out whether he did, he started down the aisle on the long walk toward the throne on which Sharbaraz sat. Abivard stayed by his right side; Tzikas quickly found a place on his left. It was as if each of them was using the eunuch to shield himself from the other. Under different circumstances the idea might have been funny.

A pair of men stood to one side of the throne of the King of Kings. Abivard presumed they were the mysterious Tus and Piran. Yeliif explained nothing. Abivard had expected no more. Then, at the appropriate moment, the beautiful eunuch stepped away, leaving Abivard and Tzikas side by side before the King of Kings.

They prostrated themselves, acknowledging their insignificance in comparison to their sovereign. Out of the corner of his eye Abivard watched Tzikas, but he had already known that the ritual was almost the same among Videssians as among the folk of Makuran. The two men waited together, foreheads touching the polished marble floor, for Sharbaraz to give them leave to rise.

At last he did. "We are not pleased with the two of you," he said when Abivard and Tzikas had regained their feet. Abivard already knew that from the length of time the King of Kings had required them to stay on their bellies. Sharbaraz went on, "By persisting in your headstrong feud, you have endangered the plan we have long been maturing, a plan which, to work to its fullest extent, requires the service of both of you."

"Majesty, if we knew what this plan was, we would be able to serve you better," Abivard answered. He was sick to death of Sharbaraz' notorious plan. Sharbaraz was full of big talk that usually ended up amounting to nothing—except trouble for Abivard.

When Sharbaraz spoke again, his words did not seem immediately to the point: "Abivard son of Godarz, brother-in-law of mine, you will remember how our father, Peroz King of Kings, departed this world for the company of the God?"

He hadn't publicly acknowledged Abivard as his brother-in-law for a long time. Abivard noted that as he answered, "Aye, Majesty, I do: battling bravely against the Khamorth out on the Pardrayan steppe." Only the blind chance of his own horse's stepping in a hole and breaking a leg at the start of its charge had kept him out of the overwhelming disaster that had befallen the Makuraner army moments afterward.

"What you say is true but incomplete," Sharbaraz told him. "How did it happen that our father, Peroz King of Kings, saw the need to campaign against the Khamorth out on the steppe?"

"They were raiding us, Majesty, as you will no doubt remember," Abivard said. "Your father wanted to punish them as they deserved." He would not speak ill of the dead. Had Peroz flung out his net of scouts more widely, the plainsmen might not have trapped him and his host.

Sharbaraz nodded. "And why were they raiding us at that particular time?" he asked with the air of a schoolmaster leading a student through a difficult lesson step by step. Abivard had trouble figuring out what to make of that.

The answer, though, was plain enough: "Because the Videssians paid them gold to raid us." He glared at Tzikas.

"Not my idea." The Videssian renegade held up a hand, denying any responsibility. "Likinios Avtokrator sent the gold out where he thought it would do the most good."

"Likinios Avtokrator, whom we knew, was devious enough to have devised such a scheme for harming his foes without risking his own men or the land then held by the Empire of Videssos," Sharbaraz said. Abivard nodded; Likinios had lived up to all the Makuraner tales about calculating, cold-blooded Videssians. The King of Kings went on, "We have endeavored to learn even from our foes. Thus the ambassadors we sent forth two years ago, just now returned to us: Tus and Piran."

"Ambassadors to whom, Majesty?" Abivard asked. At last he could put the question to someone who might answer it.

But Sharbaraz did not answer it directly. Instead, he turned to the men now back from their two-year embassy and said, "Whose agreement did you bring back with you?"

Tus and Piran spoke together, denying Abivard the chance to figure out who was who: "Majesty, we brought back the agreement of Etzilios, khagan of Kubrat, Videssos' northern neighbor."

"By the God," Abivard murmured. He'd had that notion years before but hadn't thought it really could be done. If Sharbaraz had done it . . .

Tzikas' right hand started to shape Phos' sun-sign, then checked itself. The renegade murmured, "By the God," too. Abivard for once was not disgusted at his hypocrisy. He was too busy staring at Sharbaraz King of Kings. For once he'd been wrong about his sovereign.

Sharbaraz said, "Aye, two years ago I sent them forth. They had to traverse the mountains and valleys of Erzerum without revealing their mission to the petty princes there who might have betrayed us to Videssos. They had to travel over the Pardrayan steppe all around the Videssian Sea, giving the Videssian outpost on the northern shore there a wide berth. They could not sail over the Videssian Sea to Kubrat, for we have no ships capable of such a journey." He nodded to Abivard. "We now more fully appreciate your remarks on the subject."

One of the ambassadors—the taller and older of the two—said, "We shall have ships. The Kubratoi hollow out great tree trunks and mount masts and sails on them. With these single-trunk ships they have raided the Videssian coast again and again, doing no small damage to our common foe."

"Piran has the right of it," Sharbaraz said, letting Abivard learn who was who. "Brother-in-law of mine, when the campaigning season begins this coming spring, you shall lead a great host of the men of Makuran through the Videssian westlands to Across, where all our previous efforts were halted. Under Etzilios, the Kubratoi shall come down and besiege the city by land. And—"

"And—" Abivard committed the enormity of interrupting the King of Kings. "—and their one-trunk ships will ferry over our men and the siege gear to force a breach in the wall and capture the enemy's capital."

"Just so." Sharbaraz was so pleased with himself, he over-looked the interruption.

Abivard bowed low. "Majesty," he said with more sincerity in his voice than he had used in complimenting the King of Kings for some years, "this is a splendid conception. You honor me by let-ting me help bring it to reality."

"Just so," Sharbaraz said again. Abivard let out a small mental sigh. That the King of Kings had come up with a good idea did not keep him from remaining as full of himself as he'd grown in his years on the throne, even if it did give him better reason than usual for his pride.

"You have given me my role to play, Majesty, and I am proud to play it, as I told you," Abivard said. He turned toward Tzikas. "You have not said what the Videssian's role is to be or why he should have one." If the God was kind, he might yet be rid of Tzikas.

All Sharbaraz said was, "He will be useful to you."

That left Tzikas to speak for himself, which he did in his lisping Videssian accent: "I tell you, Abivard son of Godarz, as I long ago told Sharbaraz King of Kings, may his days be long and his realm increase, that I know a secret way into Videssos the city once your men get over the Cattle Crossing and reach the wall. I did not think what I knew was worth much, because I did not think you could cross to the city. The King of Kings remembered, though, for which I thank him." He, too, bowed to Sharbaraz.

"What is this secret way into Videssos the city?" Abivard asked.

Tzikas smiled. "I will tell you—when it is time for you to send men through it into the city."

"All right," Abivard said, his voice mild. He saw a hint of sur-prise, almost of disappointment, on the Videssian renegade's face. *Expecting me to threaten and bluster, were you?* Abivard thought. Maybe the torturers could find a way to pull what Tzikas knew out of him. But maybe not; the renegade was nothing if not resource-ful and might well contrive to kill himself without yielding his secret.

In the end, though, it wouldn't matter. Before Tus and Piran had returned to Mashiz, Sharbaraz had shown every sign of being willing, if not downright eager, to be rid of Tzikas, secret or no secret. Now, with the King of Kings' plan unfolding, what Tzikas knew—or what Tzikas said he knew, which might not be the same thing—took on new value.

But suppose everything went exactly as Tzikas hoped. Suppose, thanks to his knowledge of the wall and whatever weak points it had, the Makuraners got into Videssos the city. Suppose he was the hero of the moment.

Abivard smiled at the renegade. Suppose all that came true. It would not profit Tzikas for long. Abivard was as sure of that as he was of light at noon, dark at midnight. Once Tzikas' usefulness was over, he would disappear. Sharbaraz would never name him puppet Avtokrator of the Videssians, not when he couldn't be counted on to stay a puppet.

So let him have his moment now. Why not? It wouldn't last.

Sharbaraz said, "Now you see why we could permit no unseemly brawling between the two of you. Both of you are vital to our plans, and we should have been most aggrieved at having to go forward with only one. Until Videssos the city should fall, you are indispensable to us."

"I will do my best to live up to the trust you've placed in me," Tzikas answered, bowing once more to the King of Kings. Yes, Abivard judged, the renegade made a formidable courtier, and his command of the Makuraner language was excellent. It was not, however, perfect. Sharbaraz had said that Tzikas—and Abivard, too, for that matter—was indispensable until Videssos the city fell. He had not said a word about anyone's indispensability after Videssos the city fell. Abivard had noticed that. Tzikas, by all appearances, had not.

Yeliif reappeared between Abivard and Tzikas. One moment he was not there, the next he was. He was no mean courtier in his own right, arriving at the instant when Sharbaraz dismissed them. As protocol required, Abivard and Tzikas prostrated themselves once more. For the first time in some years Abivard felt he was giving the prostration to a man who deserved such an honor.

After he and Tzikas rose, they backed away from the King of Kings till they could with propriety turn and walk away from his presence. The beautiful eunuch stayed between them. Abivard wondered if that was to ensure that the two of them didn't start fighting again no matter what instructions they'd had from Sharbaraz.

At the entrance to the throne room another eunuch took charge of Tzikas and led him away, presumably toward whatever chambers he had been allotted. Yeliif accompanied Abivard back to his own suite of rooms. "Now perhaps you understand and admit the King of Kings has a grander notion of things as they are and things as they should be than your limited imagination can encompass," Yeliif said.

"He certainly had one splendid idea there," Abivard said, which sounded like agreement but wasn't quite. He suppressed a sigh. With all the courtiers telling Sharbaraz how clever he was, the King of Kings would get—indeed, no doubt had long since gotten—the idea that all his thoughts were brilliant merely because he was the one who'd had them. That might help Sharbaraz follow through on a genuinely good notion like the one he'd had here but would make him pursue his follies with equal vigor.

"His wisdom approaches that of the God," the beautiful eunuch declared. Abivard didn't say anything to that. Sharbaraz was liable to have himself worshiped in place of the God if he kept hearing flattery like that. Abivard wondered what Dhegmussa would have to say about such a claim. He wondered if the Mobedhan Mobedh would have the spine to say anything at all.

When he got back to the rooms where he and his family were staying, he found Roshnani, as he'd expected, waiting impatiently to hear what news he'd brought. He gave that news to her, crediting the King of Kings for the scheme he'd developed. Roshnani listened with her usual sharp attention and asked several equally sharp questions. After Abivard had answered them all, she paid Sharbaraz the highest compliment Abivard had heard from her in years: "I wouldn't have believed he had it in him."

* * *

Abivard greeted Romezan with a handclasp. "Good to see you," he said. "Good to see anyone who's ever gone out into the field and has some idea of what fighting is all about."

"Not many like that around the court, as I know better than I'd like," Romezan answered. He paced up and down the central room of Abivard's suite like a trapped animal. "That's why I'd rather be out in the field if I had any choice about it."

"Turan won't let the army fall into the Void while you're away from it," Abivard answered, "and I need your help working out exactly how to put the King of Kings' plan into effect."

"What exactly is the King of Kings' plan?" Romezan asked. "I've heard there is such a thing, but that's about all."

When Abivard told him, Romezan stopped pacing and listened intently. When Abivard was through, the noble from the Seven Clans whistled once, a low, prolonged note. Abivard nodded. "That's how I felt the first time I heard it, too," he said.

Romezan stared at him. "Do you mean to tell me you had nothing to do with this plan?" Abivard, truthfully enough, denied everything; even if he had once had the same idea, Sharbaraz was the one who'd made it real, or as real as it was thus far. Romezan whistled again. "Well, if he really did think of it all by his lonesome, more power to him. Splendid notion. Kills any number of birds with one stone."

"I was thinking the same thing," Abivard said. "What worries me is timing the attack and coordinating it with the Kubratoi to make sure they're doing their part when we come calling. They can't take Videssos the city by themselves; I'm sure of that. And we can't take it if we can't get to it. Working together, though—"

"Oh, aye, I see what you're saying," Romezan told him. "These are all the little things the King of Kings won't have bothered worrying about. They're also the sorts of things that make a plan go wrong if nobody bothers to think of them. And if that happens, it's not the fault of the King of Kings. It's the fault of whoever was in charge of the campaign."

"Something like that, yes." Abivard pointed to the walls and ceiling to remind Romezan that privacy was an illusion in the palace. Romezan tossed his head imperiously as if to answer that he did not care. Abivard went on, "We also want to make sure Maniakes is away from Videssos the city when we attack it: preferably bogged down fighting in the land of the Thousand Cities the way he has been the last couple of years."

"Aye, that would be good," Romezan agreed. "But if we don't move for Videssos the city till he's moved against us, that cuts down the time we'll have to try to take the place."

"I know," Abivard said unhappily. "Anything that makes one thing better has a way of making something else worse."

"True enough, true enough," Romezan said. "Well, that's life. And you're right that we'd be better off waiting for Maniakes to be out of Videssos the city and far away before we try to take it; if he's leading the defense, it's the same as giving the Videssians an extra few thousand men. I've fought him often enough now that I don't want to do it again."

"He is troublesome," Abivard said, knowing what an understatement that was. He laughed nervously. "I wonder if he has a secret plan of his own, too, one that will let him take Mashiz. If he holds our capital while we capture his, can we trade them back when the war is over?"

"You're full of jolly notions today, aren't you?" Romezan said, but then he added, "I do see what you're saying, so don't get me wrong about that. If we figure out everything we're going to do but nothing of what Maniakes is liable to try, we end up in trouble."

"Maniakes is liable to try almost anything, worse luck for us," Abivard answered. "We thought we had him penned away from the westlands for good till he ran around us by sea."

"Still doesn't seem right," Romezan grumbled. Like most other Makuraner officers, he had trouble taking the sea seriously, even though, had it not been there, every elaborate scheme to capture Videssos the city would have been unnecessary. Then, thoughtfully, he went on, "What are they like? The Kubratoi, I mean."

"How should I know?" Abivard answered almost indignantly. "I've never dealt with them, either. If we're going to ally with them, though, we probably could do worse than asking the ambassadors who made the arrangements in the first place."

"That's sensible," Romezan said, approval in his voice. He set a finger by the side of his nose. "Or, of course, we could always ask Tzikas."

"Ho, ho!" Abivard said. "You *are* a funny fellow." Both men laughed. Neither seemed much amused.

"We shall tell you whatever we can," Piran said. Beside him Tus nodded. Both men sipped wine and ate roasted pistachios from a silver bowl a servant had brought them.

"The most important question is, What are they worth in a brawl?" Romezan said. "You've seen 'em; we haven't. By the God, I can't tell you three things about 'em."

Romezan's mind reached no farther than the battlefield, but Abivard had longer mental vision: "What are they like? If they make a bargain, will they keep it?"

Piran snorted. "They're just one band of cows in the huge Khamorth herd that stretches from the Degird River across the great Pardrayan plain to the Astris River and beyond—which means any one of 'em would sell his own grandmother to the village butcher if he thought her carcass would fetch two arkets."

"Sounds like all the Khamorth I've ever known," Romezan agreed.

Tus held up a finger like a village schoolmaster. "But," he said, "against Videssos they will keep a bargain."

"If they're of the Khamorth strain, they're liable to betray anyone for any reason or for no reason at all," Abivard said.

"Were they fighting another clan of Khamorth, you would be right," Tus said. "But Etzilios hates Maniakes for having beaten him and fears he will beat him again. With a choice between Videssos and Makuran, he will be a faithful ally for us."

"Nothing like fear to keep an alliance healthy," Romezan observed.

"If I were khagan of Kubrat—and the God be praised I'm not, nor likely to be—I'd look for allies against Videssos, too,"

Abivard said. "The Videssians have long memories, and their neighbors had better remember it."

"You sound as if you might mean us, not just the Kubratoi and the other barbarous nations of the farthermost east," Piran said.

"Of course I mean us," Abivard exploded. "Maniakes has spent the past two years trying to tear down the land of the Thousand Cities one mud brick at a time. He hasn't been doing that for his own amusement; he's been doing it to pay us back for having taken the westlands away from Videssos. If we can cut off the head by taking Videssos the city, the body—the Empire of Videssos—will die. If we can't, our grandchildren will be trying to figure out how to keep the Videssians from taking back everything Sharbaraz has won in his wars."

"That is why the King of Kings sent us on our long, hard journey," Tus said. "He agrees with you, lord, that we must uproot the Empire to keep it from growing back and troubling us again in later days."

"Will the Kubratoi horsemen and single-trunk ships be enough toward helping us get done what needs doing?" Abivard asked.

Piran said, "Their soldiers are much like Khamorth anywhere. They have a lot of warriors because the grazing is good south of the Astris. A few of their fighting men wear mail shirts in place of boiled leather. Some are loot from the Videssians; some are made by smiths there."

"What about the ships?" Romezan asked, beating Abivard to the question.

"I'm no sailor—" Piran began.

Abivard broke in: "What Makuraner is?"

"—but they looked to me as if they'd be dangerous. They carry a mast and a leather sail to mount on it, and they can hold a lot of warriors."

"That sounds like what we need to do the job, right enough," Romezan said, eyes kindling with excitement.

Abivard hoped he was right. Along with catapults and siege towers, ships were a projection of the mechanical arts into the art of war. In all such things the Videssians were uncommonly good.

How he had resented those spider-striding galleys that had held him away from Videssos the city! He hadn't thought he could hate ships more than he'd hated those galleys. Now, though, after ships had let Maniakes bypass the Makuraner-held Videssian westlands and bring the war to the land of the Thousand Cities, he wondered where his greater antipathy lay.

"If we have ships to put their ships out of action—" He frowned. "Have the Kubratoi met the Videssians on the sea in these single-trunk ships?"

"We saw no such fights," Piran said. "Etzilios was at peace with Videssos while we were in Kubrat, you understand, not wanting to make Maniakes worry about him."

"I do understand." Abivard nodded. "Maniakes needs to think all's quiet behind him. He needs to invade the land of the Thousand Cities again, in fact. The farther he is from the capital when we launch our attack, the better off we'll be. If the God is kind, we'll be in Videssos the city before he can get back." He smiled wolfishly. "I wonder what he'll do then."

Harking back to his original question, Tus said, "Etzilios assured us, boasting and vaunting about what his people have done, that their ships had stood up against the Videssians in times past."

"I know they were raiding the Videssian coast when we were in Across," Romezan said. "They could hardly have done that if their ships didn't measure up, now, could they?"

"I suppose not," Abivard said. The wolfish smile remained. "The Videssians did have some other things to worry about then, though."

"Aye, so they did." Romezan's smile was more nearly reminiscent than lupine. "We scared them then. When we come back, we'll do more than scare them. Scaring people is for children. Winning wars is a man's proper sport."

"Well said!" Piran exclaimed. "The Kubratoi, like most nomads, would phrase that a little differently: they would say fighting wars is a man's proper sport. They will make allies worth having."

Allies worth betraying, Abivard thought. If all went well, if the Kubratoi and the Makuraners together took Videssos the city and extinguished the ancient Empire of Videssos, how long before they started quarreling over the bones of the carcass? Not long, Abivard was sure: Makuran had always had nomads on the frontier and never had had any use for them.

Something else occurred to him. To Romezan he said, "We'll be taking the part of the field army you brought out of Videssos to the land of the Thousand Cities, not so?"

"We'd better," Romezan declared. "If we're going to try to break into Videssos the city, we'll need everything we have. Kardarigan's chunk won't be enough by itself. Tell me you think otherwise and I'll be very surprised."

"I don't," Abivard assured him. "But while we're in Videssos, Maniakes is going to be in the land of the Thousand Cities. And do you know who will have to keep him busy there and make sure he doesn't sack our capital while we're busy sacking his?"

"Somebody had better do that," Romezan said. His eyes sparkled. "I know who—those foot soldiers you're so proud of, the city militiamen you trained into soldiers almost worth having."

"They *are* worth having," Abivard insisted. He started to get angry before he noticed that Romezan was grinning at him. "The proof of which is they'll be able to keep the Videssians busy here long enough for us to do what needs doing there."

"They'd better, or Sharbaraz will want both our heads and likely Turan's, too: he'll be commanding them, I suppose, so he won't be able to escape his share of the blame," Romezan said. He whistled a merry little tune he'd picked up in Videssos. "Of course, if your fancied-up city guards don't do their job, the King of Kings may not be able to take anybody's head, because Maniakes may not have left him with his. One way or another, the war ends next summer."

"Not 'one way or another,' " Abivard said. "The war ends next summer: our way."

Romezan, Tus, and Piran lifted their silver goblets of wine in a salute.

* * *

Prince Peroz stared up at Abivard, who in turn looked down at the little fellow who would one day rule him if he outlived Sharbaraz King of Kings. Peroz reached up and tried to grab hold of his beard. He hadn't taken that from his own children; he wouldn't take it from his future sovereign, either.

"He's starting to discover that he has hands," Abivard said to Denak, and then, "They change so fast when they're this small."

"They certainly do." His sister sighed. "I'd almost forgotten. It's been a while now since Jarireh was tiny. She's almost Varaz's age, you know."

"Is she well? Is she happy?" Abivard asked. His sister hardly ever mentioned his eldest niece. He wondered if Denak thought of Jarireh and her sisters as failures because they had not been boys and thus had not cemented their mother's place among the women of the palace.

"She is well," Denak said. "Happy? Who could be happy here at court?" She spoke without so much as glancing over at Ksorane, who sat in a corner of the room painting her eyelids with kohl and examining her appearance in a small mirror of polished bronze. Maybe, by now, Sharbaraz had heard all of Denak's complaints.

"If we take Videssos the city—" Abivard stopped. For the first time in a long while he let himself think about all the things that might happen if Makuran took Videssos the city. "If we take the city, Dhegmussa will offer up praise to the God from the High Temple and Sharbaraz King of Kings, may his days be long and his realm increase, will quarter himself in Maniakes' palaces. He should bring you with him, for without you he never would have had the chance."

"I've given up thinking that what he should do and what he will do are one and the same," Denak answered. "He'll go to Videssos the city, no doubt, to see what you've done for him and, as you say, to vaunt himself by taking over the Avtokrator's dwelling. But I'll stay here in Mashiz, sure as sure. He'll take women who . . . amuse him, or else he'll amuse himself with frightened little Videssians." She sounded very sure, very knowing, very bitter.

"But—" Abivard began.

His sister waved him to silence. "Sharbaraz dreams large," she said. "He always has—I give him that much. Now he's dreamed large enough to catch you up in his webs again, the way he did when the crown of the King of Kings was new on his head. But I'm not part of his dreams anymore, not in any real way." She pointed to Peroz, who was beginning to yawn in Abivard's arms. "Sometimes I think he's a dream and, if I go to bed and then wake up, he'll be gone." She shrugged. "I don't even know why Sharbaraz summoned me that one night."

Ksorane set down the mirror and said, "Lady, he feared your brother and wanted a better bond with him if he could forge one."

Denak and Abivard both stared at her in surprise. The only previous time she'd spoken without being spoken to had been to keep them from touching each other. As if to pretend she hadn't done anything at all, she went back to ornamenting her eyelids.

Denak shrugged again. "Maybe she's right," she told Abivard, still as if Ksorane weren't there listening. "But whether she is or isn't, it doesn't matter as far as my going to Videssos the city. Peroz is part of Sharbaraz' dreams, but I'm not. I'll stay here in Mashiz." She was utterly matter-of-fact about it, as if foretelling the yield from a plot of land near Vek Rud stronghold. Somehow that made the prediction worse, not better.

Abivard rocked his nephew in his arms. The baby's eyes slid shut. His mouth made little sucking noises. Ksorane came up to take him and return him to his mother. "Wait a bit," Abivard told her. "Let him get a little more deeply asleep so he won't start howling when I hand him to you."

"You know something about children," Ksorane said.

"I'd be a poor excuse for a father if I didn't," he answered. Then he wondered how much Sharbaraz King of Kings knew about children. Not much, he suspected, and that saddened him. *Some things,* he thought, *should not be left to servants.*

After a while he did hand the baby to Ksorane, who returned it to Denak. Neither transfer disturbed little Peroz in the least. Looking down at him, Denak said, "I wonder what dreams he'll have, many years from now, up there on the throne of the King of Kings, and who will follow them and try to make them real for him."

"Yes," Abivard said. But what he was wondering was whether Peroz would ever sit on the throne of the King of Kings. So many babies died no matter how hard their parents struggled to keep them alive. And even if Peroz lived to grow up, his father had for a time lost the throne through disaster and treachery. Who could say now that the same would not befall the babe? No one, as Abivard knew only too well. One thing he had seen was that life did not come with a promise that it would run smoothly.

By the standards with which Abivard had become familiar while living in Vek Rud domain, Mashiz enjoyed a mild winter. It was chilly, but even the winds off the Dilbat Mountains were nothing like the ones that blew around Vek Rud stronghold. Those seemed to take a running start on the Pardrayan steppe and to blow right through a man because going around him was too much trouble.

They got mild days in Mashiz, as opposed to the endless, bone-numbing chill of the far Northwest. Every so often the wind would shift and blow off the land of the Thousand Cities. Whenever it did that for two days running, Abivard began to think spring had arrived at last. He could taste how eager he was for good weather that wasn't just a tease of the sort a dancing girl would give to a soldier who lusted after her but whom she wanted to annoy rather than bed.

As the sun swung northward from its low point in the sky, the mild days gradually came more often. But every time Abivard's hopes began to rise with the sap in the trees, a new storm would claw its way over the mountains and freeze those hopes once more.

Abivard did send messages both to the field army, ordering it to be ready to move out when the weather permitted, and to Turan, ordering him to prepare to defend the land of the Thousand Cities with foot soldiers from the city garrisons alone. He did not go into more detail than that in his message. In peacetime the Thousand Cities had a flourishing trade with Videssos. That news of what he intended might reach the Avtokrator struck him as far from impossible.

Varaz knew what Sharbaraz intended. He had even less patience than Abivard, being wild to leave the foothills for the flatlands to the east, the flatlands that were the gateway to Videssos. "You need to wait," his father told him. "Leaving too soon doesn't get us anywhere—or not soon enough, anyhow."

"I'm sick of waiting!" Varaz burst out, a sentiment with which Abivard had more than a little sympathy. "I've spent the last three winters waiting here in the palace. I want to get out, to get away. I want to go to the places where things will happen."

Pretty soon, Abivard thought, Varaz would be old enough to make things happen rather than just watching them happen. He was taller than his mother now. Before long, his beard would begin to grow and he would make the discovery every generation finds astounding: that mankind includes womankind and is much more interesting on account of it.

Abivard hadn't cared for being cooped up three winters running, either, even if conditions had improved from one winter to the next. He had borne it more easily than had his son, though. But Varaz was going to escape from Mashiz, to return first to the land of the Thousand Cities, then to Across, and then, if the God was willing, to enter Videssos the city.

"Count yourself lucky," Abivard told his elder son. "Your cousin Jarireh may never leave the palace till the day she marries."

"She's a girl, though," Varaz said. Had Roshnani heard the tone in which he said it, she probably would have boxed his ears. He went on, "Besides, her baby brother's going to be King of Kings."

"That won't help her get out and see the world—or at least I don't think it will," Abivard said. "It will make picking someone for her to marry harder than it would be, though."

"Marriage—so what?" Varaz said, nothing but scorn in his voice—he remained on the childish side of the great divide. "Your family picks someone for you, the two of you go before the servant of the God, and that's it. That's how it works most of the time, anyhow."

"Are you making an exception for your mother and me?" Abivard asked dryly.

"Well, yes, but the two of you are different," Varaz said. "Mother goes out and *does* things, almost as if she were a man; she doesn't stay in the women's quarters all the time. And you *let* her."

"No," Abivard said. "I don't 'let' her. I'm glad she does. In a number of ways she's more clever than I am. I'm only lucky in that I'm clever enough to see she is more clever."

"I don't follow that," Varaz said. He quickly held up a hand. "I probably wouldn't follow it in Videssian, either, no matter how logical it's supposed to be, so don't bother trying."

Thus forestalled, Abivard thew his hands in the air. Varaz escaped from his presence and went dashing down a palace hallway. Watching him, Abivard sighed. No, waiting was never easy.

But even Sharbaraz had been forced to wait for his ambassadors to return. In another sense he'd had to wait more than a dozen years after the Empire of Videssos had fallen into civil strife to be able to assail its capital with any hope of success. In still another sense Makuran as a whole had been waiting centuries for this opportunity to come around.

Abivard snapped his fingers. Lands didn't wait—people did. And, like his son, he was very tired of waiting.

Pashang clucked to the horses and flicked the reins. The wagon rattled away from Mashiz. Abivard rode beside it on a fine black gelding, the gift of Sharbaraz King of Kings. Romezan rode another that might have been a different foal of the same mare. Around them, almost as splendidly mounted, trotted a company of heavy cavalry, their armor and that of their horses stowed in carts or on packhorses since they were traveling through friendly territory and were not expecting to fight. One proud young horseman carried the red war banner.

Off to one side, with the group but not of it, rode Tzikas.

Abivard had been warned of all the horrid things that would happen to him if anything at all happened to Tzikas. He was still trying to work out whether those horrid things were deterrent enough. For the moment they probably were. Once Videssos the city fell, Tzikas would be expendable. And if by some misfortune Videssos the city failed to fall, Sharbaraz would be looking for a scapegoat.

Tzikas no doubt was thinking along similar lines. Abivard glanced over toward him and wasn't surprised to find the Videssian renegade's eyes already on him. He stared at Tzikas for a little while, nothing but challenge in his gaze. Tzikas looked back steadily. Abivard let out a silent sigh. Enemies were so much easier to despise when they were cowards. Yet even though Tzikas was no coward, Abivard despised him anyhow.

He turned in the saddle and said to Romezan, "We're riding in the right direction now."

"How do you mean that?" Romezan returned. "Away from the palace? Out into the field? Toward the war?"

"Any of those will do," Abivard said. "They'll all do." If he had to pick one, *away from the palace* probably would fit his thought best. In the palace he was slave to the King of Kings, for all his achievements hardly higher in status than sweepers or captive Videssian pedagogues. Away from the palace, away from the King of Kings, he was a marshal of Makuran, a great power in his own right. He had grown very used to that, all those years he'd spent extending the power of Makuran through the Videssian westlands till it reached the Cattle Crossing. Being yanked back under Sharbaraz' control would have been hard on him even had the King of Kings not seen treason lurking under every pillow and behind every door.

Romezan did not dwell on the past. He looked ahead to the east. Dreamily, he said, "Do you suppose we'll lay Videssos low? How many hundred years have they and we warred? Come this fall, will the fight be over at last?"

"If the God is kind," Abivard answered.

They rode on a while in silence. Then Abivard said, "We'll muster as far forward as we can. As soon as we have word that

Maniakes has landed, whether down in Lyssaion or in Erzerum, we move."

"What if he doesn't land?" Romezan said, looking eastward again, as if he could span the farsangs and see into the palaces in distant Videssos the city. "What if he decides to stay home for a year? Maniakes never ends up doing what we think he will."

That was true. Even so, Abivard shook his head. "He'll come," he said. "I'm sure of it, and Sharbaraz was dead right to assume it." Hearing him agree so emphatically with the King of Kings was enough to make Romezan dig a finger into his ear as if to make sure it was working as it should. Chuckling, Abivard went on. "What's Maniakes' chief advantage over us?" He answered his own question: "He commands the sea. What has he been doing with that command? He's been using it to take the war out of Videssos and into the realm of the King of Kings. How can he possibly afford not to keep on doing what he's done the past two years?"

"Put that way, I don't suppose he can," Romezan admitted.

"The real beauty of Sharbaraz' scheme—" Abivard stopped. Now *he* wondered if he was really talking about the King of Kings that way. He was, and in fact he repeated himself: "The real beauty of Sharbaraz' plan is that it uses Maniakes' strengths against him and Videssos. He takes his ships, uses them to bring his army back to the land of the Thousand Cities, and gets embroiled in fighting well away from the sea. And while he's doing all that, we steal a march and take his capital away from him."

Romezan thought for a while before nodding. "I like it."

"So do I," Abivard said.

He liked it better by the day. He and his escort made their way through the land of the Thousand Cities toward Qostabash. Peasants were busy in the fields, bringing in the spring harvest. Here and there, though, they were busy at other things, most notably the repair of canals wrecked in the previous fall's fighting and soon to be needed to cope with the sudden rush of water from the spring floods of the Tutub and the Tib and their tributaries.

And here and there, across the green quilt of the floodplain, fields went untended, unharvested. Some of the cities that had perched on mounds of their own rubble were now nothing but rubble themselves. Maniakes had made the land of the Thousand Cities pay a terrible price for the many victories Makuran had won in Videssos over the past decade.

Whenever he stopped at one of the surviving Thousand Cities, Abivard examined how well the city governor had kept up the local garrison. He was pleased to find most of those garrisons in better shape than they had been two years earlier, when the Videssians had first entered the floodplain. Before then both city governorships and slots in the city garrison had been the nearest thing to sinecures: but for flood or drought, what ever went wrong among the Thousand Cities? *Invasion* was not an answer that seemed to have occurred beforehand to many people.

Romezan paid the revived city garrisons what might have been the ultimate compliment when he said, "You know, I wouldn't mind taking a few thousand of these foot soldiers along with us when we go into the Videssian westlands. They really can fight. Who would have thought it?"

"That's not what you said when you came to my aid last summer," Abivard reminded him.

"I know," Romezan answered. "I hadn't seen them in action then. I was wrong. I admit it. You deserve a lot of credit for turning them into soldiers."

Abivard shook his head. "Do you know who deserves the credit for turning them into soldiers?"

"Turan?" Romezan snorted dismissively. "He's done well with them, aye, but he's still only a jumped-up captain learning how to be a general."

"He's done very well, as a matter of fact, but I wasn't thinking of him," Abivard answered. "The one who deserves the credit for turning them into soldiers is Maniakes. Without him they'd just be the same swaggering bullies they've been for the God only knows how many years. But that doesn't work, not against the Videssians. The ones who are still alive know better now."

"Something to that, I expect," Romezan said after a reflective pause.

"It's also one reason why we're not going to take any of those foot soldiers into Videssos," Abivard said. Romezan's dark, bushy brows pulled down and together in confusion. Abivard explained: "Remember, we want the Videssians heavily engaged here in the land of the Thousand Cities. That means we're going to have to leave behind a good-sized army to fight them, an army with good fighting men in it. Either we leave behind a piece of the field army—"

"No, by the God!" Romezan broke in.

Abivard held up a placatory hand. "I agree. The field army is the best Makuran has. That's what we send against Videssos the city, which will need the best we have. But the next best we have has to stay here to keep Maniakes in play while we move against the city."

Again Romezan paused for thought before answering. "This is a tricky business, gauging all the separate strengths to make sure each is in the proper place. Me, I'd sooner point my mass of troops at the foe, charge him straight on, and smash him down into the dirt."

"I know," Abivard said, which was true. He added, "So would I," which was less true. "But Maniakes fights like a Videsslan, so stealth makes do for a lot of his strength. It we're going to beat the Empire so it stays beaten, we have to do it his way."

"I suppose so," Romezan said unwillingly. "But if we fight like the Videssians, we'll end up acting like them in other ways, too. And they know no caste."

He spoke with great abhorrence. Abivard knew he should have felt that same abhorrence. Try as he would, he couldn't find it inside himself. He wondered why. After a few seconds' thought he said, "I've lived so long in Videssos and here in the Thousand Cities, I don't mind that nearly so much as I used to. Up on the plateau breaking people into tight groups—the King of Kings, the Seven Clans and the servants of the God, the *dihqans*, artisans and merchants, and peasants down at the bottom—seemed a natural thing to do. Now I've seen other ways of doing things, and I realize ours isn't the only one."

"That's no sort of thing for a proper Makuraner to say." Romezan sounded almost as dismayed as if Abivard had blasphemed the God.

But Abivard refused to let himself be cowed. "No, eh? Why is it you kiss my cheek, then, instead of the other way around? You outrank me. I'm just a *dihqan*, and a frontier *dihqan* at that."

"I started giving you that courtesy because you're brother-in-law to the King of Kings," the noble from the Seven Clans answered. If he'd kept quiet after that, he would have won the argument. Instead, though, he went on, "Now I see you've earned it because—"

Abivard stuck a triumphant finger in the air. "If you grant me the courtesy because I've earned it and not because of my blood, what has that got to do with caste?"

Romezan started to answer, looked confused, stopped, and tried again: "It's—that is—" He came to another stop, then burst out, "You *have* lived among the Videssians too long. All you want to do is chop logic all day. Now I'm going to be *thinking* for the next half dozen farsangs." He made the prospect sound most unpleasant. Abivard had seen that before in many different men. It always left him sad.

Tzikas, on the other hand, actively enjoyed thinking. That wasn't necessarily a recommendation, either. The older Abivard got, the more it looked as if nothing was necessarily a recommendation for anything.

Outside Qostabash men from the field army were playing mallet and ball, galloping their horses up and down a grassy stretch of ground with great abandon. Every so often a loincloth-clad peasant, his blue-black hair bound in a bun at the nape of his neck, would look up from his labor with hoe and mattock and watch the sport for a little while before bending back down to weed or prune or dig. Abivard wondered what the peasants thought of the shouting warriors whose game was not far from combat itself. Whatever it was, they kept it to themselves.

He had sent a rider out ahead of his company to let Turan know he was near. Two years before Turan had been only a company commander himself. He'd risen fast, since Abivard had access to so few veteran Makuraner officers on whom he could rely. Now Turan had shown himself able to command an army. Very soon he'd have the chance to do just that.

Now he came riding out of Qostabash to greet Abivard and his companions—he must have had men up on the walls of the city keeping an eye out for them. The first thing he did after pulling his horse alongside Abivard's was to point over at Tzikas and say, "Isn't he supposed to be dead, lord?"

"It all depends on whom you ask," Abivard answered. "I certainly think so, but the King of Kings disagrees. As in any contest of that sort, his will prevails."

"Of course it does," Turan said, as any loyal Makuraner would have done. Then, as anyone who had made the acquaintance of Tzikas would have done, he asked, "Why on earth does he want him alive?"

"For a reason even I find . . . fairly good," Abivard answered. He spent the next little while explaining the plan Sharbaraz King of Kings had devised and the places his sovereign had designated for him and for the Videssian renegade.

When he was through, Turan glanced over at Tzikas and said, "He had better make keeping him alive worth everyone's while or else he won't last, orders from the King of Kings or no orders from the King of Kings."

"Far be it from me to argue with you," Abivard said. Lowering his voice, he went on, "But I've decided I'm not going to do anything about it till after Videssos the city falls, if it does. Either way, the problem takes care of itself then." He explained his reasoning to Turan.

The officer nodded. "Aye, lord, that's very good. If we fail, which the God forbid, he gets the blame, and if we succeed, we don't need him anymore after that. Very neat. Anyone would think you were the Videssian, not his unpleasantness over there."

"Too many people have said the same thing to me lately," Abivard grumbled. "I thank the God and the Prophets Four that I'm not."

"Aye, I believe that," Turan agreed, "the same as I thank the

God—" He broke off. He'd probably been about to say something like *for making me a man, not a woman.* Considering how much freedom Roshnani had and how well she used it, that wasn't the wisest thing to say around Abivard. Turan changed the subject: "How will you know, lord, when to leave the Thousand Cities behind and strike out for Videssos?"

"As soon as we get word Maniakes has landed, whether north or south, we go," Abivard said. "At this season of the year the badlands between the Thousand Cities and Videssos will have some greenery on them, too, which means we won't have to carry quite so much grain and hay for the horses and mules."

"Every little bit helps," Turan said. "And you'll want me to keep Maniakes in play for as long as I can, isn't that right?"

"The busier he is with you, the more time I'll have to do all I can against Videssos the city," Abivard said, and Turan nodded. Abivard added, "You may even beat him—who knows?"

"With an all-infantry army?" Turan rolled his eyes. "If I can slow him down and make his life difficult, I'll be happy."

Since Abivard had been saying the same thing to Sharbaraz over the course of the previous two campaigning seasons, he found no way to blame Turan for words like those. He said, "The two things you have to remember are not to let Maniakes get behind you and make a run for Mashiz and to make him fight as many long sieges as you can."

"He hasn't fought many long ones the past couple of years," Turan said unhappily. "Brick walls like the ones hereabouts don't stand up well to siege engines, and the Videssians are good engineers."

"I know." Abivard remembered the capable crew of artisans the elder Maniakes, the Avtokrator's father, had brought with his army when the Videssians had helped put Sharbaraz back on the throne of the King of Kings. He dared not assume that the men the younger Maniakes would have with him would turn out to be any less competent.

Romezan said, "I hope Maniakes comes soon. Every day I sit here in Qostabash doing nothing is another debt the Avtokrator owes to me. I intend to collect every one of those debts, and in good Videssian gold."

"We won't be idle here," Abivard answered. "Getting an army ready to move at a moment's notice is an art of its own and one where the Videssians are liable to be better than we are."

Romezan only grunted by way of reply. He was a good man in a fight, none better, but cared less than he might have for the other side of generalship, the side that involved getting men ready for fighting and keeping them that way. He seemed to think that sort of thing happened by itself. Abivard had needed to worry about supplies from his earliest days as a soldier, when he'd fed the *dihqans* of the Northwest as they looked Sharbaraz over at the outset of his rebellion against Smerdis the usurper. If he hadn't learned then, keeping an eye on the way the Videssians did things would have taught him.

Turan said, "When you go east, I wish I were going with you. I know the job I have to do back here is important, but—"

"You'll do it, which is what counts. That's *why* you're staying behind," Abivard told him. Turan nodded but still looked dissatisfied. Abivard understood that and sympathized with it, but only to a certain degree. The Videssians weren't so apt to tack *but* on after *important.* If something was important, they did it and then went on to the next important thing.

With a small start, he realized that all the people who'd been calling him Videssian-minded lately had a point. Having spent so much time in the Empire and among imperials, he was—always with exceptions such as Tzikas—as comfortable around them as with his own people. Was feeling that way treason of a sort or simply making the best of what life had proffered? He scratched his head. He'd have to ponder that.

A sentry brought into Abivard's presence a sweat-soaked scout who smelled strongly of horse. Abivard stiffened. Was this the man for whom he'd been waiting? Before he could speak, the scout gasped out, "The Videssians have come! They—"

Abivard waited to hear no more. All the waiting was over at last. He sprang to his feet. No matter how comfortable he had grown among the Videssians, they remained the foe. He thought he could beat them. Soon he would know. He took a deep breath and shouted out the news: "We march on Videssos!"

Coming in fall 1997
from Harry Turtledove,
the Master of Alternate History

HOW FEW
REMAIN

A Novel of the *Second*
War Between the States

Published by Del Rey Books.
Available soon
in bookstores everywhere.

✎ FREE DRINKS ✎

Take the Del Rey® survey and get a free newsletter! Answer the questions below and we will send you complimentary copies of the DRINK (Del Rey® Ink) newsletter free for one year. Here's where you will find out all about upcoming books, read articles by top authors, artists, and editors, and get the inside scoop on your favorite books.

Age _____   Sex ❑ M ❑ F

Highest education level: ❑ high school ❑ college ❑ graduate degree

Annual income: ❑ $0-30,000 ❑ $30,001-60,000 ❑ over $60,000

Number of books you read per month: ❑ 0-2 ❑ 3-5 ❑ 6 or more

Preference: ❑ fantasy ❑ science fiction ❑ horror ❑ other fiction ❑ nonfiction

I buy books in hardcover: ❑ frequently ❑ sometimes ❑ rarely

I buy books at: ❑ superstores ❑ mall bookstores ❑ independent bookstores ❑ mail order

I read books by new authors: ❑ frequently ❑ sometimes ❑ rarely

I read comic books: ❑ frequently ❑ sometimes ❑ rarely

I watch the Sci-Fi cable TV channel: ❑ frequently ❑ sometimes ❑ rarely

I am interested in collector editions (signed by the author or illustrated): ❑ yes ❑ no ❑ maybe

I read Star Wars novels: ❑ frequently ❑ sometimes ❑ rarely

I read Star Trek novels: ❑ frequently ❑ sometimes ❑ rarely

I read the following newspapers and magazines:
❑ *Analog*   ❑ *Locus*   ❑ *Popular Science*
❑ *Asimov*   ❑ *Wired*   ❑ *USA Today*
❑ *SF Universe*   ❑ *Realms of Fantasy* ❑ *The New York Times*

Check the box if you do not want your name and address shared with qualified vendors ❑

Name _____

Address _____

City/State/Zip _____

E-mail _____

thousand cities

**PLEASE SEND TO: DEL REY®/The DRINK
201 EAST 50TH STREET NEW YORK NY 10022**

DEL REY® ONLINE!

The Del Rey Internet Newsletter...

A monthly electronic publication, posted on the Internet, GEnie, CompuServe, BIX, various BBSs, and the Panix gopher (gopher.panix.com). It features hype-free descriptions of books that are new in the stores, a list of our upcoming books, special announcements, a signing/reading/convention-attendance schedule for Del Rey authors, "In Depth" essays in which professionals in the field (authors, artists, designers, sales people, etc.) talk about their jobs in science fiction, a question-and-answer section, behind-the-scenes looks at sf publishing, and more!

Internet information source!

A lot of Del Rey material is available to the Internet on our Web site and on a gopher server: all back issues and the current issue of the Del Rey Internet Newsletter, sample chapters of upcoming or current books (readable or downloadable for free), submission requirements, mail-order information, and much more. We will be adding more items of all sorts (mostly new DRINs and sample chapters) regularly. The Web site is http://www.randomhouse.com/delrey/ and the address of the gopher is gopher.panix.com

Why? We at Del Rey realize that the networks are the

medium of the future. That's where you'll find us promoting our books, socializing with others in the sf field, and—most importantly—making contact and sharing information with sf readers.

Online editorial presence: Many of the Del Rey editors

are online, on the Internet, GEnie, CompuServe, America Online, and Delphi. There is a Del Rey topic on GEnie and a Del Rey folder on America Online.

The official e-mail address for Del Rey Books is

delrey@randomhouse.com (though it sometimes takes us a while to answer).

HARRY
TURTLEDOVE

Published by Del Rey® Books.
Available in your local bookstore.